DEVIL MAY CARE

BOYS OF PRESTON PREP

ANGEL LAWSON

SAMANTHA RUE

PROLOGUE

Obligation makes a person do stupid things.

Like walk into a party with dozens of people who hate my guts.

Like lowering myself to walking through puddles of beer and wafts of smoke, wading through kids whose tongues are shoved down one another's throats, and worst of all, forcing myself to talk to the Devil.

Or one of the Devils. I've only been in this house—smaller and less opulent than the usual Devil fare—for mere minutes, and I can already feel the familiar tension at the base of my spine building. It makes my stride choppy, mechanical, driven by purpose and little else.

I find Xavier first, with his swoopy hair and cute but infuriatingly smug expression. His red and black letterman jacket shines with a whole array of varsity letter pins. There's a patch with an interlocked PP on the left side, Preston Prep, the bottom of the second P extended into a devil's pitchfork; the mark of the beasts. Their identities. Xavier should know where Skylar is, though. He's the one who brought her.

He eyes me with surprise. "Oh look, Morticia's here. Didn't know they let the freaks out at night."

An Addams Family joke. Wow. How incredibly original. Perfectly elementary school. About the place Xavier's maturity stopped. I have no idea what Sky sees in him. "Where is she?"

"Where's who?" He takes a sip of beer, the foam lingering on his upper lip.

"I know she came with you, Xavier." I skim the crowded room. There's a line of people going down the hall. Headed to the bathroom, I presume. "She thinks you *like* her."

The guy next to him, another Devil, Ansel Davenport, elbows him and makes kissy faces. He's wearing the same jacket. Xavier's cheeks heat—embarrassed to be associated with Sky—with me.

"You're useless," I sneer, turning on my heel. Before I get far, a hand grabs my upper arm and stops me. I turn. Xavier followed me.

He clucks his tongue, rolls his eyes. "She disappeared, okay? Bailed on me. Once she saw there were a bunch of Northridge kids here, she started drinking with them and took off."

"Sky wouldn't ditch you for a Northridge kid," I reply. She'd been ecstatic about this date. New outfit. Hours on her shiny blonde hair. She even convinced me to help her with her makeup. It was literally hours sitting in our shared bathroom, me trying to talk her out of this while Sky just preened and gushed, "I feel like a princess!"

There's no way.

His face goes shuttered. "Well, she did, and I'm done with her," he says, walking off.

As if he ever wanted her. I'd been suspicious from day one. These guys don't slum. They don't have to. And that's what it would be considered, going out with one of the Adams girls: slumming.

"Party must be over, guys, someone let the trash in."

The voice makes my skin crawl. I'd misrepresented before. Xavier, Ansel, Emory, Heston...they aren't the real Devil—they're simply his minions. Hamilton Bates, the asshole currently standing before me, he's the real Devil. The leader of the pack. You'd know him anywhere. Face of an angel, body of a Greek god, personality of a root canal.

"Of course," he continues in a rich southern drawl, ignoring the fact a girl, some junior, is sucking on his earlobe as he speaks, "someone had already let the trash in. It's an epidemic. These Northridge kids will let anyone come to their parties. Zero standards, if I'm being honest."

"I'm not here to party."

His steel gray eyes sweep over me. "In that outfit, you're not fit to do anything but scrub floors."

I'm well aware that the oversized cardigan, ratty jeans, and scuffed boots aren't up to Preston standards. Of course, nothing about me ever has been. I push my glasses up my nose. I'd already taken out my contacts when I'd tried to contact my younger sister Skylar, who'd promised to keep in touch if she came here tonight. Six texts. No response. Yeah, I'd jumped in the car without looking in the mirror.

"Although," he gives me a sidelong glance, "the sexy secretary thing can be hot—you know, on the right kind of girl."

Right kind = pedigree.

Which, I think, no matter how wealthy and educated and successful my parents are, I'll never be, because it's about one thing. Blood. Mine isn't the right shade.

I roll my eyes, long ago accustomed to not letting it get to me. "I get it. You think I'm repulsive. Where the hell is she?"

He drinks from his cup. "Who?"

"My sister."

His mouth curves into a prickish smirk. "You mean one of the rejects your parents raised you with?"

"Hamilton, I swear to god."

His eyes dart over my shoulder to where Xavier and Ansel are standing. "I saw her—earlier—but not in a while. I think she left with some Northridge kid."

"You know how much she likes Xavier," I argue through gritted teeth. "There's no way she left with someone else."

When people look at Sky, they see someone who's beautiful. Fun. A chameleon who can adapt to any crowd. The cheerleaders, the drama kids, the dance squad, the preps. They see a girl who's bubbly and kind.

But me? I see the little girl who, at age five, was asked to clean her plate and ended up vomiting an entire serving of green beans back up ten minutes later. I see the girl who, at age six, witnessed me getting an inkling of praise for learning to swim so quickly and nearly drowning in an attempt trying to get the same. I see the girl who, at age eight, accidentally got a marker stain on the bathroom tile and scrubbed at it for five hours, until her nailbeds began to bleed. I see the girl who'd do anything to belong, to be appreciated, accepted, praised, *wanted*.

No one in this room really wants her, and it makes me anxious in some frenzied, abstract way, as if something is terribly wrong but hasn't happened quite yet.

"I may be the prince of this school," Hamilton says without a trace of irony, "but you and your sister aren't my concern. You're not one of us. You never will be. Xavier shouldn't have even asked her to this party, really. Completely out of line. Naturally, he ditched her." He jerks his thumb toward the row of kids in the hall. "The last time I saw her, she was down that way."

If Xavier rejected her, Sky would take it hard. *Really hard.* I swallow back my anger. "If anything happens to her, I'm going to—"

"Do what, Gwendolyn?"

My name makes his face pinch, like just saying it tastes bitter on his tongue. His demeanor changes, going from lazy to terrifying in a blink. He towers over me, his swimmer shoulders broad enough to cast a shadow. His glare is ice cold, void of compassion or empathy. I search them futilely for a touch of the boy I knew a long time ago, but long gone is the carefree childhood laughter shared between two imaginary pirates on a picturesque playground. Now it's just this: Hamilton's stony face and my clenched fists. I don't even know why I've wasted time talking to him.

I go in the direction he gestured, more worried about Sky than a discarded childhood friendship. The line to the bathroom is still a long, serpentine thing, and as I get closer, I realize it's also noticeably male. I see another Devil, Emory Hall, a junior, pinning in his girlfriend, the Queen of Hell herself, Campbell Clarke, just outside a closed door. A guy in a Northridge shirt suddenly exits the room, but another guy enters just as quickly, door closing behind him with a resounding 'snick'. Emory turns from Campbell to smirk at the exiting Northridge boy, their palms meeting in a congratulatory high-five.

An eerie chill falls over me.

You don't get a high five for taking a piss.

I stop by one of the Northridge kids standing in line. "Is this for the bathroom?"

"Nah," the kid says, looking nervously at his friend. They're holding forties and one takes a drag from a vape pen.

I'm about to turn away when the vaper adds, "There's a chick in there sucking dick. One after the other."

My stomach bottoms out, because I know.

I wish I didn't. For that split second between ignorance and acceptance, I hope everything would just end right here, right now, because it'd be better than knowing. But I do.

I know. I know. I know.

I lurch past them, vaguely noting they're all unfamiliar faces—all from the public school. But that red devil jacket is only a few feet away. When Emory sees me, he jerks up, grabbing Campbell's hand and bolting the other way. I glance back down the hall and all the Preston Devils are suddenly missing, including their prince.

I reach for the doorknob, but a figure blocks me.

"No cuts, bitch," a kid says. He's wearing a Northridge football sweatshirt. Number 29 stamped in the middle. I file that away in case I need it.

"Move." The word comes out shaky, hissed, a barely restrained verbal punch.

"She's sucking dick, not eating pussy," the door blocker says. "But if you wait in line, she may be willing to give it a go. 'Cause like, straight up? I don't think she's that picky."

My long, measured inhale releases in a grunt as I fist his shirt with both hands and shove him roughly aside. He slams into the guy behind him, footing lost in his surprise. The ensuing ripple effect as guy after guy gets knocked and bumped into elicits curses and complaints.

"Are you fucking kidding me?" the kid says, tipping himself to rights. "I've been in line for an hour!"

An hour?

"Get the hell out of my way," I spit, lunging for the door and flinging it open.

I stare at the scene inside. A guy sits on the bed, pants down at his ankles. My sister is bent before him, blonde ponytail bobbing in rhythm. His jaw is soft, mouth gaping. His eyes barely register me in the door.

I must say something. I must, but I don't remember anything other than the guy finally pushing my sister away and fumbling to shove his cock in his pants. Sky looks back at me with glazed, confused eyes, and I see her then. The same girl I always see. So sweet and determined and desperate like a deep, gnawing ache. For a moment, I wonder *how*. How do other people not see this?

And then I wonder if... maybe I'm wrong.

Maybe they do.

She wipes her mouth and rasps, "Gwen?" and my eyes move to the boy. The ugly, pig-faced, sweaty boy.

I want to choke him. I want to choke all of them. I want to find something big and heavy and bludgeon my way through the house. Instead, I lunge for him, screeching, "Get the fuck out of here!"

He makes a pathetic squeaking sound as he rushes from the room, fingers fumbling with his jean buttons.

I follow him out to look down the hall, but the line of guys is gone. There's only one person standing a few feet away, hands shoved in his red and black jacket; Hamilton Bates.

That deep bludgeoning urge returns in a dizzying rush, and I can almost imagine doing it, because *never*. Never in all the years he's said cruel things to me, about my family, the vicious jabs day-to-day, the unending spew of his disdain, would I have *ever* thought Hamilton Bates of something so monstrous.

The worst thing is the odd sense of loss I feel in this moment. A deep-down pang of shocked hurt. As if he weren't already lost to me, as if all the vile things he's said and done over the years could have been wiped clean, maybe, some day. I hadn't even known I'd been holding on to that, until right now. But now he's finally gone to me. Wholly. He's finally done something so entirely unforgiveable that it's easy—easy as breathing—to level him with the same cold hateful stare he's giving me.

"It might not be today," I say, voice eerily calm despite the tears in my eyes and the lump in my throat. "It might not even be tomorrow. But I swear to god, Hamilton, you're going to pay for this."

I don't give him the chance for a witty retort, because I'm scared of myself, just then. Of what I might actually do. Instead, I go back into the room, closing the door behind me, to take care of a girl who'd felt like a princess.

1

SUMMER LASTS FOREVER in the south, inching way past Labor Day and almost to Halloween. I walk out of my residence hall on November first with a sweater on over my school uniform for the first time all year. The chill still caresses my bare legs. However, I'm grateful the orange and black decorations that have infected the dorm lobby for the last month will be taken down by the end of classes that day.

I hate Halloween. It's too much of a reminder that I'm forced to wear a mask every day at this godforsaken school. For the students at Preston Prep, wearing a mask once a year is fun. For me it's about survival. I won't let these people see the real me. They can see the version of Gwen who overachieves, the Gwen who handily wins swim meets, the Gwen who keeps to herself, or most importantly, the Gwen who feels *nothing*. Because even the smallest inkling of vulnerability in this place is like blood in the water, and I won't let them.

I won't let them ruin me.

Not like they did Sky.

The good news is that I'm basically invisible anyway, especially after what happened last year. "Cancelled" is a more accurate word.

I'd been cancelled after I busted up the party. Cancelled after taking my sister home and sitting through a tearful, gut-clenched discussion with our parents about what had occurred. Cancelled after the school administrators, the board, the parents were all called in and forced to acknowledge the behavior of their star students and athletes.

I can't imagine what would have happened if someone had actually called the police.

But on some indulgent nights, lying in bed and staring at the heart-shaped stain on my dorm room ceiling, I *really do try*.

For the last six months, since the fallout from the party, a wall of silence had been wrapped around me. I'd never been that popular to begin with. I was an Adams Family Freak, after all. One of five kids adopted by Mark and Becca Adams. That was enough to mark my siblings and I as different; born out of wedlock to four different dirt-poor, uneducated, addict parents, and worst of all; my twin siblings are bi-racial, so it's not even like people can pretend. And the elite of this town, they really do love a good old-fashioned self-denial.

Sure, people put up a façade of politeness. We do live in the South after all. Manners are key. The truth is that, the twins even have a few genuine friends down in the middle school wing. But my class? Dominated by the Devils?

They'd been pacing like tigers in a cage for years, just looking for a reason. Snitching on them at the party was a gift on a silver platter.

Slinging my backpack over my shoulder, I follow the brick-paved sidewalks toward the courtyard by the carpool lanes. It really is a lovely campus, full of rich old architecture. You'd never know, just from looking at the facade, how much evil is contained in its walls. There are sprawling live oaks in the quad and behind the dorms, dressed to the nines in Spanish moss, and at just the right time of year, I can look out my window and see a delicate, pulsing swath of lightning bugs. Leaves crunch under my feet, dried from the summer heat. I briefly second-guess my decision to wear a sweater. It'll probably be seventy by lunch. I'm just determined to make fall start even if I'm miserable. But I'm always miserable at Preston Prep. Why should today be any different?

It's not long before the blue mini-van arcs through the driveway, intermingled with the Teslas and Lexuses and BMWs. It's out of place, which is fitting. The Adams kids are square pegs trying to fit in the gaping round hole of this world. Debbie's car pulls up to the curb and the back door flies open. My twelve-year-old twin siblings, Michaela and Micha, spill from inside. They run toward me as the passenger side window rolls down and Debbie leans toward me.

"Hey babe, how are you?"

This is one of the first times in my day I don't need to force my smile. "I'm good." Michaela runs toward me and gives me a hug. I squeeze her tight and tug on her twisted braids.

"We're having my famous lasagna tonight, want to come?" Debbie asks hopefully, and truthfully, it is tempting. She's a great cook, after all. It's one of the reasons my mother hired her to be our nanny. That and the fact neither my mother nor father have the slightest idea of how to actually parent.

Nevertheless, my smile tightens. "I wish I could. I have a big test tomorrow."

"Sure, you do," she replies, skeptically. There's no anger in her voice. Debbie understands why I moved on campus at the beginning of the year. She just doesn't like it. "Don't stay away too long, okay?"

I nod and the carpool monitor waves her forward. Michaela and I wave as she drives off.

"How was trick-or-treating?" I ask the twins. They had big plans for costumes and had been preparing them for weeks. They'd gone as Willow and Jaden Smith. Micha had been particularly excited about wearing a dress, which is understandable. Preston Prep has a pretty strict dress code. Individuality is frowned upon, and Micha definitely marches to the beat of his own drum. My little brother has had to learn to choose his fashion battles wisely from the start, and I doubt he understands yet just how unfair it is. Michaela can wear pants, boots, and graphic tees marketed to boys, and at most, she's just a bit of a tomboy. But for Micha, a bit of glitter and lip gloss are the makings of a full-blown scandal.

"I got so much candy," Micha says, gripping the straps of his bedazzled backpack. The sequins and glitter match the laces in his shoes, and something inside of me softens and glows. Because even with the strict dress code at Preston Prep, Micha finds his own little ways to do the complete opposite of me—not hide. "And Mom let us eat as much as we wanted before bed."

I'm sure. Why set limits?

The twins talk about Halloween the whole way to their building —the middle school wing—giving me a breakdown of the best candy. Snickers are at an all-time high, but Milky Way futures are way down. Better invest in fun-size boxes of Nerds, as the trick-or-treat economy as it relates to our particular gated community is experiencing a serious chocolate deficit.

"When are you coming home?" Michaela asks. It's a common question. My answer is the same every day.

"Not until after graduation."

She gives me a sly look. "Mama said if you don't move back by Christmas, she'll let me have your room."

It's an empty threat. Debbie already told me that Michaela moved into my room three weeks ago. She'd brought in her blanket and a least a dozen stuffed animals. If anything, this is a test to see how soon she'll have to move back into the room she shares with Micha. Because Micha is painfully earnest and unassuming, but Michaela... Michaela *schemes*.

I sigh overdramatically. "That's a risk I'll have to take. It's not that I want to stay away. It's just easier for me to do my schoolwork and swim practice when I live on campus."

Micha gives me a long look but says nothing. It's not that I haven't noticed that things have been strained between us since I moved to the dorms. The twins see all our adopted siblings as their own. As twins, they're innately used to having siblings, but to them, siblings should always *be there*. Me moving to the dorms makes the third of us to leave. Clearly, this is not proper siblinghood.

"When does the swim season start?" Michaela asks.

I squeeze her hand, giving it a jiggle. "Next week."

"Maybe once it's over, you can come home."

"Maybe," I lie, halting by the door and giving one of her braids a soft tug. "Okay, we're here. You'll have a good day, yeah?"

Michaela gives me another hug while Micha throws me a peace

sign in his wake. I push my worry aside as they disappear into the building. They're too young to really understand what happened with Skylar and no one at school is allowed to mention it.

Ever.

That was the deal my parents made with the school and the other parents. No one would call the authorities about the culpability of the Preston Prep students as long as no one discussed it ever again. Because, it was agreed, they had some accountability, even if they didn't participate. This is a problem for both the school and the kids, like the Devils that I'd seen there that night. They knew Skylar was in that room and what she was doing, and they let it happen. Maybe even worse, they stood back and had a good time, relished in it, took something sordid and horrifying and made it into a sick joke, a currency of high-fives and muffled laughter.

Sky confirmed this all long ago, that no one had intervened, but none of them had participated. Truthfully, I'm not convinced she'd admit to anything that might mean getting them into trouble. It's not about protection. It's about her need to belong, to feel approved of. I can handle being shunned. Being silenced. Being cast aside. It's not fun, but it won't break me. For Sky, this would be worse than a nightmare—it'd be an unspoken validation of her every single insecurity.

"Who was it, Sky?" I asked that night, struggling to keep my attention on the road as I drove us home. I can still remember the ache in my knuckles as I strangled the steering wheel. *"Was it a Devil? Was it Ansel? Heston? Did—"* I had to take a moment when my voice cracked, but I forced the question out through my teeth, *"Did Hamilton make you do this?"*

I glanced at her only long enough to register her frown, her eyes a mixture of confusion and innocence. *"I wanted to do it,"* she said, shocking me to my core. *"It was fun."* She touched her jaw. *"Although I am a little sore."*

Jesus.Christ.Superstar.

I walk toward the main high school building, feeling a million years older than I had that night. It was then that the shiny façade of this place was ripped away. I could never again look at it, or the students, the same way again. Not the historic architecture—arched windows, original leaded, wavy glass. The thick, carved doors, the floors; hardwood in the west wing but stone in the older, east wing. Portraits of the headmasters line the walls. The third one down has a familiar name. Hamilton.

As in Hamilton Bates' great-grandfather.

I glide through the throng of students like a salmon swimming upstream. It's bumpy and full of resistance. Despite the code of silence, the word "freak" is muttered it at least twice. I don't even try to put faces to the jabs anymore. What's the point? I just keep walking and take a breath when I get to my locker.

The first person I told about Sky was our nanny, Debbie. She's always been the rational one in our home. Our parents are smart, educated, and successful. Both Ivy League. Both lawyers. Both with hearts of gold. Both...how do I describe Mark and Becca Adams? Oh, right, they're idiots. Freedom of expression, personal conduct, individuality...that's the most important thing to them, not security or stability or safety. Not the thing kids want and need. Debbie stalked Sky's social media and found DMs between her and another girl where she bragged about what she'd done the night before. Mom was horrified that Sky's privacy had been invaded. Debbie tried to explain that fifteen-year-olds don't get privacy. The fight was huge, but ultimately Mom had to admit something was wrong. The gossip mill was churning and close to out of control.

Sky needed help, and they had to actually step up for once and be the adults in the room. The school board, my parents, and the other parents came to an agreement. Skylar would go to a residential treatment program. The Devils and anyone else at the party would not be punished, but a zero-tolerance policy was enacted. No gossip, no texts, no bullying, no whispers, nothing was ever to be discussed about that night.

To their credit and my complete surprise, everyone held up their end of the bargain. No police. No gossip. The rumor mill stopped completely. To the extreme. I don't know who made the call, although I have my suspicions, but if the students were going to pretend Sky Adams didn't exist? Then none of the Adamses existed. Particularly me.

After that meeting I became a ghost in my own school, as if I'd done something wrong by protecting my sister, by revealing that these heartless assholes couldn't be bothered to protect a fellow classmate, even if her blood isn't the right color. Truthfully, there's something worse than being openly bullied.

It's just being outright cancelled.

I rummage around for the books I need for my next class, knowing that they can pretend I don't exist, that that night didn't exist, but me? I don't have that luxury.

I remember it every time I walk down the hall. Every time I see their fancy cars and expensive shoes. Every time I see those goddamned letterman jackets. I know it when I see their smug faces —*his* face in particular. I remember Sky's mascara, running in sad lines down her cheekbones even though she swears she wanted it. I remember knowing that was a lie and I remember just how badly I wanted the steering wheel I'd been strangling to be someone's throat. I remember how I felt standing in that hallway, like a live grenade had just gone off in my chest.

I told him I would make him pay, but I haven't. How do you even begin to make these guys pay? They have everything. Money, power, entitlement...

It's the Devil's fault she was there that night. He's the leader. He has, as he brags about ad nauseum, *power*. At best, he let Xavier invite her, play with her, make her feel special, and then leave her to the wolves.

And, at worst... well.

Hamilton isn't just some random guy who sat by and watched, he's my biggest rival. We've spent the last four years vying for valedictorian and are in competition for captain of the swim team. Yeah, me, the kid without a 'pedigree', has been holding her own against the prince of the school. He can't truly ignore me because I'm the thorn in his side. The risk to his coronation. The Michael to his Lucifer.

So that's it. That's how I make him pay.

By being *better*.

Like every other morning, I glance at the tiny mirror affixed to the inside of my locker. I look beneath the mask at my dark hair and blue eyes and repeat an affirmation.

"You're better than him. Smarter. Faster. Stronger. Don't play his games. Make him play yours."

I smile and replace the mask, prepared for another day of battle.

~

I MOVED to the dorms the day after Skylar left for the residential program in Texas. Did it seem counterintuitive to move to the place I was being frozen out of? Yes. But being at home was worse. I couldn't face my parents.

Mark and Becca...I do love them. They took me in when I was three, rescuing me from a truly shitty situation of neglect and addiction. It's strange, because I know that living with them meant I had guaranteed shelter, top-notch academics, and opportunities I never would have had with my birth mother. But it takes more than money and good intentions to make a good parent.

As much as I hate the Devils' obsession with lineage, sometimes there is this nagging worry that people like Hamilton may have a point. Take my older brother Brayden, for example. He was adopted first—as a baby. He never knew anything else, just the life Mark and Becca gave him; wealth, opportunity, entitlement. He was even a Devil himself, star JV quarterback. His birth mother was, as I understand it, a thirty-something from Biloxi with a transient house-keeping job and an intense addiction to a little drug called Whatchya Got. My parents, high off of a lifelong bender of righteousness and delusion, wholeheartedly believe in open adoptions and encourage us all to make a connection with our birth family.

So Brayden did.

He met his mom. And I'm not entirely sure what went down or why, but here are the facts: Despite a long history of academic and athletic excellence, his grades began to slip. The boy who used to be one of the most promising Devils only just barely met the credit requirements to graduate. Now he's working part time at a mechanic garage, cleaning bathrooms and floors, hoping for an apprenticeship.

Then you've got Sky, two years younger than me. She was one when Mom and Dad brought her home, cute and smiley despite the cigarette burn marks on her arms. Even as a baby, I think she knew the best way to survive was to pretend everything was fine. She followed all of us around all the time. Our smiles made her smile. Our happiness made her happy, like an adorable little emotional sponge. It was cute, back then, before I realized what it said about where she came from, what had happened to her. It was cute before I realized how easily she would be manipulated, taken advantage of.

The twins were merely infants when my mom brought them home. A boy and a girl. That was the year things changed for the rest of us. There was no more pretending outside the home we were true Adamses. Their skin color told the truth. We loved them, of course. I still fondly remember sitting in their nursery, in the months after they moved in, wishing one of them would wake up and fuss so I could hold and soothe them—my very own baby brother and sister.

But outside the walls of our eclectic home, people weren't as understanding. Our classmates knew we weren't like them, with all their long family trees that dated back to the Mayflower. Sure, the Adams family did, but in the eyes of our peers we weren't really Adamses. We didn't count. We were charity cases. Rejects. Discarded and abandoned.

Mom and Dad told us not to believe it, but come on, right? At a certain age, all of us begin getting it. Brayden did. And then eventually, I did, too. The playdates stopped. Friendships grew cold. Why do they think Sky needed so much approval? Why do they think Michaela schemes and sneaks? Why do they think Micha feeds the world little bits of himself in the tiniest increments? Why do they think I don't want to come home?

Mom and Dad may have saved us from a hard, uncertain life, but they tossed us into the lion's den, and I'm not sure that's any better. Honestly, it's probably worse.

2

Hamilton

"Dude, *dude*, where did you even go last night? We looked all over for you," Ansel asks as we meet up in the stairwell leading from the boys' dormitory. "That party was fucking lit."

"You're such an idiot." I reply, "I was there, didn't you see me?"

Ansel, who has been one of my best friends since middle school, looks at me through his ridiculous hipster glasses and asks, "What was your costume?"

"Michael Phelps. Speedo, swim cap, and goggles. I even had a stack of gold medals hanging around my neck."

"Seriously? How did I miss that?" Ansel looks just like someone you'd expect named *Ansel* to look. Every part of him, from his non-prescription glasses to his manbun, has been pieced together with carefully derivative dumbassery. Sometimes the urge to slap him upside his big dumb head is so strong, it almost chokes me to death.

It's usually best to just give in to these impulses.

"Hey!" he squawks. The velocity of my palm sends his glasses lurching off his nose and he indignantly adjusts them. "Uncool!"

"You were trashed." Our smarter friend Emory explains, falling in step. Unlike Ansel, Emory has an impeccable memory. He got tested once, but it turns out, he isn't eidetic, he's just really into being a know-it-all. He's a year younger than the rest of us but fits in nicely. "You took Elana Maxwell behind Connor Hall. She showed up thirty minutes later with puke all over her tits, screaming about what a dickhead you are. Xavier and I hauled your ass up to your room before security found you."

"Ah," Ansel says, as if it all suddenly makes sense. "That explains the messages from Elana on my phone." He glances down at his phone, warily. "Thirty-six so far."

Xavier not-so-subtly coughs, "*Stalker*," and even I smirk.

Elana Maxwell *is* a stalker. Classic Stage 5 Clinger. Once she gets her hooks into you, it'd be easier to get rid of the clap. But Ansel, being the insufferable dumbass of the group, is our peak romantic. He's always on the lookout for love, although a consistent fuck buddy has never gone amiss. Elana's been around for a few months now. It was only a matter of time.

Truthfully, I didn't stick around the party long at all. I made an appearance—as was expected—fooled around with Reagan for a bit —as was expected—and then went back to my room. I've got too much on the line over the next few weeks to blow it all on one night of Halloween partying. I can celebrate after I've been named captain of the swim team. Then I can add that detail to my college applications and solidify once and for all that Gwendolyn Adams is done at this school.

It'll be the final nail in the coffin, and I can't wait to pound it in.

"What's with the weird look?" Emory asks me. "You look like an evil villain or something."

I shrug, smirking. "Just plotting to overtake the world."

He snorts. "From you, I believe it. Geez, I wonder who's pissed you off this time?"

It's a rhetorical question. Everyone knows who is number one on my shit list. She's been perched there for six months now. To be fair, maybe even longer.

We reach the main landing and I look around the crowd, making sure Reagan's not around. She's clingy—not as bad as Elana—but she's looking for something. A date to the winter formal? A relationship commitment? A ride on my cock? None of those things are going to happen. Don't get me wrong—she's hot. Sexy. Not to mention, seriously good at giving head. But sometimes at this school, it's like shooting fish in a fucking barrel. Absolutely zero challenge. Sometimes it's almost like I want a chase. Which doesn't make sense, either. Easy pickings is what I really need.

Zero distractions, right?

I breathe a small sigh of relief when I don't see her anywhere, but I do catch sight of a pale face and dark wavy hair cutting through the crowd. Her eyes are focused straight ahead, oblivious to everyone around her. Mine narrow.

Xavier's fingers snap in front of my face. "Hamilton!"

"Huh?" I ask, dragging my eyes away from the girl.

"I asked if you wanted to use the box seats this weekend. Dad's out of town on business. He said I could have them."

"The United game?" I raise an eyebrow, and he nods. If Ansel's thing is being a dumb hipster and Emory's thing is being a smartass know-it-all, then Xavier's thing is being the guy with connections. "I'm in, definitely."

"Awesome. I'll text you details. We can get there early, there's a full bar."

We bump fists and Xavier heads off to his first period, but I hold back a minute, skimming the room.

"You're doing it again," Ansel says.

I blink at him. "Doing what?"

"Looking for her."

We both know who "her" is.

Dark hair. Big blue eyes. Puffy pink lips.

"Well, duh? Because I fucking hate her and want to do everything possible to avoid her."

Ansel rolls his eyes. "You're not the only one who got in trouble over that bullshit."

"No," I agree, jaw tightening, "but I'm the one with the most on the line."

After the meeting with the board and Skylar's parents, everyone agreed to The Terms, and trust me, capital Ts are necessary here. Most of the parents thought The Terms were punishment enough. Not my father. There's never a problem too small for his emotional sledgehammer. Being at that party, letting the Devils get out of control, not having a handle on everything; these are all a clear sign of weakness. Well, at least to him. Apparently, the fact that I'm the best—academically, athletically, genetically—makes me responsible for everyone else, and it's bullshit. But a 'real leader' wouldn't have let that happen. A *Hamilton* wouldn't have let that happen.

A Hamilton would *never* let someone inferior, with no name, no legacy, dictate my future.

In typical fashion, he completely overreacted by cracking down. In his opinion, I never should have been around the public-school kids from Northridge in the first place, and I sure as hell shouldn't have been anywhere near the Adams family. My father's perspective is that if I want to play with commoners, there are *avenues* to make that happen. The worst of the fallout was that I had to move out of the estate and into the dorms for "extra supervision." Additionally, he took my BMW away; it's locked up in the student lot with a tracker affixed to the bottom, only to be used to travel to and from home. The explanation is that my singular focus was to be on academics, swimming, and tending to my tarnished reputation. This was followed by a demeaning lecture about 'girls like that' and how it's best to stay clear of them, and concluded with the promise that, if I needed someone so desperately to suck me off, he'd hire a reputable escort.

Jesus.

My kingdom for the ability to bleach *that* conversation from my memory.

"Once I make team captain, he'll lay off," I assure. "It's just really important to him that I succeed."

And maintain the legacy.

Preston Prep is just the first step of many. Next is getting into one of the southern Ivies. Vanderbilt, Washington and Lee, UVA, or Wake Forest. And then, joining my father and grandfather's fraternity, which would lead to me being invited to "The Machine," a secret society that would be the key to all future relationships and successes. I had the bloodline, the money, and the family prestige, but if I tarnished it—fucked with it in any way—all of that could crumble. I'd be *done*—not just socially, but also where my father was concerned. I'm under no illusions. Unconditional family love and all that other fluffy bullshit might be enough for trash like the Adamses, but my family? Not a chance.

"You should take Reagan home," Ansel suggests. "Isn't her dad a senator or something? Maybe she can calm him down."

I don't want to give my father *or* Reagan any ideas, but yeah, Reagan with her luxurious blonde hair and impeccable make-up—not to mention perfect tits that she inherited from her beauty queen mother—would distract my father for a little bit, even if only for the conflict of wondering if he liked her for me, or himself.

Fucking gross.

I shake that off before it devolves into physical nausea. "No, it'll be fine. Coach is making the big announcement next week. I think things will chill from there."

Ansel lifts a dubious eyebrow. "And if not?"

My eyes follow the sway of Gwendolyn's hips as she turns down the hall. My fingers twitch, sparked by the anger boiling low beneath the surface.

"Then shit is going to get very real."

I SLIDE into my first period seat, opening my backpack and dropping my book on the desk.

Heston Wilcox, another Devil, follows me in and takes the seat next to mine. Our fathers are both leaders in the business community, members of the same clubs, and alumni of Preston. As a result, Heston and I have been tossed together since preschool. It's a good thing we like one another. We've swam competitively together and against one another since we were four, which means a lot of long weekends and practices spent with each other. This will be our last year on the team. We started the academic year with a pact to make this one the best, and not even this stupid

Adams drama could dampen our determination. If anything, it's just driven us harder.

"How's the shoulder," he asks, opening his own book.

I rotate it, out of reflex. The pulling ache has receded since last semester, leaving a tightness in its wake. "Better. The PT seems to be working. It's stronger."

"Good," he replies, slouching in his seat. "I need my anchor."

When we're not competing against one another, Heston and I are on the same relay. He's the first leg and he swims hard, pulling us ahead of the pack early. I'm the last leg, the anchor, the one who brings it home. It's like this: if he fails, it means I need to work that much harder. But it's not necessarily over. I'm clutch. We can come back from it. But if *I* fail, that's it. All his effort—everyone's effort—is wasted.

Story of my life.

We've won the state championship three years in a row, so we both need me to be healthy if we're going to get a fourth.

I glance at the clock on the wall. There's one minute left before class starts. Dr. Ross is already at the front of the room. She's an old hag with a hard-on for punctuality and will assign detention if you're even a single minute late. My gaze jumps a row and two seats over to the seat that's always empty until right before the bell rings.

At twenty-five seconds 'til, *she* walks into the room, skirt swishing against her long legs. She doesn't look at anyone, not even Dr. Ross, before hooking her bag on the back of her chair. She sits, smoothing her skirt underneath her. She's got a swimmer's body. Lean, strong, long. When the bell rings a second later, she tosses her hair over her shoulder and stares straight ahead.

I flinch when I feel a sharp kick against my leg. Heston smirks at me and mouths, "Obsessed."

"Fuck off." I glare at my book and flip to the page written on the board.

"I will if you stop looking at her like you want to peel off her skin." He whispers, but the laughter is clear in his voice. "Your name is Hamilton, Bates. Not Norman."

My jaw tenses. Am I pissed at Gwen? Fuck yes. Do I want to make her pay for dragging me into all this? Absolutely. But obviously Heston is right. I seriously need to chill the hell out. I just don't think she realizes how much she's messed up my life. My dad wasn't the only one upset about the party. My mother was convinced I was going down as a sex offender, that this will hit the news, that "people" (AKA: the women in at the club, at her charity groups, the Junior League) will know.

Bad PR?

Heaven forbid.

Gwendolyn Adams and her siblings are garbage picked up by her hippie parents out of some unfortunate need to show the world how charitable and virtuous they are. It's a freak house over there. You can take the trash out of the trailer, but you can't take the trailer out of the trash.

If anything, I blame the school board and my parents—all of the parents—for letting this happen in the first place. I remember when Brayden and Gwendolyn showed up at Preston Prep, back when we were all in the elementary wing together. Hell, we played on the playground together every day at recess. Brayden was cool, good at football. And Gwen—Jesus Christ. She was so pretty and unassuming... right up until she opened her mouth. The girl would fight about anything. I'm pretty sure she had whole treaties solving the line to the swing sets, and some of the kids were just outright *over* trying to use the monkey bars when she was around.

I figured, even then, she'd inherited that trait from her lawyer parents. We thought they were like the rest of us. Mark Adams' name was on the alumni list. Why wouldn't we assume? No one realized the truth until the twins appeared. Becca Adams just showed up one day with two new babies, and like, come on. It was obvious she'd never been pregnant, not like Ansel's mom two years before. Instead, Mrs. Adams was as skinny as ever. But when she showed off those babies, she called them her own.

They weren't hers. Not with the green eyes and creamy brown skin.

That's when we knew.

All of the Adams kids were adopted.

They weren't like us, they weren't legacies.

They didn't deserve to be here, to absorb our knowledge, to win our awards, to dictate our behavior. Gwendolyn Adams is the worst of the worst. That little play with her hot mess of a sister? That was aimed at us. The Devils. The popular people. The ones who belonged here. She's determined to topple our system, our history, and anything else that makes us who we are.

I'm sure as fuck not going to let her.

3

THWWWIIIICK

The dome of mac n' cheese on my tray wiggles once it's released from the scoop. Bev, the lunch lady, adds a watery spoonful of green beans and plops a greasy piece of chicken next to it.

You'd think rich kid school would have better food, but cafeteria fare may be one of the world's great equalizers.

"Here you go, hon," she says, after adding a large, square brownie.

"Thank you." My voice sounds small and weird. It may be the first thing I've said since seeing the twins that morning. Exiting the line, I turn and face the room. Every move has become a landmine. This is part of the plan, obviously. They can't get back at me and Sky the traditional way, but they can make every little thing as difficult as possible. I kind of have to hand it to them. It's almost impressive how these people truly excel at the art of ostracism.

As I walk past each table, empty seats are immediately swallowed by shifting bodies. There's no eye contact. No invitation. For a while there, I secretly ate in the library. I could get my homework done and have a little respite from all the intensely aggressive being-ignored. But that came to a sharp and sudden end following an announcement over the intercom letting the student body know that eating outside the cafeteria was now prohibited. Now, to the casual observer this might have seemed like an unfortunate coincidence.

I know better.

I make my way across the room to a small table by the vending machines. It's not the worst seat. There's a window that looks over the middle school wing's garden and sometimes I can catch a glimpse of the twins. Opening my juice, I peer out the window and—*what the hell?*

A reflection hovers on the glass—like I'm staring right at him.

Hamilton Bates.

It's not like I don't know he watches me. I feel his laser sharp gaze on me all the time. At first, I was inwardly pretty paranoid about it, but now it's like an eerie comfort. Keep your enemies close, right? Hamilton is definitely my enemy. He loathes me, blames me. The feeling is mutual.

I always make an effort not to look, no matter how much I want to, how much my instincts itch or my spidey-senses go on alert. I pretend like I'm not even aware of his focus on me in the hallway, or in the classes we share. I pretend like he's not tracking my times at swim or observing me across the quad. It's Hamilton. He's a raging asshole, but he knows not to cross a line, or his daddy will crack the whip.

He'd also never, ever touch me.

God, he may get infected by my *inferior genes*.

But in this moment, I can see him in the reflection. As he's completely unaware of this, I take a moment to resentfully soak in the Devil. He's tragically beautiful, truth be told. He has the face and body of a god, and these cold eyes that could pin you even when they *aren't* trying to drill a hole into your skull. As someone who's been exposed to his nearly naked body since we started swimming together, I can definitely attest that he's genetically superior—there's no doubt about that. He's got the perfect swimmer's physique; long, lean, and ripped with muscles. His wing-span allows him to glide across the pool like he was born in the water. His entire torso is just frankly ridiculous.

And his face?

Well, his features are striking, created from generations of perfect unions. The guy is basically a walking, talking CW star, like...it's just obnoxious. But his looks are diminished by the perpetual, unnerving scowl on his face. His eyebrows are always pulled low in anger, making his eyes seem even darker than usual. Soulless. Lost. And his full bottom lip is always raw and chapped from worrying it with his teeth.

I stare so long, so hard at his reflection that I don't realize the moment our eyes meet, caught with one another, until it's too late. His lip curves up into an evil smirk, as if I'm the one being busted by watching him. The heat of embarrassment rushes up my neck, but I don't blink, I don't look away, he's not going to win—

"Can I sit here?"

I blink, poorly recovering my flinch. "Huh?"

The stranger repeats, "Is it cool if I take this seat?"

I glance back at the window, searching once again for Hamilton's reflection, but he's already gone, vanished like a spiteful mirage. With a steeling inhale, I finally take in the guy standing before me. He's not incredibly tall—compact, but the fit lines of his upper body are visible through his white button-down shirt. His tie is askew and I smell the hint of chlorine when he moves.

"Who are you?" I ask, not unkindly.

"Tyson Riggins." He brushes his blond hair out of his eyes and offers me his hand. I stare at it for a moment and then remember my manners, shaking it. He explains, "I'm new. A transfer from Northridge."

"A transfer?" *From Northridge?* I study his face, trying frantically to draw a memory of him from that line of boys waiting to have a go at my sister. Fortunately for both of us, I come up blank.

I glance around and wonder if this is some kind of setup. Typically, no one pays me any attention, so it has that faint whiff of deceit.

"I got a scholarship for the diving team. My coach pulled some strings and got me on the Red Devils. Seems like you were short a diver this year and they needed to fill the gap."

"Oh," I say, still a little confused. "Okay?"

He sits across from me and picks up his plastic fork. "You're Gwendolyn Adams."

"Gwen," I correct, feeling the pull of tension in my shoulders. "Do we know one another?"

He shovels a spoonful of mac n' cheese into his mouth, talking around it. "I watched you swim at the state finals last year and take the record in the two hundred free. You're really good."

I search his eyes for a long moment, looking for any sign of malice or artifice. But the gaze that holds mine is warm, casual. I look away, clearing my throat. "That's... I mean, thank you."

He tears off a piece of chicken, pops it in his mouth and licks the grease from his fingers. "Sorry you have to see this. I'm starving. Morning practice and all."

"I have brothers," I reply, fighting a smile. "I'm familiar with the repulsive eating habits of growing boys."

He grins and bites off a chunk of roll.

I lean forward, deciding he seems earnest enough. Probably a nice kid. Probably fun to hang around. Probably not someone who wants their reputation ruined on the first day at a new school. "Look, it's nice of you to come over and everything, and I don't want to seem like a bitch, but I'm not really sure sitting with me is going to put you on the right foot around here. You may want to find another seat."

"Oh, the fact you were sitting alone was a big plus for me." His blue eyes scan around the room. "I might not go here, but trust me, I know these assholes. Been competing against them for years. It's like all those generations of in-breeding turned their brains into toxic mush. When I walked in here, recognized you, and saw you sitting alone, it was like a sign from god."

He lifts the chain on his neck, revealing a silver cross, and presses it to his lips.

Interesting.

I sigh down at my lunch tray. "You're putting such a massive target on your back right now, you have no idea."

By now, enough people have noticed the new kid. And they've definitely noticed him talking to me.

"Eh," he shrugs and wipes his mouth with a napkin. "I don't really care what everyone else thinks, do you?"

A bubble of laughter bursts from my throat and escapes in an awkward squawk. I know it's not exactly that easy. But hey, that *is* my usual mantra, isn't it?

"No." I pick up my fork, supposing an appetite won't be the hardest thing to muster.

"Good. I mean, I'm new and I'm going to need a friend. You're not new and," he looks around and makes a face, "well, it looks like you've got some wiggle room for friends. If you want, I mean. You may totally be into this isolated, hot-girl thing, though. Which is also perfectly respectable."

A wave of warmth floods my cheeks at him calling me hot. Years of diving practice must have deprived his brain of oxygen at some point, because no one thinks I'm hot. I've never been anything but the human embodiment of shoe-scum to these people, and it might be fine and well to decide not to care what everyone else thinks, but it doesn't make it any easier to look in the mirror every morning and see myself as anything but.

"If there's one thing I want," I decide, shaking off the negative mood before it can find a toehold, "it's to have the best senior swim season yet. Diving included. And yeah, it'd be nice to have someone to hang with."

He grins, tucking back into his lunch, and my grin comes strangely easy, natural. I lean back and marvel at how such a minor thing can change an entire psychological trajectory. I don't know who or what sent Tyson Riggins into my life. I'm not religious, but who knows? Maybe it was divine intervention. My eyes skim the room for the red and black jackets, seeing them clustered across the room, and I know one thing for sure.

It definitely wasn't a Devil.

~

I LIKE COMPETING, and I genuinely enjoy swimming with others, but there's nothing better than facing an empty, still pool. The flat glassy surface, as if suspended in time, the whirr of the pumps, the sharp scent of chlorine; this is home. Most swimmers and divers prefer just jumping in, but me? I like toeing the surface before I take the plunge, feeling that first zing of cool water and following the ripple it creates —our fond 'hello'.

My toes push off the side of the wall and my body slices through the water. Each stroke gets me closer, each turn an opportunity to get ahead. Down in the blue, where the water is clear and the only sound is the muted *whoosh* of my strokes, I can finally and truly escape it all. I don't think of anything but cool enamel blues, the burn of my muscles, and water rushing against my sides. I don't think of Sky. Of Hamilton. Not anyone.

Although I guess I do think about Tyson a little bit.

His arrival had been a surprise.

After we parted, I did my research by checking him out on social media. To my relief, he actually does seem entirely legit. Photos on ChattySnap show him at dive competitions all over the country. There are a few pictures of him at Northridge's homecoming a few weeks earlier. He looked adorable in his tux and was obviously having a good time with his friends, particularly the cute girl that seemed to be his date. He's a junior—not a senior—which makes the school transfer far less suspicious. Truthfully, even I had flirted with the possibility of transferring when everything happened with Sky. Mom and Dad offered, but really, I didn't want to start over. I just want to move on.

I finish my final lap and check the clock on the wall. Coach James will be by soon to lock up, and I'm not supposed to be in here—not exactly. There's no guard on duty and it's against school rules to swim without one. I know the schedule, though, and I know if I get in between 8:15 and 9:20, after water polo practice finishes but before lockup, no one will be the wiser. The clock says 9:13.

Plenty of time.

Water rushes down my body as I pull myself out of the pool. I grab my towel, wrapping it around my midsection, and then enter the small co-ed locker room. The main one is always closed once activities are over for the day, but this one has a combination lock, allowing for after-hours entry. I walk in and head to the locker where I left my towel and a change of clothes. After hastily drying off, I pull on my flannel pants right over my suit, hoping they'll warm me, then bend over to wring the excess water out of my hair. I'm just like that—head between my knees, hair all tangled in a towel—when the door opens.

I freeze.

Shit. If Coach James catches me, I'm beyond screwed.

I fling my hair back, prepared to twist it into a bun, but instead yelp when I realize that I'm not alone.

And it's not Coach James.

I still with my hands over my head, blinking at the scowling boy in front of me. His eyes dart down to my chest, and *hey*. I just got out of a pool that isn't heated particularly well. It's *cold*. I don't have to look to know my nipples are peaked.

His cold gaze slithers up to mine, mouth slanting into some unholy marriage of sneer and smirk. "Well, well, well. Happy to see me?"

I don't even grace him with a reply.

"Using the pool after hours? With no guard on duty?" Hamilton's smirk transforms to an amused sort of satisfaction. He shakes his head, *tsk*ing. "This doesn't seem like the kind of behavior befitting a student vying for team captain. I'm thinking it might be my duty to report this to the coach."

His hair and T-shirt are dark with sweat. The sleeves of his shirt have been ripped off, allowing my eyes to take in his wiry biceps, glistening forearms, and the weight-lifting gloves covering his hands.

I raise an eyebrow. "I could say the same about you. The gym closed an hour ago."

His eyes flash in anger, weightlifting gloves rumpling as he fists them. But his anger is just as quickly gone, replaced by the same cool demeanor. "Go ahead and tell whoever you like. You'll find I have permission for extra gym hours for physical therapy."

I have no idea if he's telling the truth or not. His poker face has always been eerily immaculate. It's one of the reasons he's so dangerous. It's one of the reasons my nerves are always on edge around him, constantly trying to find my footing, but never quite able.

"Of course," I say, twisting the band around my hair. "Nothing you do is ever against the rules. There are always special circumstances, always an excuse for your behavior, right?" I level him with a look of utter disgust. "The Devils are always covered."

His eyes spark once again, but I avoid them by reaching for both my shirt and the flimsy pretense that I don't sense his absolute hatred of me—hatred simply for failing to be a perfect clone of every other student here. Closing my eyes, I pull my shirt over my head, relieved to be hidden from his glower, however brief it may be.

When my head emerges from the shirt, however, he's inches from my face.

I jerk back, crashing into my locker.

"Here's what you don't get, Adams." His voice is carefully controlled, but even still, I can detect the barely restrained growl of anger in his words. "There is no room for mistakes, excuses, or bad behavior in my life. I follow strict rules, codes, and procedures. I surround myself with people who adhere to the same values. The same ideals. The same understanding of how life works—what it takes to succeed."

He's so close that I can smell the mixture of sweat and deodorant on his skin. I try shifting away from the locker handle stabbing into my back, but I'm pinned by his glare and the solid wall of him.

His eyes narrow at the movement, eyes tightening as he continues, "I know you think I was involved with what happened to your sister, but let me make something perfectly clear." His jaw flexes as he tilts his head closer, voice pitched low and harsh. "She's trash. You're trash. Your whole goddamned family is a bunch of feral, abandoned rejects. Your blood, your saliva? It's all dirty. There's no way I'd contaminate my dick or any other part of my body with it. Understand?"

God, he's so predictable and childish and... well, just so utterly *lame*. His words don't even graze me, they're just that over-the-top ridiculous. A laugh bubbles from my chest and escapes in a snort before I can stop it. Hamilton's eyes flash even hotter, and then—because god, I just can't even help it—I reach out and caress his cheek, running my fingertips down his chiseled jaw.

He jolts back as if being burned.

"What the hell are you doing?" he spits.

I smile serenely. "Soothing you like a child. That was a tantrum, right? I'm fresh out of binkies or blankets, else I'd give you one."

He lunges, completely closing the distance between us, his two palms meeting the metal of the lockers with a resounding *bang*. His muscular arms pin me there, one on each side, but I hide my shock enough to fight back a flinch.

Instead, I raise my chin.

The dark pupils in his eyes are blown with anger and I'm surrounded by him. Too close, too tall, too big, too *Hamilton*. In all the years I've known him, been forced into classrooms and gyms with him, I've never been this close to Hamilton Bates. I'm not sure why, but the first thing I notice about his proximity is the annoying lack of flaws on his face, even this close. You could probably put this guy under a microscope and find the answer to the universe or something.

My eyes track a drop of sweat as it falls from a lock of his inky hair to clutch at his eyelash. "You think baiting me is funny?"

"You want to know what I think?" I hold his gaze, completely calm despite the percussion of something hot and frenetic in my veins. "I think you're a joke, Bates. I think you're weak and painfully unoriginal. I think you're so transparently pathetic that you believe controlling your minions might make you look stronger, even though it really doesn't. But mostly I think one of them dared to show up with my sister instead of raiding your Approved Bitches stash, so you showed him what you really thought she was worth."

He reacts, by grabbing my wrists and slamming my arms up and over my head.

He leans his hard, powerful body against mine, pinning me with all his crazy heat. "Shut up." His warm breath washes over my face, the sharp scent of old cinnamon gum making my throat bob with a swallow. "Jesus fucking Christ, do you ever just *shut the fuck up*?"

His grip, damp and slippery against my wrists, flexes once, twice, and for the life of me I just can't stop myself. "Nope."

His nostrils flare on a long, sharp inhale, eyes closing as if he's asking some higher power for the strength to put up with me. It must not work, because when he opens his eyes again, for the first time, I almost feel genuinely afraid of him.

If you asked me if he would have ever gone this far, I'd say no. I'd say that he was all bluster and pedigree, just a chess piece playing the board he was raised to dominate. But now I'm not so sure. His carefully composed poker face is crumbling, I can tell, and behind it is something crazed and red with intent, a sharp edge that trembles down my spine.

No, he's just trying to intimidate me. He can't control me like he can the others, this is nothing more than a last-ditch effort. That realization gives me renewed strength.

I fight against him, hiding my wince as the bones in my wrist strain against his grip. "Let go."

But his grip just tightens. "Come on, Gwen. Admit it. You'd love it if I caved—just once—for a piece of trash like you, wouldn't you?"

I freeze, not even sure who he's arguing with right now. Me or himself? Either way, it's clear that he's not releasing me. Now it's just the two of us caught in some battle of impulses, a battle I'm not sure I entirely understand. If he hates me so much, if I repulse him so deeply, why is he holding me like this? Touching me?

The same question is clear in his eyes, eyebrows tightly knitted together as his gaze dips to my parted mouth.

He's wondering the same thing.

His face tilts and I see the muscle in the back of his jaw twitch. But then his palms finally loosen around my wrists, and it's like a cord has been cut, because I figure this is the end. He's about to release me, and then we can both walk away from this whole awkward, strange, bewildering encounter.

His lips twist into a sneer as he mutters, "I hate you."

I roll my eyes. "Well the feeling is mutual, you gigantic assho—"

His lips crash into mine.

Briefly, I ponder string theory.

Because you see, the Gwen in any other universe would be so shocked, so grossed the hell out, that she'd probably vomit all over his dumb, wet, obnoxiously perfect mouth. Probably, she'd knee him in the balls. Likely, she'd screech and shove him away. Whatever she'd do in that other universe—the Alternate Universe of Sense-Making—it definitely wouldn't be *this*.

I'm wholly unprepared for the jolt that runs through me—this spike of white-hot, senseless *want* that consume me so forcefully, I actually whimper against his mouth.

His *mouth*, what the actual hell, warm and soft and hard, all at once.

Lost in the hot, confusing tangle of it all, I'm only vaguely aware of him releasing my hands, but I feel it like a lightning bolt when he shifts his grip, one clutching my hip while the other winds itself in the hair at the base of my neck, pulling our bodies flush.

An inkling of sense manages to make it through the fog, long enough for me to be aware that he's not pinning me anymore. I should definitely run. Or like, that whole 'kneeing him in the balls' thing that Alternate Universe Gwen was so fond of? That's pretty good. I should totally do that. I should escape.

I do none of those things.

Instead, I part my lips and deepen the kiss, hitching a breath when our tongues finally meet. My spine does something weird and liquid when he licks into my mouth, all slickness and heat and sharp edges.

My hands glide over his chest, exploring the hard muscles from years of intense competitive swimming. He feels solid, hot and alive. Not like a cold-hearted demon, at all. From here, all pressed against his skin, our tongues sliding together, I can feel his pulse beneath my palm.

It's racing.

Just like mine.

His abs jump when I graze his taut lower belly, and his groan sounds ragged at the edges, like it's being torn from his chest. He surges forward in response, hips pushing mine into the lockers, and there's no mistaking the length of him against my belly, hard and eager and willing. I gasp into his mouth at the feel of it, going still.

He jerks back.

His eyes are hooded and glazed, but I can still see the creep of hysteria in them, and I know that—for the first time maybe ever—me and Hamilton Bates are on the exact same page.

This has gone too far.

Way too far.

Actually, it passed 'too far' a hundred miles back and is now crossing an Atlantic-sized ocean of weird.

The door to the locker room suddenly creaks, and it's like an ice-cold bucket of water. Our eyes widen and I freeze, trapping a tense breath in the pit of my chest. The sound of distant, shuffling footsteps fills the room, right before the lights go off. Darkness shrouds us, but only briefly, before the bright 'exit' signs above the doorways on either side of the room bathe us in a buzzing ominous red.

Shakily, Hamilton exhales, and I follow. I feel his chest dip under my hands, but my pulse fills my ears until I can hear little else. If we're caught like this... Hamilton Bates and Gwendolyn Adams? Obviously, the consequences would be unbearable.

Our eyes meet, the knowledge of that truth passing between us. What would the Devils say? Oh *god*, how would I explain this to my family? To Sky?

The betrayal drops like a stone in my belly. "I won't tell," I whisper, although I'm not sure why.

Then, as fast as this all started, it ends.

He jumps back, swatting my hands away. "Go," he says in a low, rough voice. "Just get the hell out of here."

I stare at him owlishly for a long, suspended moment, fighting the impulse to touch my abused lips.

His responding glare is probably meant to intimidate me, but it's a bit dampened by the way he reaches down to adjust himself in his shorts. "What the fuck do you want, Adams? Go! I told you, I hate you. I hate everything about you. You're ugly. You're stupid. Your sister is a goddamned whore."

The insults that spill from his mouth are limp, like he's just pulling from muscle memory at this point, but the last one is enough to finally shake some sense into me.

I slap my palms onto his bare chest and *shove*. Clearly caught off guard enough to lose his footing, the back of his knees slam against the bench, toppling him backwards. While he's down, I grab my bag and leave, putting as much distance between me and Hamilton Bates as I possibly can.

4

IF ANYONE FINDS OUT...

The thought throbs through my mind as I rush across the quad. Thankfully, it's dark out and nearing curfew, which means that there are few, if any, people to see my walk of shame. A gust of cool, November air sends a shiver rippling across my limbs. I left without my workout bag, which included my sweatshirt. Doesn't matter. That was the very least of my fuck-ups tonight. I need to cool the fuck off anyway, from head to toe. And—*shit*—yes, that apparently includes my dick, because *Jesus Christ*.

What just happened?

No fucking idea.

One minute I'm taunting her, just hoping to put her off all this shit, and the next thing I know, I'm kissing her.

And she kissed me back.

I come to an abrupt stop as a gag seizes my throat. My stomach twists in disgust, but I luckily manage to keep the contents down. I drag a wrist over my mouth in a futile attempt to rid myself of the ghost of her kiss, the taste of her mouth.

Fuck.

What have I done?

The thought that responds to me is, annoyingly, my father's voice. If he ever—god fucking forbid—found out about this. It's what he'd think. It's what he'd say. It's what I'd be.

Weak.

She'd said it, too. *"I think you're weak..."*

My hands clench around the thought. Is that what set me off? Her calling me out like that?

It'd be easy to say it was. But I'd been on a hair trigger from the instant I'd accidentally walked in the room and saw her in that tight swimsuit. The girls always wear these racing suits, low in the back and cut high on the hips, revealing plenty of skin, leaving nothing to the imagination, and come on. I'm only human. Her nipples were pebbled from the cool air.

That's not what I saw first, though. It'd been her wide blue eyes and her flushed cheeks. Her full, pink lips. Not like the other girls— no need for pounds of makeup or hushed procedures over spring break.

Just seeing her, knowing how much trouble she'd caused me, made my blood boil. And the thing is, she doesn't care. She never has. She calls us all cruel, heartless sociopaths, but in reality? She's no better. And now that I've had time to really turn it over in my brain, I remember that whole situation in the locker room was *her* fault. She'd baited me. Humiliated me. Basically, dared me to scare the hell out of her.

I push open the door to Cresswell, and take the stairs two at a time, passing the first three floors, up to the fourth—the senior hall. I cast a furtive glance down the hallway to be sure no one is around. If anyone found out...

Fuck, I'd never live this down. *Never*. Not after years of ruling the Devils with an iron fist. Not after setting such an immaculate standard on who we associated with, and how we treated those we didn't. Sure, I'd been cruel to those who stepped out of line, but it was for good cause, no one could fault me for that. That's what leaders do. They lead.

They definitely don't make out with trash like Gwendolyn Adams in the co-ed locker room.

If anyone heard I'd done such a thing, every ounce of my credibility would be gone. All the work I've done up to now, wasted.

My unit was down at the end, with a view of the lake. My father may have made me live with the commoners, but no Bates was ever going to live in a dorm's shitty single. Nah, I unlock the door to my suite, and something within me unwinds, even if only slightly. Even when it came to punishment, I had the best.

"Yo!" Xavier peers at me over the back of the couch. "Where you been?"

I clear my throat, hoping my voice doesn't sound as rough as it feels. "Gym."

I make a beeline for my own room, grabbing a banana and sports drink from the kitchenette's counter along the way.

But Xavier isn't far behind. He leans casually in the doorway as I toe off my shoes. "Hey, you good?"

What? Why? Can he tell?

Hoping he doesn't notice the way I freeze, I twist the cap off my drink. "Sure. Why?"

"I don't know." He shrugs and finally enters the room. "You've just been distracted all day. Emory said you were coming to play Madden with us after dinner, but you never showed."

"Ah, right. Sorry about that." I peel the banana and take a bite, talking around my mouthful. "I just forgot I had some PT scheduled."

His eyes shift to my shoulder. "You worried about making captain?"

I scoff. "Against Adams? Fuck no. That shit's in the bag."

My father's donated so much money for the new natatorium that there's no way they pass me up. Is she a good swimmer? Sure, I guess. For a chick, at least. But Adams doesn't have the leadership qualities needed to take us to state. The team needs someone who understands how important it is to win.

Against my will, my mind flashes back to the memory of her underneath me, all soft curves and hard edges. That soft, eager mouth. That hot, slick tongue. The way she panted through her nose against my cheek. How her body responded to me, surging up into the kiss.

Shit shit shit.

I grab the drink and down half of it so fast, I nearly choke.

Feeling half-crazed, I clumsily offer, "Let me shower and I'll come down and kick your asses, okay?"

Xavier rolls his eyes and starts for the door.

But before he leaves, I give in to the impulse to call, "Hey, wait."

He looks back at me. "What?"

I glance around like a paranoid lunatic, as if someone could be listening. "So, like." I wet my lips and keep my voice low. "That night. You know, at the party..."

Xavier's eyebrows hike up his forehead, and then he turns, easing my door shut. None of us talk about that night. Ever. No one. The board, the headmaster, our parents—they made it clear what would happen if we did, but I just...

I need to know.

"Why did you invite Sky to the party?" I ask.

Xavier's expression is cautious, wary. I don't blame him. He's my best friend. I shouldn't be digging it up, it's not good for anyone. But I know if I don't ask, the question will just keep bouncing around inside my head until it drives me batshit.

I genuinely want to know. "Like, for real. The truth."

Xavier crosses his arms and looks away. "I thought she was hot. Funny. Kind of naïve, easy to get in bed. You know?" He looks embarrassed to admit it, which is enough to make me know it's the truth. "Why?"

I chew my lip, thinking. "So how did she go from being your date to being in that room... doing that?"

"We had a fight," he admits. The wariness is back, his jaw tense. "She wanted us to leave the party, go do something else. But I wanted to hang out with you guys for a while. I..." He pauses, dropping his gaze.

"You what?"

He shrugs. "I didn't want it to look like I was that into her. Because.... well, you know..."

I guess, "Because she's an Adams."

Xavier's eyes narrow. The name is like a slur. "Yeah, because of that. I knew how you and the other guys felt about her. It just—" He makes a sharp gesture. "—escalated, probably from the booze. She got mad and started flirting with some dopey Northridge kid, which just pissed me off, so I called her a slut. She said, 'If you think I'm a slut, I guess you don't care what I do with any of these guys.'" His expression turns sour. "I guess I just assumed she was going to hook up with the Northridge kid. But turns out she was in that room, doing...well, you know."

He also glances around like someone may hear us. I get it.

I shouldn't need to say it, but I do. "You know I didn't know what was going on in there that night, right?"

He nods. "Yeah, I know."

Gwendolyn didn't.

She honestly believed I'd been in control of the whole thing. That I'd set the whole thing up, let those Northridge kids do a train on her sister. I'm a lot of things. I'm controlling, and sometimes cruel, and probably often an entitled prick.

But I'm not a monster.

Xavier sighs, finally letting his arms drop to his sides. "Why are you asking?"

But what he's really wondering is, *why now?* And I can't tell him the truth. I can't tell him that, fifteen minutes ago, I'd been pinned underneath the fire of pure hatred in Gwendolyn's eyes. And I definitely can't tell him that it somehow stoked my libido enough that I came *this close* to creaming my shorts as I kissed her.

I run my hand through my hair. *What the fuck is wrong with me?* "I guess with the swim season coming up, and being forced into close proximity with her sister, it was just on my mind. No big deal." I tip the bottle to my lips and down the rest of my drink, waving him off.

This must appease Xavier because he nods, turning back to the door to open it. He pauses with his hand on the knob, though, adding, "Look, don't sweat all this shit with Gwen so much. It doesn't do anyone any good." With that, he leaves.

After a long moment spent glaring at his wake, I toss my trash and peel off my shirt, headed into the bathroom to shower. Xavier confirmed what I thought—*what I knew*—that Skylar Adams had put herself in that situation to get back at him.

Just like tonight, when Gwendolyn had the chance to run, and she didn't. She kissed me back. She touched me. She leaned into it.

Into me.

She wanted it and that's got to be it. Having a hot willing body under me, someone who's shaking with it, wanting a piece of me? Like I said. I'm only human. Any other guy would have done the same.

That's gotta be why I caved.

I just can't seem to wash it off. The scent, the humiliation, the shame. I'm on my third shower, but I still feel all of it.

I showered once when I got back to the dorm. And then again, after kicking everyone's ass in Madden. And then I took a third shower when I woke up at six a.m., covered in sweat and caught in the spider webs of a familiar dream. I lather the soap, trying to scald that girl off my body. My mind wanders to the dream. It's one I'm used to having, but it's been a while, old memories tugging me back under.

It's summer at the beach. Twilight. Lights blinking on the pier.

"Tell Mama and Daddy I'm meeting some kids at the marina, okay?"

It's my older sister, Hollis. She's sixteen. I'm twelve.

"Can I come?"

She peers into her compact's powdery mirror as she paints her lips a bright, angry pink. "Sorry, bro. You're too young."

"I'm not that young!" I argue, feeling this is the absolute worst insult. "I'm in middle school now. Come on, Holl! I can hang. I won't tell Mom or Dad if you're drinking."

She cuts her eyes at me. They're thick with black mascara. She looks like a cat. "Like Mom and Dad care if I drink or smoke?"

I frown. "Then what do they care about?"

She squeezes a bottle, and even in my dream I smell the flowery scent.

"Legacy," she says simply. "That's it—that's all. Trust me, one day you'll understand."

She ruffles my hair and goes to the door that leads to a balcony off her room. The rush of the ocean fills the room, all salt-sharp scent and humid air, and she waves over her shoulder before vanishing over the railing. I follow her to the balcony, peering down to the beach where a shadowy figure meets her. I can't see their faces, but I do see them kiss before walking hand in hand down the beach.

I turn my face into the showerhead, drowning out the imagery. It's a beach. Two teenagers sneaking out. Who cares?

My father, that's who.

That night, when Hollis left, was the catalyst to the skeleton in my family's closet—our biggest shame. It's why I have no choice but to be the best. It's all on me, now. I'm the only one left to carry on the family legacy. There isn't anyone else to share the weight with. Not anymore.

I scrub my hands through my hair and reach for the body soap, squeezing it into my shaky palm. The long and short of it is this: the pressure of perfection is a crushing weight. Like how some nights I wake up from this dream, but then other nights I wake up choking on it all, barely able to draw in a breath, my chest's so fucking tight.

Don't get me wrong. I'm up to the task. I know it. I was bred for it, raised for it, but any slip... any mistake. There are nights I could lay there in bed and come up with lists of things that could ruin it—and they go on forever. Not fucking up? It's like threading a needle, only the needle's in a haystack the size of China.

If my father knew about last night...

My spine goes rigid at the thought.

And at the same time, I wonder... maybe that's why I did it? Am I cracking under the pressure? Do I just need a release?

My mind replays, over and over, Gwendolyn pressed against those lockers, the flicker of fear in her eyes when she finally realized that maybe I could be dangerous, and how scary I could be. And the frisson of power I felt when she did. She'd fought back longer than I'd expected. She'd held her own physically and mentally, matching my strength, my wit, my bite.

Until I'd stumbled—*caved*—given in to the impulse of imposing myself on her. Winning the only way I could, by force.

Except she didn't freak out, or panic, or cry.

Her whimper against my mouth had nothing to do with fear. She just liked it *that much*.

My dick twitches, rising at the memory.

I press my forearm against the tile and exhale. I'd been hard since storming out of the locker room the night before—hard every time I thought about the feel of her body, the taste of her tongue.

What's wrong with me?

Oh, right.

I'm eighteen. Horny. Wound up. Completely, annoyingly normal.

And hey, a pair of tits is a pair of tits.

At least that's what I tell myself as I take my length into my hand, giving it a long, slow stroke. It doesn't matter who they belong to. Like, I think of Reagan. Cute, perky, willing-to-please, Reagan. Reagan with the shiny blond hair, with the senator father, the girl who is more than happy to get on her knees for me. She doesn't fight me. She doesn't push back. She's not...

Fuck. Fuck. Fuuuuuk.

Gwendolyn fucking Adams.

That's who these tits belong to; a freak, a reject, a snitch.

But, still, my mind offers unwillingly, *beautiful, strong, determined.*

My balls tighten, my breath catches, and I'm just so fucking tired of holding back all the time, of always being in control. I lather the soap and tug against the tip, imagining a different hand. I think of a girl in a bathing suit, her body lean and strong and soft. I imagine a pair of hot lips, kissing along my neck, down my chest. I *vividly remember* those eager fingertips grazing my abs, and my strokes grow shorter, faster, hips pushing into it just imagining what it would have been like if they'd traveled lower, if she'd cupped me in her hot palm, pressing and moving as she licked into my mouth.

Leaning my forehead against my arm, I grunt and come hard enough to shake with it, gasping as my release paints the tiles.

Maybe that was it. Maybe this was just an exorcism, releasing these inconvenient, pent-up hormones, all the stress and emotions that'd built up overnight.

Had to be.

I shut off the shower, finally feeling slightly satiated, and I tell myself that was it—the encounter was over. Done. I'm not thinking about Gwendolyn "Freak" Adams for another second. I have to forget about it.

And she had better forget about it, too.

If not, I'd be forced to definitely make her regret it.

5

I spend the entire night tossing and turning in my bed, cringing with constant flashes of memory. The little sleep I get is on and off, disturbed by dreams of angry eyes and a burning mouth, of consuming fires, of falling into the cool blue of Sky's accusing eyes and still burning—maybe burning even hotter. Each time I surface from one, another smoky tendril seems to pull me back under.

I wake up earlier than usual, ready to be done with the nightmares, but when I dress, I can't even stand to look at myself in the mirror. I know what would be looking back at me: betrayal. There'd be no hiding from the neon flush of my cheeks. There'd be no denying that these are my lips. These are what they look like after kissing Hamilton Bates. These are my hands, the hands that touched him with intent. This is my body, the one that responded to him, *wanted* him.

When I'd declared war against the Devils, against Hamilton Bates in particular, this wasn't what it was supposed to be.

I shouldn't be surprised he's an aggressive sexual predator. Sexual assault fits with everything else about his entitled, demanding, and controlling persona. No, the only thing truly shocking here is that I kissed him back. I didn't run when I could. I didn't knee him in the balls or slap his pretty face.

As in all things, I met him beat for beat.

And I liked it.

Every step toward the carpool line feels like a walk to the guillotine. The twins are smart, annoyingly observant. What if they can tell?

I snort at myself, even if only inwardly. God, it was just *a kiss*. It was nothing but the last-ditch effort of a bully's struggle to intimidate me. Nothing more, nothing less.

Debbie's van swings through the line, and I try to shake the vestiges of smoky tendrils from my mind. I have a game face, and while I almost never use it around family, I can adapt it, right? Shoulders straight, face relaxed, lips tipped up into a grin. Nothing wrong here.

When the twins jump out, Michaela bounces forward to clutch me into a hug.

Debbie watches through the open window. "You look tired. Are you sick?"

"No." I hug Michaela back just as hard, explaining, "I just didn't sleep very well."

"Here," she says, holding up her morning latte. She gets them from the coffee shop down the street on the way to school; I know it's a morning ritual for them. Hot chocolate for the twins. Latte for her. Back when I'd ride with them, my order was always a mocha.

I frown as Michaela releases me. "I don't want to take your drink."

But Debbie just shrugs me off. "I'll stop for another. You definitely need a jolt of caffeine to get through the day." I know it's futile to argue, so I lean in to grab the paper cup. But she snatches it just out of reach before I can. "I know this is about more than just lack of sleep."

I freeze, staring back at her with wide eyes. "What?"

How did she know? Dammit, *this* is why I don't use a game face around family. They can always tell.

"I'd know that face anywhere, Gwendolyn Adams," she continues, inspecting me closely. "Ever since that time when you were four, and I caught you sneaking downstairs for candy during nap time. And I've been seeing it for months now. That's your guilt-face." She sighs, eyebrows pulled low in a frown. "I've told you this before, what happened to Sky is not your fault. If anything, you're the reason she got the help she needed."

Sky. She thinks this is about Sky. And I suppose she's not even completely wrong.

"I know." I tuck my hair behind my ear, grimacing at how obvious I am. "It's just... sometimes being here makes it hard not to remember, that's all."

"You're welcome to come home any time, baby girl. You know you can change schools, too. Your mama and daddy will be happy to do that."

Oh, I know they will. There's nothing they love better than pushing the past behind them and moving on to something shinier and new. New school, new house, new family.

"I can't," I insist, "swim season starts next week."

The look she gives me is hard and wise, like she knows this is about more than just the team. Fortunately, a horn blares from the carpool line, people fed up with waiting or driving around. Debbie finally hands over the drink, offering me a comforting smile. "Just call me if you need me."

I try to muster a smile. "I will."

I step back and see the twins have already started toward their building. Checking my watch, I realize that Debbie and I spoke too long, pushing me perilously close to the bell. Now I'll have to run, or Dr. Ross will give me detention for being late.

The main hall is already clear by the time I get there, which is a nice break from the usually packed hallway of people ignoring me. *Shit.* But I have to stop at my locker for my book—another thing Dr. Ross is a stickler about. It's not exactly like I can ask someone to share. The whole student body has frozen me out.

I make a beeline to my locker, furiously spin my combination, grab the book, slam the door, and rush down the hall. This is cutting it close, even for me. It'd taken me weeks of careful calculating, but

I'd created the optimally timed routine, all orchestrated for my arrival to class at the exacting moment of the bell's ring. It's an economy of tolerance. The less time I have to be subjected to silent scorn and spiteful stares, the better.

I pass a clock outside the science room and glance at it just in time to see the minute hand shift to 7:58. I mutter a curse under my breath, but I see the classroom from here. If I run, like *really* run, I can totally make it.

My legs come to a sudden and jolting stop when I turn the corner.

Hamilton Bates is waiting outside the door. Those broad shoulders are rigid, eyes wild, and his hair is just a bit sloppier than the usual bedhead style he probably spends an hour in front of the mirror perfecting every morning. When he sees me, he straightens, throat bobbing with a swallow.

I hesitate. *Is he waiting on me? What? Why?*

Every nerve in my body stands on end as we hold a frenzied, extended gaze in the empty hallway.

I force my feet to move, because I sure as hell don't want to add detention to the list of things going wrong in my life. I make it to the door just as the bell rings—eyes pointedly forward—and ignore him.

I pass Heston, who's got a slimy grin plastered on his face, and slide swiftly into my seat. Reagan looks past me, eyes focused on her boyfriend who I know is merely a few steps behind. I can't help but notice the purple bruise at the base of her throat—the Devil's Mark. Seeing it—seeing *her*—makes my stomach flip. He has a girlfriend for god's sake. That just makes what happened even worse.

Hamilton's backpack makes a noise behind me as he drops it to the floor, but I barely hear it over the sound of my heartbeat echoing in my ears. I'd already been dealing with shame, regret, and guilt. Now add the humiliation of being late to class to the top of the list.

I wait for Dr. Ross to drop the hammer, but to my surprise, she jumps right into the lecture. Maybe the rumors are false. Maybe she's not so strict after all. The urge to turn around and see what Hamilton is thinking is strong—but not strong enough to throw self-preservation out the window, not to mention whatever tattered shreds are left of my dignity.

At that thought, a memory of Hamilton flashes through my mind. His firm abs beneath my fingertips, the darkness of his hooded eyes, the way his brows were knitted tightly together when I opened mine, just for a moment, in the middle of our kiss. But the clearest part of the memory is definitely the heat of him, the anger thrumming beneath the sweaty surface of his skin, the way he surged into me, commanded me with his body and mouth...

I squirm in my seat, feeling both flushed and completely aghast at myself. Who am I even kidding? There's no tattered shreds of dignity left. If there were a single thread left, I just blew that sucker away.

My stomach churns uncomfortably the whole class, and I don't hear a word Dr. Ross says until the bell rings, finally allowing for escape—

"Ms. Adams, Mr. Bates? Please see me before you leave."

I freeze in my path to the door, stomach plummeting. I don't move until the rest of the class leaves. Only then do I dare a glance at Hamilton. His expression is downright murderous, so overwhelmingly severe that I actually get the feeling his day is going worse than mine. I may have betrayed my sister last night, but he betrayed something that, to him, is a lot bigger and far less forgiving; legacy and his own identity. He dared lower himself to kissing me, a nothing. Well, less than a nothing. A nothing is completely neutral nothingness. It's not even there. But I'm the freak of Preston Prep. And he made out with me.

That's gotta cut pretty deep.

Dr. Ross is a tiny African American woman with reddish hair and glasses twice the size of her face. With her size, it'd be easy to dismiss her. But that would be a mistake. She has a Ph.D. from Harvard, is credited in multiple published papers, and is frankly a huge feather in Preston Prep's cap. She's a total badass.

She levels us both with a look. "I know you're both aware of my tardy policy."

I fidget, answering, "Zero tolerance."

Hamilton says nothing.

"My time is valuable. If I can get here on time, fighting through the traffic of this god-forsaken city—*after* getting my two children to school every day—then you two can roll your privileged behinds out of bed and *walk* the two blocks from the dormitory."

I swallow the lump in my throat. "Yes, ma'am."

Her eyes flick to Hamilton. His jaw twitches but he finally relents, "Yes, ma'am."

"Two weeks of detention," she says, looking down to shuffle papers. "After school."

My jaw drops.

Two weeks?!

Some of the anger on Hamilton's face transforms into a similar sort of shock. He recovers quickly. "With all due respect, Dr. Ross, I have a standing physical therapy appointment, and swim starts next week."

She pushes her glasses up her nose and looks at me. "And you?"

"After-school tutoring in the library and yeah," I shuffle my feet, "also swim."

"Fine. Weekend detention. Two hours every Saturday morning for five weeks." She grins the grin of a woman who knows just how much this sucks for us, but also knows that we aren't in a position to complain.

Clearly, she doesn't know Hamilton very well.

"Five weeks of Saturday detention?!" He gapes at her. "Doing what?"

"You can meet with Mr. Dewey." Mr. Dewey is the dean of discipline for the residents in the dorms. He's here all weekend. "He'll coordinate your punishment."

"Like, together?" Hamilton blurts.

She blinks at him. "You walked in together late. You can do your punishment together."

"But—" he starts.

"That was just a coincidence," I say anxiously. "Totally by accident."

"You'll survive." She stacks papers on her desk. "I'm not asking Mr. Dewey to implement two different punishments when I'm already accommodating your schedules." She jerks her chin toward the door. "Go. Before you're late to your next class, as well."

It's a dismissal and even Hamilton knows not to argue. With my hand clenched around my backpack strap, I follow him out the door. Any thought that I had about him waiting for me before class has vanished. There's no chance. Not with the way he just reacted to spending time in detention with me.

The feeling is mutual.

Reagan, who's waiting for him in the hall, immediately clings to his arm. She pulls him into an empty space next to the trophy case, just out of sight.

"Hey, you," she says, "how bad was it?"

"Five weeks." The anger in Hamilton's voice is unmistakable. "Saturday mornings."

"Ouch. With *her*?"

I stop, pressing my back against the wall just enough to see them through the trophy case.

His grin is tight and sarcastic. "Yep."

"Damn, babe. That's like double punishment."

He thrusts his hand into his hair, and that ball of muscle tics at the back of his jaw. "I don't want to talk about it."

"I mean, because she's always causing drama for you—"

"Reagan." His voice is low and hard. "I said I don't want to *fucking* talk about it."

Hurt flickers across her face. "Geez, fine. I just thought you may want some commiseration for having to spend that much of your free time with a total bitch."

"I spend time with you, don't I?"

Damn.

The hurt vanishes as quickly as it'd come. She touches his chest. "Look, babe, you've been under a lot of stress lately. You've been all tense and distant. You even went to bed early on Halloween. I know I could make you feel so much better, if you'd just let me."

His eyes drop down to hers and a strange feeling twists in my belly. Disgust? Revulsion? I don't wait to explore it further, or risk finding out exactly what Reagan might do to help him "relax."

∼

To my surprise, Tyson is already at the lunch table when I arrive, halfway through a massive plate of spaghetti. "Oh my god, Gwen. That lunch lady? She's the best. Said I needed some meat on my bones and gave me extra. Were I not already happily committed to another, I'd get down on a knee."

I smile, some of the tension falling from my shoulder. "Yeah, Bev is good people. And FYI, if you're nice to her, she'll slip in extra dessert, too."

He looks back at me, slack-mouthed. "Yes. *Yes*. I'm so completely all over that."

I hook my backpack on my chair and glance across the room. The shiny blonde of Reagan's hair catches my eye and I notice she and Hamilton are sitting close together, her hand resting on his thigh. I study his face and notice some of the harsh, tense lines from earlier are gone. Maybe she *had* helped him relax.

Ew.

"Who's that?" Tyson asks.

"Who's who?" I focus on my lunch.

"That girl you're watching." He nods in their direction, "Blondie."

I give a weak scoff. "I wasn't watching her."

He gives me a face that says just how believable that isn't. "Whatever, just humor me anyway. Who is that? Who are any of these people? Give me the dirt, Gwen."

I grimace. "I'm not really much for the whole gossip thing." That's what happens when most of the gossip is about you and your family.

He rolls his eyes. "If gossip makes you uncomfortable, consider it my new student orientation. It's just information to make my day a little easier. Who to admire. Who to avoid. Who's dating who so I don't get punched out for talking to another dude's chick."

I look at him in disapproval. "Did you just say 'chick'?"

"I did and I stand by it."

Tyson is different. Funny. We don't have a lot of funny moments around here—just cruelty and intimidation. At Preston Prep, jokes are made to humiliate, not entertain. And statistically, if one is being made here, then I'm probably the butt of it. I weigh what my new friend is asking of me and decide that it would be nice to have a few guidelines as a new student, if I were in his shoes.

"Okay." I survey the room. "The kids at Preston Prep aren't defined by one thing; academics, jocks, or nerds, for example. Everyone here is smart. Everyone has money. A few are gifted academically, musically, or athletically. A few are genetically superior when it comes to looks. But, of course, that can be paid for as well."

Tyson nods knowingly. "Plastic surgery."

"Yep. It's pretty common for someone to go off for winter break and come back with a new nose." I glance around the room at my attractive classmates. "The biggest currency here is power."

Tyson repeats the word. "Power."

"These kids... they're obsessed with it. Their parents are politicians, CEOs, college presidents, Fortune 500 board members, partners at the biggest law firms, lobbyists, and don't forget the secret societies. They're part of a machine that's been running since the invention of language, and it only commodifies one thing." I twirl the spaghetti around my fork. "Legacy. Pedigree. Bloodline. That's what matters most here."

He leans back and studies me. "And you're not a part of that, for some reason."

I shrug. "My parents are, but I'm not."

His eyebrows pull together. "Wait, how does that work?"

I shrug, opting to be completely honest. "I'm adopted. So are all my siblings. We live in the right home. We have the right parents who have the right careers. We have money and privilege. But we don't share the same blood."

"Damn." He looks bewildered. "Are you serious?"

"As a heart attack."

"Well these people are going to hate me," he decides, looking around. "I have two moms."

I let out a surprised laugh. "Really?"

He nods. "One's a teacher, the other's a psychologist. So I'm poor, I'm a bastard, and I have gay moms."

"Yikes, that is a pretty bad draw." I bump his knees with mine to let him know I'm joking. "Guess we'll have to stick together."

He takes a bite of garlic bread and chews slowly. "So back to Blondie. Where does she fit in?"

I roll my eyes. "Her father is a Senator. Her mother was Ms. South Carolina. She got those tits naturally, by the way. No plastic surgery for her—at least not yet." I take a sly look in her direction. "Otherwise, she's just like any other girl in that group. I like to call them 'the Devils' playthings'."

He chokes on his bread and laughs. "Like the mascot! I like it. Out of curiosity, how exactly does one attain the status of Devil's plaything?"

I think of Reagan promising to help Hamilton relax earlier. "Okay, this is total gossip... but it's pretty well known that each Devil has a test they put their potential girlfriends or, you know, *playthings* through."

He leans forward, interested. "A test?"

"Most of it's sexual. Threesomes or whatever. But a few sound a little less deviant."

A memory flashes in my mind.

Sky was in the kitchen, the hand mixer she was holding dripping with batter. It was two weeks before the party.

"What on earth are you doing?" I asked, taking in the state of the kitchen.

"Making cupcakes for Xavier." She looked down at the mess on the counter, cheeks pink. "Either that, or damning myself to a whole night of doing dishes. Time will tell?"

I quirked an eyebrow. "Cupcakes?"

"Well," she explained as she spooned batter into a muffin tin, "Caitlyn Rogers told me that sweets are Xavier's favorite. It's kind of mandatory if you're his girlfriend."

"What kind of test did Blondie pass?"

I blink, back in the cafeteria, and feel my mood darken. "Ah, yeah, her Devil is notorious for the blow-job test."

He gapes at me for a moment before gesturing. "Continue."

"They say that any girl interested in him has to get on their knees and service him. If he likes it, I guess you can stick around. If not..." I shrug.

It's one reason I'm suspicious of Hamilton's involvement with Sky that night. Blow jobs? I know it's not unique to him—he is a guy, after all—but it's his signature brand of power play. It's meant to be demeaning and degrading. I also suspect he favors this particular act because he's lazy as hell and completely uninterested in showing another person any actual pleasure. Probably too much effort.

"I'm assuming the guy she's literally clinging onto for dear life is the Devil?" He casts a dubious glance down at the cross pendant around his neck. "That's probably not sacrilege or anything."

"Well, there are a few." I nod at the table. "The main ones stick together like a club. Ansel Davenport, baseball player. Emory Hall, football. He's a junior, but tight with those guys. His best friend Reynolds got sent away a few years ago and they kind of adopted him. It doesn't hurt that Campbell is into him." I look around the room and my eyes land on a pretty blond girl two years younger. "That's his sister, Vandy. She was in a bad accident a few years ago—caused by Reynolds—and is like, the most protected girl in school. Don't mess with her."

"Why would I mess with her?" He asks, forehead furrowed.

I shrug. Why would any of these guys do any of the things they do? "Just a warning."

"Noted."

"The guy next to him? That's Xavier Ward." I swallow over the name, still bitter about his brief 'interest' in Sky. "He also plays football. Then there's Heston—"

"Did you just say Heston?" Tyson laughs. "Oh my god, I know that guy from swim. At first, I thought his name was a joke, because like... wow, pretentious much?"

"Right? Most pretentious name ever." I laugh along, feeling heard and seen for the first time in a long while. "But yeah, Heston Wilcox is an incredible swimmer."

"I saw him." Tyson concedes, "He's good. Same with Bates."

My eyes jump to Hamilton when he says his name. Unfortunately, he happens to be looking my way when I do, and we make eye contact. Whatever "relaxation" method Reagan used earlier has lost its effectiveness. His scowl is firmly back in place, jaw tight, eyes narrowed.

Heat prickles the back of my neck, and I glance down at my food, shoveling in a mouthful of pasta to give myself a moment to re-orient. On the long, long list of reasons I hate Hamilton Bates—and it could probably cover an entire CVS receipt—that one is definitely up there. How one look from him is enough to tangle me up in anger, distraction, or just downright agitation is beyond my comprehension, but here I am.

All tangled up.

"Okay, that look..." Tyson stops just short of visibly gesturing between me and Hamilton. "That look means something. What's going on between you two?"

I force myself to swallow the spaghetti. Then I force myself not to bring it all back up. "That's nothing."

He scoffs. "Yeah right."

"I hate him," I say simply. "And he hates me. We're always somehow forced to compete with each other, either in the classroom or on the swim team. We're both hoping for captain this year."

Tyson leans back in his seat, crosses his arms and watches me.

I stare back at him. "What?"

"Look, Gwen, I know competition. Really well, actually. I'm on the diving Olympic Development team. It's about as cut-throat as it can get. That look he gave you?" He cuts his eyes sideways, toward Hamilton. "That's not about competition. Real competitors take the emotion out of it. It's based purely on drive, motivation, and success."

Oh Tyson, too insightful. It's going to get him into some serious trouble.

"Fine," I relent, crossing my arms in a mirror pose. "He hates me because of my background. He thinks my whole family, and me especially, are trash. He—" I pause here, reluctant to bring it all up, but ultimately decide that the wide berth I've been given means no one is around to hear me. "We have a history. Something really, really bad happened to my sister last year and it was his fault. He let his idiot bootlickers get out of control."

Tyson must sense the ugliness and pain beneath the surface of my words because he doesn't ask for details. Instead, he pries open his carton of milk and offers, "The good news is that he's a swimmer and I'm a diver. We aren't competing against each other. I'm perfectly happy to take on some of that hate for you."

I look at him skeptically but can't hide my grin. "I don't think it works that way, but thank you."

"We'll see." He looks over his shoulder, back at the cafeteria line. "You really think I can talk her into extra dessert?"

My smile grows wider. "I have a feeling you can talk almost anyone into anything."

"No time like the present to test that theory." He hops up, striding across the room.

Sometimes being here is like carrying around a duffel bag filled with lead, every day, every class, every night. And although whatever happened with Hamilton in that locker room probably increased the weight of my baggage to the power of a gazillion, having someone to talk to—someone who understands, even if only on a surface level— has taken some of that weight off. And that's...

I watch Tyson lean against the glass case and charm the pants off of Bev. Lo and behold, a moment later he returns with *two* extra desserts and a wide smile on his dimpled face.

Well, that's *something*.

6

I STARTED this utter cluster-fuck of a day squeaky clean from the shower, ready to forget about Gwendolyn Adams and her mouth. And her tits. And her hips. And her hands against my—

Well, moving on from that.

Obviously, one final and very necessary interaction had to be arranged.

I had to put the fear of God into her.

I'm not proud of how I'd left the locker room that night. Running away had been a clear sign of weakness. Really, I should have owned it. I should have picked up my bag, properly explained what I would do to her if she told *anyone* what happened, and then strutted out of that gym with my chin held high.

As it happened, my bag is still in the locker room, Adams is walking around there with a figurative H-bomb pointed at the very concept of my existence, and I'd spent the entire night whacking off like a panicked, hormonal moron.

That wouldn't do.

It's like my dad's always said: The best time to prevent a scandal is right before it happens. The second best time is right after it happens. The third best time is *right fucking now*.

So I waited for her before first period, perfectly aware that by the time she slipped into the classroom, the halls would be empty. Obviously, no one could see me talking to her. That was a risk I wouldn't take.

It was the perfect plan, except for one thing.

She was late—really, annoyingly, uncharacteristically late—for the one fucking class that has a zero-tolerance policy on tardiness. When I spotted her running toward me, down the deserted hall, I could instantly tell that she'd slept less than I had. She had dark smudges beneath her puffy, bloodshot eyes, and her long hair had been twisted up into a sloppy bun that had worked itself free enough to bob clumsily along behind her as she sprinted. Her unzipped hoodie had slouched itself down one of her shoulders, pinned to her arm by the straining strap of her book bag.

Jesus, she looked *wrecked*.

As if kissing me was actually horrible. As if Adams were the one lowering herself in that exchange. As if getting kissed by easily the most attractive and successful guy in this school was such a *burden*.

Fucking spare me.

In any case, we were both late because of her bullshit, so now I'm looking down the barrel of five Saturday detentions and ten hours of isolation with her. Not happening.

Probably, I could call my father and he'd have this shit taken care of by sundown. Well, normally. But I'm already up shit-creek with him. The last thing I want to give him is more fodder to fuel the crushing depths of his disappointment in me.

No, I'll have to deal with Mr. Dewey myself. How hard can it be to get him to put us in separate rooms or something?

Of course, there's a far more pressing matter, in that Gwendolyn has made friends with the new kid—that diver from Northridge brought in on scholarship. He's sat with her two days in a row and for the last fifteen minutes, it's obvious that she's been giving him the run down on the school. I don't necessarily give a shit about that. What concerns me is the fact they've both looked this way more than once.

I can practically hear her voice in my head, whispering to him about it, lying about it, embellishing it; telling him everything about what happened between us last night.

"Babe, want to go take a walk by the lake before next period," Reagan whispers, her hand running down my thigh. This girl. I can't shake her. She's been riding me all day. Does she know? How would she know?

To be fair, I'd intentionally sought her out earlier, following a truly depressing jerk-off session. I'd just wanted to get my game back, re-focus my hind-brain. So I'd made out with her behind the main building, spent a few long minutes sucking on her neck, giving her the mark. It was an effort to stabilize myself—to pretend everything was normal.

And fine, sure. I'm man enough to admit it.

I'd wanted Adams to see it.

Now, the regret cringes inside me. It's only going to encourage Reagan's interest in me more. Last fucking thing I need.

I take her wrist between my forefinger and thumb and ease her hand aside. My tight smile probably doesn't do much to lessen the sting. "I actually need to grab something in the... uh, library."

Reagan's fallen expression instantly perks back up. "I can come with! Let me get my stuff."

I shoot Campbell a pleading look. She's kind of their Queen Bee. She's with Emory now, but we dated sophomore year. It was a disaster. Campbell and I are way too much alike. But it gave her the social leverage she needed to dominate over the other girls. And, like me, she knows how to keep them in line.

"Reagan," she says, her green eyes cutting away from mine, "come to the bathroom with me. I need a tampon."

The guys groan. No one wants to hear about shit like that, which is exactly why she said it. I send Campbell a subtle nod in appreciation.

"Sure," Reagan says, quickly gathering her things. She's more scared of Campbell than me. "Later?"

"Maybe. I've got a lot of shit to do this afternoon." Grabbing my backpack off the floor, I bolt before she can say anything else.

I fuck around in the hallway for a minute trying to figure out what to do. Not one person can know about this. I know how gossip spreads in a place like Preston Prep—like chlamydia in a whore house. Fun while you're doing it. A pain in the ass to recover from.

Ducking into a small storage closet off the main hall, I crack the door and wait. My heartbeat pounds in my ears, some weird thrum of adrenaline. Fear? Worry? Something's got me wound up, and the rising tide of it fills my chest in a rush when I spot her exiting the cafeteria, parting ways with the new kid. That non-emotive mask slips back on, like the blinders horses wear not to get distracted. Oh, *Gwen*, Preston Prep is not the place to let down your guard.

Just as she passes the storage room, I reach out and grab her arm, yanking her out of the hall. I shut the door with an ominous *click* and stand in front of it, blocking her escape.

"What the—" her blue eyes widen with alarm. "Seriously, Bates!"

"Shhhhhhh!" I press my palm over her lips. They're warm and moist and puffy. I instantly yank my hand away, giving my palm a long wipe on my thigh. "Shut up."

"You shut up." She looks around like she's just realized where we are, eyebrows knitting together in confusion. "Oh, my god, are you going to assault me again?"

"Assau—" It's my turn to go bug-eyed. "I *did not* assault you."

She hisses, "You attacked me in the locker room! At least with your mouth. That counts as an attack."

"Oh, fuck off." I sneer down at her. "I can't be the first person driven to extreme measures just to shut you the hell up." My eyes narrow. "And let's not forget the part where you *enthusiastically* kissed me back."

Her jaw drops. "You were holding me with those... those..." her eyes dart down to my hands, which I'm desperately trying to keep from throttling her, "*animal paws*! I had no choice."

A derisive laugh escapes me. "That's such creative editing, you should consider joining the AV club. Remember how I let you go? You could have left at any point."

She blinks, jaw opening and closing like a fish. At first no words come out, so it's pretty clear I'd one-upped her. I smirk in amusement.

But then a flicker of light sparks in her eyes and her upper lip curls. "You had a boner, Bates. I felt it."

That bit of information clings to the air like an undeniably bad scent.

"So what?" I shrug it off. "I'm a guy, that's what happens. If my dick doesn't get hard while kissing a girl, then one of us is broken."

"So I should be flattered that you were grinding into me like a horny dog." She snorts.

"Oh please, definitely fucking don't flatter yourself. I live with teenage boys, Adams. A wet rag could get us hard." My eyes take her in, head to toe. "You're nothing special."

"What, like you are?" Oh, she's really getting worked up now, all steely-eyed and straight-backed, nostrils beginning to flare. "Maybe having so efficiently starved me of human interaction that your disgusting mouth actually seemed quasi-appealing for the five seconds you forced it on me seems like a big win to you, but trust me, it's not." She eyes me in much the same way I'd eyed her. "You're repulsive."

I shoot back, "And you're a bitch."

"And you're a sociopath!" she seethes. "I say that, by the way, with deepest apologies to the sociopath community!" She growls, thrusting her hands in her hair. "What is it that you really want, Bates? Why did you drag me in here?"

I watch her, her cheeks flushed from anger, chest heaving, and it takes me an infuriatingly long moment to remember. Why *had* I brought her in here?

"I thought so," she replies to my silence. "You're just fucking with me again." She moves to leave, which snaps me back to reality.

"I needed to talk to you," I blurt, stopping just short of grabbing her arm. "To make something clear."

Her arms cross over her chest. "What?"

"What happened between us last night?" I don't grab her arm to stop her from leaving, but I do lean closer, eyes narrowed in threat. "If you tell anyone, even that new kid—"

"You'll what? Make my life miserable? Give me the silent treatment? Oh, wait, I know, you'll convince the entire school not to speak to me and treat me like a pariah." She rolls her eyes. "Trust me, Bates, you don't have to worry about me telling anyone what we did. I know it must be hard for you to imagine, but it's actually more embarrassing for me than you."

My responding laughter is jagged with hysteria. "Yeah, right."

"What, you think I'm joking?" When our gazes meet, the corners of her eyes are pinched. "Last night was the most humiliating moment of my life. Not just because you kissed me, but because—" She pauses here, looking away. "Fine, okay? I kissed you back. You gave me the chance to leave and I didn't go." She looks as untethered and confused as I've felt all day. "And I don't even understand *why*. I don't even *know* myself right now, do you have any idea how that feels? I didn't just demean myself, I betrayed everything I believe in, including my family." She swallows, finally looking at me again. "Trust me, I don't want anyone to know what happened between us. That secret is going with me to the grave."

It's quite the rant, self-pitying and delusional. Oh well. Whatever she needs to tell herself. "Fine. Just make sure it stays that way."

With that I exit the closet, refusing to let her be the one that walks out first this time. It's petty and juvenile—this whole thing is, really—but Gwendolyn Adams has always had an irrational effect on me, whether I want to admit it or not. Those days are long past and things have changed. That girl is kryptonite—the ultimate derailment of an already derailed senior year. One thing is for certain, I will not let her be the catalyst of my undoing. I'll make sure she runs from Preston Prep long before that.

7

THE NEXT FEW days pass without incident, falling into a typical pattern of meeting the twins for carpool, and being ignored in the halls and classroom. I tutor a few elementary kids in the afternoons and sneak in extra swim practice in the evenings. Every now and then, Tyson will accompany me to the pool to practice his dives in the deep end, but other than that, everything is comfortingly, horrifyingly, normal. There are no more run-ins with Hamilton, who has just as easily fallen back to pretending I don't exist.

Balance is restored.

That said, I can't help but notice the subtle winds of change. Daylight savings rolls in and it gets dark earlier, the air a bit crisper, cooler. Madam Okausa gives us extra French homework. And, not that I notice overmuch or anything, but Reagan and Hamilton seem closer than usual. Like right now, as I walk across the quad from the dorm to the library for a tutoring session. I see them wrapped up in one another, leaning against a locker. She's got her back pressed to the red metal and he's leaning over—into—her, moving a lock of her shiny blonde hair away from her ample cleavage.

Not that I care.

Because I don't. It's just curious. He'd always seemed pretty aloof about her, blowing her off and snapping at her all the time, but now he's giving her all this obvious attention. Maybe, I think, his brush with being a cheater made him realize he liked her more? Whatever. Not my business.

Except...

Except now I can't un-know what I *know*. Like how Hamilton kisses with his tongue in these really elegant looping sweeps, or how his fingertips feel when they're pressing into the flesh of my hip, and how the little crescent impressions from his fingernails take approximately an hour to completely disappear. And I know other things, too. Like how when he's turned on, there's this little divot between his eyebrows, like he's confused but also really impatient. Or how he apparently likes to guide a girl's head with the fist he winds into the hair at the base of her skull, but he also doesn't pull it.

But the biggest thing I can't un-know is definitely the shape of him pressing into my belly, hard and eager. He felt big, which is just stupidly predictable. Of course, he has a big cock. And it's probably gorgeous, too. It probably performs magic tricks and solves complex algebraic equations and holds the answer to the universe or whatever. A perfect cock to go with the perfect body and perfect face and perfect trust fund. There is truly no justice in this world.

But not being able to un-know these things—and the unfortunate consequence of *knowing* them frequently, and with a frankly concerning amount of fascination—makes me ponder the rumors of the blow job test and whether or not it's true. Does he really make potential girlfriends take a test? The sordid locker room gossip about it varies, the veracity of which verges perpetually on the edge of urban legend.

Most believable is the gossip that one girl took the test and gagged, therefore failing. And another, who used too much teeth. And a third, who refused to swallow.

Far less believable is the gossip about one girl getting it stuck in her throat. And another, who ended up spraying his spunk out of her nose.

If the test *does* exist, then Campbell Clarke obviously passed. They were *the* couple sophomore year. Even a break-up didn't hurt either of their reputations. If anything, it just made them more popular, like when those huge crime families split up into different but symbiotic factions.

Even hours later, I'm still lost in some bizarre train of thought about the blow job Costra Nosta as I enter the fine arts building. The library is on the other side of campus, but it's cold and much warmer to cut through the music hall. Preston Prep has an incredible fine arts program—theater, orchestra and band, visual arts, even dance. Micha is in the dance program, and he's incredibly talented. It's also his happy place. It's like every worry, every thought, every distraction melts when he steps on the stage.

I don't have a creative bone in my body, but I feel the same way when I get in the pool. There's something about the silence, the cool embrace of isolation, that just sets my mind into a singular, comforting focus. All I have to do is swim. I don't have to think about who is looking at me, or what they're saying about me or my family. No one knows my pedigree. The judgement is purely merit-based. There's just a time at the end, and it's not subjective, not based on who your parents are, how you look, what you say. You win or lose, it's that simple. And typically, I win.

I turn the corner into a long hallway of private music rooms. These rooms, booked by students in advance for practice or individual tutoring sessions, are state of the art, and mostly soundproofed. Although, as I pass, I can hear the faint strains of different students as they work. Their faces are visible through the windows. One girl is playing a flute, her posture perfectly straight. Another boy is playing a trumpet, and from what I can hear of it, really badly.

Toward the end of the hall, I feel a vibration before I hear any actual music. I peek in the window just enough to discern the warm, curved wood of a cello. I pause, leaning against the wall there, watching, mesmerized by the deep reverberations and the quick slim fingers of the musician. There's an innate confidence in the movements, quick and nimble, something I long to possess, but never will. I'm satisfied to just appreciate it, watching as the bow moves gracefully, with competent intent, coaxing a dark, haunting melody from the instrument. The fingers glide over the strings, pressing down hard when needed, then switching to a gentler touch to get the desired result. There's never a break in the music, never a skip. It's deep and powerful, and yet, there's also a vulnerability to it—a longing, wistful sound to the dips and keens.

Reluctant to give up my personal show but knowing that I can't afford to be late for my tutoring session, I push away from the wall and finally pass the window. Unable to help myself, I dare to shoot a glance at the person cradling the instrument.

My stomach sinks like a rock.

Palms growing sweaty, I rush away, the musician never distracted from his play.

Forget being late. I duck out the next door to feel the cool breeze on my cheeks and try—really hard—to reconcile the Hamilton Bates I just saw in that music room with the one I know, intimately. How can someone so evil, so dark and depraved, create something so beautiful?

Saturday rolls around with a gray, overcast sky, and a bitingly chilled wind. It's the perfect backdrop for the first day of Saturday detention. While the rest of the dormitory sleeps in, I cross the campus toward the athletic fields. Mr. Dewey had replied to my email the night before.

Hollbrook Field, 8 AM. Dress for work.

I wear my rattiest jeans and Brayden's old Preston football sweatshirt. A thick headband works both as a way to keep my hair out of my face and insulate my ears. Despite that, I still feel a surge of jealousy when I see Hamilton walking from the boy's dorm with a steaming cup of coffee from the local café clutched in those long fingers.

Mr. Dewey waits for us by the front wall of the stadium, dressed in a heavy wool coat and a red and black plaid scarf. Next to his feet is a box of supplies.

"Mr. Bates," he greets as we walk from opposite directions, "next time you get coffee delivered before detention, make sure you bring enough for everyone."

I press a snicker into my sweater sleeve at the admonishment, which earns me a steely glare from Hamilton's tired eyes. Jaw clenched with annoyance, he removes the lid and holds my gaze as he tips the cup, pouring all that hot, delicious coffee onto the ground.

I guess we'll all go without.

"Dean Dewey," he starts, using the voice he reserves for teachers and administrators. "Thank you for working around my rigorous schedule to meet on the weekend. As much as I appreciate your dedication to the school disciplinary system, I assure you that being tardy to Dr. Ross' class was a one-time occurrence. I'm perfectly willing to submit to whatever punishment you're got in mind, but I do have one request."

I gape at Hamilton, because, like.... how much bullshit can one guy can muster at eight a.m. on a Saturday? Apparently, *a lot.*

"And what is that?" Dean Dewey asks, already sounding annoyed.

"I would prefer to take my punishment alone. To, uh, you know. Reflect on my failures."

I roll my eyes. Jesus Christ.

"Unfortunately, Mr. Bates, the work required is a two-person job, and I assure you, this isn't something you'd want to do alone. It would take far longer than the five weeks detention." Hamilton opens his mouth to argue—he'd probably take thirty weeks of detention if it meant not spending them with me—but Dean Dewey cuts him off with a sharp gesture to the wall next to the stadium entrance. "As you know, the football team won the state title this year. The Headmaster wants a new mural on the wall for next season. That means the current mural needs to be cleaned, primed, and painted for the artists.

We both gawk up at the massive wall, which runs the entire length of the concession stand.

"The whole thing?" I ask, gulping at the size. Like Hamilton, I'd hoped this would be a task we could complete quickly, and then go our separate ways. Like picking up trash from the quad or covering up bathroom graffiti. But this? We'll be lucky to get this done in five weeks.

Hamilton huffs, rubbing at his forehead in a way that always signals an impending conniption. "Isn't this the kind of work Preston Prep pays for? Don't we have staff for this kind of project? Is the school not even solvent anymore?"

It's like watching a train wreck and the secondhand embarrassment *burns*. In five point zero seconds, he's going to flip his lid, and that won't go well—for either of us.

I step forward.

"We'll get it done," I declare. "Between the two of us, it should be a quick job." Hamilton levels his glare at me, but I ignore him, adding, "I assume all the tools and supplies we need are in that box?"

Mr. Dewey seems delighted, either at my compliance or ability to head off one of Hamilton's tantrums. "And in the shed. Ladders, paint rollers, scrapers, drop cloths." He rattles off the list. "Make sure you clean up when you're finished. We need to maintain a clean appearance while you're not working."

"Yes, sir," I reply. Hamilton takes a moment to chew on the words that even he won't allow himself to say, and ultimately nods.

Once the dean leaves, I hear the boy next to me mutter, "Kiss ass."

I turn to glare at him. "Seriously? You're calling me a kiss ass? Three minutes ago, you were basically groveling at his feet to weasel your way out of this." I mock in a dumb jock voice, "*I appreciate your dedication to the school disciplinary system.* Do you even know how embarrassing you sound?"

"About half as embarrassing as you." He tosses the empty coffee cup on the ground. "Let's get this done."

I keep my glare leveled on him as I walk to the cup and make a big show of picking it up. "Slob."

He stuffs his hands into his pockets and shrugs, uncaring.

While I spread out the massive drop cloth, he rifles through the box and pulls out scrapers for the peeling sections of paint. He throws them carelessly on the cloth.

Once again, I make a big show of picking one up. "Well?" I challenge, waiting. There's no way I'm going to let him stand there and watch me do all the work.

He glowers off into the distance with a stubborn, pinched expression. A gust of wind whips his hair from his forehead, and he holds out long enough that it flops right back, all mussed and agitated. With a grunting breath, he stomps over and takes a scraper, and even though he's holding it the wrong way—like a serial killer stalking someone with a knife—I'm appeased enough to get started.

My scraper makes moderately difficult work of the loose paint and dirt splashed up during the last hard rain. For a good five minutes, there's nothing but the scratchy sounds of us working and the shuffle of the wind in the grass.

Suddenly, Hamilton yelps in pain.

"What?" I ask.

He snaps, "Nothing."

I glance up from where I'm squatting, scraping the paint off the bottom of the 'P', and see a trail of blood dripping down his finger. That doesn't stop him, although it should. He's completely useless with the tool, still holding it down-fist and allowing his knuckles to bang against the concrete wall. I spend a long-suffering two minutes weighing the pros and cons of coaching him through this.

Before I can even come to a decision, he shouts again.

"Dammit! This fucking thing doesn't work!" He kicks the wall then hurls the tool halfway across the parking lot. His tantrum doesn't end there. He lunges for the box, lifting it over his head and tossing it down the sidewalk. Supplies bounce and scatter everywhere.

"Dude!" I shout, "Are you an actual toddler? What the hell are you doing?"

Rollers spin down the slight incline headed down toward the parking lot, while the lid off a can of turpentine pops off, and the fluid gushes all over the ground. Hamilton does nothing to stop this of course, just curses and kicks the wall again. I race over to keep the environmental damage to a minimum.

"A little help would sure be nice," I snap, trying to sop up the turpentine with a bunch of rags. He just nurses his finger, frowning down at it with an expression so intense, I almost fear for the fate of my own scraper. I mutter, "Or not. Whatever. I've got it, you gigantic baby."

I do the best I can at mopping up the liquid, but I don't have nearly enough rags for such a task and my hands smell terrible. I shake my head. "Seriously, Bates, have you ever done any kind of hard work? Did those seven minutes of back-breaking *scraping* actually bring you to ruin?"

All that crazy-eyed focus shifts from his finger to me. "I've done hard work before, *Adams*. Two summers ago, I had to clean my father's entire fucking yacht after Heston and I threw a party."

I stare at him blankly. "Let me get this straight. Your one notable moment of manual labor was cleaning a yacht. With Heston Wilcox."

"What?" he asks, as if there was nothing ridiculous about that entire summation.

"You really do have a negative sum of self-awareness, don't you?"

His lips twitch in a sneer. "And what exactly have you done?"

"Well for starters, at my house we all have chores. That's what happens when you have a lot of kids and no maid—"

"Bullshit!" He has a smug gleam to his eye. "I know you have a nanny. I've seen her."

I narrow my eyes. Has he been *watching* me? How does he know about Debbie?

"I don't deny that we have a nanny. My parents both work. They've had five kids. Of course, they need help. But even so, it's not like we have a staff or anything."

"So you sort your own laundry. How heroic." He turns to address a fake crowd. "Get a load of Mother Theresa over here! She probably washed a fork once."

"Two years ago," I begin, teeth grinding, "while you were throwing parties on your yacht, my whole family went to Puerto Rico on a humanitarian project to help clean up after the hurricane." I hurl the wet rags into the box and start picking up the other supplies scattered all over. "We helped rebuild a school for a community ravaged by the storm. We brought medical supplies and books for the children."

He stares at me for a moment, eyes hard and unreadable. The lines of his face are a dichotomy of harsh and beautiful. The lure of the Devil. His long lashes flutter when he rolls his eyes. "This is why people hate you, you know."

"What?" I ask, taken aback. "Why?"

"Because of shit like that." He gestures to the air between us. "That doesn't make you better than anyone else."

"I never said it did!"

He shrugs. "You sure act like it."

"No, I don't," I insist, crossing my arms. "Helping others is just something we were raised to do."

"Obviously," he says dryly.

My skin pricks with anger. "What does that mean?"

"It means your whole family is one big charity case, looking for more charity cases to mount on your shoulders while you climb the hill of mount martyr."

"First of all, that's ridiculous. Second," I push the headband off my ears. They're suddenly hot. "You say that like helping others is a bad thing."

He looks at me incredulously, as though I'm missing something.

I continue, "It's *not* a bad thing. My parents decided to use their wealth and privilege for something other than just furthering their own position in society. They saw a need and they wanted to fill it. Why is that so terrible? Do you really think that people—children in particular—don't deserve a better life? An opportunity to make more of themselves than what they were raised in?"

"You know what I believe in? I believe in the American dream. I'm a fucking capitalist, I believe in meritocracy," he says, without a trace of irony. "If people want to waste their hard-earned time and money pulling people from gutters, then I've got no problem with that, just —" He goes suspiciously silent here, mouth snapping shut.

"Just *what*?" I say it like a dare.

His face screws up into the mask that transforms him into the Devil, the Prince of Preston Prep. It's cruel and calculating. "Just not in my backyard, or my school, or my fraternity. Keep it somewhere else. Like over at Northridge or wherever the hell it is you people frequent."

A bark of laughter escapes my throat. I can't help it. It bubbles in my chest and explodes from my lips in a harsh bark.

He raises an eyebrow. "What's so funny?"

"You, Bates. You have absolutely no idea how ridiculous you sound. Just look at you." I wave a hand at him. "Your whole life is one big vanity project. I bet even your shits are hollow."

"No, *Adams*, I'm sane. I sound like every goddamned Bates that came before me. Reasonable. Rational." He tips his chin up, head high. "Look, you grew up your way—with your whole 'it takes a village' hippie shitshow. I grew up my way, where we've learned to protect our way of life, where we're taught to preserve our lineage." Something dark flickers in his eyes. "I've learned that when you don't tow that line, there are consequences, and I'm talking about actions, choices, that can't be undone."

He's breathing heavy, agitated. He's always on the edge. One step from crossing over. Tantrum. Rage. There's something strange in the way he's standing, the dull heat of his eyes. I suspect, though I couldn't begin to explain why, that Hamilton Bates has been very badly hurt.

There's something dark in the boy in front of me. I can't help but wonder how deep it goes and what's caused it.

Without thinking I ask, "What's your deal, Bates? Who's hurt you?"

He blinks, like maybe he's just seeing me for the first time. But the reprieve only lasts a moment before the curl of his upper lip is back. "Let me guess, this is the part of Saturday detention where we huddle in the library and tell each other why our lives secretly suck, therefore discovering that, despite our differences, we're actually a lot alike." He mock-frowns at me. "Sorry, this isn't Breakfast Club, and you're sure as fuck no Molly Ringwald. I'm not going to let you drag me into the swamp with you like you tried to do the other night."

My jaw drops. "When I *what*?"

"You know what you did."

"Wow." I laugh, pushing my hair from my face. "Are you accusing me of something? Because if memory serves, you assaulted *me*."

The tips of his ears turn red and his jaw locks. His frame seems to expand, hulking over me, and a shiver runs down my spine. It's an instinctive reminder of how dangerous this boy is, how much harm he could do, if he wanted. He stares down at me, so full of hate that I can almost taste the tangy, bitter edge of it. I'm so aware of his gaze dropping to my lips that my tongue darts out to wet them, something instinctive and involuntary. For a heartbeat, I worry that he's going to do something to me.

For more than one heartbeat, I really want him to.

"Forget it." He lurches back. "I'm not doing any of this bullshit. I'll just deal with the fallout later. You can tell Dewey I'm out."

I watch, stunned, as he walks back across the campus, shoulders tense and angry. I don't follow him. I don't even really care that he only managed a measly seven minutes of actual work, and somehow ended up making more work for me in the process. Hamilton Bates is a spoiled brat, and I'm better off without him.

8

WHO HURT YOU?

The question throbs in my mind like a headache, and it's still less infuriating than her having the *nerve* to even ask.

My response had burned hot and sour in the back of my throat. The raw, feral edge of me wanted to hurt her in return, make her pay for believing me some secretly weak and damaged little boy. It wanted to lash back, warn her to be worried about who was hurting *her*, threaten and intimidate. How fucking dare she look at me like I was less?

Like I was one of her *charity cases*.

But a much, much smaller part of me, one that I admittedly didn't have control over, wanted to tell her that I *did* hurt. That for all my talk of the importance of family and lineage, the line I walked was precarious and painfully thin. It wanted to tell her that it was all stupid—that I *knew* it was stupid—but it was *mine*. And that I'd already seen my sister fall from the tightrope of it all, clutching and clawing, and all the worse for wear because of it, and how was that stupid? It wanted to tell her that the future of the Bates' line fell on my shoulders, and that I follow it out of fear just as much as responsibility.

Mostly, it wanted to tell her—to singe all her softness with the truth of it—that my whole life is nothing more than a never-ending string of frantic attempts to achieve the next stupid fucking thing, because I naively believe it'll get better once I do.

It'll be better when I pass exams.

It'll be better when I finish the year with the highest GPA.

It'll be better when I make captain.

It has to get better.

And it never fucking does.

But as much as I'd love to sting her with it, Adams doesn't deserve that truth—not from me.

The problem is that she just won't stop arguing. She won't stop pushing. She's got zero fucking common sense, just standing before me with that face and body and argumentative little mouth like a gust of wind threatening to blow me right off that line.

What is it about this girl, and why the hell does she keep tripping me up?

It'd be so easy to just blame it on hormones. She's beautiful, with that shiny, sweet-smelling hair, her full lips and round tits. The thing about Adams is that she's pretty—she's got this soft, open-looking face—but she's also nice and sturdy. She's got a great figure, of course, but she's not fragile and delicate like some of the other twigs around here.

I could probably bend her over something. Hell, I could probably bend her in half. I could probably slam my dick into her over and over again, and she'd be able to handle it. No, she'd probably *give back* just as good. She could probably ride me hard and put me away wet. She'd probably twist that hot, annoying little mouth of hers into an evil smirk while she wrings it all from me, tits bouncing, hair swaying as she screws herself down onto my—

"*Fuck.*"

Warm jizz drips over my fist, and I scramble for a dirty shirt to clean up, panting.

That's right. I jerked off. *Again.*

To Gwendolyn Adams.

Again.

I can't keep doing this. It can't be healthy. I've got Reagan so ready and willing to do whatever I want, but I just... don't. No, my mind, my libido, my fantasies, and my fucking nightmares keep going back to Gwendolyn over and over again. I just can't shake it.

If it's not hormones, then it has to be nothing more than a simple case of a spoiled little rich boy wanting what he can't have. That makes sense, right? She's the chocolate cake on the highest shelf. The forbidden bottle of Scotch in my father's liquor cabinet. The Porsche I took out on a midnight spin before I had a license.

She's just off limits, that's all.

It's completely logical to want it.

Right?

Sighing, I toss the dirty shirt into the hamper and zip up my jeans. My knees aren't *weak* as I dig around the closet for my United shirt, but I do need to take a moment to regain my bearings. The game is in a few hours and Xavier's dad is sending a car to pick us up to take us to the stadium. Couldn't have happened at a better fucking time. Some time away from here, some fresh air and excitement, will be just the thing to exorcise her from my mind.

My injured finger brushes against the inside of my shirt as I pull it on, and I wince. The wound isn't a big deal, it's just a scrape, even if it bled like crazy. But something about it had really pissed me off. It wasn't the work. I mean, am I used to performing tedious labor? Hell no. Why would I be? Am I ashamed my family can afford a staff—which, I sneer inwardly to Gwen, creates gainful employment for skilled workers, *thank you very fucking much*? Nope.

It wasn't the work that pissed me off.

It was that she was doing it faster, easier, *better*.

I walk into the bathroom and fish around for a Band-Aid to cover the raw scrape. Unfortunately, I don't have any. Instead, I find a roll of gauze, which I use to wind around my finger a dozen times, tucking the end under. It's sloppy and will probably annoy me all night, but it'll work.

Out in the lobby, the guys are sitting around playing video games.

I know that Emory and Heston will meet us there. Xavier lives on campus primarily, because his parents travel a lot, but mostly because of the big party he'd thrown at their lake house over the summer. He blames me. My dad had already demonstrated that such a punishment was becoming of the community's unruly boys, so it suddenly became a viable option to any parent with an axe to grind. Ansel also lives on campus, but that's only because he's a lazy fucker who can't be bothered to drag his ass out of bed any earlier than seven—although I'm sure being in close proximity to girls 24/7 is probably a significant part of the appeal.

Xavier glances over from the screen. "Hey, ready?"

I nod. "Yeah."

"Did you have detention today? How'd it go?"

I hold up my poorly bandaged finger. "It was a fucking riot."

Ansel laughs, but never looks away from the game. "I bet Adams had a good time, too."

My teeth clench together at the sound of her name. "What's that supposed to mean?"

"Because, you know." Ansel shrugs. "You may be an asshole to all of us, but to her? You're just downright evil, bro. That's gotta be like the double-decker taco of punishments for—aw, you fucking son-of-a-bitch, Xave!" He throws his controller down before picking it right back up.

I stare blankly at the side of his head. "Did some obscure paint-based neurotoxin make it into my bloodstream this morning, or are you seriously defending *Adams*?"

Ansel's avatar explodes once again, but when he tosses down the controller this time, he doesn't bother picking it back up. He looks up at me. "I just think she bothers you way more than the rest of us."

"He's got a point," Xavier says, putting down his own controller. "You've got a real hard-on for fucking with Gwen. It's not like it's a secret."

Well, I don't have a hard-on anymore, I've already taken care of it. But, I exhale, trying to release a little of the building anger that's so close to the surface right now. This is the last thing I need. If the guys have noticed I've lost control, then the teachers and administrators can't be far behind. If Coach James catches wind of it, then I can probably kiss that captainship goodbye. And that won't do.

It'll be better when I make captain.

"Listen," I say, "I need to do something before we go. Meet you at the car?"

"Sure," Xavier's already booted up the next game and Ansel's grabbing for his abused controller.

I head back down to the athletic field, knowing Adams should be long gone by now. If Mr. Dewey finds the mess I made, he'll give us another day of detention—or worse. If this morning was proof of anything, it was that I can't handle being around her any longer than absolutely necessary. Why can't people see that? Why does the universe keep trying to throw us together?

It's obvious even from a distance that the supplies I'd thrown around like the Hulk have been cleaned up. Same with the drop cloth and all the mess from scraping the walls. On closer inspection, it seems the walls themselves have been cleaned, Adams having obviously done the work alone.

What a fucking martyr. Hopefully someone will let her down from that cross soon.

A text buzzes on my phone, informing me that the car has arrived.

I'll find out soon enough if Adams told the dean I'd walked out earlier, and what sort of fallout will come from it. I mean, of course she did. Snitching really is her forte. I'm sure it gave her nothing but pleasure to rat me out for a shiny new opportunity to look better than me.

I jog across the campus toward the limo waiting for us. Xavier's driver opens the door and I slide inside. I've barely settled in my seat before Ansel pushes a beer in my hand, and something within me slowly begins to unwind at the promise of hedonism laid out before me. I screw off the cap and take a long drink.

There will probably be hell to pay tomorrow for walking off like that from detention, but until then I'm going to enjoy the rest of the afternoon with my friends, a good soccer match, and a lot of beer.

～

THE CAMPUS IS dark when we get dropped off, hours later. United won, which only added to the celebratory energy on the way home.

"I can't believe Menendez got that final penalty kick. I thought for sure Duncan would stop it." Ansel steps back to recreate the kick while Xavier plays the goalie. An imaginary scene follows. I play the part of the adoring crowd, cupping my hands around my mouth to simulate raucous cheering.

"Menendez is unstoppable," Xavier says. He loops his arm around Ansel. We're stuffed with free food from the box and pretty drunk. Well, I'm drunk. I don't know about the others, but I've got enough of a buzz that I stop on the way back to the dorm to take a piss right against the giant tree where the sidewalk diverges into two.

"Ham, come on," Xavier calls, "if Buster finds you..."

Buster is the campus security guard. He's pushing 80, and I'm pretty sure there aren't even any bullets in his gun. What's he going to do, call my dad? The thought makes me laugh as I rest my forearm on the trunk and relieve my bladder. My phone vibrates as I'm zipping up.

It's a text from Dean Dewey, thanking me and Adams for our hard work that morning. Evidently, he was impressed with our progress, particularly with the level of care we took cleaning up.

Confused, I look up from my phone only to see that Ansel and Xavier have run across the quad and are headed toward the soccer fields—probably to go recreate the game. I stumble clumsily forward, not even realizing I'm on the wrong path until I reach the dormitory and can't get the code to work. I jam in the digits again, and again, and a third time, having the fleeting thought that somehow, I've been locked out. Or am I so drunk that I've forgotten the code?

Two girls approach from behind, giving me looks of combined wariness and gawking as they sidle up to me.

That's when it hits me.

I'm not at Cresswell, I'm at Hayden. The girls' dorm.

They enter the correct code and reluctantly, I follow them in, giving a slight nod of thanks.

I've been in here before, naturally. Different girls, different rooms. Hell, I lost my virginity in room 306. I was a freshman, she was a junior, and it lasted approximately the length of the commercial break during a rerun episode of CSI—not that anyone knows that.

The two dorms are almost exact clones of each other. The seniors are on the fourth floor here, just like over in Cresswell. I take the stairs, two at a time, fast enough that I feel lightheaded when I reach the top. Truthfully, I'm not a big drinker, especially when I'm trying to stay in top physical shape. Obviously, the booze hit me harder than I thought.

At least that's my excuse for walking down the senior hall, fingers dragging down the wall as I scan the names by the doors. Until I stop abruptly.

418.

Gwendolyn Adams.

My stomach flutters in warning, but I knock anyway, leaning against the wall as I wait. She appears in the open door only a moment later, dressed in an obscenely tight shirt, no bra, nipples on point. Her shorts are these tiny clinging things, probably halfway up her ass. Very little is being left to the imagination here.

I drag a hand down my face.

This was the *worst* idea.

Her eyes widen. "What the hell are you doing here?"

I fumble my phone from my pocket, holding it to face her. "Just got the text from Dewey. Apparently, we did a great job." My sneer feels limp. "What's your angle, Adams? You think I need you to cover for me? You think I need your help?"

"Jesus," she mutters, casting a nervous glance down the hall. Her hand fists my jersey and she yanks me in the room, shutting the door behind her. "You smell like a brewery, Bates. Are you drunk?"

"Wow, nothing gets past your keen observation skills, huh?" I lope into the room. It's a small single, tidy to the point of boredom. Where are the fairy lights? The color-coordinated curtains and bedding? The photos of friends? Oh right, she doesn't have any. I snicker at her bare walls before turning to face her. My gaze instantly fixates itself on those pert tits. "Well? Why'd you cover for me?"

She crosses her arms over her chest. I smirk at the still-visible outline of a nipple.

"I didn't cover for you, Bates. I did the job we were assigned. Believe it or not, I'm just as ready to be done with this as you are. Probably more than."

"Not fucking likely," I mutter. I roam over to the bookshelf, fingers running down spines. Mostly assigned reading. Ah, Stephen King. For the kind of girl who flirts with having a dark side but is never quite willing to put out. How apropos. I hook my finger into the spine and pull it from the shelf. "Plus, isn't that a bit too selfish a motive for an Adams? You don't do things for yourself. Nah, you're too *good* for that."

"This again?" She drops her arms in her annoyance and my eyes dip back down. "I'm so sorry you're intimidated by my service work. I know this may seem like a really radical statement, but not everything in life is about you."

I inhale, which is stupid, because I'm overwhelmed by a blast of her scent—something sweet and homey and feminine. I tumble gracelessly onto her bed and stretch my legs out, flexing my ankles as I open the book. A quick flip through the pages reveals creased top corners. Gwendolyn Adams, abuser of books, isn't so perfect after all.

She stands over me, expression slightly murderous, and snatches the book out of my hands. "Please, make yourself *uncomfortable*."

"You're telling me," I begin, crossing my ankles, "that you have no desire to turn me into one of your little charity ventures? Fixing the poor little rich boy would be quite the pet project." I lean back on my elbows, finding her mattress surprisingly soft. "Whatever, Adams, you can build me a house if you want. For the record, I prefer platinum fixtures and a double-headed shower feature."

"I think you're drunk." She tosses the book aside and my eyes follow, raising an imperious brow at the untidiness of such an act. "I also think that you're—and I cannot stress this enough—the biggest self-centered idiot I've ever met. And we're both going to get in *more* trouble if you're caught in here."

"Tell me why you covered for me." I'll keep asking until she answers. What the hell, right? I have all night. I want her to admit that she just can't stop trying to one-up me.

Unfortunately, Gwendolyn Adams doesn't give a shit about what I want. Instead of answering, she frowns at the injured hand pressing into her bed. The bandage is ratty, dirty from an afternoon of gluttony and not giving a fuck. I'd forgotten about it, really.

She gestures to it long-sufferingly, "Is that seriously the best bandage you could manage?"

"Do I look like a nurse?"

"You don't want to know what I think you look like," she answers in a terse voice.

My eyebrows climb my forehead. "I bet I fucking do."

We're locked in a suspended, challenging stare that goes on long enough that she eventually sighs. "Do you want me to rewrap that for you, or what?"

"See?" I grin, victorious. "I knew you wouldn't stop until you could fix something about me."

"Oh my god, how can one person be this insufferable," she mutters, but walks across the room and retrieves a large pouch. Returning to me, she unzips it and I see a red cross on the front. "Move." She shoves me aside with her hips and drops next to me on the bed.

"Take off the old bandage," she demands, rifling through the pouch. I unwind the gauze, wincing when the fabric sticks to the wound, a stinging tug that would probably hurt a lot more, were I sober. I rip it off quick, revealing a raw, crimson scrape wound. "Does it hurt?"

I shrug. "I don't know. Maybe a little." Actually, it probably hurts a lot, and I don't even want to think what it'll feel like in the chlorine at swim practice in two days.

"The gauze stuck because you didn't put any ointment on it. You need to keep it moist," she explains, tearing the edge off a little disposable packet of goo. She squeezes a glob of it onto the wound and after a moment of slight hesitation, takes my hand in her own and uses her finger's delicate touch to smear it around. The cool, greasy medicine brings an instant relief, and I don't bother fussing as she rewraps it with a smaller strip of gauze. Once she's secured it with actual tape, I hold it up to inspect it.

"Don't tell me," I say, "you learned how to do that by treating the ailing children of some remote third-world village after an earthquake ravaged their community."

"Actually," she says, packing back up the supplies, her actions stiff and agitated, "I learned how to do that on myself, back when my mother left me home alone for three days and I sliced my hand open on a can of rancid ravioli." She levels me with a frosty look. "But of course, the ceiling of knowledge as it pertains to the absolute basics of caring for a *scrape* is pretty low."

Her eyes hold mine—daring me to come up with a smart retort. Strangely, what emerges is, "Just because I don't do a bunch of dumb charity shit doesn't make me a bad person."

She blinks at me for a moment, eyebrows pulling together. Slowly, as if speaking to a small and very dumb child, she says, "No. The way you treat people makes you a bad person."

I hold up a finger. "That's up for debate. Arguably, I'm morally grey at worst, and at best—"

"What the hell are you doing here, Hamilton?" she bursts. "Because if I have to hear you drunkenly extol your own virtues, so help me god, I will fling myself out that window."

I look around the room as if seeing it for the first time.

What *am* I doing here?

Well, I couldn't tell her the truth, could I? I couldn't say that I just want to prove that she's nothing special. That the fact I can't stop thinking about her all the time is just some stress-induced psychological fluke. That what transpired between us in the locker room was an anomaly. A moment of weakness. My mind playing tricks on me.

Instead, I lift my hand, raising it to slip a finger below her chin, and look at that. She doesn't even flinch, doesn't resist at all when I nudge her face upward. Her wide eyes meet mine for only a split second before dropping to my mouth.

The kiss is slow and gentle, entirely void of the rage and intimidation of the first time we were together. There are no jagged edges here. This is all softness, so delicate and careful that even the soft sound of suction as our lips retreat threatens to shatter the moment.

The girl in front of me isn't fighting back. She's stunned silent as I sit here exploring the curiosity of it all. The lack of heat and anger should make this kiss different, I think. It should make it vacant, less intense, nothing more than any other mediocre kiss.

But *fuck*. It's just as good as I'd remembered. Better, maybe, because here I have the bandwidth to really take it in and feel it. This isn't going even remotely how I expected. I pull back and see her wide, confused eyes. Before she can form the question, I return to her lips, eager to dive in for more. But this time, I allow my hand to rest on her waist and slide up, rucking her thin tank top as it ascends.

Her hands land on my chest and she pushes me hard enough that I have to shoot out a hand to avoid falling off the bed.

I let out a surly, "Ow," as I land on my injured hand.

Having already lurched herself from the bed, Gwendolyn gapes down at me. "*What* are you doing?"

I shrug, feigning casualness even though my heart is racing like a hummingbird's wings. "Thought I'd try it again. See what all the fuss was about."

"You're fucking with me, aren't you?" She darts a nervous glance out her window, then toward her door, and I don't even know what she's expecting to find. A gaggle of Devils standing in the hall with their ears pressed up against the door? A camera capturing the whole thing to share on social media? "You totally are! You need to leave."

"Why?"

"*Why?*" Her question comes out shrill, incredulous.

"Why do I need to leave?" I know perfectly well that I'm being an ass, but I just can't help it now that I've reclaimed the upper hand. I really hadn't been messing with her before, but now? How could I possibly help myself?

"Because, because..." She's got that pink, flustered sheen all about her, cheeks and neck splotched with red. I've seen her flushed with anger before, and the Gwen standing before me doesn't have nearly enough of the wide, apoplectic eyes to signal anger alone.

She's so fucking hot for this.

Gwendolyn marches across the small room and throws open the door, but I clear the room in all of two strides, slamming it shut again with the splay of my palm, pinning her in.

I lean close enough that every inhale bombards my senses with the scent of her hair. "You like it, don't you?"

"What?" her voice is a whisper.

"Kissing me," I say, dipping close enough to brush the tip of my nose across her cheek.

"I hate you," she breathes, but she's almost there, her eyelids nearly dropping. "I pity you."

"Yes." I run my palm down the hot length of her neck, feeling the crazy flutter of her pulse, and then down her collarbone, over the side of her breast, until I rest it on her waist. Her nipples peak, confirming that at the very least, her body doesn't hate me. Not in the least. "You do hate me. Maybe even you even pity me. But you *want* something else." My mouth hovers on the precipice of meeting hers, not kissing her but close enough that it'd take almost no effort at all, just a small push, to take it if she wants. The air gets thicker and thicker with the energy between us, our breaths coming faster, louder. Her eyes flick down to my mouth. That's not what really seals it, though. I know I win when her hips shift under my grip in a squirm that she tries—and utterly fails—to suppress.

Gwendolyn Adams wants more than a kiss from me.

So much more.

I brush my lips against hers then—gentle at first, little more than a whisper—and then pressing forward harder, coaxing her lips to part for me. I can taste the tremor that runs down her spine, the soft sound she makes, just as clearly as I can the mint on her tongue. I deepen the kiss, licking into her mouth, but as soon as it retreats, her teeth close on my bottom lip in a shock of sting and bitterness. I jerk back with a wounded sound that I won't admit to making tomorrow, but I'm greeted only with her roguish smirk. Her fingers wind themselves into my hair and, for a long moment, we just stare at one another.

Enemies. Opposites. Forbidden.

This is wrong, *so wrong*. But every nerve in my body is sparking and pushing, begging me to go in for another kiss, an impulse so strong that I can barely hide how I'm shaking with the liquid hot need for it. One thing is decidedly clear.

I can't stop.

I don't want to stop.

Which is exactly why I jolt away from Gwendolyn and shove her roughly aside. Praying that no one sees me exiting the room, I flee, and don't look back. I don't dare, because if I do, there's no telling what will happen.

9

Usually, going home is a bit of a respite. I can take off the mask and just be Gwen for a day. That's a big part of the reason why I don't do it as often as I could.

Taking the mask off is difficult, sure. There's always a period where I feel more shut down than I should, like I'm just waking up and still trying to adjust my eyes. Sometimes, I feel my family's awareness of it, their furtive looks when a joke whizzes by me, or my dragging smile, lagging just a bit behind where it should be. It doesn't take long, not with Michaela's hugs, or Brayden's playful teasing, or the way my mom runs her fingers through the length of my hair. It just slides off like a muck.

But putting the mask back on after a day of feeling comfortable in my own skin—slipping into my carefully controlled state of nothingness—is almost torture.

It's Sunday and I'd agreed to come home for the day. From the instant I walk in the door, giving Michaela a hug, hip checking Brayden by the refrigerator, and fielding a dozen questions by my mother, what happened the night before looms heavily at the forefront of my mind. Those stiff moments between my state of nothingness and getting back into my own skin are filled with a muted panic that, when the mask comes off, they'll be able to tell. Do I look like a girl who's kissed Hamilton Bates, my sworn enemy, twice?

More than once I've stopped in front of a reflective surface, searching for the answer. I don't look any different, and I don't know how. How can the utter tangle of my insides not be visible in any way? It doesn't seem right.

Mail from colleges all over the country waits for me on the table by the front door. A new pair of shoes sits next to them, the result of a sale that Debbie couldn't pass up. Fried chicken crackles in a frying pan in the kitchen—my favorite dinner—one my mother is trying to painstakingly recreate since Debbie's visiting her own kids today.

Everything is just horrifically normal.

I always feel wistful and guilty when the family goes all out for me like this. It's not uncommon for me to feel antsy to get out of here, but tonight seems worse than normal. I don't discount the weird week I've had to be part of the reason.

"Gwen, Gwen." Michaela taps my arm to get my attention. "After dinner, you should come see my new bedspread, okay?"

I raise an eyebrow at my younger sister. "A new bedspread, huh?"

"Yep." She gives me a sly grin. "It's purple with white checks. Mama let me pick it out."

For a moment, I'm achingly grateful that Michaela's whole 'reverse psychology' schtick is so artless and obvious. The second she's refined it into something effective, we're all doomed.

I meet her cunning smile with my own. "Can't wait."

What Michaela doesn't get is that I'm already planning to leave for college next year. That room is already as good as hers.

"We're home," Dad calls from the entry by the garage. Micha walks in first, dance bag over his shoulder, the sparkly cape tied around his neck fluttering in his wake.

"Hey, dude," I say, offering my fist. He bumps it. "How was dance?"

"Good, I guess." He grabs a handful of nuts off the kitchen table. "Except Gloria is determined to get the solo. Like every year."

"You think you can beat her?"

"Oh, I know I can. I just need her to back off and stop being so bossy. She thinks she's the queen." He rolls his eyes overdramatically. "As if."

This kid lives for drama, on and off the stage. A good feud will keep him going for months.

"Sweetie," Mom admonishes, hovering over the stove. Her hair is a braided rope of graying hair down her slim back. "Dance isn't about competition. It's about expression, sharing your inner beauty to the world."

Inwardly, I have to laugh at this. That's a losing battle. Micha may be even more competitive than I am.

"Yeah, Micha," I mockingly agree. "There are no rivals in dance."

His eyes twinkle at me right before he casually drops, "So Gwen, I heard you got detention."

I narrow my eyes. What a little punk. I try to step on his toe, but he dances out of the way, laughing. "Touché," I mutter.

"Detention?" my dad asks, eyebrows raised in surprise. "What on earth for?"

Instead of answering, I turn to Micha. "Where did you hear that?"

"Dena Clarke is in my Sunday class." He shrugs. "Her sister told her."

"Why is Campbell Clarke talking about me?" I ask, more to myself than Micha. "God, I shouldn't even be on her radar."

"Hello, is this thing on?" My dad taps an invisible mic, which makes all of us roll our eyes in unison. "Why did you get detention?"

"She was late," Michaela answers, happy just to be part of the conversation. "With Hamilton Bates."

My jaw drops.

She heard, too? Jesus Christ, what kind of gossip train is running down to the middle school?

The room falls ominously silent, everyone's gaze shifting to me. Even Brayden, who's now in the living room watching football on the big screen TV, cranes his head around the back of the couch to shoot a questioning gaze at me.

"I was not late *with* Hamilton," I explain, his name feeling foreign and abrasive on my tongue. Or maybe it was his tongue that felt abrasive on my tongue. *Shit*. Conjuring up that image is nothing but trouble. My ears heat. "We were both late. Separately. To the same class."

"And what class was this?" Mom asks, tongs dripping grease onto the floor as she stands there all shocked and dismayed.

"Dr. Ross."

Brayden makes a sharp, sympathetic sound through a mouthful of chips. "God, Dr. Ross. She's the biggest hard-ass about tardiness," he explains to my parents.

"Language," Dad gives my brother a stern look. "Was it just one day of detention?"

"No." I sigh, slumping dejectedly in my chair. "Five Saturdays in a row. She made an exception for our afterschool activities, but it came with a compromise."

Mom gives me a long, worried look. "Do you need me to call the dean? I'm sure they can work something out. I know being around Hamilton makes you uncomfortable."

This is so tempting that it's almost a physical battle to keep my mouth shut. Being around Hamilton *does* make me uncomfortable. And angry. And flustered. And hot. And crazy. And super confused. No one person should ever be exposed to as many emotions as Hamilton Bates makes me feel. "No," I ultimately decide, shoulders dropping, "it's not a big deal. I don't want to cause a fuss."

"It's not a fuss, Gwen. You two have a complicated history. I know he's not always nice to you—not anymore."

My teeth clench. "Mom, it's fine."

She turns back to the kitchen, metal tongs turning the chicken. "Okay, but if he says anything—"

"He won't." Mom and Dad both look at me with concern. I sense Brayden paying too much attention, as well. Six months ago, I would have set fire to the school before being alone with Hamilton Bates. Hell, he probably would have, too. I assure them all, "Seriously, it's fine. We're both busy and honestly, it's kind of funny watching him try to perform manual labor. It's like watching a monkey try to use a screwdriver."

Michaela honks a laugh at that, and I go about the business of taking the food to the dining room table, feeling better now that they know about the detention. I have plenty weighing on me, and at least that's one less thing. Luckily, it's not brought up again during what's shaping up to be a civil dinner. There's no talk of Chakras or karmic balance or how eating food grounded in the Earth can help center your mind. Sometimes that 'woo' stuff can get really grating, as if our parents make sure we're so well educated that we can argue with them over the table about how science, like, exists. But conversation this evening mostly revolves around Micha's upcoming dance performance and Brayden being promoted from sentient toilet scrubber to hesitant apprentice at the garage.

We're clearing the table when Mom says, "Oh, I talked to Sky this morning. She's sad she can't be here but wanted me to tell you she's doing well. And Michaela, she said to tell you that she got to ride Chestnut today. She sent a picture."

My sister is meticulously picking out slices of strawberry from her bowl of fruit, strategically avoiding all melon. But at this, her face lights up. "Really?" She hops up from where she's attentively *not* helping and runs over to see the phone. Sky's residential program is on a ranch in Texas and taking care of the horses is part of the therapy. Michaela has been green with envy for months. It probably helps that she has no idea why Sky is even there. "Look, Gwen! Isn't it so pretty?"

She thrusts the phone at me, the screen showing a photo of a horse with a tan coat and a flowing blonde mane. My eyes skip over the horse and focus on my sister. She's smiling in the picture, green eyes bright and crinkled in the late fall sun. Her hair is longer now, blonder even, almost matching the horse's mane. For a moment, I'm struck with a random memory of her sitting on my bed, her hair catching a halo of light from an open window as I braid it so carefully, the way her nose would crinkle with a laugh, the sharp scent of nail polish as she begged me to choose between Lavender Luck and Woman Scorned.

I hand the phone back to my mom. "She looks good. Sky, I mean." I promise Michaela, "The horse is nice, too."

Mom smiles, and something in the sadness of her eyes makes me suspect she knows that I was remembering the better times.

But she doesn't know that I often wonder just how much better those times even were.

"She sounds so good during our phone sessions, too. Really balanced. I think the dry heat really helps her." Mom and dad have weekly family therapy via video with her. "Next week she's supposed to have a call with Amanda."

"Amanda," I repeat, going still. Amanda is Sky's birth mother—the one with the boyfriend and the cigarette burns and everything else. "Are you sure that's a good idea?"

Mom shrugs, spooning the leftover green beans into a container. "You know I've always encouraged a relationship between you all and your birth parents."

I glance over to make sure that Michaela has joined my dad and the boys in the living room. "Yes, I do know that. I also know it doesn't always turn out for the best."

Obviously, Brayden's relationship with his birth mother hadn't been successful, but there's also the twins. They were meeting with their birth mother once a month for a long time. It went pretty well until, one day, Micha showed up wearing a skirt, glittery sneakers, and a long stack of plastic bracelets on his arm. His mom threw a complete fit, calling him names, making fun of him, throwing around slurs. The whole thing was awful and probably scarred the poor kid.

"Amanda is clean now—"

"So she says."

"And is getting her GED."

I roll my eyes. "Of course, she is."

My mom gives me a look. "Gwen."

"*Mom*," I reply, "it's like you never learn. There's a reason these people gave up their kids. At the very best, they don't want to be parents. At worst, they literally just don't have what it takes to try. Why can't you just accept that?"

She wipes her hands on a dishtowel and looks at me with kind, loving eyes. "Gwen, I've been reading more and more about how the bond between birth mother and child is so important. You all lived and breathed in another woman's womb. It's a role I wish belonged to me, but it doesn't. I want you to feel free to nurture that part of yourself."

I swear to god, if she breaks into some kind of hippie-mother Earth song or waves incense over my head, I might actually stab her with a dinner fork.

"Don't you get it?!" My voice is almost at a growl at this point. "Skylar is incapable of making decisions that are in her best interest! Do you think she can even say no to that woman? Did it ever occur to you that she's a big part of the reason Sky let all that shit happen to her last year?"

She frowns. "You know I don't like that kind of dirty language. It's the lowest form of expression."

"Oh, that?" I laugh in frustration. "*That* is what upsets you? 'Shit' upsets you, not exposing your emotionally and psychologically compromised daughter to the person responsible for her abuse. Maybe we should get the Devils in on the call, too. Some of the Northridge boys even, why not?"

"Gwendolyn!" My mother's eyes are alight in anger now, too. "That is quite enough!"

I drop the stack of plates I'm holding on the counter. "I don't know why we're even talking about this. It's not like you ever listen to me anyway."

I storm off, stomping up the stairs to the second floor. I pass the long hallway lined with photos of all us kids, years' and years' worth of school and family photos, lifetimes of progress and adjustments captured in time. It's like it means nothing.

I enter my bedroom, slam and lock the door, and then turn to thrust two middle fingers at it.

How's that for expression?

It takes me a minute to realize that Michaela really wasn't kidding. When I do, it interrupts my silent fuming so entirely that it's like whiplash. She's *seriously* taken over my room. The purple bedspread is joined by fuzzy pillows and at least a dozen stuffed animals, including one that I'm pretty sure is a taco in the form of a cat. My books have been pushed aside for *Pop!* figurines and the top of my dresser is covered with her hair accessories. It's not like I'm mad or anything. It's just jarring. I made the choice to move to the dorms, and how long has she been warning me what would happen if I didn't come back home?

Still, I sink onto the bed—the same bed I'd had the memory of Sky on before—and feel like something small but fundamental has been pulled out of me.

The outburst with my mom wasn't exactly unusual. Although the other kids had willingly seen their birth parents when Mom organized it, I'd refused. The idea of letting that kind of toxicity into my life was unappealing—scary, if I was being honest. Why open the door to someone who effectively threw me out? Hamilton was right about that. My mom saw me as garbage. Easily disposable. Why would I want to foster any kind of relationship with someone who thought of me like that? How could that be healthy?

I move to sit in the soft fuzzy chair by the window. There's a streetlight outside that made this corner perfect for reading after dark. For weeks I'd huddle in the corner, reading books before passing out on a pile of blankets. Mom obviously decided if I was going to fall asleep while reading, I could at least do it in a comfortable chair. It wasn't as though we had bedtimes or anything. Mom believed in the body's natural rhythms. If Brayden wanted to go to bed at three a.m. on a school night, no big deal. If Micha fell asleep on the way home from school in Debbie's car, fine.

Again, maybe Hamilton was right. We're feral.

That's the third time I've thought about him tonight—probably more, if I'm being honest. Also, if I'm being honest, Hamilton Bates has been on my mind for a long time, way before the last week or even the last year. On a whim I jump up and go to my closet, pushing up on my toes to reach for the shoe box I kept in the top corner. I grab the edge, and pull it toward me, catching it before it tips. Carrying it back to the chair, I sit, crisscrossing my legs and settling it in my lap. I take a deep breath before opening the dusty lid.

Inside are what I used to call my treasures. It's mostly swim-related; a rainbow array of ribbons, awards, and certificates. There are a few abstract things—mementos from important races, a rock I think I found after winning a big race, the napkin from the diner downtown near the natatorium that has the best milkshakes. I search until I find what I'm looking for—what I think is in this box. It's possible I made the moment up, but I don't think so. In my mind, there's a photograph. Proof. I sort through a stack of pictures until—

Yes! It's real.

It's a picture, taken during one of my mom's intense phases with photography. Sometimes she gets a whim and decides to document nearly every moment of our lives. The phases don't usually last long, so there are certain points in our childhoods that have a borderline obsessive photographic record. Actual photographs can be hard to come by—digital is easier and also easier to wipe away, to pretend never existed. But the picture in my hand is scarily tangible, as are the subjects; me and Hamilton.

We'd both spent a month practicing long-course racing, essentially flipping the lanes on their sides, doubling the distance. The races are slower, a bit more tedious. Pacing is important, because if a swimmer starts with a burst of speed, they'll flame out quickly, making it hard to complete the race. It was the summer before the twins came home, before Hamilton knew the truth about us all. We'd spent the training period egging each other on, trying to best one another. But we'd also relied on one another. Cheering for better times, a perfected flip-turn, a well-executed dive. We were team-mates, not enemies. Back then I was just Gwen—or Gwendolyn. He always called me by my full first name. He was just Hamilton, the funny kid with a bright smile. That's who I see in the photograph I'm holding. Gwendolyn and Hamilton—happy. Gold medals of accomplishment hanging around our necks, arms wrapped around one another.

When I think back on the downy nostalgia of childhood, these are the moments that make it golden. These were the moments I was happiest.

I stare at the photo for a long time, trying to reconcile the broadly grinning Hamilton in the photo with the one I know today. The boy who hates me. Torments me. Ignores me. How strange to think, back then, that I thought I knew enough of Hamilton to be so sure of his character. And then again, later on, to have placed him so easily into the role of a monster. Now, he's the boy who won't stop kissing me.

If I thought his prior mindfucks were top-tier, then I was wrong.

This shit takes the cake.

Unbelievably, it's the second kiss that bothers me most. There was something about the way it started—gentle, almost *sweet*—that makes me want to turn away from the memory. It was an uncomfortable earnestness, as if we were just two regular, equal people, and I wanted it. I liked it. But the whole thing was dishonest in its honesty.

And that's the thing about kissing Hamilton Bates; every kiss brings out warring emotions. Guilt, desire, betrayal, want.

Is that his plan? To confuse me?

I lean back and stare at the ceiling, letting my eyes flutter shut.

I don't like him, and I *really* don't trust him, but his mouth? His hands? After seeing him play the cello, I shouldn't be surprised at the accuracy of his touch or why I'd want more. I wonder what it would be like to really have his hands on my body. Would it feel as good as his mouth does on mine?

No.

My eyes pop open, narrowed.

No, I am not going down this road or entertaining this one bit more. He was drunk. He's a dick who's trying to manipulate me, and acting as if it could ever be anything more isn't just doing my family disservice. It's doing *me* a disservice.

Closing the lid, I stand and return the box to the closet, sliding it, and my conflicted feelings about Hamilton, back where they belong —hidden and in the past.

10

Hamilton

"Ham—are you even listening to me?"

"Huh?" My eyes dart down to Reagan's. Her hand, clasped around my neck, tugs me to face her. I answer, "Yeah, I'm listening."

Obviously, I'm not listening.

I try to now, angling my face to hers, but it's such a struggle. Every time she opens her mouth, it's *blah blah blah*. The girl is just dull as dirt. If she's not trying to find out where I've been, where I'm going, or what I'm going to do *with her*, it's just the most basic ass gossip imaginable. I do actually have a life.

She rolls her eyes, well aware that I'm lying. "I said, good luck today. I know it's a big one." Her other hand runs down my arm, feeling my bicep. "Are you nervous?"

"About what? Practice?" I scoff. "This is like my millionth swim practice, Reagan. No. I'm not nervous."

"I mean about the captain announcement."

Well, fuck.

I *wasn't*.

I narrow my eyes. "Why, have you heard something?"

"Ah, no?" Her fingers tickle my neck. "It's just... I got really nervous before cheerleading announcements last fall. I'd worked really hard for my position, and you know how Campbell can be about playing favorites."

"Ah, right, cheerleading." My grin must not look as condescending as it feels, since she just nods in response. Some schools that cheer competitively might be comparable to the pure athleticism of swim, but Preston's squad is nothing more than hot pieces of ass prancing around in short skirts with their tits bouncing all over. "The coach makes this call, not some status-conscious bitch. Our captains are based on experience and leadership. I'm the obvious choice."

The bravado is only a little false. I know good and well that Adams has a chance of sliding in and stealing my spot. But I have a little insurance in the form of my father's gracious donation to the swim club. A little extra security in case Coach decided to make a decision based on empathy rather than merit.

Speaking of...

I can see Adams turning down the hallway from over the top of Reagan's head. She's got this small but sunny smile on her face, which is weird. I lift my head to watch her, that small smile growing. Where's the blank sadness? The stoic indignation?

That's when I notice Tyson Riggins, her new little friend, loping along beside her.

My hand curls into a fist, teeth clenching.

God, I hate that guy.

He's only been here for a week, and he's already upsetting the established social order at the school. Someone needs to explain to him that Gwendolyn Adams is strictly persona non grata. She's kryptonite. Off limits.

Mine.

"Babe!"

"*What*?" I snap, glaring down at Reagan. She looks almost as annoyed as I feel. Good. It'd sure be nice if she stopped buzzing around me like a pesky fly.

"I *said*, I've got to get to Econ." Despite her annoyance with me, her face tilts up, like she's expecting a kiss.

My eyes dart back over to Adams and our gazes instantly lock. Normally, she'd never let that happen, and if she did, she'd probably look away.

She doesn't.

Knowing her eyes are on me, that something about this has gained her interest, makes me wrap my arm around Reagan's waist and pull her close.

"Thanks for stopping by," I say, flipping on the charm. I touch her chin and plant a kiss on her mouth. She reacts with zeal, kissing me back passionately, like she's trying to crawl into my skin. Almost instantly, I regret all of this.

Down girl, that's enough.

I try not to grimace when I see that Reagan's eyes are glazed, but she ultimately walks off, nearly tripping over her feet. I feel the heat of Gwendolyn's eyes boring into me and wish I didn't. What, did she think there was something going on with us? That she meant something to me?

If anything, my lapse in judgment cemented the fact that I need to just stay away from alcohol.

And Adams? I really, *really* need to stay away from her. Which, I realize fifteen minutes later, after a rousing welcome from Coach James, is going to be more challenging than I think. We're sorted into the same competitive lane.

I lower my goggles and dive in, immediately setting the pace. Heston follows, then Gwendolyn, and a junior who's fast as hell. Even in the water I want my distance from her, so I push too fast, and I know—I *know* I'm working my shoulder harder than I should, but I don't let up, not an inch. I take a breather at the end of the lap, rotating my stiffening shoulder to ease out the burning tightness. Heston stops when I do, always looking for a short cut.

"Did you see Adams?" he pants, water dripping down his grinning face. "I think her tits got bigger since last year."

I shoot him a glare and duck under water, pushing off the wall with the balls of my feet. What the hell is it with everyone? Is Adams suddenly not off limits anymore? Has she been uncancelled? Did all it take was one kid from Northridge showing up and talking to her to undo everything we'd established over the last six months? It's bullshit.

Fucking Heston, I think, switching from freestyle to backstroke in one easy flip. I keep my eyes on the ceiling, counting the little flags that hang overhead so that we don't crash into the wall. Heston's a trust fund baby who will spend his freshman year of college on the beaches of Italy at his family's villa, fucking local housewives and keeping the winery in business. If he decided to get his hands on Gwendolyn, he'd absolutely destroy her.

In fact, I already have suspicions that he'd had some involvement in the set up with her sister at the party. Sky was always known for being so easy to manipulate—like clay in anyone's hands, really—and Heston's a lazy fuck. The utter lack of effort necessary to inflict as much damage as possible has his name written all over it. It's just a feeling, although I don't really put it past any of the Devils. They've just been too quiet about it—too cooperative. They definitely haven't wanted to talk to me about it, no matter how many times I've casually broached the subject.

Slam!

I jerk out of the water, arms tangled, pushing hard. Adams flails in the water beside me, eyes accusatory. "What the hell, Bates! Stay in your own damn lane!"

"*My* lane? It's those goddamned gangly arms of yours taking up all the space!"

She opens her mouth like she's going to say something, but she snaps it shut, drops under water and swims away.

Satisfaction swells within me as she backs down first.

That's right. Know your place.

Of course, it's all dampened when I look over my shoulder and see Coach James watching us with a frown on his face.

Shit.

We make it through the rest of practice without further altercations. While everyone finishes their final cool-downs, I grab my towel and wrap it around my waist. Heston and the others in my lane do the same.

"Do you think he'll announce captains now?" Heston asks, drying off his face.

"I thought so, but... I don't know." I look around, stomach dropping. "Maybe not."

James is standing with a few of the assistant coaches, glancing at the swimmers and taking notes. It's not unusual. There are new swimmers on the team. People grow over the summer—sometimes a few inches—it can completely change their score. We also occasionally lose a swimmer or two. There are a lot of factors when creating a team roster, but something about the delay makes me antsy and uncomfortable. That feeling multiplies when he blows his whistle and says, "Good first day. I'll see everyone back tomorrow," and then adds, "Bates and Adams. I need to see you in my office."

Heston's eyebrows shoot to the top of his forehead, mouth spreading into a jaw-dropped grin. He slaps me on my back. "Oh, fuck, this is it! Good luck, bro."

Rigid with frustration, I pull a pair of shorts over my Speedo before walking over to the office. Gwendolyn is already there, towel wrapped under her armpits, skin pebbled with goosebumps. Her teeth worry away at her bottom lip. Without my even wanting them to, my eyes dart down to her tits. Fucking Heston. He's totally right. They may be bigger. My dick twitches in confirmation.

"Thanks for waiting," Coach says, striding into the room. He drops his clipboard on his desk and folds his arms. Coach James is young, fit. He swam at Princeton and made it to the Olympic Trials. I respect the hell out of him. There's something about him. He just knows how to get the best out of the team. He's not a dick, either, which is not always the case in competitive sports. "I know you two thought I was going to make the captain announcement today, and you're right. I was." He rubs his chin. "But then I saw you two have that little fuss in the lane and I knew I needed to talk to you directly first."

For the first time since I walked in the room, Gwendolyn looks over at me. I don't give away the fact that my heart is suddenly banging against my chest.

"What's going on?" I ask. "Is there a problem?"

"You two are my best swimmers," he begins. "I think we all know that. Each of you bring a different strength to the team. Gwen, you're consistent, hardworking, focused. You take the time to encourage younger swimmers and foster a team mentality." She beams reluctantly at the praise. I manage not to roll my eyes, and look attentive when he looks at me. "Hamilton, you've got the right kind of competitive nature this sport requires, strong leadership abilities, and unwavering spirit."

There's a 'but' lingering in there somewhere. We both know it.

"I don't like the friction that's been going on between the two of you for the last year. I know there are extenuating circumstances, but it goes beyond what happened with Gwen's sister." It's like all the air is suddenly sucked out of the room. Our backs go ramrod straight so simultaneously, it's like we're two marionettes on a single string. *No one* mentions Sky. Not even teachers. "I can't have this kind of division on my team, especially not from my two best swimmers. I need unity and cooperation in the team leader. And I think deep down, you both know I'm right."

"What are you saying?" Gwendolyn asks quietly. "That neither of us are going to be captain?"

"I won't deny that the thought crossed my mind, but if I did that, I'd be losing a really great asset for this team. And that's not exactly fair, is it? So, I had another idea." He looks between us. "Co-captains."

"Excuse me?" I blurt.

Gwendolyn's jaw drops.

Coach holds up his hands. "Do it together or don't do it at all. It's your choice. If you can't work together, I'll find someone else to do it."

"I—I—" Gwendolyn seems unable to speak, instead blinking owlishly at the coach.

My vision narrows until I'm seeing nothing but the red of the wall behind the coach. This can't be happening. It *can't*. My hands fist and I feel the tension building in my neck, in the shoulder that's already smarting from swimming too hard. This was supposed to be *it*. Things were supposed to get better after this. I was supposed to be captain and make my dad proud and finally, *finally* be better.

"Coach," I start, trying to regain some semblance of composure, because I have to. I *have to* fix this. "I understand where you're coming from. I do. But is there anything, *anything*—"

"Bates, I've spoken to the headmaster and some of the other faculty, and we all agree. It's time for this feud to settle down. It's lasted for months and it's affecting the quality of life at Preston for students and teachers alike."

"With all due respect," Gwendolyn finally speaks up, "Bates isn't the only problem I have at this school."

"I'm aware," he gives her a sympathetic look, before shifting his gaze on me. "As much as I hate to admit it—Hamilton, you have a lot of influence with the student body. They're looking to you for cues. It's a power structure I'm not a fan of, but it's how the culture of this school operates. You have power here."

It sounds like a compliment. I'm not sure it is.

"Coach..." Doing this in front of Coach James is humiliating enough, but Adams having to see the way I beg him with my eyes is just a cherry on top of this shit cake. "I have less power than you think."

"You have enough," he argues. "And I think it's time you use it for something worthwhile. Nothing changes if you don't agree to get along and work together. You're both gifted students and skilled athletes. You can achieve so much more together than divided." He sighs, shaking his head at the open door, where the team is still milling around the halls. "I know it's more complicated than that, which is why I'm giving you this chance. You can blame me for making you work together, if that makes this easier on you. Or you can walk away. It's up to you." He grabs his clipboard. "Let me know before practice tomorrow, what you decide."

He walks out of the room, a heavy silence falling between the two of us. Anger burns under my skin, but hotter than the anger burns the bone-deep shame of failure. It should have been guaranteed. I should have been so good, so proficient, that there was no question. I should have had this shit in the bag. And now my best-case scenario is coming in tied with someone who doesn't even belong here. This is not what I want. It's not what my father will want.

But walking away from the position would be worse, wouldn't it? I need it for my applications. For my pride. Even if I have to share it with a she-witch in the process, it's still...

It's still *something*.

"Look, Adams..." I start, trying to figure out how in the hell I'm supposed to talk her into something I don't even believe in.

"I ain't looking at shit." she replies plainly. "This is going to be a hard pass for me. You can forget it."

"Let's talk about this—"

She storms out of the room, leaving me standing there like a fool.

I swallow down a new swell of anger and follow her out. I watch as she ducks into the girls' locker room and pause for a hot second, dithering only a moment before following her in. A few girls are still in there, all dressed, just gathering their things. They gape at me intruding on their space.

I bark, "Leave."

They scurry out like mice, leaving the two of us alone.

Gwendolyn breathes out a dark laugh. "Nice show of leadership, already treating people like minions. Heil Bates."

She gives me a Nazi salute.

I will myself not to lose my shit, instead sweeping a sneering gaze down her body. "Who's being the childish, entitled toddler now?"

"I can't believe you seriously want me to do this," she says, readjusting her towel around her narrow waist. "No, actually, it makes perfect sense. You need to be in control, even if that means sharing it with me. Mostly because you think you can control me, too. But I already have to spend my Saturdays covering for your ass. I have no interest in taking on your half of this assignment, too—all so you can claim on your college applications that you did all the work. And," she continues haughtily, "don't even try to pretend this is going to change anything. We both know things will be business as usual, only instead of just making everyone ignore me, you'll probably get the other swimmers to treat me like dirt, and then your flunkies will have new and interesting opportunities to mock me behind my back —or worse—to my face."

I shake my head, laughing bitterly. "God, you're so delusional."

She rests her hands on her hips. "How am *I* the delusional one?"

"How am *I* the control freak?" I gesture to her. "Your entire life is about controlling everyone and everything you meet. Look at you, you couldn't even let me get in trouble for blowing off detention the other day. God forbid Dean Dewey think you let a situation—let *me*—get out of hand. Even the twins. You hover over them like a mother-fucking hen, as if they can't find their own damn classroom without your careful guiding hand." I grin cruelly, fueled and fired up, ready to burn it all down. "And you know what else? *Sky.* Yeah, I said her name. You probably baby her, too, don't you? It's obvious enough you blame yourself for what happened to her, despite not even *being there.* Because Gwen must be all-knowing and all-powerful. That's why you were so bent on blaming the Devils. Because if that whole mess had been nothing more than her own decision, that would mean you never had control to begin with."

I have no time to react. It's like one second she's standing there getting redder and redder, and the next, my head is whipping to the side, face stinging. The sound of her palm slapping against my cheek echoes off the tile walls with a hard *crack.*

My tongue slips out to nurse the spot where my tooth has punctured the skin. The bright, coppery taste of blood fills my mouth, but I don't flinch. I just look right into her eyes, wide with a mixture of shock and horror, and step closer, until our faces are inches apart.

My heart bangs a dark, enraged rhythm against my ribcage when I whisper, "How does it feel to lose control?"

I expect her to hurt me again, and I wonder what it's going to be. Maybe a punch this time, maybe even a knee to the groin. I'm ready for it, whatever it is.

The push is only briefly amusing, her two wide palms coming up to my chest and shoving me down onto the bench behind me. Her towel slides off and she's standing before me in nothing but the thin Lycra of her swimsuit, so understandably, my brain goes kind of fuzzy at the edges.

That's just playing dirty.

Before I can even halfway parse my lap being full with the weight of her suddenly straddling my thighs, she's pressing our mouths together.

Truthfully, a punch would have probably been less violent.

Gwen kisses like a freight train, all teeth and tongue and unstoppable momentum. I don't even have time to brace myself for one attack before the next comes—a suck at my lip, fingernails digging into my shoulders. It's a sharp, hot hurt that makes my dick swell until it's a throbbing ache trapped between us.

Her kiss is warm, disturbingly familiar. I didn't even know I craved the taste of her until her tongue pushed against mine—that hard pang of wanting and having and feeling drunk on the taste of it. Her body is lean and strong, soft and hard in all the right places. I run my hands down her exposed back, fingers tripping over the criss-crossed straps of her swimsuit. I yank at the end, loosening the tie, and somewhere buried deep in my hindbrain is a sort of warning— that I should prepare for another slap.

Instead, she arches her back, letting the straps fall from her shoulders.

It's possible something in my brain breaks because I have to be delirious to think I have Gwendolyn Adams' bare tits pressing into me.

I break from the kiss just long enough to look, and fuck. There they are. Her tits are absolute perfection. I cup them in my hands while she tugs at my bottom lip with her teeth, grinding down against my erection. The friction is good, *ridiculously good*, and my mind goes to that special, fuzzy place where I momentarily forget anything that isn't my aching dick or the tits in my hand.

It all comes back in a snap when Gwendolyn rolls her hips, forcing the damp, narrow section of her bathing suit—the one barely covering her pussy—to slide eagerly against my cock. She drops her face into my neck and I suck the soft skin beneath her ear, groaning into it.

I run my hand down her smooth back before tugging on her long mane of hair, forcing her to look at me.

"Does that feel good?"

She looks at me with glazed eyes for a beat, cheeks aflame, lips puffy and red, before nodding. Her eyes dart to the side but she says, "Y-yes."

"Do you want more?"

She doesn't answer, face hardening as she keeps rocking against me.

I still her hips, grinding us both to a painful halt. She exhales in a shudder. "Tell me you want it, Adams, and I'll let you have it."

Her eyes clear, then narrow, and I figure....

That may have been a step too far.

Except, apparently not. With her nose pressed against mine, her eyes drop closed and she breathes, "I want it."

I release my grip, and she resumes the motion of humping against my cock, tits bouncing just below eye level, and for all semblance of control, I am completely and thoroughly enraptured. It takes everything I have not to yank off the rest of that suit—and it'd be so fucking easy—and bury myself inside of her. But even I know that's too much, too far.

"Fuck," she moans against my lips, and I kiss her again, wanting that ragged edge of sound inside of me. With every rock of her hips, her breath grows shorter and shorter against my mouth, until eventually we're just panting into one another, hips driving us mindlessly forward.

Suddenly, her head falls back, and I want to suck my mark into the long, pale column of her throat—God, I really do—but more than that, I just need to see. I need to see what she looks like when she finally lets go of all that self-righteous control and comes on my dick. Her nails dig into my back and my balls tighten, making my own breathing grow ragged.

"Come on," I grunt, feeling the sharp swell of my own release rapidly approaching. "Come on, Adams. Let it fucking go, come on."

Her teeth bite down into her lip, muffling her cry as she suddenly seizes, shuddering hard against me. I pull her face to mine in a kiss, swallowing her moan, and then follow her directly over the edge. It feels like it goes on forever, spilling into my shorts, grinding up into her a little more roughly than intended. She doesn't seem to mind. She just keeps rocking into me, letting us ride it out together, panting hot and wet against my mouth.

Soon we both still, nothing but the harsh sounds of our breath filling the room, and I don't know what to do with the hand tangled in her hair or the one clutching her hip. I know the second one of us flinches, it's over.

The sound of my swallow is apparently all it takes for reality to come crashing back.

"Oh my god," she gasps, clambering off of me with shaky legs. She hastily wraps her arms around her bare chest. "That—oh my god."

I shift, wincing. "Tell me about it." My Speedo is filled with cum, and the tip of my dick is chafed raw. I try to sort out my situation while Gwendolyn darts around the locker room, throwing on her clothes and gathering her things.

She pauses and looks at me, eyes raking over the length of my body. I'm pretty sure she left marks on my back. Just like I'm pretty sure I see a hickey under her ear.

"That," she begins, but I hold up my hand.

"Never happened."

"Never.

Sing me another tune some time.

"But hey, you know what *did* happen?" I stand on my own wobbly legs and can't help but smirk. "I think we just kind of proved that we can work together."

She stares at me blankly. It's not a threat, it's just the truth. But I see the worry in her eyes. She can't help it. She doesn't trust me, and frankly, she shouldn't.

"Adams." I hold her gaze, and I'm not proud of what comes next any more than dry humping her in the girls' locker room. I shouldn't have to do this. But desperate times and all that. "Please," I ask.

She watches me, and I'm not sure what she's looking for. Even I can't manage the artifice of deception three minutes after coming my brains out. Whatever she was looking for, she must find it. She runs her hand down her shirt, like she's cleaning it off, and thrusts it toward me. "Co-captains?"

I offer her my own and we shake, her fingers still trembling— either from the orgasm or from the horror of what we'd just done.

Either way, I got mine.

11

"Debbie made you this!" Michaela produces a muffin from her backpack with a crumb-flying flourish. "It's chocolate."

"My favorite." The muffin looks as squished and lopsided as I feel. "Thanks."

I'm being a total coward, having pretended at being late to avoid talking to our nanny. I couldn't face her after what I'd done. I can barely even face myself after what happened last night.

"How does it feel to lose control?" Even now, I can call up the memory of his face perfectly, inches from my own. If I thought kissing him that first time tangled me up, then what happened yesterday just took a sledgehammer to it all. This time, it wasn't the dark creep of nightmares that made me squirm all night. It was the near constant, hyper-realistic, Imax-sized internal replay of what he felt like beneath me, around me, against me.

How does it feel to lose control?

Starting alphabetically, agonizing. Amazing. Appalling. Awesome. Awful. I have plans to get through the Bs during homeroom. By the end of the day, I should have enough for a whole storybook on the cautionary tale of hot boys and the neurotic girls they torment.

"So, how's dance going?" I ask Micha, welcoming the distraction. "Did you get the solo?"

"Our teacher hasn't decided yet. The final audition is tonight. I've been struggling with this one move..." He pauses to drop his bag and assume a dancing posture. I was never good with dance, myself, so I'm not really sure if the twirl he pushes into is technically as perfect as it looks, but it's quick and graceful.

A few of the high school kids walking past slow to gawk at him, and I don't know if they're impressed or about to say something really shitty. My hackles rise, regardless, ready to push back if they so much as snicker at him.

Micha's oblivious, thankfully. He just completes his last step with a dip and turn, and then falls out of the posture, shrugging. "But I think I've got it down better than Gloria. She's my only real competition."

"Mom says we can go out for ice cream if he gets the solo," Michaela explains to me. She hands Micha his bag and adds, "You'll get it. Or *else*."

I laugh at the glare on Micha's face. "Come on, guys. We all know Mom will take you for ice cream regardless. It looks like you've got it down, anyway." I tuck a piece of hair behind my ear and start to unwrap the muffin. I glance up and notice Michaela watching me closely. "What?"

She touches beneath her ear. "What's that?"

My hand reaches for the spot. It's tender and red. I know that from seeing it in the mirror this morning. I'd tried covering the hickey with concealer, but that obviously didn't work. I'd sure like to know what the hell he was thinking, leaving evidence like that. My first thought was that Hamilton had tried to give me a Devil's mark, but that's just insane. He'd never want anyone to know. *Ever.* "Just a bruise. I got hit by a kickboard at swim last night."

But a small part of me is glad it's there. I have solid, tangible proof that last night happened. It wasn't some messed up fever dream that my brain created. His mouth was *there*. It's all at once some strange, erotic, horrifying relief.

"Ouch," she says, satisfied and sympathetic, but I'm inwardly filled with dread. Michaela documents everything just in case she needs the information for later.

When we reach their classroom, they both say in that creepy twin unison, "See you later!"

"Bye! Good luck, Micha! Text me and let me know how it goes, okay?"

He probably won't, but Mom's guaranteed to give me a documentary-level video and photo account of every moment. Eating the muffin on the way to class, I furtively pull my hair over my shoulder in an attempt to hide the hickey. Every day for the last six months has been the same; I walk in, go to my locker with a negative sum of acknowledgment, and I go to class to the same treatment. The wall of silence follows my each and every step like a hostile but ever-faithful dog.

But today isn't like every other day.

Today is the day after Hamilton and I gave each other orgasms. And neither of us hated the orgasms as much as we hate each other.

And that's the weird thing. It's not like my feelings toward Hamilton have changed. It's not like I rubbed all up on his dick for a few minutes and suddenly think he's worth the light of day. Not a bit. He's a petty, mean, egotistical asshole. But my body? Well, I quickly learn it has a mind of its own.

But it's not how it was supposed to be. The first guy I ever did this kind of stuff with was supposed to be nice. He was supposed to be sweet and caring, or—at the absolute bottom barrel of standards— not be the person responsible for making my life a miserable, isolated mess.

I walk down the hall toward first period and it's like whatever happened between us has raised my awareness of him tenfold. I instantly spot him lounging against the wall near his locker. Images of him from the night before flash before my eyes, unbidden. Hamilton leaning over me, daring me to lose control. The want in his heavy-lidded eyes when my bathing suit fell. The way his hands felt, cupping my breasts, brushing against my nipples. How hard and hot he felt beneath me, the way I could feel him twitch against my center when he came. The part of his lips as he panted against my own, face twisted in the same sweet ache of release I was feeling, too.

Now, he's talking with Reagan, which is... good. It's fine. I'm not laboring under the delusion that what we did meant anything. The faculty at this school are clearly hell-bent on forcing us into these frustrating situations together, and what else could be expected? No, all of this—the kissing, the making out, the orgasms—was simple physical catharsis, that's all.

A one-time thing.

Okay, a two-time thing.

Well, a three-time thing, at absolute maximum.

I cram the last piece of muffin in my mouth as I walk toward him into the classroom, stopping at a trashcan to toss the wrapper. But now my fingers are covered in sticky chocolate and I don't have time to go wash my hands. I look woefully down at them before deciding to just lick off the residue. I start toward the classroom, my eyes being drawn toward the door. Hamilton stands there, stormy gray eyes zeroed in on my mouth. The knuckles of the fingers clutching his book are bone-white.

When our gazes meet, we both seem to just freeze. The heat in his eyes sends a white-hot spike of want down my spine, but I finally pass him, grazing his arm in the process.

A three-time thing, I repeat to myself.

That's all.

I BEAT Tyson to the cafeteria and intentionally sit on the opposite side of the table. Thankfully, he doesn't notice, just slides his tray across the table, a piece of pizza already hanging from his mouth.

"How long did that meeting with Coach James go last night?" he asks after swallowing. "I waited for you, but I had to get back to the dorm."

I take a deep breath. "He wants us to co-captain."

Tyson's eyes pop. "Wait, what? The two of you? Isn't that like asking those Oasis brothers to make another album?"

"That's what we told him." I roll my eyes. "He didn't care. He thinks that our feud is causing a problem for the team, and if we can't work together, then he'll pick someone else."

"So what did you say?" he pushes the hair out of his eyes and glances over to where I know Hamilton is sitting. "From the looks of it, I'm assuming 'no'."

I frown at him. "What do you mean?"

"Because Bates has been shooting daggers over here since I sat down. I figure he's pissed at you for turning it down."

I steal a glance. It's a dumb move because he's not looking, but Reagan is. Her fingers are playing with the curls at the back of his neck. She might as well just pee on him.

I pull a face. "Well, actually…"

"Seriously?" He honks a disbelieving laugh. "You're going to co-captain with him? Is it even possible for you to work together? The way I hear it, if the two of you meet in this timeline, you might cause some kind of world-ending cataclysm."

That's certainly one way of putting it.

I shift in my seat. "We're going to try, I guess. We managed to get through the first day of detention without killing one another, at least."

Barely.

"That doesn't seem like a very high bar."

"I know." I push my salad around with my fork. "Coach had some pretty good arguments, and I'm not the only one making concessions. We both have to cooperate."

He shrugs. "If this is what you want to do, I've got your back."

"You may be the only one." I give him a tired smile. "Hamilton has been an ass to me for years. Way before shit hit the fan last year. He and the Devils have carefully groomed the entire student body into hating me."

"Then why are you doing it?" He wonders, eyebrows pulled together in confusion. "Is it worth it?"

Why? Because he talked me into it.

No, he *orgasmed* me into it.

I realize now that I probably just fell into his trap. I handed him the perfect opportunity to humiliate me on a weekly basis. None of the faculty or students could blame him for suddenly acknowledging my existence—Coach James was taking all the blame for that. This is just giving him VIP access to be a bigger dick to me than usual.

Except, of course, if it was a trap, he wasn't the one setting it. I'm the one who hit him. I'm the one who jumped him. I'm the one who grinded on his dick until I came.

Shit. Shit. Shit.

"I don't know," I tell Tyson, stabbing my fork into my salad, "maybe it'll be fine. Or maybe it'll be the dumbest decision I've made yet."

This is doubtful. I'm pretty sure that ship already sailed last night in the locker room.

How much worse can things get?

PRACTICE WAS HARD. Everyone is tired and distracted once they're gathered together following cooling down, hopefully enough that this goes more smoothly than I'm expecting. Hamilton's already out of the water, the trainer strapping a bag of ice over his shoulder.

"Meet me after?" I whisper nervously to Tyson when he and the other divers join us.

"Sure," he says, squeezing my hand.

It's not enough to settle my nerves. I have a feeling this isn't going to go well and my stomach twists anxiously. It only gets worse when I step up to stand next to Hamilton, which is better than facing him, because I don't actually have to see his expression when Coach tells the team the decision.

Unfortunately, I *can* see Heston Wilcox's face, along with most of the team. Heston looks absolutely floored, his regal blue eyes darting to Hamilton's. It's a mixture of shock and disbelief. I feel a little surprised, myself. I'd thought Hamilton would have told him.

My teammates are smart enough to keep their mouths shut while coach is around, but on the way back to the locker room, I hear whispers.

"Her? Seriously? What's she going to do, guilt us to a championship?"

"God, we'll have to watch everything we do now. Fucking snitch."

"I feel so bad for Hamilton, now he's gotta work with that bitch. She probably just wants to fuck him."

"Heh, right? Who doesn't?"

"You know Coach just did it because he feels sorry for her."

It gets progressively worse. Snide remarks about my body, my hair, my face. Then they go into my swimming abilities, how I'm not nearly good enough to be captain of a kiddie pool, let alone varsity-level. And eventually—as it always does—they start in on my family, how we're mutts and trash. They don't say Sky's name specifically, they can't. But the word slut is tossed about in enough hissed inflections that they don't even need to.

Hot tears prick at my eyes—something that rarely happens. But I know why. I put my mask on for a reason. I lay low and stay out of the fray. *This* is why. If I ignore them—if on some level, even superficial, I don't exist—then I can't get hurt. But the second I pull off that mask, the instant I try to be present.... here I am. A target all over again.

I duck into the captain's office, which is a perk that comes with the position. It's just a small room with a desk and two chairs. A big board hangs on the wall with the season's schedule and a graph to plug swimmers into position. The nicest addition is being able to leave my suit and other accessories here between practices, as there's a private bathroom with a shower. This is a big deal after having to share common facilities in the locker room.

I can't even really take it all in and enjoy it. I can't feel proud. I can't even push my shoulders back and lift my wobbling chin. I barely dry off, tugging on my shorts and a shirt and hastily packing my bag. I'll shower later. I want to get out of there as fast as possible.

I will *not* let these people see me cry.

Movement shifts in the doorway and I freeze, trying desperately to swallow down the lump in my throat.

I will definitely not fucking let *him* see me cry.

Wiggling my arms into my bag's straps, I keep my eyes on the ground, avoiding his gaze, but he blocks the door with the solid wall of his bare-chested body. I stare at the fine trail of hair snaking down from his belly button and clench my teeth.

"Running off?"

My voice is thick and low. "Move."

"I thought maybe we could go over the new roster, divide up the duties and shit."

"I'll do whatever. I don't care," I say to his sternum.

There's a beat of silence before two fingers press under my chin, forcing my eyes upward. His hard gaze wavers when he takes me in, face going slack. My nose is probably neon-red by now, and I can't stop my eyes from swimming. He grows blurrier with each passing second, until finally, the tears run over, tracking hot, embarrassing lines down my cheeks.

His jaw tics, the muscle in the back tightening into a hard ball, then he drops my chin like he's been burned and steps aside.

I bolt out the door like an animal being released from a cage, instantly catching sight of Tyson and darting toward him.

"Hey, whoa." Throwing his arm around my shoulder, he quietly asks, "You okay?"

"No."

"Did he say something to you?" His voice is harder now, dark with the promise of retaliation.

"No," I promise. "I don't want to talk about it."

"Okay." Tyson frowns, giving my shoulder a squeeze. "But I told you. I've got your back. You can do this, got it?"

I nod, hating how this feels, but thankful I have a friend supporting me. A couple months ago, this would have been unbearable. But I'm not alone anymore. I may not have on my mask, but Tyson provides a shield, one I won't refuse.

Stairway to Hell, 3pm

I take a slow, incredulous glance around the hallway, but no one's watching me to see it. The note was sitting on top of my history textbook, had obviously been slipped into the slats on my locker. I don't need to really wonder, though.

I know exactly who it's from.

I crumple the paper in a tight fist and spike it into the locker before slamming it shut. I don't know what possibility makes me angrier about Hamilton summoning me to the Devil's notorious campus make-out spot—the thought of him actually trying to schedule a hook up with me, or the thought of him just wanting a nice private place to rub salt in my wounds from yesterday's co-captain announcement.

Weirdly, it's the first possibility that vexes me most of all. Like I'd ever be one of his playthings. Like I'm just going to drop what I'm doing and climb seven flights of stairs in the south wing's bell tower for the privilege of hooking up with him. I'd sooner gouge my own eyes out with a spoon. It's completely *vile*.

I'm planning to tell him this and so much more as I stomp up the steps of the tower. I have a whole essay planned in my head. A lot of it goes into the fact that he might not be used to girls who actually harbor even a trace of self-respect, but here's what it looks like. And that our last time together wasn't even all that good—who cares if it's a lie—and that I know what he's doing. He saw that one moment of weakness from me as I left practice and thinks he can wriggle in and get another piece of me, but he's wrong.

"You're wrong," I seethe as I enter the top of the tower. He whips around from where he's standing, gazing through one of the open arches to the campus below. There's a pile of leaves in the corner, but I can still see where someone tossed a spent condom. *Gross.*

"I'm probably not," he answers, lounging casually back against the wall. It's windy up here and his hair is all mussed. "But what am I not being wrong about, specifically?"

I drop my bag, feeling sweaty and sore from the long climb up. "I'm not one of your fucking bimbos, Bates. You can't just call me up here like I'm some rank booty call. For one, it's disgusting, and for two, the answer is no."

He lifts an eyebrow. "You think I asked you to come up here so we could fuck?"

I open and close my mouth a few times, stunned a little speech-less, because that—us *fucking*—hadn't even crossed my mind. I just figured he wanted to make out or something. But now the idea of it invades my mind, the thought of the two of us up against this stone wall, my legs wrapped around his waist as he—

I try to shake it from my head. "Whatever you wanted, it's not happening. That's all I came here to say."

Before I can even pick up my bag, Hamilton is laughing. "You're really full of yourself, Adams."

I whip up to gape at him, open-mouthed. "*I'm* full of myself?!"

"I didn't bring you up here to fuck you," he clarifies, eyes dragging snidely down my body. "I can get pussy any time I want, I don't need to waste my energy arguing with you to get some."

"Then what?" I swallow, my face heating. "What the hell do you want, Bates?"

He pushes off the wall, loping toward me. "Yesterday, at swim practice—"

Now it's my turn to laugh. "So it's the second one, then."

"The second what?"

"You want to rub salt into my wounds," I explain, crossing my arms. "Hate to rain on your parade, but I'm already over it. So go ahead, give it your best shot."

He stops in front of me, his expression some tight marriage of exasperation and annoyance. "You know what? In case you missed it, I didn't do anything to you yesterday. I was the one trying to actually get some shit done while you scurried away. I just wanted to know who was fucking with you."

"Who was fucking with me?" I look around the tower, gesturing widely toward the window where, below, the entire campus is milling about. "Why don't I tell you everyone who isn't fucking with me? It'd take two seconds as opposed to all night."

He rolls his eyes, shifting his weight. "Yes, your persecution complex is still in fine form. I'm glad to see you haven't forgotten to oil it daily. Doesn't really give me anything to go off of, though."

"Oh my god, you're so dense that light bends around you." I can feel my anger swelling until my nostrils are flaring, and I'm probably already getting red again. At this point, any anger at Hamilton has somehow connected itself directly to my freak of a libido. "It's not one person. It's an entire culture. I can't even tell you who said my ass was fat, or that Coach only made me co-captain because he pitied me, or who called my sister a slut, or who said I'm not even good enough at swimming to captain a kiddie pool. It's everyone, Bates. Because you might suck at treating people like human beings, but when it comes to turning the whole school against someone? You're the master." I bow mockingly. "Master Bates."

He seems to be getting just as worked up, that muscle in his jaw getting tenser and sharper. "I didn't come here to fight with you. Believe it or not, I was actually trying to make shit better. Which is pretty big of me, considering that ridiculous lecture you gave me about not wanting to carry my half of another responsibility, and here I am carrying yours."

I scoff. "What do you even care?"

"Because this is half my job, too!" he insists, jabbing a finger into his chest. "This is my first year as captain and my last season swimming for this team. I want us to get a title, and we can't do that if you're running off crying after every fucking practice."

I go rigid, furious with myself for giving that to him—for giving him the ammo he needed to regard me as some weak little crybaby. "That's not going to happen again. I don't need you to save me."

He drops that rigid defensive posture, face going blank. "Wait... you came up here to fight with me, didn't you?"

"Well..." I try adjusting to the weird, sudden shift in energy, but can't quite manage it. "*Yeah*."

"Yeah," he says, breathing a laugh as his gaze shifts toward the open windows. "We could do that, or..." He steps closer, and closer, hand slipping forward to brush against the hem of my skirt. When his gaze meets mine again, his mouth is curved into a mean smirk. "Or we could skip the part where you hit me or push me and just get right to the good stuff."

My jaw drops at the realization that he thinks *I* want to hookup. It makes me indignant enough that my palms come up to his chest, shoving—

Oh, shit.

He stumbles back a few steps, eyes flashing in triumph. "I fucking knew it," he says, stalking his way back to me. "That's why you're here."

"Is not!" I insist, but it's a laughably weak denial.

I take a moment to internally panic, because did I? Did I really come up here hoping to get in a fight with him, knowing where those fights have been leading?

No, my mind provides sarcastically. *You got a note asking you to come to the prime make-out spot and decided to show up, just to talk.*

I'm such an *idiot.*

"You know what I'm going to do for you, Adams?" He steps closer, until he's near enough to smell, until the heat of his breath just barely washes over my mouth. His eyes are heavy-lidded now, knowing. "I'm not even going to make you ask for it this time."

The kiss is some bastard amalgamation of the one in the dorm room and the ones from last night. It isn't tender, but there's no fury in it, either. When his tongue seeks entrance, I give it to him, letting him lick into my mouth, licking back into his.

As we kiss, I wonder if this is what I came for. And then he starts backing me up, guiding me until my back meets the wall between two of the opened archways. We're still hidden from view—if anyone looked up to the tower, they wouldn't see a thing. But I can still hear them all down there beneath us, the raucous sounds of campus life, laughter and yelling.

He pulls back from the kiss with dark eyes and a red mouth. "Well?"

I swallow, letting my head fall back against the wall, and then close my eyes in shame. "I thought you weren't going to make me ask for it."

He lets out a low laugh. "I won't. But you have to give me something." His fingers reach down to touch my bare thigh, skimming it up until it's just beneath the hem of my skirt. "Just say 'yes'."

I open my eyes and see the massive bell behind him. A faded, graffitied Devil has been scrubbed off the bronze—marking the territory. I wonder how many girls have been here before, how many people have had sex right where I'm standing? My eyes dart to the fabled wooden beam holding up the bell. Dozens of initials are gouged into the century old wood, under those notches. If gossip is to be believed, each one represents a conquest.

Gwen Adams isn't the kind of girl that would ever be up in the Devil's Lair.

Yet here I am.

I meet his dark gaze. "Yes."

His fingers drag up at the same time our mouths meet, and it's almost impossible to track any one thing. The press of his nose against my cheek as he deepens the kiss, the tickle of his fingers as they climb my thigh and go... *inward*, between my legs. When he finally touches me—finally rubs his fingers against my damp, hot center—I moan into his mouth, my nerves suddenly more alight than ever. It's different from the other night, those nimble, skilled fingers of his able to find my clit even through my panties.

I rock into it, urging him forward. He responds by fisting the crotch of my panties and yanking them down my thighs. I throw my head back against the wall, gasping wildly for air, and the fingers return, skin to skin this time, nothing between us.

He buries a long, ragged sound into my throat. "God, look at you. Fucking soaked for me." I can feel it in the way his fingers glide deftly between my folds, my toes curling at the sensations. "Come on," he says, nudging my face to his before taking my mouth in another kiss. He doesn't close his eyes, and neither do I. We trade kisses like that as his fingers explore me, pressing harder when my knees shake, pulling back when I try to grind into them.

He's still holding my gaze when his finger finds my entrance. We stop kissing. I can tell he's waiting—waiting for me to say 'no', waiting for me to push him away, to tell him it's too far, too much.

I don't.

His finger sinks slowly into me and I feel like if I shook any harder, I'd just fall to pieces right here in the tower. He watches me closely, almost carefully, our mouths barely touching. I'm not sure what he's looking for, but when I feel the heel of his hand meet my mound, his breath comes out in a hot rush.

"Fuck," he growls, eyes dropping closed. "Knew you'd be tight."

I rock into his palm, testing the feel of him against me, *inside* me. "Oh, god," I breathe, but my moan is swallowed by his kiss.

The whole thing is so entirely ridiculous—me fighting to rock against his palm as he fights to fuck me with his finger—and it's still the most erotic thing I've ever felt. When his other hand takes mine, I know instantly what he wants. He doesn't even need to guide my hand to the obscene bulge at the front of his pants, but he does it anyway, pressing my palm against it. I curl my fingers around him through the fabric of his pants and he groans, breaking the kiss to rest his forehead against mine, rocking against my hand the same way I'm rocking against his.

"Should have worn one of the red shirts," he pants, eyes staring down the neck of my shirt. Preston has a small variety of uniforms, but the red one is the only fully button-down shirt for girls. The one I'm wearing would have to be pulled over my head to be taken off. No way am I doing that up here.

I bite my lip, remembering how good it felt the night before, his hands cupping my boobs, thumbs rough against my nipples, and mutter a curse.

I struggle to pull the tail of my shirt from the waist of my skirt one-handed, but once I do, Hamilton's ready. He shoves his hand up the front of it and it's not quite as good—over my bra—but it's thin enough that the pad of his thumb flicking over my nipple makes me shudder.

All of it combines into this wicked maelstrom of heat building in the pit of my stomach and I know I'm close. I can feel it in him, too— how he gets impossibly harder in my hand, the way his breaths grow into these little punches of air against my mouth, the little crevice that forms between his eyebrows, almost like he's in pain, but I know better.

My own orgasm comes upon me in a hot shock, thighs clamping hard around his hand. I make a sound that's too loud and surprised than I have any right to be, but I can't help it, I just grab two tight fistfuls of the shirt covering his shoulders and go over that edge, shaking.

He buries his face into my shoulder, and I feel more than see him take a biteful of my own shirt and gnash it between his teeth as he begins jerking beneath my hand.

"I cannot fucking believe," he says, wetting his lips as he stumbles back, "that I just came in my pants again. Jesus Christ, I'd forgotten how much this sucks." He crams a hand in his pocket and seems to.... adjust things, face twisting into a grimace.

I hastily pull up my panties, feeling red and embarrassed and sore and so fucking good that it's a legitimate miracle I'm not visibly fluorescent with the glow of it.

Still a bit breathless, Hamilton meets my glazed eyes and ticks off with his fingers, "Never happened. All my fault. You hate me. I'm the worst. Hasty post-coital exit." He sweeps his own bag from the ground, throwing it over a shoulder. "There, covered all the bases for you. I'll go ahead and take the last one."

And then he's gone.

12

I HEAR a long whistle as I walk out of the bathroom.

"These are some sweet ass digs."

I pause, steam billowing from behind me, and see Heston sitting in one of the chairs with his feet kicked up on the desk. He's wearing plaid flannel pants—red and black—with 'PP Swim' stamped on the hip. That had been quite the meme back in Freshman year.

"I don't remember inviting you in." I knock his feet off the desk, and they land with a thud.

He picks up a dry erase marker and spins it between his fingers. "I can't believe you didn't tell me about the co-captain thing."

"Coach wanted to make the announcement." I rub my hair with the towel, shrugging. "It's not a big deal."

He snorts. "You're kidding, right? You and Adams partnering up? This, plus detention? You're spending more time with her during the week than you are with Reagan."

I turn to hide my grimace. He doesn't know just how right he is. "It's not like I'm choosing to." Although it'd be really nice to spend less time with Raegan. Unfortunately, this is the most inconvenient time to break up with her, what with all the awkward shit going on between me and Gwendolyn. It's better that she thinks I'm already attached, that our little... *encounters* weren't anything special. Just flukes.

Were they?

Of course, they were.

"Have you told your dad?" Heston asks, interrupting my thoughts.

"Not yet." That's something I plan to do in person. This is a particularly delicate situation, which will no doubt require improvisation strategy. I've been thinking on it for days now, weighing the different outcomes. I'd rather get a feel for what he's really thinking, and I can't do that over the phone. "We're having dinner tomorrow night. I'll let him know then."

"Smart." He swivels in the chair, taking in the small space with a thoughtful expression. "You know, it's too bad Adams is such a freak. Any other co-ed captain situation and this would be the perfect hook-up spot." He spreads his hands on the desk, testing the sturdiness. "A little sexy secretary action? Damn, I bet her pussy is tighter than Beyonce's jeans."

I react so fast, I don't even have time to consider it. I lunge toward him and shove him against the wall, chair clattering over. I press my forearm against his throat and his eyes bulge, hands instantly struggling against me.

He grunts, "What the *fuck*!"

"This fucking hard-on you've got for Adams is getting real old," I hiss, heart thundering in my chest.

"What?!" His eyes grow wider, this panicked little crinkle growing between his eyebrows. "I don't have a hard-on for Adams!"

"No?" I press harder, my voice low and dangerous. "Because with the way you're always talking about her tits and pussy, it's starting to feel like maybe you do." I hold him there for a second longer, our eyes locked, and then release him.

"What the hell, Bates!" He rubs his neck. "I know you hate her, but seriously, I can't even joke about her?"

"No," I reply, trying to tamp down this insane fucking *urge* to just beat this fucker bloody. "You know the rules. She doesn't exist. She's fucking cancelled."

Heston rights the chair, and we both know he literally can't be pissed off at me. Not outwardly. Regardless, his movements are jerky and curt, eyes ablaze. "And how exactly do you plan on pulling that off while you're working with her all the time?"

I take a moment while my back is turned to stare blankly in the direction of the bathroom.

Shit.

How am I supposed to keep her in her place—keep fucking letches like Heston away from her—while doing this job? How am I supposed to tell people she's cancelled when I'm talking to her every day, listening to her, doing shit with her?

More importantly, why is the faculty so determined to ruin all my efforts? Don't they see that Adams being an invisible nobody is better for everyone?

"Dealing with that is my job," I decide, pulling a shirt from my bag. "Yours is to fall in line." I level him with a warning look.

I can count on one hand the amount of times I've pulled rank like this. It's known that I'm the leader of the Devils, I rarely need to. Whipping out my dick every week and lording it over them has never been appealing to me. Not since last spring, when everything went down with Sky, have I had to step up. But Gwendolyn? No way I'm letting these assholes talk about her like that—especially not Heston, who's already sketchy enough.

"Act the way I act. That means if I ignore Adams, you do, too. If I listen to her, so do you. Coach wants us to look cohesive and cooperative, and that's doable. But it also means you can't act like a fucking degenerate. Understood?"

"Yes, Jesus." He stalks toward the door, but thankfully, most of that angry energy seems to have been sapped. "Next time just use your words instead of your fists, bro."

"Yeah, well..." I cram my towel into my bag and throw it over my shoulder. "Next time use your brain and not your dick."

Before we walk out, he insists, "I don't want to fuck her." The thing about Heston is that most people think he's a really good liar.

He has this way of turning on the charm, of sounding perfectly sincere. When it's down to strictly voice performance, Heston is second to none.

But face-to-face, I know his tells.

There's the smallest wrinkle near his left eye, almost like a crow's foot. It's only ever there when he's lying.

"No one does," I tell him, flipping off the light. "And I'm here to make sure you don't forget it."

THE NEXT DAY AT PRACTICE, it's pretty clear that Gwendolyn is drowning—figuratively, not literally, because even I have to admit she's a fucking fantastic swimmer. This is drowning of the purely social variety.

It's not that she doesn't try. She comes in all bold voice and straight posture, and the strong commanding artifice is only *mostly* obvious. I watch from the shallow end as she stashes her belongings in the office and strides across the pool deck with her chin lifted, clipboard clutched to her chest.

As she gets near, John Martin, fastest in breast-stroke, mutters something vaguely crude and elbows Heston. Heston's responding smile is enough to earn my cold, sharp glare. His jaw snaps shut, and he busies himself with putting on his cap.

"What's that?" I ask, pointing to the clipboard in her hand. Best to get the train-wreck over with.

"I want to get everyone's phone number so we can start a group text," she explains. "I'll split it down by subcategories, like relays and strokes. It'll be easier to contact people that way and might also be good for reminders if people start slacking off or skipping practice."

It all seems a bit tedious to me. I mean, most everyone on the team already follows each other on ChattySnap or some other social media. Why reinvent the wheel? I open my mouth to tell her that, but then I remember. Gwendolyn doesn't participate in social media, *at all*. Not after what happened with her sister. She's completely out of the loop.

"Go for it," I sigh, reaching for my goggles.

"Listen up!" she calls, her voice drowned out by everyone talking. "Hey! I need your attention, please!"

She visibly flounders for a moment, eyebrows knitting together, teeth beginning to worry at her lip. I can see the wheels in there moving. Her insecurity is being broadcast like a fucking billboard, and the second they see it, they'll eat her ass alive. I just can't watch it any longer.

Turning toward the crowd, I bark, "Devils!"

The room falls silent.

I make a gesture to Gwendolyn, who gives me a look of reluctant appreciation, but doesn't waste the opportunity.

At least a little of her poise has returned. "Before you get wet, I need you to fill out your information on this clipboard. It'll make communication a lot more efficient," she says. Her voice wavers a bit halfway through, nerves obviously getting the best of her, not that she'd ever acknowledge it. Not stubborn-as-nails Gwendolyn Adams.

The diver is the first one to step forward, of course, loping forward with a fond grin. She smiles at him so gratefully that it's like the tension just pours right out of her frame. Like *he's* done something heroic. Like *he's* the one who got everyone paying attention and spared her from an afternoon of being ignored. What's with him anyway? Does he want to fuck her, too? And why is everyone suddenly wanting under Adam's swimsuit?

She smiles at him appreciatively and a stark realization hits me like a punch in the gut.

Maybe she's already screwing him.

I yank on my cap and adjust my goggles, diving into the water to cool off. I should be focusing on training. Nothing else.

Nothing else.

~

"Tight enough?"

I wince, more from the cold than the pain. "Yeah, it should hold."

Icing my shoulder is part of the daily process and Janet, the trainer, attaches the heavy bag over my shoulder with tape. Truthfully, now that we're back to regular practices, there are days where the pain is bad enough that just looking at my book bag in the mornings is enough to make me want to scream.

Obviously, no one can know this.

"Twenty minutes," she says, and I nod in reply.

I walk out of the training room and down the empty pool deck to the office, willing my shoulder to stop aching. I'm somewhere between 'grin and bear it' and 'just ignore the pain' when an object flies from out of nowhere, landing inches from the edge of the pool.

Or... not from nowhere. From the office I share with Gwen.

Upon closer inspection, the object in question is the clipboard from earlier. Out of curiosity I go over, pick it up, and skim the list.

Tyson Riggings
Neil Down
Harry Dong
Anita Dick
Ben N. Syder
Curley Pubes
Eaton Beaver
Buster Himen
Ima Hoare

I take a deep inhale.

Assholes.

After running a long-suffering hand down my face, I carry the clipboard back into the office. Gwen's wearing an oversized sweatshirt, but her legs are still bare underneath and her hair is still wet, a dark lump that's been twisted into a knot on top of her head. I get this sudden, weird feeling at the notion that I'm the only one who can see her like this, all crazy-eyed and sexy-frumpy, storming around.

Her wild-eyed look of fury transforms into a narrow scowl when she sees me. "I told you," she growls, thrusting a finger at me, "I *told you* I didn't want to do this. And now, look!"

I toss the clipboard on the desk. "Are you forgetting the fact that we're in high school? They're assholes. Everyone in high school is an asshole. It's not a big deal."

"No one respects me. They think I'm a joke. If they're not mocking me loudly enough to barely be considered 'behind my back', then they're doing shit like this. There's no point in me being co-captain if no one wants to listen to me." She exhales, all of the anger seeming to drain out of her at once. "You want this title so bad, then you take it."

Oh, if only. Coach made it clear it's both of us or neither of us. "Don't you think you're being a little dramatic?"

Her arms cross over her chest, making the hem of her shirt rise. It's a legitimate battle not to drop my gaze to the milky expanse of her thighs. "You wouldn't understand. None of them ever step out of line with you! Like today. You speak and they jump. Even Heston follows your orders."

"Jesus, get off the cross, Adams." I roll my eyes. "I didn't ask to be in charge of the Devils. It's not like it's the best thing to ever happen to me, either. They might be quick to look to me for leadership, but I also know that when something goes wrong, they're just as quick to blame me for it. Like, fucking Xavier, right?" I gesture behind me, even knowing he's not here. "When my dad forced me to move onto campus, his parents figured... hey, why not? If the Bateses can do it, so can we. So now he's looking at me like it's my fault. Do I take the blame? Hell no. Do I act guilty? Not a chance. Like, Jesus, if they only knew—"

My mouth snaps shut, lips forming a grim line.

She tilts her head curiously. "Knew what?"

About what you and me do together. About my moments of weakness.

No, I can't give her that leverage. "Nothing. If you ask me, you need to just not let it bother you so much. You getting all worked up like this is just blood in the water. And while we're at it, the other extreme isn't much better."

"What other extreme?" She seems genuinely interested.

"That thing where you turn into a fucking robot. It's weird! If you walk around acting inhuman, that's exactly how they're going to treat you. Just act normal. Casual. If they don't think you care, they'll chill out. But at the same time, don't let them run you over. I'm not sitting next to a co-captain with no balls."

Her eyebrow raises and I see a hint of a smile on her face. "I don't have balls, Bates, you of all people should know that."

Our eyes hold one another for a moment and that flicker of energy ebbs between us. I pull at the tape and yank off the ice. "Put on some pants," I say, halfway to get out of this little room, halfway because I have a genius idea, "and come with me."

"Where are we going?" she asks warily.

"If these jackoffs want to play games, then they picked the wrong people." I pick up the clipboard and wink.

13

Gwen

"This is your car?" I ask, running my hands over the smooth leather. I'm not one of those girls who gets all hot for nice cars, but if I were? I'd probably be fanning myself or something. The leather smells new and the seat warmer is making me warm and all relaxed—a perk after being in the water for practice. It usually takes me an hour to shake the chill.

"Yep." He flashes me a smug grin. "Technically I'm not allowed to drive it anywhere but home. But this is an official team duty, so I feel like it qualifies as acceptable."

Between the comfy seat and the exhaustion of a crappy practice, I don't even have it in me to muster anything more snide than a sarcastic smile when I say, "You can justify anything, can't you?"

His eyes sweep over me so furtively, that if I would have blinked, I might have missed it. He hums in response, clearing his throat. That weird feeling I keep getting in my belly around Hamilton these days starts swelling up. It's some unholy mixture of excitement, nausea, and embarrassment. I just don't even know what's going on with me and Hamilton right now. Every interaction we have is fraught with so many conflicting emotions, it's like daily whiplash.

"Where are we going again?" I casually ignore what his reaction seems to be suggesting. Hamilton can justify a lot. But he can't justify what he does with me any more than I can.

Against all my instincts, I agreed to sneak off campus with him, to get in the car with him, to go somewhere unspecified with him. I discreetly check the GPS tracker on my phone, because seriously, if this were an elaborate ruse to get me somewhere isolated and do shitty things to me, it just might be the most normal thing to happen this month.

Hamilton doesn't answer but pulls into a parking lot ablaze with light. It's the 24-hour print shop. He takes the clipboard off my lap and a spark rushes through my body when his fingers graze my legs.

Nope.

No.

That is not what this is about.

He unbuckles and I do the same, but then he reaches across me suddenly, and my heart lunges into my throat. I can't help but think that this is it. He's going to do something to me—hurt me.

I flinch.

I know he sees it when he freezes, our gazes meeting just long enough for the strange, shocked look in his eyes to register. If I didn't know better, I'd almost say he looks guilty when his long fingers pull at my door lever, opening it from the inside. While I'm processing the gesture, he exits the car.

He stops to lean back in. "Look, they wanted to be assholes," he says in explanation. "We're just going to give them what they asked for. That's all."

Payback?

Well, that's something I can get behind.

I follow two steps behind him through the parking lot toward the shop, and I only gawk at him a little bit when he holds the door open for me as I enter.

"How can I help you?" the guy at the counter asks, pushing his glasses up his nose.

Hamilton pushes the clipboard toward him, looking annoyingly self-assured as he leans against the counter. "We're going to need sixty custom shirts with these names on the back. Black shirt. Red print. Preston Prep Devil logo on the front. I'm sure you have it on file." Hamilton speaks with absolute authority as though what he's just asked for is completely reasonable. "Oh, and I need it tomorrow by four."

"By four?" the guy says, already shaking his head. "That's not possible."

Hamilton slaps a black credit card on the counter, sliding it forward with one long finger. "I think you'll probably find it is."

The guy makes a complicated face—one part sour, one part weary, two parts exasperated—and finally concedes, "Let's see what we can do for you, Mr. Bates."

I'm dumbfounded as I watch him negotiate size and a final price, all for an elaborate prank for the team he's supposed to be leading—all to get them back for being jerks to me. This is way beyond what's required.

"You shouldn't have to pay for all that," I say when we're back in the car.

"I'll turn in the receipt."

I worry my lip between my teeth. "I'm not sure that's what the team budget is for…"

"Adams," he says, voice deep with exasperation.

"What?"

"Would you just chill out? It's going to be fine. This doesn't even rank in my top thirty stunts."

The truth slips out. "What if they just hate me more?"

He looks at me, mouth turning down. "Trust me. They won't. This is exactly the kind of thing that'll show them you're more than an overachieving, badly dressed, buzzkill of a goody-goody with a stick up her ass."

"Hey!" I squawk. "Fuck you, you—"

He leans over and pushes his mouth against mine, effectively shutting me up. The kiss is warm and gentle, his jaw strong, and despite myself I sink into him, letting all the nerves and worry dissipate with every stroke of his tongue.

I don't know what's happening, or *why* it keeps happening.

But I know I don't want to stop.

He pulls away and his eyes are dark, but the curve of his smirk is amused.

I swallow. "What was that for?"

"To shut you up. It seems to be the only thing that works." He starts the car and tosses his arm over my seat, presumably to look over his shoulder before backing out. But he winces suddenly, making a pained sound as he pulls it back. "*Fuck.*"

"Your shoulder?" I realize, mouth pulling into a frown. "That... that doesn't sound good. Are you working it too hard?"

"Of course I'm not." But his mouth is set into a thin, grim line as he pulls out of the parking space. "It's nothing. Just a little tight."

He peels out of the parking lot, tires squealing. I hold onto my seat like my life depends on it, but really, I just need to do something with my hands. My heart thunders wildly in my chest and I know it's more about the kiss than the fast driving.

If tonight showed me anything, it's that Hamilton Bates may know me better than anyone else at this school.

And that's more terrifying than anything else.

"HOLDEN!" a voice calls across the cafeteria. "Holden McGroin! You down there?"

"Nope," another voice replies, "but I saw him with Jenny Tayla a few minutes ago."

A ripple of laughter passes down the tables and I see two of my teammates high five. It's been like this for two days, ever since the print shop delivered five boxes of shirts to the natatorium and Hamilton and I passed them out to our stunned and delighted teammates.

When there were two left, Hamilton handed one to me and

pulled the other over his ripped, muscular upper body. He turned and I saw written across his broad shoulders, "Master Bates."

I looked down at my own. "Ivana B Cumming. Seriously?" I asked, unable to smother a laugh.

"It was that or Helda Dick." He shrugged but I knew he thought he was hilarious. The truth is that he kinda is. Who knew?

The most impressive part of it all was that Hamilton didn't take credit. We'd handed them out together and ultimately, as much as I hated to admit it, he was right. The kids looked at me differently after they realized I had a sense of humor about their bullshit. If it'd been a test, then I passed.

"I still can't believe you did that," Tyson says from across the lunch table. "I thought Coach James was going to have a heart attack."

"Me too," I laugh, "but he was pretty cool about it."

He did make Hamilton and I swim an extra 200 for being smart-asses, but all in all, I think he's just happy to see Hamilton and I working together. He did make it clear we're not allowed to wear the shirts anywhere but at practice. It's not the kind of joke other schools or the officials would find amusing.

"Oh, I wanted to ask you something," Tyson pipes up.

"Yeah?" I scrape the remains of my yogurt out of the container. "What's up?"

"I have this diving competition on Saturday afternoon. My girl-friend is coming and I kind of wanted you to meet her."

I realize this must be the girl from the homecoming pictures. "Aw, you want me to meet your girlfriend?"

"She's been bugging me about introducing her to some kids from school. You're really my only friend so far."

I pause, considering. "Is she from Northridge, because—"

"No no no," he says quickly. "She goes to Holy Innocence. She's a sweet little Catholic girl." His grin is wicked.

I point to his chest. "Is that why you wear the cross?"

He touches the charm around his neck. "Kind of. Her mother likes it."

I gather my trash and stand, deciding, "I guess I can come after I do my detention hours. Other than that, it's not like I have a huge social calendar to rearrange."

"Awesome—not about your detention or lack of social life—but because you're coming," he says, wrapping his arm around me and giving me a tight squeeze. I start across the cafeteria and look up to see Hamilton watching me, and even though his expression is perfectly blank and aloof, the intensity of his gaze trips me up. Literally. I fumble my yogurt container—which I catch—but the spoon falls, skittering across the floor and echoing loudly around the room. The universe being the cruel mistress that she is, it lands two feet from where Hamilton sits.

"Crap," I mutter, feeling all the eyes in the room suddenly shifting to me.

I dart over and quickly bend, eyes now level with Hamilton's crotch. Reagan's hand is resting possessively on his thigh, her sharp red nails pressed into the fabric of his khakis. I grab the spoon and lurch upright, smoothing out the back of my skirt as I go. The hair on the back of my neck stands on end when I realize he's still watching me.

Closely.

"See you at practice," I tell Tyson, parting from him in the hallway. I duck into the bathroom and silently berate my reflection in the mirror. Before that little scene in the cafeteria, this had been shaping up to be a really good day. The swim team was treating me... well, not *good*, but they weren't making snide comments around me all the time, and that was a pretty big upgrade.

When I exit, I notice that the hall is pretty empty, which makes sense, since most everyone is still at lunch. I'm passing by one of the science labs when the door opens and I'm yanked inside.

"What the f—!" I shout, heart pounding. I'm not even surprised to see Hamilton standing a few feet away with a strained expression, back to the door. It's not the first time he's cornered me alone. "I know you don't want to be seen talking to me in public, but seriously? A text would work—"

A heartbeat later, he's closed the distance and has his hand tangled into my hair.

Hamilton's mouth crashes against mine, and it's an increasingly familiar feeling, just as warm and insistent as ever. But he doesn't stop there, not like in the car. His hands roam down my backside, tickling the back of my thighs. A flash of red fingernails flits through my mind and I jerk back, gasping.

"Shouldn't you be doing this with Reagan right now?"

He licks his bottom lip. His voice is gravelly when he replies, "Reagan didn't prance around in front of me in the cafeteria in that tiny little skirt, flashing me her panties."

"I did not," I insist, aghast. "I barely even—"

"They're white," he rattles off simply. "Utilitarian, yet disturbingly sexy."

I stare at him evenly, throat bobbing with a swallow, which is enough of an admission for him.

"You drive me crazy," he breathes in a rush, burying his face into my neck, pushing his wet mouth against my jaw. "God, I fucking hate it, and it's like I can't stop. You acting completely clueless about what you're doing to me every time you walk by doesn't make it any better."

His hands move again, this time under my skirt. My whole body is warm and the spot between my legs is well past that—damp and hot.

"So this is my fault?" I accuse, but it must seem pretty weak given the way my hands instantly roam up his shirt. "Typical."

His fingers push under the edge of my panties, invasive and intruding. I should be affronted—annoyed at the very least—but just like last time, I can't feel much of anything beyond that liquid-hot, bone-deep *need* to feel him touch me. I want to feel the wind up and the impending implosion. I want to combust, to be consumed, to feel him around me and inside me, over me and beneath me, and it's all just *insane*.

Him knowing exactly how to accomplish this is a mystery— stupid freak of a libido—but he plays me like the strings on his cello. The pads of his fingers graze against the hot bundle of nerves in between my legs and I shiver, knees buckling. His strong, muscular arm wraps around me, holding me up.

"Careful," he says, pushing a breathy chuckle against my mouth in another kiss. "We're not finished yet."

The bulge in his pants pushes against my thigh and I reach for him without much thought, sliding my hand down his length. He hisses and returns his attention to my neck.

I knew he was big, even before what happened in the Stairway to Hell. I'd felt him, and geez, I'd basically *seen* him through the thin, clingy fabric of his Speedo countless times. But holding him like this, it's just not the same. It's not the same, and it's not enough.

I tug frantically at his shirt, freeing it from his pants, and then shove my hand under his waist band. He exhales raggedly when I slide my hand down the hot, smooth skin. It twitches in my hand, his hips pushing eagerly into my palm.

He pulls back to look me in the eye when he says, "I'm not coming in my pants again."

My hand goes still, because I can't give Hamilton a blow job. I *won't*. I won't fall in line like the other girls he hangs out with, the ones that want to be his girlfriend. I will not take the *test*.

"I just wanted to make that clear," he adds, fully unaware of my mental war. And then he drops to his knees, forcing my hand to slide abruptly away.

Even with him on his knees in front of me, his hand tugging down my panties, it still takes me an extended moment of disbelief to understand what he's about to do.

"Bates." My voice is reedy and panicked, and I'm not actually sure why. Here I am about to get eaten out by Hamilton fucking Bates, and I can't seem to pry my damn knees apart.

"Hey." He looks up at me, mouth red and swollen, and gently guides my hips back, until I'm leaning against the lab table. "Just relax," he says, running his warm palms down my bare, trembling thighs. He licks his lips. "I just want to taste you."

I swallow hard and press my weight into the table, casting a worried glance at the door. It takes a few moments of Hamilton touching me like that—hands stroking gently between my thighs—before he finally coaxes my legs to part.

He holds my gaze as his fingers return to my center, thumb pressing against my clit, and then licks his lips again and disappears beneath my skirt.

My knuckles go white as I grip the table.

His tongue is so much hotter and wetter down there that the first touch startles me. I have to fight to keep my thighs from clamping around his head, because it just seems like the polite thing to do. He must sense this, because his palms run back up my thighs, kneading into my muscles before gently pushing them farther apart.

I'm grateful for it when I do, because it gives him more access, that silver tongue of his lapping at my clit, and then farther back. From this vantage, all I can see are the muscles in his back working beneath the fabric of his shirt as he moves. And he seems to be moving, like, *a lot*.

More than necessary.

But my brain is too muddled to really focus on anything but the machinations of his mouth, and *God*. It's like someone bottled tingling heat and sunshine, and for some reason, I can't seem to catch my breath. My head keeps falling back and if I grip this table any tighter, I'm convinced I'll crush it.

The orgasm is like none other—a slow rolling wave of crashing heat, my walls clenching and nerves coiling, winding tighter and tighter—and it comes upon me so intensely that I don't even realize I'm clutching his injured shoulder until I feel him grunt against me.

It sounds more pained than anything.

I snatch my hand back, gasping, "Sorry, sorry," but his tongue never stops, he just eases me through the crest and fall of it.

I squirm away when I start feeling too sensitive, and he finally emerges from beneath my skirt, red-cheeked and shiny-mouthed. He doesn't meet my gaze, though, eyes clamped tightly closed as he—

I bite down hard on my lip. He's pulled himself from his pants and his hand is flying over his erection, these sharp little breaths punching from his chest with every stroke. His whole torso clenches when he comes, spilling over his fist and onto the white floor below.

The sound he makes is guttural, breathless.

When he's done, he leans back on his heels, head thrown back. "Fuck, *yes*."

We're both hot and sticky messes. We untangle and I try to decide how a girl usually takes care of cleanliness in a situation such as this, but my mind is totally fogged. I turn away to awkwardly pull up my panties. The shake in my hands is different from the quiver in my knees.

He adjusts himself behind me, obviously needing to clean up his own mess.

"What was that?" I ask him, pushing my hair from my sweaty face. "Why does it keep happening?"

Why do I let it keep happening?

His voice is languid. "I don't know. Because it feels good?"

Is it as simple as that? No. He's not a good person. He's hurt my family, my sister, *me*. Maybe it does feel good, but after the whole tangled sex fog settles, it mostly just feels super shitty.

"Why is it okay for us to do *that*, but not for you to look at me in the hallway? Or speak to me in class?"

"I don't make the rules." He tucks in his shirt.

"That's bullshit and you know it." I face the sink and scrub my hands. I've already learned you can't wash out shame or regret, but I try anyway. The heat is scalding, burning my skin, and I sense him behind me just before he turns off the faucet.

His chest presses against my back. Gentle fingers push aside my hair and I feel his breath on my ear. "You're right, it is bullshit. I don't know why, but I can't stay away from you, and I think... I think maybe you can't stay away from me, either." His mouth presses a slow, wet kiss into the spot below my ear. "If you ask me, we're doing this because it feels good and we're both in a place where that's hard to find. Can't that be enough?"

His teeth tug at my earlobe and my hands clench the side of the sink.

I want him to go away.

I want more.

I want...

The lunch bell rings shrilly, shattering the fragile warmth of the moment. I duck away, grabbing my backpack and slipping out the door. I merge seamlessly with the tide of kids headed to class and try to ignore the heat of his kiss, just below my ear, like a brand.

Although I'm put back together and no one would ever guess, I feel naked, dirty... *exposed*.

Knowing Hamilton Bates, that's exactly what he wants.

❧

OTHER THAN BASIC swim captain duties, I resolve to avoid Hamilton for the rest of the week. Without giving Tyson any details, I ask him to stick around and wait for me after lunch, after practice. He's happy to do it, and if it means I won't suddenly find myself alone with Hamilton in the captain's office or anywhere else, then it's working.

Frankly, I don't trust myself.

All that comes to an end on Saturday when it's time to show for detention. There's no buffer or escaping this one. Dread paralyzes me as I put on my work clothes and shoes. I stare at the bag hanging from the back of my desk, which contains something I brought from home last weekend. At the time it didn't feel like a big deal, but now, any gesture, any interaction, feels like some kind of involuntary acceptance of it all.

Clearly, it's dumb. I'm being absurd. It's just my ridiculous hormones. He's Hamilton Bates. He's like the epitome of attractiveness. Hamilton is hot, and I'm big enough to admit that. He's sexy and genetically perfect, the ideal physical specimen. It only makes sense that my body reacts to his body, to have some evolutionary biological imperative triggered when he's around. I've always been aware of his muscles and the way he's performed as an athlete. He walks around nearly naked at swim. There's no ignoring his ripped abs and strong legs, his lean biceps and powerful back. So we apparently have some latent sexual chemistry going on. Who *wouldn't* be attracted to all of that?

Because, damn. *Seriously.* The guy is smoking hot, and I'm...

I'm just one woman.

It's a perfectly valid weakness.

I repeat all of this to myself like an affirmation, doing my best to convince myself that it's just surface deep. With a steeling inhale, I grab the bag and leave.

146

The morning air is cool and humid, and the campus is quiet in that eerie, hushed blanket it always transforms into on early morning weekends. I'm surprised when I realize that Hamilton has beaten me to the athletic field, his silhouette standing stark against the vacant expanse. As I approach, I see he's at least better dressed for the task this week in worn, faded jeans and an old Devil hoodie that's already ratty and frayed. He's even wearing a pair of old, battered sneakers. The clothes make him a lot less intimidating, like he's just any other normal high school guy who rolled out of bed at the crack of noon and pulled on the first items of clothing that entered his sightline. He and Dean Dewey watch me approach, waiting. I notice a cup of coffee in the dean's hand and two in Hamilton's.

Hamilton thrusts one to me, his gaze diverted.

Huh.

After a pause, I reluctantly take the warm cup in my hands. "Uh, thank you."

Well, the dean did tell him not to bring coffee for himself if he didn't provide it to everyone.

"If you two are ready to get started, I'll leave you to it," the dean says, looking between us. When neither of us replies, both avoiding the other's gaze and awkwardly cradling our drinks, he nods and walks off.

I take a hesitant sip of the coffee, surprised to taste the dark, sugary goodness of a mocha—my favorite. I frown into the cup, then back at Hamilton, who has begun pulling out the drop cloth. How on earth does he know what I like to drink? Fluke, I assume.

I fidget with the cup for a belated moment, trying to figure out how to approach him. I ultimately just blurt, "I have something for you."

He spreads out the cloth, his long arms billowing it wide. "Do you now?" He spares me a quick glance over his shoulder, and the knowing glint in his eye is enough to make my cheeks heat.

I do my best to ignore him, knowing he's just trying to rattle me. Without any ado, I toss him the bag and it lands limply at his feet.

He bends to retrieve it, peering inside with a frown. "What are these?"

"Gloves, Bates. I'm sure you've seen them before."

"Yeah, no shit, smart ass," he mutters. "Why are you giving them to me?"

"To protect your dainty, cello-playing fingers. I found them in the garage at home."

"Hm." He tugs them on and stretches his fingers, a slow smirk spreading across his face. When he meets my gaze, his eyes are dark and glittering. "Well, I guess you *would* be invested in the welfare of my fingers."

My jaw drops, but I'm at a loss for any sort of retort. He has actually stunned me speechless. Instead of trying, I focus on finding the little key-tool to open the can of primer, doing my best to pretend like my body hasn't just lit up like a Christmas tree at the thought of just what those fingers can do.

Thankfully, he doesn't seem interested in goading me about it any further.

For about three minutes.

"So I'm thinking," he begins, taking in the wall with a pensive expression, "we can split this fucker in half. I'll take the bottom—" That smarmy ass grin returns. "—you can take the top."

And that's how, ten minutes later, I find myself on the ladder, fighting the wobble of the uneven surface as he paints the lower portion of the wall. It takes me a while to realize just how deftly he's manipulated me into taking the harder part of the job. When I do, I pause, my paint roller stuttering to a stop against the wall.

He's *whistling*.

Insufferable fucking jerk.

I set my jaw and keep painting.

The best part about it is that, since we start on opposite sides and agree to meet in the middle, we're far enough apart that there's no encouragement to speak. Hamilton solidifies this by placing his phone on top of the box of supplies and cranking up his play list.

Perfect.

As the sun rises, it grows warmer, and the first hour goes quickly. Hamilton finishes his first coat before I do and lazily drops his roller into the pan, but I continue with the final section at the top. I try to ignore him in my periphery, pulling his sweatshirt over his head and laying it on the ground before dropping onto it. He stretches out languidly, legs crossed at the ankles, leaning back on his elbows. It's impossible to tune out my awareness of him. His gaze sweeping over me as he watches me work is like a constant heat on the back of my neck.

Nope.

Not today, Satan.

I paint faster.

"Yo, Bates," I hear a distant voice call. I look back over my shoulder and see a pack of Devils coming our way. Xavier's twirling a baseball bat and Heston's clutching a glove to his chest, while Emory and Ansel each hold a ball and glove. Heston swings a bat hand to hand. It's not uncommon on the weekend for the students on campus to use the athletic fields recreationally if they aren't in use. "So this is what Dewey has you doing at the ass-crack of dawn on a Saturday? Lazing around while you let Adams do all the heavy lifting."

I'm well aware that it looks like Hamilton's fucking off while I do all the work.

"Hey, I did my share. It's not my fault I'm just better at everything," he says, smirking meanly at them, "but I guess that's par for her course."

"Well, the view's not bad," Ansel says, eliciting laughter from the others.

Hamilton waits a beat before responding. "I guess I am pretty lucky that Adams is my partner for this. Her background makes her more prepared for shitty menial labor. Isn't that right, *Morticia*?"

"It is nice to get through one of these without you bleeding all over the place because of your massive levels of psychosis and incompetence, *Norman*."

The guys howl with laughter, and I swipe the roller over the last section before starting down the ladder. They snort themselves into silence when I walk over, roller hanging limply in my hand. Hamilton gets to his feet, spurred on by my insult, but I speak before he has the chance. "If anyone's unlucky to be out here, it's me, having to deal with such a pathetic, privileged, sorry excuse for a human being. I sincerely hope you manage to stay in your daddy's good graces, Bates, because if he snatches away that trust fund and you have to rely on anything other than your face or dick to get by in this world, you're completely screwed."

Hamilton stares at me, the familiar twinkle of evil in his eye. It sends a physical reaction through me, and I don't even know what the hell. This Pavlovian response I've developed to pissing Hamilton off can't possibly be healthy. He's wearing the same expression he had before I slapped him in the office. Or before he kissed me in the locker room.

Fuck.

Not the result I was asking for.

"Dude," Heston says, when Hamilton doesn't have a snappy comeback, "I think she just said you should be a whore."

Unfortunately, Hamilton's had time to think. "At least I have people willing to fuck me, Adams." He takes three stalking steps toward me, his eyes narrowed. "Because *you'd* have to pay someone to stick their dick in your haunted, dusty, self-righteous, death trap of a pussy."

"Damn," Emory says, eyes bulging.

How fucking dare he.

I move without thinking, inches away from him, "I swear to God, I'll..."

"You'll what?" His eyes flicker with excitement and his tongue darts out to wet his bottom lip. "What exactly will you do, Adams?"

I feel the Devils watching us, drinking us in like a fine wine, but I'm not giving them one ounce of satisfaction. I take the roller in my hand, push it against Hamilton's forehead, and spin it down his pretty face, leaving a trail of white primer across his flawless skin.

Everything goes quiet. He doesn't even move. He could slap it away, but it just rolls over his chin unimpeded.

Hamilton gapes at me, frozen.

The other Devils do the same.

I drop the roller onto the cloth and storm away.

He must try to come after me, because over my thundering heart,

I can hear a commotion between the guys—shouts and demands for Hamilton to calm down.

"You know how she is… she's a fucking snitch, it's not worth it, you'll just regret it," one of them says, their words bouncing off the stone facade of the building.

They've got one thing right.

Hamilton Bates *will* regret ever fucking with me.

14

I LEAN against my car to avoid my impulse to pace. Something about my house always makes me want to pace. Maybe it's the shrieking silence of it all, the stillness, the lack of life. Or maybe it's the coldness of it, the starkness, like nothing is ever really touched—like you can never really make a mark on it. Like you could live in this fucking place for seventeen years and it'd never really have a trace of you. It wasn't always something I realized or understood—not until I moved to the dorms.

Sure, I complain about living in a 500 square foot shoe box versus my father's 12,000 square foot home overlooking the lake. But the dorm has *life*. I'm able to mark it up with bits of myself, here and there. I can put my jacket on the couch and it'll still be there in the morning. It remembers me.

Slowly the dorm began feeling more and more like home. Now I'm standing in front of my house, its wide empty windows staring down at me, and I know the second I cross the threshold, it'll feel like a vise is squeezing the life out of me.

This time is worse, of course, because I know what's coming. And

I can stand out here all night, staring up at the gaping windows and dreading it, but it won't change a fucking thing.

I already know what's coming. Disapproval. Disappointment. Pity. And that'll just be his reaction to the things he knows about. If he found out about Gwendolyn?

That can never happen. Even imagining makes my blood run cold.

It takes me a few more minutes of not-pacing before I man up and finally approach the front door. It feels strange to walk in without knocking now, as if I owned some part of this place that never remembers me.

I walk into the main hall, aware that being here should feel like home, but the house is ridiculous, even by Bates standards. It's big enough for a family of fifteen, yet now it's just my mother and father rattling around with a housekeeper. I know why my parents bought this home: expectations. Obviously, my father couldn't have been regarded as truly successful without the excessive mansion in the gated neighborhood on the north side of town. And my mother, well. It's her staging area, isn't it? Her way of proving her value, that she can entertain guests with the finest snobbery a Chanel wallet has to offer. It's as sterile as the dormitory, maybe even less. The kids, at least, provide entertainment and companionship. Here, it's like walking through a museum with a single exhibit: twenty-first century upper-class showmanship.

The back doors are open, so I head out to the patio where the outdoor dining area is set for three.

"There you are," my mother says, placing her drink on the table. My mother is probably a beautiful woman to most people. Her long blond hair is always impeccable. I half suspect she goes to bed with it styled. There was a time, years ago—back when Hollis' name could still be spoken in this house—where I'm pretty sure I could remember her smiling without the wrinkles spreading out from the edge of her eyes. Before the Botox, back when her eyebrows could still make an expression, she used to look sort of annoyingly sly.

Really, if I think about it, she almost reminds me of... Reagan.

I super do *not* think about it.

She stands and gives me a kiss on the cheek, but frowns as she studies me. "Goodness, what's wrong with your face?" She touches my chin and moves it back and forth before rubbing at my eyebrow. "What is all that muck?"

"It's paint." I shrug, trying to tamp down my nerves at the thought of my father walking in, at any moment. "I got a little on me."

'A little' is the understatement of the year. Gwendolyn fucking coated me. It took me hours to get it off and I only managed that by calling Reagan. She arrived quickly with a carrying case of makeup supplies, particularly some sort of industrial strength remover. I didn't want to call her—every interaction with her only confirms that I need to break off whatever this is—but I didn't have many options. I've never really been that into her, no more than the other girls I've dated at Preston. Campbell was probably the last girl I really liked—goddamn, she's a spitfire—but too into petty stuff like looks and social status. Reagan's just a follower, though. A sheep. I'm not even sure how I let her latch on.

She'd tried to hang out this evening. Thankfully, I had this awful fucking dinner with my parents as an excuse. If I were smart, I'd do what Xavier suggested and bring her with me to get them off my ass, but I couldn't make myself do it. It would give *everyone* the totally wrong impression.

"Are you taking art?" Mom asks cluelessly.

My father takes that moment to stride in, carrying his own drink, and comments, "I'm assuming it's from your detention, correct?" I stiffen, eyebrows knitting together in confusion. He scoffs at my surprised reaction and takes his seat at the table, gesturing for me to do the same. "Weekly reports, son. I've been getting them since you moved on campus."

Ah, of course. Why loosen the reins?

He continues, "I'm well aware of your detention. I'm also aware of the fact you've taken your car out recently. Past curfew."

I take my own seat, my shoulders already tightening in frustration. I realize that he knows about the captainship. He's just drawing it out, trying to trap me. "I had an errand to run for the swim team. It's not like I was out joyriding."

Renata, our housekeeper, walks in pushing a cart full of food. Conversation pauses as she places plates of food in the center of the table. She glances at me and smiles warmly. She's always been kind to me. Not like a second mother so much as a gentle aunt. She's the only source of sincere warmth I come home to anymore, and the thought makes my face darken.

I bet when Gwen goes home, there's laughter. There's probably a big meal, all of them sitting around the table, sharing smiles and stories. It's probably a whole event, all of them being happy to see each other. Hell, I bet they even look forward to it. Her parents probably just *ask* her about her week, and I doubt she stands in her driveway for an hour dreading her own answers.

I have Renata, who is nice—who smiles at me—and who I, in some sense, pay to do so. When she finishes plating the food, and walks back into the house, my father resumes speaking.

"So," he folds his napkin into his lap, "when were you going to tell me about the coach's decision?"

I smile bitterly at my plate. *Ah, there it is.* "Doesn't seem like you needed me to tell you anything. You've got your minions doing it for you."

"Don't take that tone with me." He cuts into a big piece of steak, bloody juice gushing over the bone white china, then looks across the table at me. It's worse than I thought. If he were merely disappointed, he'd push his plate away to talk, one-on-one, giving me all of his attention. I guess it's difficult to make someone feel two inches tall when you're not completely focused on the task.

No, this isn't disappointment.

It's fury. "You know why I have people keeping me informed? Because I don't want to get blindsided again. It's not like you're going to tell me when shit's about to hit the fan. I learned that lesson with the Adams incident last year."

I suck in a sharp breath, stomach churning uncomfortably. Even knowing that this isn't school—that we're free to talk about it here— it's like I'm conditioned to recoil at the mere mention of it.

"Do we have to do this now?" Mother asks, pushing her salad around.

My plate is still empty.

"Bridgette, your son is floundering." He punctuates this by stabbing his fork in my direction. "He's insolent, he's inadequate, and he keeps screwing up. I don't know when the time is right to discuss it. Over his rejection letter from UVA? Maybe Duke?"

"Jesus, Dad, I am not going to get rejected from college because I got a detention for being thirty-seconds late to class." I stretch my neck in an attempt to ease the tension in my injured shoulder. "I'm also not going to get rejected for being awarded co-captain with the most competent female swimmer on the team."

His gaze is like a dagger, barely veiled rage burning in his eyes. "You don't know that. Word travels. The Adams girl and her family have already done their damage by getting their tentacles into Preston Prep. I won't let her ruin you or your chances for future success. Working with her as co-captain is detrimental to your academic and athletic career, not to mention the personal implications of being around a family with such—" He flounders here, mouth turned up in a sneer.

"Such *what*?" I ask, voice harder than I'd like. There's a threat in there. Against me? Against Gwendolyn? I may want to throttle her for what she did today with the paint, but Jesus Christ. She's just *Gwen*.

He gives me a warning look and continues, "Such different values and expectations. Gwendolyn may seem competent, or even high achieving, but after what happened with her sister, I don't think you can let down your guard." He eats belligerently, like the steak he's cutting into has caused some great offense. "It is entirely possible she may try to destroy you out of vindictiveness and revenge. There is nothing she or her family would like to see more than a Bates be taken down. Or worse, *infiltrated*."

Infiltrated.

I glance into the house through the open French doors. I can see the massive fireplace from my seat and the painting hanging above the mantle. It's of the three of us; my mother, father, and me. It used to be a different painting, one that included my sister Hollis. A guest would never even know she existed, because this house—*this fucking house*—doesn't *remember*. She's just been erased. Or rather, in my father's opinion she was 'infiltrated,' and therefore removed like an infection.

Like a tumor.

Like we can't even talk about her anymore, because it would give her power, and there would be nothing worse than that.

My dad cut her out, erased her, *cancelled her.*

Something uncomfortable clicks in my head when I think about it. I realize that what happened to Hollis is what's happening to Gwendolyn—all at my father's insistence. As an entire school, we'd just erased her from our school society. And we were so fucking good at it, too. *I* was so good at it. Almost like I'd had practice. I'd done exactly what he did to Hollis.

Holy shit.

I shove my chair back with a loud scrape against the slate floors, something in the pit of my stomach roiling. I shouldn't even be surprised. This is what he's always wanted, isn't it? A little clone of him to show off like a pony—a son who is just as successful as him, but not a single iota more. He'll lift me up while all at once holding me back.

I press my palms to the table, leveling my father with an open-faced look. "I know you think that your way is the only way. That the way you handle things is how to get shit done. You may be right, but you also may be wrong. I'd think that after proving that I have control over the Devils, and control over the swim team, and control over every aspect of my life at that school, you'd back the fuck off."

His face grows red, nostrils flaring. "The detention—"

"Is bullshit!" I slap my palms on the table. "Do you realize that half the reason I'm being punished is because the hardline attitude you suggested we take on Gwendolyn Adams makes me look petty and immature? The administrators and coaches don't like it. The detention, the captainship, it's all just damage control. It's me, cleaning up your mess. But I have some good news for you. I've got *everything* under control; the Devils, the swim team, and, yes, even Gwendolyn Adams. I tried it your way. Now you need to let me handle it on my own terms. Preston Prep is *my* domain, not yours."

With that I walk off, not wanting to give him any more of my time or energy.

He doesn't deserve it.

～

HUNGER STRIKES HALFWAY BACK to campus, once the tightly wound ball of anxiety starts to unravel in the pit of my stomach. There's a party tonight out on the lake, but I have zero interest in going to it. Reagan's already texted me three times asking if I'm going to come. That's enough to solidify the decision for me.

On a whim, I pull into the parking lot for the Northridge Diner. The place is packed, but that's not a surprise. It's a Saturday night. Northridge Diner—or 'The Nerd', coined by the unfortunate acronym of NRD—has always been a hot spot for the local kids to hang out. They make killer burgers and milkshakes. It's worth the wait.

What I'm not sure it's worth is running into Gwendolyn on the way in.

We both reach the front door at the same time, but then stop abruptly.

"Oh," she says, eyes sweeping over my face, obviously looking for the remains of her paint job, "go ahead." She doesn't even have the good grace to look contrite about the primer still glued to my eyebrows.

"No," I hold open the door, inhale hissing through my flared nose, "after you. *I insist.*"

The diver, Tyson, walks up with a small girl at his side, their hands linked. A strange sensation flutters in my chest at the sight of them—obviously a couple.

"Hamilton," he says, eyes shifting between us. "Ah, what's going on?"

"Just headed back from a firing squad disguised as a dinner with my parents," I say, uncharacteristically honest. "You guys?"

Tyson looks at Gwen, and when she doesn't answer, takes the reins. "I had a competition today." The girl squeezes his hand. "Oh,

158

sorry, this is Presley. Pres, this is Hamilton. He and Gwen are co-captains of the swim team."

"Oh, you made the shirts!" she says, face breaking into a beaming smile. "Those sound hilarious."

"Thanks," I say, shifting awkwardly. My eyes flick to Gwen, who looks similarly uncomfortable, like she's waiting for a bomb to drop. Makes sense. I've devoted the last six months to destroying any vestiges of her social life and here she is with two new friends. I'm a wildcard. "It was a team effort, though. Gwen helped."

Her eyes finally meet mine, eyebrows pulling together in confusion.

A customer walks out, prompting us to walk in and get in line. There's no way to avoid one another, and although Gwen and I both feel the tension thickening between us, Tyson and Presley seem so into one another that I don't think they notice. Luckily, the line moves fast and their group orders first. When I step up to the counter, Presley insists, "Come find us and sit with us, okay?"

"Nah, that's okay. I don't want to intrude." Tyson looks at Gwendolyn, who just shrugs before walking off with Presley. I exhale and study him, trying to find what tack to take with this guy. Ten minutes ago, it probably would have been some form of aggression. But I'm suddenly feeling a lot less like I want to punch him in the face, so I decide my sense of earnestness could probably use some exercise. "She and I... we kind of had it out this morning at detention."

"So I heard." He bobs his head. "By the way, you uhhh, have some paint on your eyelashes there." He grins, pointing at my face.

I roll my eyes, not even bothering to pick at it. "It was either keep the paint or lose the eyelashes."

He snorts a laugh. "Seriously, you two need to chill out and work past your shit. The Nerd is neutral territory. None of your Devils will see you fraternizing with the enemy or whatever. Can't you just give it a break for one night?"

I run my hand though my hair, nodding. "That could sound doable."

I think.

He leaves me to place my order, and soon, I'm walking toward their booth in the back. Tyson and Presley are on one bench and Gwendolyn is on the other. The sheer awkwardness of the moment almost makes me leave. Sitting next to the Freak? The bitch who, just hours ago, covered my face in paint?

Well, I did say she had a haunted, dusty, self-righteous vagina.

I sigh, shoulders dropping.

I guess that maybe makes us even.

Approaching the table, I quickly slide onto the bench, like pulling off a Band-Aid. Gwendolyn doesn't even spare me a look when she shifts away, nearly clinging to the wall. I only just barely restrain my eye-roll. As if she hasn't let me, *wanted me*, to touch her body before. I know this is different. This is real life, not some pent-up, ragey grope-fest in a dark room.

Seriously, why are the lights so bright in here?

"You said you had a family dinner?" Presley says, chewing on a fry. "But here you are eating another meal. I know Tyson eats a lot, but…"

"No," I admit, "dinner with my parents was a disaster. I left before the food could even touch my plate."

"Sounds tense." Tyson asks.

"Tense is an understatement." I nod, putting some ketchup onto my burger. "We haven't gotten along for a while now. Like six months."

Gwendolyn fidgets next to me but keeps her eyes on her food.

I'm dreading further questions, but thankfully, Tyson's girl seems to have a short attention span because she blurts out, "I figured it out!" She stares at Gwendolyn. "I knew you looked really familiar. You were at the Community Service Day, a few months ago, right?"

Gwen looks at her pensively. "Down at the park?"

"Yes! I knew it!" Presley's grin is wide and bright. "Wait. Your mom is the one that started the summer meals program for school kids, right?"

"That's her." Gwen smiles fondly. "It's kind of her passion project."

I take a bite of my hamburger and only distantly listen to them ramble on about their good deeds. Swallowing and wiping my mouth, I raise an eyebrow at Tyson and say, "Guess we can't compare to these two do-gooders."

Presley turns to me, winding her arm around his. "Tyson volunteers his time down at the pool in the summer giving the kids diving lessons. It's so amazingly adorable. Actually, that's how we met."

I take a long drag on my milkshake while Gwendolyn asks for more details. Presley happily complies, going into some nonsense about watching the kids at the pool and Tyson needing a volunteer. Meet-cute ensues, blahblahblah...

Fucking gag me.

"Anyway," Presley continues, "he spent two hours trying to teach me how to do a basic dive off the dock—"

"I'm pretty sure she was faking," Tyson adds, "just to get me to stick around."

"Yeah, right," she laughs, touching the tip of his nose with her finger, "you're just a terrible coach."

"Hey! I never claimed to be a good coach, just an amazing diver."

"You're good at a lot of things, baby." The two of them grin soppily at one another. I grab my hamburger and cram it into my mouth for another bite. Gwendolyn stabs her milkshake with her straw. Under the table her knee bounces nervously. My foot accidentally bumps hers and she flinches, shifting uncomfortably.

"So how long have you two known one another?" Presley asks, looking between us.

"Oh, um," Gwendolyn starts, "I don't know. A long time."

I lower my burger and nod. "Since grade school."

"We were just thrown together a lot because of swim," Gwendolyn adds, smiling tightly. "Forced companionship."

I get a flash of memory of her from back then, skinny as a rail with two askew pigtails. She wore the same red and white team bathing suit every day and habitually lost her goggles. After so long, I took to packing two, so she could always borrow one. In return, she'd always bring me a snack, because her nanny always packed extra. Neither of us had to ask. Things were different back then. Simpler. At that age, having friends wasn't about status or cliques or posturing. It was just two kids, sitting with their feet dipped into the deep end, trying to see who could kick the biggest splash.

Once, I even let her win.

I blink, coming back to the present.

Presley is still talking. "Wow, really? That's cool, though. You guys have, like... *real* history. I only moved here three years ago, so I'm not sure I'll ever really feel like I fit in with the girls at Holy Innocence. All their friendships were formed long before I started."

Tyson tosses his arm over her shoulder and pulls her in for a hug. I can't help but watch them and wonder if his actions are genuine or just a play. He seems genuine, like an actual 'nice guy', which is about the only annoying thing about him. The only time I'm overtly nice to a girl like that is when I'm hoping to get some later.

The cross hanging around both of their necks kind of makes me wonder if that's even on the table and, if it's not, then what's even the point?

"Just because we've gone to school together for years and swim on the same team doesn't mean we're in the same group of friends," Gwendolyn says, her knee bouncing even faster. "That's not how Preston Prep works. Isn't that right, Hamilton?"

I narrow my eyes, putting my burger down. *Does she really want to start this here?*

Tyson frowns, looking between us. "If I understand correctly, these two have a bit of an ongoing feud."

His girlfriend's eyebrows arch. "Oh, seriously? I guess I noticed a little tension, but I wasn't sure if you two were like, exes? Or maybe you're into each other? There's a whole vibe happening."

Gwendolyn barks an obnoxious laugh before I get a chance to. Her knee moves like a jackhammer, driving me nuts. I clamp a hand down on her thigh, stilling her completely.

"That vibe—" she begins, trying to pry my hand from her thigh. To spite her, I press down harder. "—is called mutual loathing. Hatred. Disgust. Distrust. Because the thing about Hamilton is that he's a complete prick—"

"And she's a complete bitch," I add, tossing in my own jab as I dig my fingers into her knee.

"Also, he's a pretentious, spoiled man-baby."

"And she's a self-righteous control freak."

"And despite billing himself as a competitive hard-worker," she digs her nails into my wrist, "he absolutely crumbles at the faintest whiff of anything resembling adversity."

"Whoa, vicious!" Presley laughs in that awkward way where she's clearly trying to dispel the tension. She gives Tyson a playful look, "What are we going to do with him?"

"I mean, we could technically kill him." Gwen leans forward with an open, earnest face. "But it's just that we'd have to hunt down all the horcruxes first, you know?"

"As you can see," I conclude to Presley, refusing to acknowledge Gwendolyn just compared me to Voldemort. I mean, obviously, if we're making Harry Potter comparisons, I'm the Draco Malfoy of the group. "Voluntarily spending time with her is an obscene form of self-torture."

"Exactly." Gwendolyn looks at me for the first time that night and I see the flicker of fire in her eyes. A deranged smile creeps onto her face and I feel the tug of a sharp grin pulling at my own lips.

"Ooookay," Presley says from across the table, jabbing Tyson with an elbow. "That's...um, babe? Ready to go?"

The two grab their trays and hover over the table while Gwendolyn and I continue our silently hostile standoff.

"Gwen?"

She blinks twice, removing her hand from mine, then looks up at Tyson. "Yeah, coming."

I ease out of the booth, standing to give her room to pass. When she brushes by me, her curvy ass grazes my groin. Accident? Maybe. On purpose? God knows. Neither option stops the heat that rushes through me or the way my pants suddenly get tighter.

"It was nice meeting you, Hamilton," Presley says. "Hopefully I'll see you at some of the meets."

"Nice to meet you, too," I murmur, dragging my eyes away from watching Gwendolyn toss her trash into the bin a few feet away. "Thanks for the company."

Following them out, I part from them and head to my car. In the rearview mirror, I watch them approach Riggins' beat up truck. He holds the door for them both, like a gentleman, and Presley gives him a kiss on the way in. Adams smiles in appreciation.

That's who she should be spending her time with, anyway. Nice, regular people. People who get her and her need to help others. Not assholes like me.

I start up the car and peel out of the parking lot, tires squealing on the pavement. All this time I thought Gwendolyn Adams was wrong for Preston Prep. In reality, Preston Prep was wrong for her.

15

THE KNOCK COMES ONLY a few minutes after I walk into my dorm. I instantly regret answering it, because there he is.

Hamilton's broad form darkens my doorway.

I tiredly ask, "What do you want, Bates?" and turn back to my room. After the last time, I'm smarter than to think he won't invite himself in, and he does exactly that, closing the door behind him with a soft *snick*. "If you're looking to get your face drenched with primer again, then I'm sorry to inform you I'm fresh out."

It was a shock to see him at The Nerd, to say the least. Devils typically don't lower themselves to eat at any establishment that lacks a bare minimum of two chandeliers. But Hamilton just looked so *off*, his whole demeanor slack and subdued. Dejected. It wasn't a look he wore well. When he said he'd come from his parents' house, I figured that explained it. I suppose even spoiled brats get frustrated with their parents at some point. For once, I could actually relate.

"I was on the way back to my room," he says, long fingers trailing over my dresser. His face is shadowed by the low light of my lamp, but the blank hollows of his eyes look just as tired as before.

When no further explanation is forthcoming, I sigh in annoyance. "And?"

He pulls a book from my shelf, just like last time, and fans through the pages. "Instead, I came here."

I lean against my desk, arms crossed. "*Bates.*"

"Adams."

All it takes is one look from him and that flickering spark between us—that weird mixture of anger and lust—flares instantly to life.

I just want to pull my hair out.

It isn't *fair.*

It isn't right that he can walk in here and, with a couple words and a single semi-hostile glance, send my body alight. Is this how it's going to be? Has he completely ruined me for other guys? Will I ever be able to feel this painfully alive with a nice, normal guy, or are hostile glances and the quick-fire exchange of barbed insults all that will ever do it for me?

Damn it.

"You should go," I tell him, hugging my middle, "or someone might see you. A Devil, or someone else. Maybe even Reagan."

He turns and looks at me, hands stuffed into his pockets. His tongue darts out to wet his lower lip. "I don't want to."

I drop my gaze. "Keep hanging around like this, some of my freak may rub off on you."

After a beat of silence, he asks, "You really want me to go?"

"Of course, I want you to go." I drop my arms, exhaling in an angry rush. "I didn't invite you here. Why would I? Wasn't thirty minutes ago, you were calling me a bitch!"

"And you called me a prick." He stalks forward and my heart jumps, banging wildly against my ribs. "And then you rubbed your ass on my cock."

I gape at him, wide-eyed. "I did not!"

"Did too."

"It wasn't—I didn't even—" I huff a breath, feeling warm-cheeked and flustered. "It was an accident!"

He gives a low chuckle, head tilted curiously as he takes me in. "Sure it was."

"It was!"

Not even I believe it.

"Just admit it, Adams." He's inches away, jaw clenched, eyes darting to my mouth. "Admit that you want me."

I roll my eyes. "Fuck off, Bates."

"I'm not afraid to say it," he challenges, pushing close enough that I can feel the warm wash of his breath against my ear when he whispers, "I want to fuck you."

My breath hitches and I know he hears it, feels it. I want to tell him that it'll never happen. That I have standards. That I'm not even interested. That I definitely don't lay in bed some nights and think of him doing that—fucking me—while getting myself off.

All I manage is a hard gulp.

He pulls back far enough to meet my gaze. "Just admit it and I'll leave."

My chest clutches in panic, but I don't let him see it. I just lift my chin and glare him down. "Why? So you can lord it over me for god only knows how long? So you can brag to all your douchebag Devil friends about how you duped The Freak into spreading her legs for you? So that you can finally run and tell daddy that he was right; all of the Adams girls really are sluts?" I take a deep breath and exhale. "Or does your ginormous ego just need the affirmation that every girl at Preston Prep wants you, even a piece of trash like me?"

He stares at me for a long moment, his stormy gaze fixed to mine, and then finally turns and strolls to the door. I turn to my desk, fingers trembling, the sounds of the door opening and closing seeming almost distant against the whooshing in my ears. I'm not scared of Hamilton. I'm *not*. I'm scared of how I feel around him. I'm scared of slipping in a way I can't come back from.

I suspect he has the same fear.

I wanted to murder him at detention for calling me out in front of his idiot friends, for belittling and demeaning me while we both knew that he could barely keep his hands off of me. But he also brought me coffee, and my favorite kind, at that. How did he even know? And he helped me with the swim team by buying those shirts. He also made my entire body light on fire when his hand clamped around my thigh earlier tonight, and if I closed my eyes and really focused, I'm pretty sure I could still feel the heat.

It's that conflict—that crazy-making mess of confusion—that makes being around him unbearable.

Unbearable and *terrifying*.

It's also a big part of what propels me to the door. I swing it open, his name on my lips, but he's already there. He's standing only inches away, like he'd wanted to leave but couldn't. He seems genuinely shocked to see me standing there—to have been caught.

"Fine," I say, the word coming out low and hissed. "I admit it."

His expression transforms slowly, from shocked stupor to victorious, creeping smirk. "Admit what, exactly?"

My eyes narrow. "Seriously, you're going to make me—"

'Say it' is how I'd finish that sentence if he doesn't lunge at me, lips crashing against mine. His wet mouth swallows a low sound that feels ripped right from my chest. His arms come around my middle and he half guides, half carries me back into the room, door slamming shut behind him. The journey to my bed is muddled with the hot sensation of him licking greedily into my mouth, one of his hands coming down to palm at the swell of my backside.

Our fall to the bed is graceless and messy. He doesn't land on top of me so much as he sort of *surges* into me. The weight of him is almost too much. It doesn't last long before he tears his mouth from mine and ducks his head, his lips burning a fiery trail down my neck to my collarbone.

I push clumsily at his shirt, because if I'm going to do this, then I'm going to do it right, and that means finally getting to see and touch all of his ridiculously perfect body. I get his shirt up around his armpits before he finally lifts his head and yanks it off, muscles rippling in the process. He removes mine just as fast, his palms skittering up my ribs as he tugs it up my body.

He throws my shirt aside. Quick, nimble fingers remove my bra as though he'd practiced the move as much as the cello. The lacy fabric gets tossed aside next, and then he sits back.

His gray eyes drink me in, slow but greedy. I can almost feel the searing circuit they make down my neck, over my chest, my ribs, my tense belly. He reaches out and his fingers follow the same path, gliding down my body.

"Jesus Christ, your tits..." He flattens a palm to my ribs, sliding it up to cup one in his hand. His thumb rubs over my nipple and I arch into the touch, teeth digging into my lip. It feels like it takes an eternity for him to finally lower his mouth to it, his lips and tongue looking stark and red against my pale, flushed skin.

I wind a hand into his hair, gasping at how his mouth feels on me. His hand comes up to fondle my other breast, and if he'd wanted to make me want him, then this was definitely the way to do it.

I feel him tugging at my waistband in a foggy, abstract sort of way. Every nerve in my body is pointed right toward his mouth, his tongue laving against my nipple. Eventually, it's clear that they're going to need a little more attention. With a soft, annoyed grunt, he pulls away.

"These fucking things, swear to god," he pants, rising to the end of the bed to peel the clingy fabric down and over my feet. "Blessing and a curse."

The tent in his jeans is obscene, and I prop myself up on my elbows to watch as he thumbs his button open, pushing them to the ground and kicking them away. I take a moment to really drink him in. The broad chest, the chiseled abs, the firm thighs, the corded arms. It's almost too much—too good to be true.

What am I doing? What are we doing?

I can feel the phantom creep of panic taking me, legs tensing, knees pressing together, and I hardly register the way he's looking at me with those dark, hungry eyes.

He keeps his black boxer briefs on and bends, pressing a slow kiss into my ankle, my knees, the tops of my thighs. He wedges a hand between them, coaxing them apart, and if he feels the fine tremors in my muscles when I reluctantly part my legs, then he at least does me the favor of ignoring it.

I fall to my back and stare at the top of his head as he ascends, trailing his lips closer and closer to my center. The closer he gets, the tighter my body feels, like it's just thin skin stretched over a pile of embers waiting to explode.

I exhale when his kisses move up to my hip, and then my belly, and I'm... surprised at all this slow attention. I'd always imagined him to be the fast and greedy type, only concerned about chasing his pleasure, but this is—

Intent.

And I instantly realize why I'm panicking. This isn't some quick, impulsive, fury-driven catharsis we're chasing here. This is *intent*. This is something we both mean to do. This is something we both *want* to do—outside of arguments or pressure or competition.

This changes everything.

I think perhaps he can feel it, too, because when he dips between the apex of my legs, his hand is shaking almost as badly as my legs are. He finally meets my gaze again, finger playing at the edge of my panties, and he watches me closely, like he's waiting for me to slap him across the face or knee him in the balls.

I could, but I won't—can't, really. For some insane reason, my mind and body have both decided that I need to see this through. I push at the waistband of his briefs, wanting him freed, and he lends a hand, rearing back to shimmy them down his thighs.

I finally get a good look at him, and yes. That is definitely a dick. It is definitely *Hamilton's* dick. I could have probably picked it out of a line-up long before this. I can tell it's his, because photos of it belong in textbooks. It's long and thick, and doesn't even have the good grace to be disgustingly veiny or anything, it's just...

It's just so *Hamilton*.

He plants a hand onto the bed beside me and bends back over me, hovering. His gaze doesn't leave mine when he presses our hips together, the long, hot length of him rocking itself against my core.

My mouth parts on an inhale and I clutch his biceps, legs clamping around his hips. "Wait, wait."

"Fight with me tomorrow," he says, ducking his head to press a biting kiss into my neck. "Fight me all week, for all I care. But don't fight me right now, Adams. If you don't relax, it's going to hurt." His low rasp sends a chill up my spine. Is that Hamilton Bates showing concern? Tenderness? His voice is low and quiet, like he's sharing a secret. "I don't want to hurt you. You're a virgin, aren't you?"

I'm not sure how I can flush any harder than I already am, but it feels like that's what happens. As much as I want to say no, that I'm experienced and have had plenty of lovers, I don't. I can't. It's not something I can hide.

"There's a box of condoms in the nightstand," I blurt, not even bothering to avoid his eyes when he looks at me with a raised eyebrow.

"Is there, now?" His eyes dart to the drawer and he reaches for it, pulling it open and searching blindly.

"I bought them. Not for this—not for you, I mean. Just to be safe, so I wouldn't end up like those girls—like my mom. The kind of girl who's stupid and impulsive and unprepared and—"

I pause and watch him open one of the condoms, rolling it over his thick erection. It's a quick, practiced motion, something he's obviously familiar with. He tosses the wrapper somewhere on my floor and leans back over me, taking himself in hand. I feel the pressure of him pushing at me, nudging, ready to get inside, and I'm looking at the size of him and thinking...

"I don't care how relaxed I get, there's no fucking way that won't hurt." My stomach flip-flops and I have to battle not to let the hysterical laughter trapped in my chest burst forth. Because I'm realizing that maybe losing your virginity to a dick that big isn't the greatest experience.

Not so perfect, after all.

His nose nudges mine until I meet his gaze. His eyes are hooded, the muscles in his jaw flexing. "You're not like those other girls, Adams. You're strong. Resilient. Smart. Bossy." He distracts me with a slow, wet kiss, and something just... *gives*, his erection pushing just barely past the resistance.

I gasp and dig my fingers into his back, toes curling.

"You can handle all my bullshit," he continues, "and if you can handle that, you can handle anything."

He finishes his thought with another deep kiss, and pushes the rest of the way in. He part groans, part growls, burying his face into my neck as he stretches me out, filling me up.

It does hurt.

But I think, later, I probably won't remember that part. What I'll remember is the shift of his back muscles as he waits, seated inside of me, for me to adjust. I'll remember the wash of his breath against my mouth when he pants at the feeling of being inside me. Mostly, I'll remember the look on his face—the pucker in his brow, the tick in his jaw—and how the look in his eyes was something lost and completely undone. I'll remember how it felt to know that it was because of me.

I'll remember that there's power here. That there's triumph here.

I try to relax as he starts to move, gently pulling back out before pushing in again. We watch each other as he rocks into me, testing, careful, and it's not the feral lust from the times before—it's a slow-building heat. Each time we meet, I feel my anxiety unwind, my belly loosening, my desire building. It isn't long before I start raising my hips to meet his, tentatively at first, and then spurred on by the ragged sound he makes in the back of his throat.

Soon I match him thrust for thrust, all senses lost about what I'm doing, who I'm doing it with and what kind of hell I'll have to pay when it's over. I follow the dance of our bodies—and it is a dance. I can't even remember why I was so nervous. It feels so natural now to lock my ankles around his waist, just blind instinct to hook a hand around his shoulder and hold on as he plunges into me, the sweet friction and new, full feeling taking my breath away with each pass.

I can't help but watch Hamilton over me, *in me*. His jaw gets tighter and sharper, eyes falling closed, shoulders eclipsing me like the sun. He's beautiful—consumed—a side of him I've never seen before.

His control starts slipping gradually, driven by something primal and animalistic, his movements growing erratic, relentless. I can see his hand in my periphery, curled into a fist in my bedsheets, and the sounds he makes—these breathy grunts that sound like they're being forced through his clenched teeth—are doing things to me. I lose myself to the sounds, the sensations twisting deep in my own core. It's easy to lose myself in the rhythm of our bodies, in the closeness, in the bitter energy that fuels us. I come in a hot burst of white behind my eyelids, heels digging deep into his back, pushing him closer as I grind up into him. He hisses a sharp, *"Fuck,"* and slams into me, his massive frame shuddering with his own release, his skin hot, his cock pulsing inside of me.

Sheer exhaustion—physical and emotional—crashes over me as my legs slide limply from his waist. Hamilton rests there, on top of me, for a suspended moment, forehead resting against mine, face strangely serene. My mind is too numb to think of what'd just happened. Of the consequences...

Jesus Christ.

I jerk awake a few moments later, sharp clarity coming into focus.

What had I done?

I thought the kiss was a betrayal, but this... how do I explain this? How do I justify it? Hell, I'd gone after him! I'd admitted that I wanted him!

Hamilton shifts, the look of contentment gone, face going shuttered, eyes darkening. I recognize the expression instantly.

Resentment.

"I should go," he says, untangling himself from me. I look away as he cleans up, wrapping my blanket around me like a shield. He starts, "That was—"

"A mistake."

He nods in agreement, plucking his shorts and jeans from the floor. He tugs them on quickly, then his shirt. As skilled as he was getting my clothes off, he also seems practiced in making a... what did he call it? 'Hasty post-coital exit'?

He crams his feet into his shoes and heads to the door, stopping to say, "If you—"

I cut him off. "You don't need to threaten me. I won't tell anyone."

His eyes hold mine, but there's more exhaustion than threat in them. "Good. Trust me, I won't either."

The door opens and shuts, and then I'm alone. There's no risk of him returning nor of me going after him. I burrow under the covers, caught in the mixed emotions of everything that just happened. I feel both full and empty—both relieved and hurt.

I shouldn't expect anything better after tangling with Hamilton Bates.

By Sunday morning, I know for sure that there's no way I'm facing my family. My paranoia reaches a fever pitch and I call my mom to tell her that I don't feel great, that I'm really sorry I won't be home, that I'm going to spend the day resting.

"Do you need some soup?" she asks, concerned. "I can bring some over. I know you like Pho from the 24-hour place."

"No, it's fine."

"Okay, well..." She sighs and her disappointment is palpable. "Just a reminder about Micha's dance. It's in two weeks. Mark your calendar, okay?"

"Got it, Mom, wouldn't miss it. Tell the kids I'll see them tomorrow morning, okay?"

"Go to the infirmary if you don't feel better."

"I will."

I won't.

Pretty sure the infirmary doesn't have a cure for massive regret.

"Love you."

"Love you, too," I say and hang up the phone. I drop it on the bedside table. My eyes fall on the box of condoms halfway out of the drawer, and then to the torn wrapper on the floor. I slam the drawer and snatch the wrapper up, tucking it deep into my trash bin.

Seriously, what have I done?

It's not that I think he'll tell anyone—god forbid. He'd probably slit his throat before he admitted to even being able to stand my presence, let alone sleeping with me. It's just the fucking mind games.

That, and the fact that I lost my virginity to a complete douchebag. My 'precious womanly flower' has never been worth much to me. I don't necessarily subscribe to some puritan concept of anyone's first time needing to be perfectly planned with the love of their life. But not getting dicked down by the guy who's spent the last six months making me miserable would have been a nice start to the sexually active era of my life.

Hamilton can have sex with any girl at this school. Most, if not all, would be more than willing. Reagan alone can probably satisfy his urges. But he keeps coming back for me, over and over, and now things have gone absolutely too far. That was an act that couldn't be undone. He doesn't like me, and I don't like him.

So, what is this?

That's the part that keeps hanging me up.

EVEN THOUGH I'M not sick, I do feel feverish. Lethargic. Fragile. Doomed to an eternity of shame. All the usual side effects of regret, I guess. I do what I always do when I need to clear my mind.

I head to the pool.

There are open hours on the weekend, so after leaving my belongings in the captain's office, I dive into the water and let the monotony of swimming laps ease my spinning mind.

As usual, exercising helps. The dull ache in my belly grows less obtrusive as my arms and legs begin to burn from the exertion. I get into the rhythm of the stroke, gaining confidence with each push off the wall. I know who I am, what I'm good at, and what I want to do.

I'm not just some dumb girl who lost her virginity to the school asshole. That was never my destiny. And denying my own agency in this isn't useful, isn't fair, and isn't me.

I admit it.

I wanted it.

Is that so bad?

The truth is that I can handle my side of this. But what about his? What does Hamilton really want? Every move he makes is about power and control. But he had power over me long before we started getting hot and heavy. So how does this factor in? What is his endgame?

I climb out of the pool, trailing rivulets of water behind me, and enter the office. If Hamilton wanted control last night, then I'm not sure he succeeded. He looked pretty out of it when he came inside of me. And he didn't look particularly happy with himself when he fled.

I promise myself while showering to just let it go. Forget about it. We can do that, right? Forget this ever happened?

That resolve comes crashing down when I walk out of the tiny bathroom and see him sitting at the desk, broad shoulders hunched over the calendar. He glances back, eyes always assessing, then resumes his work.

"What are you doing here?" he asks, shifting uncomfortably. "I thought you went home on Sundays."

How does he know that?

"Are you stalking me or something?" I ask, hanging my towel on the hook. "Because if this is some kind of stalker fetish—"

"I'm not stalking you, Adams." He rubs his eyes. I can't help but notice the dark circles underneath. A thick layer of stubble covers his sharp chin. "As someone stuck here on the weekend, it's just pretty obvious that you take off every Sunday. And before you ask, no, I didn't follow you down here. Coach asked me to fill out this heat sheet before time trials on Monday and I forgot."

His story checks out. I'd filled out my sheet on Friday, and he's right. This campus is small. I know way more about my classmates' schedules than I'd like. But could anyone blame me for being a little paranoid the day after having sex with Hamilton? This little game with him is making me lose my mind. I slide my feet into my shoes and reach for my jacket.

"What do you think?" he asks suddenly, angling toward me with his sheet in hand. "Pierce or Bearman for the fifty-free?"

I stop mid-zip and blink. "You... want my opinion?"

He lifts an eyebrow. "I just asked you for it, didn't I?"

The hair prickles on the back of my neck and I discreetly look around for a camera. If anyone could pull a long-con, it'd be Hamilton. Is that what this is about? Him making me feel comfortable, then getting evidence to prove me and my sister are sluts?

He drops the paper onto the desk, sighing. "I don't know what's running through that head of yours, Adams, but you seriously need to stop."

"Stop what?"

He leans back in the chair, his long legs sprawled in front of him, and rubs a hand down his tired face. "Look, there's no way to avoid fallout from last night. I get it, trust me. But you look like you're waiting for a bomb to drop."

"Are you saying there isn't one?" I cross my arms, watching him skeptically. "Because that's the problem, Bates. I don't trust you, and I don't trust the Devils. I don't get why you're doing this, or why I'm caught up in it."

"It's sex." He raises his hands, palms out, hapless. "There's not much more to it than that." He runs his hand through his hair. "It's just... it's a distraction. That's all."

"Distraction from what?"

He glares at me for so long that I think he won't answer. But he does. "From school, college applications, my parents, boredom. Pick one. Predictably, you're overthinking it."

"I'm not predictable and I'm not overthinking it."

He laces his fingers behind his head, eyebrows raised. "Every day you get up and go to the carpool line to meet your brother and sister before school. You walk them to class. Then you put on that battle armor and head into the main building, where you get to class with exactly zero time to spare to interact with anyone. At night, during the off season, you sneak down here after water polo practice for extra swim time. You don't go to parties. You don't do social media. You don't really like going home on weekends, except you clearly feel obligated. You're obsessed with your grades. Probably more horrified at the blemish on your record for getting detention than having to do it with me. You're so hung up on your fucking savior complex that you hardly have time to get off the cross to live your life." He swivels in the chair. "You're predictable and you need a distraction as much as I do."

His summary hits me like a punch in the gut. I can't dispute any of it. I narrow my eyes. "I thought you weren't stalking me."

He rolls his eyes. "I'm observant—particularly with the people trying to ruin my life. Don't tell me you don't keep track of me the same way. Know your enemy, isn't that the saying?"

There's something wrong with me, because as he speaks, as he admits that he's noticed me, watched me for all these months, something inside me flares to life again. Hamilton and I have been circling one another for ages, the push-pull of whatever keeps dragging us together impossible to ignore.

Every interaction we've had has been on his terms. Every kiss, every touch, every meeting. But as I stand before him right now, it clicks.

He's right. I'm overthinking it. It's just sex.

Sex, with a little practice, that could be really, really good.

Heart pounding, I walk to the door and close it, pushing the lock in with my thumb. I'm done being the poor little embarrassed girl all the time. If I want to fuck Hamilton, then why shouldn't I?

I turn and feel his gaze tracking my motions closely, carefully, as I throw caution to the wind and climb into his lap, straddling his hips.

His eyes widen, hands flying up. "Adams, what the—"

"You really don't need to talk for this." I grab a fistful of his hair and say, "Shut the fuck up." I register his shock, the way his mouth parts on an inhale, and then the slow transformation as his eyes drags over my body, hands landing on my hips.

He meets my gaze, mouth twisting into dark smirk. "Make me," he replies, hands sliding down to cup my ass.

I do, crashing my mouth into his, sinking into this boy—this trouble—pushing aside my fear and paranoia. His tongue is hot and his hands are greedy, and he's right.

Hamilton Bates is very, very distracting.

If I'm going to play with fire, I figure I may as well do it with the Devil himself.

HAMILTON

"HEY MAN, where were you all weekend? You missed a killer party at Mason's lake house on Saturday night."

Xavier falls into step as we cross the quad. It's the Monday morning following a weekend mostly spent with Gwendolyn, and a good portion of that spent in Gwendolyn's pants. In short, it's really fucking surreal to be walking around like it's any other day when I've clearly fallen into some twisted alternate porn-universe.

I'd totally forgotten about that party. "Busy," I reply, not explaining further.

"Getting all that paint off?" Ansel says, catching up. "How long did that take?"

I roll my eyes. It seems like a lifetime ago that Gwendolyn covered my face in paint. Since then, I've confirmed that her pussy is definitely not haunted or filled with cobwebs.

Twice.

I confirmed it twice.

"What are we talking about?" Heston asks, walking over from the student parking lot.

Ansel gestures to me with a nod. "Hamilton's paint job the other day."

Heston grins. "She completely nailed you with that one. Although, you shouldn't be surprised. You're lucky she didn't cut your balls off, too."

I open my mouth, ready to tell them that she didn't cut off my balls, but she certainly knew how to handle them. I stop myself, grinding my teeth together instead. Normally, I would have been chomping at the bit to brag about having banged a girl over the weekend. Yes, I'm one of those guys. Sue me. My sexual exploits are pretty well known. Honestly, usually the gossip travels for me. Girls want people to know they slept with a Devil. *The Devil.* That's how that idiotic "blow job test" rumor got started in the first place.

Obviously, Gwendolyn is different. They can't ever know. She wouldn't want them to, that's for sure, and I don't want them to, either.

Not because I'm embarrassed. She's hot, and frankly, quite the conquest. It just figures I'd bag someone actually interesting and then have to keep my mouth shut about it. If she didn't have the "Freak" label, she'd be a hot commodity. She's gorgeous, athletic, smart. I'd put her notch beneath my name on the Stairway to Hell beam in a skinny fucking minute. No, it's not because of that. It's because right now she's mine, and I want to keep her like that.

I hadn't lied to her in the office the day before. I needed a distraction, and Gwendolyn Adams was doing the job.

"I had dinner with my parents Saturday night. Once it was over, I wasn't in the mood to party," I say, trying not to grimace when I see Reagan walking over. "I wouldn't have been good company, anyway."

"So it wasn't just me you blew off," she pouts, tugging at my collar.

"Nah, just—family shit." I smile tightly, trying to subtly extricate myself from her clutched. "It got intense. My dad is pissed off about me getting detention, and don't even get me started on the co-captain bullshit."

"Can't he just call the school and tell them you can't work with her." When she says 'her,' Reagan's eyes dart across the quad to where Gwendolyn's walking, returning from the middle school building.

"Especially after that bullshit with the paint. She could have blinded you or something."

I try to ignore my weird hyper-awareness of Gwen in my periphery, rolling my shoulders to shrug it off. "Right now, my plan is to lay low and just get through it."

"Seriously, Reag, don't make a stink," Heston says. "Adams is proving to be a pretty worthy co-captain with the whole t-shirt stunt. Which, now that I think about it, really reeks of a Hamilton Bates stunt."

I shrug. "I guess she has more game than we realized."

The bell tower chimes, which is a five-minute warning. As a group we start toward the main building. I keep one eye on Gwendolyn as she enters the front door, barely aware that Reagan has linked her fingers with mine.

"When you didn't come to the party," she says, pressing against my side, "I came by your room to make sure you were okay."

I glance down at her arm, her hand, clutched to me like a fucking monkey. "Captain duties. I was in the office."

"I'm just kind of getting the feeling you may be avoiding me lately." She squeezes my hand and blinks at me with those wide blue eyes. She's a cute girl. She's... fun. She's more than willing to do whatever I want. Yet, when I focus on the way her hand feels in mine, there's nothing. No tingle. No flicker of want. No desire. It's like holding hands with a cousin.

"Hey," she continues, eyes twinkling, "maybe you and I could make use of the office some time?"

A wave of images crashes over me. Gwendolyn climbing into my lap, her mouth pressed against mine, the quiver in her belly as she stood before me, letting me drag her panties down her legs. The slack look of rapture as she sank down onto me, hair tumbling down her shoulders. The way she gave a few experimental rocks against me before lifting and dropping, learning way too quickly exactly how to ride my dick. How her tits looked—god, her tits—right in my face, and how she arched them into me, urging me to lick them. And then later, when we were both completely on the edge, how it felt to come inside of her again as she tightened and shuddered around me. The sound she made—this little jagged mewl—and how flushed she looked after.

"Hamilton." Reagan yanks my arm.

"Huh?" I rub my neck and feel the prickle of sweat that's beaded there, my pants feeling tight just from the memory. Reagan looks beyond irritated. I clear my throat. "So that's a 'no' on the office. Coach would kill me. The last thing I need right now is more detention, or to lose my *half*-captainship."

"Then figure something out, okay?" She blows out sharply, eyes narrowed. "Because you're the one with all the limitations and parameters. I'm here for you—ready and willing—but if you're not into it..."

I nod, not knowing what to say or do. Usually, if I'm distant or sharp toward a girl, she just fucks off. For someone with as long of a sexual rap sheet as me, I somehow have developed zero rejection skillsets. And Reagan just isn't taking the hint.

"I'll see what I can do."

That seems to appease her, which is all I want at the moment. I'll just kick that can down the road. Once we've entered the classroom, I brace myself for Gwendolyn's entrance. I'm going to have to sit mere feet away from her for the next hour, all the while somehow pretending I don't know what it feels like to be inside of her, to see the way her face spasms when she comes, as if I haven't tasted her, taken her.

I cast a furtive, exasperated glance down at my swelling dick.

I slouch in my desk, tapping my pen on the notebook in front of me, doing my best to remain calm and casual. Reagan leans over to unzip her backpack and her collar shifts, revealing a fresh hickey on her neck.

I raise an eyebrow.

Maybe she didn't miss me this weekend as much as she claims.

That line of thought vanishes when Gwendolyn walks in and all my attention is focused on pretending like I'm looking at anything —*anyone* but her.

There's no doubt she's under my skin and for the first time in my life, I feel completely and totally out of control.

The crazy thing is that I kind of like it.

∿

FOURTH PERIOD. Library. I spot Gwendolyn across the room with her headphones on, as usual, blocking out the world.

I'm supposed to be researching for a history paper on the Battle of Gettysburg. Instead I pull up the Preston Prep instant messaging system.

H: Hey.

G: Hi?

H: So listen… can we meet?

G: For what?

H: You know what.

G: You're seriously IM'ing me about this.

H: I don't have your phone number or I'd text.

G: No, you wouldn't.

H: Sure I would, why not?

G: Because your friends would find out. Or your girlfriend.

Ouch.

H: Anyway, let's meet.

G: I have tutoring today, then swim, then I'm busy.

H: You're getting tutored?

G: I *am* the tutor, asshole.

H: Of course, more good deeds to add to your karmic martyr list.

G: Shut up. I'm signing off.

H: WAIT!

G: What?

H: I have the music room reserved from 3-4.

I wait, having put it out there. A time and a place. Private. Secluded. All manner of things could go down in there.

After a minute of no response, my hands start to itch and *shit, shit, shit,* what if I pushed too hard and fucked this up for good?

My finger hovers over the icon to go offline, to lick my wounds and pretend this never happened.

Ding!

G: We'll see.

It's not a yes, but it's not a no. I sign off and gather my things, leaving the library to get some air. No girl has ever given me a maybe before.

Why does that make her even more impossibly hot?

THE MUSIC HALL is a safe space. None of the Devils play an instrument. They're all focused on sports and girls. Not that I'm not focused on those things, too, but the best colleges like a little culture added to the mix. Plenty of kids with high GPAs are either athletic or creatively gifted, but few check all three boxes. Playing an instrument was my mother's idea. She had grand ideas of me performing on the piano for her friends at junior league functions, so naturally, I chose a string instrument. I'm already my father's show dog, there's no way in hell I'm being hers, too.

I don't mind playing, though. It's kind of chill, despite being another way of challenging myself. Not everyone can do it. It's just one more step toward being elite—part of a small few with specific skills.

The rooms are private, padded and soundproofed not to bother the rest of the musicians. There's a small desk and a couple of chairs, but not much else. I open up my case and remove my cello. I sit, positioning the instrument between my legs, and place my music on the stand. I pick up my bow and test the strings, making sure it's in tune. It's probably some great tragedy that I find playing music more centering than swimming. There's no competition here—not even against myself. It's all about creating sound, following the notes, letting it sweep me away. But swimming has totally ass-fucked my shoulder, which means that I can only stand to play for an hour, at most.

Today, it's not so easy to settle into the song. I'm frustrated when I miss the first few notes, distracted as I have been for days, by the thought of Gwendolyn Adams. What if she doesn't show? What if I made a fool of myself? Seriously, I can't remember the last time I even asked a girl to meet me.

Not that this is a date.

It's definitely not a date. Hook-ups come naturally. I could snap my fingers and Reagan would be there. Everything about this situation with Gwendolyn is confusing. Infuriating. Goddamn frustrating.

My bow drops, producing a loud, earsplitting screech.

"Goddamnit."

"Wow, I expected better of you, Master Bates."

I whip my head around and see Gwendolyn standing in the doorway, bag hanging casually from her shoulder. She enters and closes the door behind her quickly, pulling down the shade. That move alone clears up any question I had about her wanting to be seen with me.

I run my hand down the neck of my cello. "I guess I don't play well when I'm agitated."

She leans against the desk, skirt rising slightly up her thigh. "What's got you so bothered?"

"Well," I carefully place the cello in its stand, "there's this girl. My nemesis, really. I asked her to meet me and she was pretty non-committal."

Her eyebrows lift. "That must have been catastrophic for your ego."

"Don't worry, it takes a lot more than that to bruise my ego." She's so sexy like this—bantering and smart, without all the righteous artifice. It makes my pulse quicken and my dick hard. "But surprise, surprise, she showed up after all."

"Yeah." She frowns, gaze falling to her shoes. "She must be a real moron, right?"

The room is small. We're close together, while at a distance. It'd be so easy to flip her over and bend her over the desk, bury myself in her, but it's clear that she's skittish today—enough that I know I could blow this completely if I'm not careful. I'll have to treat this delicately. What I've learned over the last few days is that I need Gwendolyn Adams, in a way I never could have anticipated.

"Tell me something," she says suddenly, eyebrows furrowed as she studies me, "did you really mean it?"

I search my mind, half convinced I missed some important part of the conversation while I was fantasizing about banging her against that desk. "Did I mean what?"

"What you said to me the other night, before we..." She flushes, looking away. "You know."

I've said a lot of shit to a lot of girls to get in their pants. It's not something I'm proud of, but it's just the way the game is played. Gwendolyn, in particular, is quite effective in making my brain melt.

I squint at her. "Yeah, I'm going to need a little bit more to go on."

She exhales and looks up at the ceiling, as if asking some higher power for the strength. "You said something about me being stronger than other girls. Did you mean that?"

'You can handle all my bullshit— and if you can handle that, you can handle anything.'

The words echo in my head, the memory crystal clear. She'd been under me, her body hot but soft. *My* body hard and thrumming. And I just remember thinking 'nothing about this feels wrong'.

"Yeah, I meant it," I reply, clasping my hands between my knees with a shrug. "It's true."

She studies my face, as if looking to find the truth in my response. I'm not sure what she finds. "What about Reagan?"

I know what she's asking. What I'm doing with Gwen... it makes me a cheater. A liar. Do I tell her that I haven't slept with her? That I spend more time avoiding her than anything else? Would that make it any better, make me any less of a dick?

Probably not.

"Look, here's the truth." I run my hand through my hair and admit, "Reagan is a nice, sweet, compliant little sheep who doesn't interest me one fucking bit. Our relationship is purely superficial, but it's also socially acceptable. She's too easy for me. She's predictable. She's not like—" I stop, but it doesn't matter.

"Like me?" she snorts and rolls her eyes.

"She's nothing like you. You're a pain in my ass. You drive me crazy. All you ever do is argue with me. And as much as I hate it—"

"You like it."

God, I really, *really* do.

I love the way it feels, the trouble and the electricity. It's not like it was with Campbell. With her, it was *drama*. With Gwen, it's a *struggle*. I can't just have Gwen. I have to fight tooth and fucking nail for it. It makes my balls ache and my heart pound. Gwendolyn Adams is a need more than a want. And I have no fucking idea what to do with that except try to pound her out of my system.

I'm not so sure she'd be keen about that.

Except, she's here. And we're talking about it. And everything's turned upside down.

"One last thing," she says, arms crossed over those perfect tits.

I nod, curious enough.

"What about the test?"

"Test?" I can't ever follow her train of thought. See? *Struggle*.

"You know, the test." She quirks an eyebrow at me, her eyes darting down to my crotch. "The blow job test."

Ah, right. The infamous test. The test Campbell made up sophomore year to make herself look bad ass. The test that somehow evolved into a weird, unspoken rule for any girl who wanted to date me. The entire charade propelled us in popularity and power, and yeah, I got a few blow jobs out of it, for sure. As far as sexual rumors went, I'm pretty sure I hit the jackpot on that one.

All this talk of getting my dick sucked makes it a physical battle not to study her mouth too hard.

"You auditioning for my girlfriend, now?"

She laughs, loud and honking. "Yeah, right, Bates. As if being your shady, illicit hook-up isn't bad enough."

Her blunt honesty hurts more than expected, like a sharp stab to the middle of my chest. It's not something I feel often, and I don't particularly like it. She pushes off the desk and heads toward the door, making it clear that any hopes of a hookup right now are wildly misplaced. It isn't going to happen. Maybe ever.

She takes a quick look down the hall, making sure no one sees her leaving, and then vanishes down the hall, plaid skirt swishing behind her. I fall back in my chair, heart thrumming, body on edge, one thought flitting through my mind.

Maybe this girl can bruise my ego, after all.

17

Gwendolyn

"Gwen! We brought you something!" Michaela rushes from the car, coffee cup clutched in both hands.

"Careful!" Debbie calls, eyeing Michaela's trot worriedly. I quickly rescue the drink from my sister's hands.

"Thank you!" I say to both Michaela and Debbie, the latter obviously having been the one responsible for the coffee. Debbie honks her horn in reply and drives off.

"You look better today," Micha says, squinting up at me from where he's kneeled, adjusting one of his pink shoelaces.

I frown. "What's that supposed to mean?"

"You looked tired on Monday," Michaela explains. She gives Micha an impatient look, huffing when he finally falls into step with us. "That's why we brought you the mocha. Sugar and caffeine. It's your favorite right?"

"It is." I take a demonstrative sip. It's delicious, perfect for a cold morning. Thanksgiving is only two weeks away, so the air is growing crisper, and the ancient trees around the campus are dressed up in vivid yellows and deep oranges.

"Good," she says in relief, smile widening. "Because that's what I told that boy the other day when he asked."

I come to a stumbling halt, head whipping toward her. "Wait, what? What boy?"

"The cute one—"

"He's not cute," Micha says, giving his sister a wise look, "he's *hot*."

Michaela doesn't bother disagreeing. She adds, "Anyway, he said he was on the swim team."

"Hamilton?" I take a panicked glance around the courtyard. "You talked to Hamilton?"

"Yeah." She grips her backpack straps with both hands and starts to walk toward the building.

"Whoa, whoa!" I grab her by the arm, pulling her back to me. "Michaela, tell me *exactly* what happened."

The twins share a confused glance before she explains, "We were waiting in the carpool line after school. He just walked up and asked what your favorite coffee was."

I rear back in surprise. "Really?"

"Yep." Michaela nods.

I consider her for a moment, worrying my lip between my teeth. "That's it?"

"That's it." She shrugs, and I fight back a wave of frantic frustration. She asks, "Did he bring you some coffee?"

"Actually, he did." Saturday morning. Before our little meltdown. "Did he say anything else?"

I know Michaela, who is scarily detail-oriented, can do better than this. Where are the specifics? What was he wearing? What was his demeanor? What day was it? Was he already on his way off-campus, suggesting a spontaneous gesture, or was it the day before?

Set the fucking scene, child!

"No, but he was nice. He said he liked my braids." She grins, reaching up to twirl one around her finger. She breathes a giggle. "His eyes are dreamy."

Hell yeah, they are.

"Okay, well, if he talks to you again, let me know, okay?"

Micha's eyebrow raises dramatically—something he's no doubt been practicing in the mirror for the last year. "Are you two hanging out?"

"No!" I reply, a little too abruptly. From the look on his face, my brother isn't buying it. "We're co-captains on swim together. Sometimes we do nice things for each other. It's no big deal."

"Whatever you say, sis," he replies.

The bell tower chimes, cutting the conversation short. I wave and they take off into the middle school. If Michaela is telling the truth—and there's no reason she wouldn't—Hamilton went out of his way to make sure he brought me a coffee I specifically would like. And this was before we had it out at detention. Before he humiliated me in front of his friends. Before we even had sex.

Traffic control devices get less mixed signals than this.

I walk toward the main building, coffee cup warming my hands, and feel my eyes pull magnetically toward where Hamilton stands with his friends. Micha's right. He *is* hot. His hair is gently blowing in the breeze, and he ducks his head down against it, grinning with half his mouth as he talks. His tie is a little loose at his neck, and he's propped up against one of the low retaining walls, hands pushed into his pockets. I look at him and get all these *thoughts*, like his shoulders shifting under his shirt as he shrugs, and how I've had my hands hooked around them while he was thrusting into me. Or how when he reaches up to fidget with his earlobe, remembering that my teeth have been there. Or when he wets his bottom lip with his tongue, I get this striking awareness that it's been buried between my legs.

The conversation we had with one another in the music room was all at once awkward and disorienting. He wanted to hook up—it was written clear as day on his face—but I was such a mess of nerves and self-doubt that we'd talked instead. The whole conversation felt like we were setting clear parameters; this isn't dating and I'm not lining up to be his girlfriend. After what he admitted about his current girlfriend, I'm not sure Hamilton Bates is designed for commitment at all, least of all with me.

Across the quad, I watch him as he laughs at something Xavier says, his face glowing in the early morning sun, and I'm acutely aware when his eyes dart my direction, before flicking away just as quickly. If I blinked, I would have missed it.

No, the coffee gesture wasn't loaded. It was a minor peace offering, nothing more. The unspoken agreement we seemed to have come to yesterday was obvious. We're both in this to fulfill a need—a need that apparently neither of us have been able to quench—and that it doesn't need to be fraught with hatred and resentment to work. It can just... be.

It just can't be anything more.

"I NEED ALL the seniors to come meet by the bleachers," Hamilton announces once practice is over. We're wrapped in towels, muscles and skin hot from swimming, but pebbled with goosebumps from the cool air outside the water. There are twenty seniors, and, after a moment of dawdling, they all huddle obediently around me and Hamilton.

"The first meet is coming up and that means it's time for locker decorating," Hamilton says, while I pass around cards to each swimmer. "Gwendolyn is giving you a list of the swimmers you're responsible for, and I don't want to hear any bitching about who you get."

"Everyone should have about four teammates that you're responsible for. There are a few details about each swimmer, such as favorite color, candy, drink—that kind of thing. We have art supplies and paper in the office for you to use, including a metric fuckload of glitter, and don't be afraid to go the extra mile by adding personal touches."

I'm not quite sure how locker decorating—which should by all accounts be scorned as a lame waste of time by the popular kids—became something that got the entire team excited, but even Heston seems eager, nodding along. Though I shouldn't really be surprised. It's tradition, one that's upheld seriously. This is more than just a silly craft project. It is, in its own way, a competition itself.

I'm just glad they're cooperating.

"The administration is leaving the building open tomorrow night for the sole purpose of decorating. Go in, find the locker, and decorate the fucking thing. That's it. No sneaking into classrooms, petty theft, or vandalizing anything." Hamilton's grey eyes sweep the crowd before narrowing at Heston, who holds his hands up innocently. I don't think either of us miss the wicked smirk on his mouth. Last year there were some problems, but Coach was able to smooth it over. I doubt we'd get a third chance. "We'll meet at the main doors at nine sharp, got it?"

As a group, they nod, and break off to begin discussing their ideas. Most head into the office to avail themselves of the supplies to take back to their dorms or home. When we're alone, Hamilton scratches the back of his neck and turns to me, eyes averted.

"So," he asks quietly. "Want to knock this out together?"

I eye him warily. We have eighteen lockers to decorate between the two of us and something tells me that, much like manual labor, creative arts probably aren't part of Hamilton's wheelhouse. There's also a part of me that suspects he's using this as a way to get me alone so we can do more hot, sweaty things. It's not even that I don't want to. It's just that I'm still unsure what to make of it all, and it doesn't seem like a good idea.

"*If* I agree to come, I'm not doing all the work," I tell him, avoiding his gaze when I carefully add, "And that's all we'd be doing. Working."

"Fine. You can come by my suite, if you want." I give him a warning look and he rolls his eyes. "Jesus Christ, we'll leave the door open, okay? It's not about that, I just have a lot of space there. We can spread out, have plenty of room to work with."

I nod toward the group of Devils walking into the locker room. "Won't certain people have something to say about that?" He and I both know that just waltzing up to his suite will be making a particular kind of public statement.

But Hamilton just shrugs. "This is the kind of thing Coach wants us to do, right? The dean, too. We're supposed to be putting aside our differences for the sake of good leadership or whatever. So, I have no problem with it getting around. It's the kind of thing that gets them off our back." He meets my gaze, the curve of his mouth spreading into an impish grin. "It'll also get back to my dad, which will make him absolutely fucking furious." He cocks an eyebrow. "You game?"

While he waits for me to decide, he pulls on a shirt, covering his ridiculous upper body. I don't miss his wince, nor the way his body goes rigid for a split second while working his shoulder.

"That's getting worse."

"Nah." He shakes his head, and I think if I listen closely enough, I can hear the undercurrent of the pain he's clearly trying to hide. "Just tight. It's not an issue."

I dither for a moment, and I don't even know. It's like I have this sudden impulse to sit him down on the bench and give him a massage or something, which is preposterous. Hamilton's a fantastic swimmer, and I don't know what his plans for the future are—maybe it's all riding on his athletics, though I doubt it—but I do know that nothing good can come from ignoring an injury like this.

I tell myself firmly that it's not my problem to fix. If he wanted help, he'd ask for it like a big boy.

Which is why I can't ignore it when he does—such as help with decorating lockers.

The truth is that for all my bravado, I'm not sure I want to put myself in a situation where I'm alone with Hamilton in his dorm room. Far riskier situations haven't stopped us.

But he's right. It would make the coach happy, and upsetting his father is a really tempting flavor to ice that cake with.

I take a breath and turn to him, holding his slate-gray gaze. "I'm game."

I STAND OUTSIDE of Cresswell long enough to draw stares. I have a box of art supplies wedged under my arm, and I'm wondering if maybe I've finally lost my mind. Agreeing to come here was foolish, like walking into a set trap. When we're alone, I know Hamilton can be civil. I've seen it. But in front of his dormmates? I just can't see it happening. It'll probably be just like the other day at detention. For all his talk about putting aside our differences for the sake of leadership, I've yet to see proof that Hamilton has it in him.

No. This feels exactly like walking into enemy territory.

What would Skylar think?

I'm overwhelmed by a sudden moment of clarity that I can't do it. For some reason, going into the Devil's lair feels even worse than what we've already done. The making out, the sex, had all been hormonally instigated impulse. This is something else. *This* is willing fraternization.

I turn on my heel and crash into someone before I can even take a step.

"Oh, shit, are you—*Gwen*?" Xavier looks down at me with wide eyes.

"Sorry," I mumble, taking a wide step back. "I was just—"

Understanding seems to dawn over his face. "You need the code?"

Dammit.

My face twists up into a grimace. If I leave now, he'll know that I chickened out. "Yeah, I guess so." He steps past me and punches it in. I exhale, shoulders dropping in defeat. "While you're at it, can you point me to Bates' room? We have this swim team thing to do."

Xavier looks at me over his shoulder and doesn't seem surprised at all. "Sure, it's on the fourth floor. Here," he takes the box from me easily, "you can just follow me."

The hairs on the back of my neck stand on end, every nerve going suddenly on high alert. Why is Xavier being nice to me? Once again, suspicions of a setup tickle my spidey-senses. I have no idea what I'm walking into.

On the second-floor landing, two underclassmen pass us. One gives me a long, curious look, even slowing to watch me. He looks nervous. My fight or flight instincts take over.

There's no way I can fight off a guy like Xavier.

I stop, voice shaking when I start, "You know what? I think I forgot—"

Xavier turns to me. "Hey, can I ask you something?" He lowers the box so it's resting against his hip. And the thing is, he doesn't look angry, or aggressive, or even like he just doesn't like me. He looks perfectly casual.

"Um..." I glance around nervously. "I guess so?"

"I know we're not supposed to talk about this." He takes a furtive glance over his shoulder, but we're alone now. "But I was wondering how Skylar is doing. Like, for real."

I stare blankly at him. In the seven months since the party, no one at Preston has mentioned Skylar to me. It's against the rules, for one, but mostly I've just assumed that no one actually cares.

But of all people with the nerve to ask...

Xavier frowns at my silence, at my blank stare, and then nods at the ground. "Yeah, that's fair. I never should have taken her to the party that night. It was stupid and risky. I knew the guys wouldn't want her to be there, but I just thought..." He trails off for a moment, eyebrows pushed together. "I guess I just thought if they spent some time with her like I had, they might come around, you know? See that she was cool and nice and smart and... you know, *Sky*. And then we had that stupid fight." He shifts closer, his voice dropping into a fervent, shaky whisper. "I had no idea what was going on that night, Gwen. I really didn't, I'll swear on my own life. I really did like her. I mean..." he gives me a sad smile, "not that I ever stopped liking her. And it's just that I never got a chance to say goodbye, or that I was sorry."

Wow.

He shifts the box to his other hip, sighing. "Just... if you talk to her, could you let her know that?"

I nod silently, at a complete loss for words while I try to reconcile this guy with the one I've spent seven months hating. Because there's no way—there's *no way*—that was an act.

Without me needing to tell him, he seems to sense that I'm not going to talk about her. He nods once more, as if accepting that the conversation is over, and continues up the steps. When we reach the top, he says, "Bates' room is down here. It's the biggest one, of course."

He quiets as we pass the lounge, where a few guys glance my way. Whatever moment Xavier and I shared on the stairs has left me unprepared for the discomfort of Ansel and Emory's lingering gazes. They don't look hostile, but they don't look friendly, either. My skin feels prickly and hot and I can't stop my shoulders from curling protectively inward. As we approach the—as promised—*open* door, I take a deep breath and give Xavier's sleeve a small tug.

I wait for him to meet my gaze before quietly offering, "She's doing... better. Healing."

He smiles at me, but his eyes are sad. "Good. Thank you."

With his foot he "knocks" on the door and calls, "Yo, Bates! Gwen's here."

Hamilton emerges from a separate room and I roll my eyes, because seriously, how does he have more than one room? I'm assuming it's a bedroom, because the one we're in now is clearly is a living room, with its couch and recliner. A flat screen hangs on the wall. A small kitchenette is even attached. It's ridiculous, but it's clear he has no idea how much so as he strolls over barefoot. He's wearing obscenely loose sweatpants and a Preston Prep Swim hoodie.

His gaze darts between me and Xavier, eyes narrowing at whatever he finds there.

Xavier ignores this and dumps the box unceremoniously into his arms. He says, "Good luck! And remember, attempted murder charges don't look good on college applications." He throws us two thumbs-ups and leaves.

Hamilton's eyes slide to me. "Did he say something to you?"

"No." I fight the urge to hug my middle, still feeling spooked. "Why?"

He drops the box. "Your cheeks are red, and you've got that line on your forehead that you only get when you're freaking out or something."

"Probably has something to do with me walking in here," I tick off on my fingers, "alone, with a room full of guys, who have never been anything but vocal about despising me, who blame me for their disciplinary problems, and are all bigger than me."

"*Bigger* than you?" Hamilton's expression grows more and more incredulous. "What the fuck did you think we were going to do, attack you or something? Jesus fucking Christ!"

"Excuse me for having a basic sense of self-preservation." I throw my hands in the air, frustrated. "At least Xavier was nice enough to walk up with me."

His jaw clenches. "I didn't think you needed an escort. Especially *me* as an escort. If anything would start the rumor mill, it'd be me walking a girl—*any* girl—up to my room."

"The fact you think that's normal tells me more about you than anything else, Bates."

He shrugs, blank-faced, as though being a basic asshole is perfectly fine. For him, I guess it is. I'm not saying he doesn't deal with any expectations in his life. Obviously, his father has plenty. But none are for standard manners or consideration of other people. No wonder he's such a jerk.

Yet, as I'm unpacking the art supplies, he walks over to the little kitchenette and returns with a bag from the local market. He dumps it on the table. Inside, there is candy, protein bars, crackers, and a variety of other snacks.

"What's all that?"

Those long fingers reach into the pocket of his hoodie and pluck out the cards I handed out earlier that day. "Since you don't have a car, I went to the store and grabbed the stuff we needed."

"Oh. Well... good," I say, refusing to thank him for doing what needed to be done. "I should have everything else."

He peers into the box. "Yeah, I'm going to have to establish one rule now: no glitter."

No glitter.

"Okay, first of all?" I hold up a finger. "How dare you."

"It's a fucking nightmare, Adams. I don't want to have to clean that shit up for the rest of the year."

I chuckle under my breath, but it transforms into a peal of mocking laughter.

He blinks at me. "What?"

"Like you clean."

His eyes flash, and just like that, I feel the tell-tale tingle of a spark igniting in the pit of my stomach. This is what gets us into trouble. The bickering and challenges and little prickly jabs. It escalates into something bigger, snowballs, evolves into something frantic and desperate.

I take a deep breath and say, "Fine, no glitter. But I'm using as many paint pens as I want."

His eyes narrow, but he takes the compromise, fully aware that keeping the peace also means keeping our clothes on.

I think.

THE NEXT NIGHT, all twenty of us meet at the main hall, everyone weighed down with supplies for decorating the lockers.

"I'm serious about not making a mess, sneaking into classrooms, or any other bullshit, got it?" Hamilton says.

"Loud and clear, Master Bates." Heston gives a dramatic salute. His brilliant blue eyes pass between me and Hamilton when he adds, "That goes for ya'll, too, right?"

I freeze, eyes darting to Hamilton.

"What does that mean?" Hamilton asks, coolly.

"You're the two delinquents around here. Are we sure we can trust you not to get in more trouble? Maybe you like all that Saturday detention."

"Fuck off," Hamilton mutters, before adding to the rest of the group, "we get an hour, don't waste it."

I don't speak—don't even breathe—before Heston and the others have turned the corner toward the underclassmen hallways.

"What was that about?" I ask in a rush. "Do you think he—"

"No." He runs his hand through his hair, sighing. "He's full of shit. He just loves getting a rise out of me, he does this shit all the time."

"Oh." I let myself relax, falling into step beside him. "So, there's dissension among the Devil's ranks, huh?"

He stops in front of our first locker and sets the box on the floor. I grab the poster we made, woefully sans glitter, while he fishes out the tape. "Heston wants it both ways. He wants to be in charge yet have no accountability."

"And you're accountable?" I scoff. "In what way?"

He pulls off a piece of tape, dragging it across the sharp edge to cut it, then hands it to me, eyes pensive. "It's complicated."

"I sincerely doubt it is, but okay."

He leans against the bank of lockers and pulls off another piece of tape, waiting for me to need it. "I know you think the Devils run wild, but trust me. Things could be a hell of a lot worse. There's plenty of shit I put a stop to."

I attach the poster, jaw clenching. "Like not letting Xavier date my sister?"

"I *did* let him date your sister." He looks away, something cold and dark passing over his face. "Look what happened."

I'm instantly taken by a tide of white-hot anger. He's so blasé about it. At least Xavier had the guts to apologize, to man up and admit his faults in it. That's more than I ever expected from any Devil. But Hamilton? It's like he just doesn't get it. He doesn't understand that his actions have consequences, and that people outside his little circle of hell are worthy, too.

We both sense that this isn't the time to go into it, so we move on to the next names on our lists. Regardless, the tension ebbing between us is a thick, palpable thing, and not the kind of strain we've grown used to lately. This one is filled with a much darker bitterness and the awareness that neither will budge.

The hour ticks by, silent save for the sounds of tape and paper, the crinkle of wrappers, our footsteps in the empty hall, the clanks of lockers opening and closing.

When we get to the last locker, he hands me a candy bar to tie to the handle. Our fingers graze each other's, and he suddenly says, "I'm the one that told them to cancel you." His voice is even—matter-of-fact. "It was a punishment for squealing about the Devils being at that party."

"No shit," I mutter, trying to fight down a hot prickle behind my eyelids. "Tell me something I don't know." The admission isn't a surprise, but it still hurts to hear, and my hands shake as I struggle to secure the candy bar with ribbon.

He takes it from me, our fingers brushing once again. Facing the locker, he loops the string through the small hole of the handle.

While he works, he says, "What you don't know is that being canceled was a mercy. What some of the guys wanted to do..." His eyes flick over to me and I see dark rage in the steel gray. "Wiping you from the collective consciousness of the student body was the only way to keep you safe, Gwendolyn, and I used every bit of leverage I had to enforce it."

He secures the candy and picks up the empty box, holding it like a shield between us. His expression is wary.

It should be.

"I'm sorry." I laugh meanly. "Are you trying to be the *hero* in all this? Like what you did to me for the last seven months was some kind of fucking favor?"

"No," he shouts, voice bouncing off the metal lockers, "I'm not a goddamned hero. I let shit get out of control. I let Xavier's eye wander. I let him have his fun. I had no fucking idea that your sister—" He clamps his mouth shut.

My voice is pitched dangerously, violently low when I ask, "My sister *what*?"

He works his mouth silently for a moment, as if carefully choosing his words. "I had no idea that she had so many problems. You're sisters, okay? I thought she was tough, like you. I thought she could handle herself. I had no clue shit would go wrong, and I'm not a hero." His smile is sharp and bitter. "I'm a fucking idiot for letting it happen. You think I don't remember the way you looked at me that night, in the hallway? You think it makes me happy that you're scared for your own fucking safety just being around us now? That you thought I somehow orchestrated the whole thing, because you actually think that low of me?" He flings his arms out, letting them fall limply, loudly, against his thighs. "And the thing is, you're right to. I can't even blame you. Because even if I didn't set it up, it was still on me."

He turns and walks off, shoulders curved dejectedly.

I stare at the locker in something akin to shock. I've seen him naked, I've even seen him in the throes of an orgasm, but *that*. That was Hamilton Bates, stripped bare. And fuck.

Fuck him.

Fuck Hamilton *fucking* Bates.

I kick the nearest locker, taking a moment to rearrange the shape of the universe in my head. It's not a neat and tidy thing, not like having Hamilton to blame for what happened to Sky. But that's the way it always is, isn't it? Messy and complicated and completely maddening.

I turn and follow him, walking at first, and then breaking into a sprint to run him down.

When I do, darting in front of him, he stumbles back, looking down at me with dark, stormy eyes.

"Skylar does have problems," I begin quietly, putting a hand on the box he's holding between us as a gesture. *Stay, listen.* "And what happened that night proved they were worse than I knew—than *any* of us knew. And if you want to beat yourself up for treating us like dirt all these years, then trust me, I'll find you a bat myself. But if what you're saying is true—if you really didn't have anything to do with that—then you can't take the blame for her being there." I inhale, chest shuddering. "I'm the one who could have stopped her. I never should have let her go."

He stares at me, hard, eyes boring into me, searching. And then he bursts into a long, wheezing laughter. He laughs so hard he nearly doubles over, back convulsing with it.

I gape at him. "Are you *laughing* at me?"

He rears up, snorting. "Adams, you've been blaming this shit on me for seven months. I finally take a little responsibility and you want to take the blame yourself? You are the most fucking self-righteous martyr I've ever met." He drops the box and it lands with a thud, the remaining supplies clanking together. He steps over it and approaches me. "What do you want me to do? Fight you for who should take the most blame?"

"No." My heart hammers, because I know that look in his eye. It's evil. Twisted. Aroused. I feel it in my belly.

He swipes a thumb over the corner of his lips, eyes scanning me. "What do you want then?" He looms over me, my back pressed up against the lockers, and his searching eyes lock right on my mouth.

All I have to do is ask for it.

I take a shallow breath. "I want—"

"Bates!" Heston's voice carries down the hall. "Where you at, fucker? We're all finished, and nobody drew dicks on the girls' toilet stalls." After a suspended moment of Hamilton and I staring at one another, Heston cautiously adds, "But if they had, the artistic rendition would have been impeccable."

"Yeah," Hamilton says, tongue flicking out to lick his bottom lip. "We're finished, too."

He bends and picks up the box, not giving me another look. They turn the corner and walk down the darkened hall. I follow behind, far enough that they can't see me, but not too far that I can't hear Heston ask, "What the hell was that all about?"

"Nothing. You know how she is. That goddamned mouth never stops flapping."

"That's what you get for talking to her like she's real people."

"Wilcox, I swear to God."

Heston shrugs. "I've said it before, I'll say it again. That bitch needs a good hard fuck. Something to knock her down a few pegs, put her in her place. I would've taken a shot at her by now if it weren't for—"

I don't get to hear what comes out of his mouth next, because all I hear is the crack of Hamilton's fist crashing into Heston's jaw. The snap is loud, jarring in the dark silence of the hallways.

Heston lets out a pained squawk, and then, "Motherfucker! Are you kidding me?"

Hamilton doesn't answer, he just keeps walking, leaving Heston leaning against the wall, holding his jaw. He spits on the floor—*gross* —before ducking into the bathroom. I use the opportunity to run down the hall and burst from the doors of the school. My feet stumble on the steps and I fall, except I don't. Strong arms catch me before I hit the ground. I barely have time to regain my balance before he drags me off the sidewalk and under one of the massive living oaks.

"Did you hear that?" he asks, hand flexing around my shoulder.

"Yes." I swallow. "Thank you."

"For what?" I can see the outline of his features in the moonlight, his eyebrows pulled together. "Punching Heston? I'd do it every day if I could."

"For... defending me," I say, "and for looking out for me, even if I didn't know or understand it."

"It wasn't just for you." He sounds stilted, uncomfortable. "If they came after you and something happened... we'd all pay the price."

I press my back into the tree, sliding my hands around his waist. The move makes him look down at me, gaze meeting my own. I concede, "You were right. Being a Devil, being an Adams—it's complicated."

He laughs darkly, running his hands down my back until they rest just above my waist. "The less questions, probably the better, don't you think?"

Making a point, he cuts my reply off with a soft and coaxing kiss. I return it, despite my fears and reservations, my fingers slipping to the nape of his neck, pulling at the fringe of hair there. His movements are restrained, gentler than usual, like he understands that this is a delicate, fragile thing, like he's afraid of scaring me off. If only he could hear the crazy percussion of my heart or feel the ball of tension in my belly, he wouldn't play it so safe.

Who knew his soft kisses were as tempting as the harder ones?

He breaks away, moving his lips to my neck. His hot tongue flicks out to taste me, and I release a gasp as his fingers toy at the hem of my shirt. I squirm when he touches a ticklish spot, and he does it again, grinning mischievously against my collarbone. He surges into me, pressing into the bark hard enough that I feel his desire, hard and excited against my hip.

I feel myself slipping, flooded with the sudden awareness that I'm thoroughly unopposed to having sex right here, against this tree. To having sex with Hamilton Bates, at all, anywhere. I don't care.

Wait, no, I *do* care.

I want this. I want him.

His hands wander lower, to the swell of my backside and further, just below, to the backs of my thighs. He hooks his palms around them and lifts me up. It's pure instinct to wrap my legs around his hip. I feel his erection against my core and throw my head back against the scratchy tree trunk, exhaling a keening moan.

It's the creak of the thick, wooden door from the main building that halts us—an anomaly in the quiet night. Hamilton freezes, his mouth inches from mine. We look into one another's eyes as footsteps carry down the steps and onto the sidewalk a few feet away. I hold my breath, which only seems to make my heart pound harder. Hamilton fingers gouge into me with the strength of his death grip.

Sure, we both may want this, but having someone else find out—having Heston find out?

Not a chance.

Time passes—seconds, maybe minutes—and Hamilton tilts his head to peer around the trunk of the tree. He exhales and says, "He's gone."

"That was close," I reply, and he nods, releasing me gently until my feet touch the ground. "Probably a good thing—"

"No."

I bite my lip. "No?"

"Well, you're right. It probably was a good thing." The pang of hurt I feel doesn't even make any sense. He's just agreeing with me. Except he's not done. "We shouldn't do this here," he explains, tucking a piece of hair behind my ear. He trails his fingers down my jaw, hooks one beneath my chin, and tilts my face to his. "I don't want to screw you against a tree, Adams. I want you in a bed where I can take my time and there's no risk of interruption."

"Oh." Heat rushes through me and I try to comprehend what he's saying.

"I mean," he smiles devilishly, "I *will* take you right here if that's the only option, but—"

"We'll figure it out," I reply, voice a little shaky, but still sure. "But I think we should go. Neither of us can miss curfew."

He seems in agreement, although his jaw is clenched so tight, I'm not sure what he's really thinking. But then he reaches for me, pulling me against the solid breadth of him, and presses another one of those slow, tender kisses into my mouth. His tongue sweeps against mine, hot and hungry, but before it can get too far, he releases me with a shudder.

He commands, "Go."

I do as he says, opting not to fight with him for once, and head across the quiet campus, back to my dorm. At the door, I stop to enter the code, sparing a paranoid glance over my shoulder. That's when I see him, barely visible under the shadow of the trees, watching and waiting for me until I get inside.

18

THE NEXT FEW days begin something new—strange and exciting.

For years, I've been in the spotlight. A golden boy who everyone looks up to, the kid they want to be. I didn't come into my popularity honestly, I was just bestowed it, simply by being a Bates. It's in my genes, my blood, and my name. Stepping into the role of leading the Devils was natural. Excelling in sports, academics, was always a given. Things came easily to me.

Gwendolyn Adams isn't easy, which is exactly why I can't get enough of her.

Sending her away that night below the tree was a feat of strength —an amount of sheer willpower that I had no idea I possessed. I'd wanted her so desperately that it was borderline masochism the way I kept pulling back. I've jerked off ten times since then using the memory of her pressed up against that tree. The way she felt, warm and frantic up against me, the scent of her, the sounds she made. What I'd said to her was the truth. I wanted more than a quick bang in the shadows of the quad. I wanted to take my time, do it right, take and have everything, and that required self-control.

At first, we ignore one another like usual. We slide into our assigned seats without meeting each other's gaze. We avoid one another in the hall. I continue hanging out with my friends, keeping Reagan at bay. My interest in her has dropped to zero, maybe even less. Her touch does nothing for me, and my excuses are growing shorter and increasingly flimsy as the days pass. I just don't care. After having something I actually want, the thought of Raegan is just disappointing. My focus is on something bigger, brighter. Something addictive.

I'm doing my best not to stare at her in the cafeteria, where she sits at her usual table with Tyson, when Campbell walks in and tosses a stack of tickets on the table.

"What's this?" Ansel asks, picking one up. He pulls a face. "A dance performance?"

Campbell shoots daggers at him. "My sister is in it and she has to sell a dozen tickets. My mom bought those, but we have to fill the seats. I need everyone to come," Campbell explains, sitting diagonally from me. "Just show up, clap, and she'll let us have a party at my house. My dad will provide the alcohol and everything."

"Can we use his boat?" Heston asks. His jaw is bruised and swollen. He's been treating me so coldly that we haven't spoken to one another in days. This is just fine by me. As far as I know, no one has asked about the bruise or my red knuckles. Some things are best left unsaid.

"Not if you're drinking," Campbell replies, "but he did install a new hot tub, and that's fair game."

Heston picks up a ticket and tucks it in his jacket pocket. "I'm in."

The others grab their tickets while I'm distracted by Gwendolyn's fingers, lazily scratching just above the hemline of her skirt.

"Ham!"

I jerk my eyes to Campbell. She's holding the last ticket in my face. I take it from her with a long-suffering sigh. "Sure, I'll go."

Her gaze darts over to Gwendolyn and then back to mine. "You know, her little brother is in the program. He's got the leading role. My sister was so pissed about it. She's pretty sure he only got it out of pity."

I give her a bored look. "And you're telling me all of this because..."

She shrugs. "You just seem so focused on her lately, I thought you may want to know."

Every stare at the table lifts to me. Everyone but Reagan, who is fastidiously interested in her salad. Heston watches me more closely than any of them, the muscles of his bruised jaw hard and tense. "I'm not interested in her. Between swim and detention, she's making my life miserable."

I suspect most of them don't buy it—Heston and Campbell, especially—but at this point, what can I do?

The gods seem to be on my side, because the cafeteria is filled with the sudden shriek of the fire alarm. A collective groan rumbles down the table.

Xavier mutters, "Fucking stoners in the bathroom again. Why can't they smoke up behind the dumpsters like a civilized person?"

He's probably right. This happens once a quarter and is almost always traced back to someone hotboxing in the third-floor boys' room. It makes it pretty hard to take any alarm seriously, except...

Dean Dewey stands at the front of the room, announcing in a strained, but artificially calm voice, "I need everyone to follow directions. Please proceed to the nearest exit, this is not a drill."

"Definitely the stoners," Ansel sighs. Emory's already standing, eyes skimming the room. No doubt he's looking for his sister. The instant he locates her across the room, he's bolted from the table, taking off to make sure she's okay.

I glance at Campbell and she shrugs. "You know how protective he is."

"Overprotective," I add. Sometimes I wonder if it's less about the injury she sustained in the accident and more about keeping his increasingly hot sister away from the degenerates at the school.

Whichever, I use the distraction to break away from the others by just hanging back. They're almost instantly swallowed by the crowd, giving me a much-needed reprieve. We're squeezed into a narrow line as we exit the cafeteria, bodies bumping into one another. Some idiot sophomore wearing a gallon of Axe elbows me in the side, and then cringes away at the heat of my glare. With the cloud of bad body spray, it takes me a moment to catch the scent of smoke—something woodsy and plastic-bitter. Definitely not weed.

That's when I see the top of Gwendolyn's head, bobbing along in the crowd. She's far ahead of me, to the west of the room, and I track her with my eyes.

Then, she disappears.

One second, she's there, and the next, she's gone.

I surge forward, pushing past people who mutter curses at me.

"Everyone stay calm," a teacher announces, "head to the nearest exit. Don't panic. Everything is under control; you just need to follow protocol!"

That just makes it worse, and I'm caught in a throng of increasingly nervous students, the air around us growing denser with smoke with every passing second. People start to push. A few girls cry out in panic, and I don't recognize any of them.

Until I do.

I know it's Gwen's cry I hear, something shrill and pained. I can't see her, though. She was there, I know she was. I keep my eyes focused on where I saw her last. She was on the other side of a tide of people, getting pushed down one of the halls. My heart hammers as I work sideways, not caring who I shove aside or run into. They yell at me to move, but I don't, not until I'm there, not until I—

She's crouched on the floor, arms shielding her head, and I have to push someone with an obnoxiously bulging backpack out of the way to reach out and grab her wrist.

Her hand balls into a fist, fighting against me—*always fighting against me*—but I don't let go.

"It's me, it's just me!" I yell over the din. Finally, her blue eyes raise to mine, and my mouth parts in shock.

There's blood.

"He kicked me." She cups a shaking palm over her nose, eyes wide with a wild mixture of fear, anger, and hurt. "I fell and he kicked me in the face."

I tear my eyes away from her bloody face to look around, vision going red. "Who?"

She tugs my arm, using it to pull herself upright. "I don't know, I only saw his shoe."

Our palms flatten, fingers linking, and I pull her with me through the mob, shielding her as we go, and I keep searching for the person responsible, despite having no information to go off of. Whoever it was, he better hope it stays that way.

It seems like it takes forever until we finally spill outside, the glare of the sun seeming too stark and bright. I instantly whirl around to her, tilting her face.

"Jesus Christ," I breathe as I inspect her. The blood has run down her mouth, over her chin. She looks ghoulish. "Does it feel broken?"

She blinks at me owlishly, lifting her free hand to prod at it. "I don't know?"

"It'd feel crunchy," I say impatiently, "like a bag of pebbles."

She prods it again, wincing. "I don't think so. I don't know, it just stings."

I exhale. "Did he get you anywhere else?" I ask, eyes sweeping down her body.

She shakes her head. "I don't even know how I fell. I was fine and then everyone was freaking out."

My heart slowly starts to get back to a normal rate. "It was like you got swallowed."

"Hey," a voice says and we both turn, seeing Tyson appear from the crowd. "I got stuck in there—" His eyes take in several things in quick succession. Her bloody face, our linked hands, the blood on my sleeve from where she grabbed me for leverage.

His jaw locks, eyes growing wide with ferocity. "Oh, I know you fucking didn't." He drops his bag and stalks forward, but Gwen steps between us, dropping my hand like a hot poker.

"No no no," she tells Tyson. "I fell in there and someone kicked me. He just helped me up, pulled me through the crowd."

Tyson looks skeptical at first, eyes darting avidly between us. "If he did something to you—"

I gape at him in disbelief. "Why does everyone think I'm an abusive piece of shit this month?"

Gwen swipes the back of her hand over her mouth. "Ty, seriously.

You know if he'd done this to me, I'd have his balls in my pocket right now. The guy had orange shoes. That's all I know."

Tyson's gaze drops to my shoes.

"They're black!" I lift a foot to prove it.

Tyson ultimately sags, bending to retrieve his bag. He pulls out a travel-size bag of tissues, handing them to Gwen. "Sorry, that was just kind of a fucked-up thing to see after all that. Are you okay?"

"Yes, we've already determined it's probably not broken." Gwen presses a wad of tissues to her nose, eyebrows furrowed. Her voice is firm and sure when she adds, "It wasn't an accident. It was like he literally went out of his way to kick me."

I ask, "Are you sure you didn't notice anything else about him?" as my narrowed eyes take in the scattered crowd. No one's looking our way that I can tell.

She sighs, dropping the hand with the soiled tissue. She looks exhausted, probably from the adrenaline crash. "Just that it was a guy."

I slide my hands into my pocket, at a loss for what to do. I look at Tyson, who seems in the same boat. Except, he can do stuff like this:

"Come on." He cups her by the elbow and leads her toward where the faculty are congregating. "Let's see if we can get a nurse to check that out, yeah?"

She nods, sparing me a glance over her shoulder as they walk away.

Thanks, she mouths.

Tyson gives me a look over his shoulder, too, but his is a mixture of curiosity and suspicion.

Better him than any of the Devils, I think, going the opposite way. What was I thinking, going after her like that? Touching her like that? They're already suspicious enough, and the fallout would be catastrophic. There's no way my father wouldn't find out, especially after what happened to Hollis.

But I do know what I was thinking. I was thinking that whatever the hell is going on with me and Gwendolyn right now, it's simultaneously the most thrilling and terrifying thing that's ever happened to me.

I'm not ready to give it up.

19

"So, what was that between you and Hamilton?"

I flex my hand, because it's like I can still feel his skin against mine. Confused, hurt, angry, and overwhelmed, I didn't know it was Hamilton grabbing for me in the hallway at first; but then I felt the tell-tale tingling that charged between us whenever we touched, and I knew.

Even without him saying it was him, I knew.

I don't know how he knew to come for me. But thank God he did.

Now Tyson stands before me with a million questions. I don't have any answers—at least not any that I want to give.

"Nothing," I reply, sitting on a bench away from the crowd. The nurse has already checked me out and determined that I'd probably have a nice big bruise bloom in the next few days, but for now it's just swollen and sore, otherwise unbroken. "I was on the floor bleeding all over the place, and I guess he saw me. He just helped me get outside."

Tyson's eyebrows climb his forehead. "Dude, he was totally holding your hand."

"Yes." Fact. He was.

"Why?"

"Well, he was leading me through the hall because I was hurt. It was just chaotic—even you got stuck, right?"

He nods. Tyson is a new friend—my *only* friend. He doesn't know everything that has gone on between me and the Devils over the years, but he knows enough. Enough to actually try getting up in Hamilton's face when he thought he'd hurt me. There was no doubt in my mind that Tyson would have thrown down to avenge me. The memory makes me even more fond of my new friend.

"You'd tell me if something was going on, right?" Tyson studies me, frowning. "Because I told you before, I have your back. You don't have to keep secrets from me."

"There's no secret," I assure him, even though I feel bad about lying. That's not a great start to a friendship, but whatever is going on between me and Hamilton right now, it's no one's business but ours. "We're on better terms now with the whole co-captain thing. Honestly, he probably helped me so that he doesn't get stuck with my half of the work."

He barks a laugh. "That, I'd believe."

A fire truck rolls into the parking lot and a flurry of men rush into the building. I'm struck with another memory: Hamilton asking who kicked me, and the look of blind, controlled fury on his face as he searched the hallway for him. Just as baldly as I know Tyson would have pummeled Hamilton for hurting me, Hamilton would have definitely kicked the shit out of that guy.

I would have probably given it a go myself.

"It's just scary," I say, staring pensively into the distance. "That someone would want to hurt me like that." And I am hurt, physically, but also it just hurts in general. "I'm not, like, a bad person. I never bother anyone. I go out of my way to not make a splash here. It's just..." I rub my temples, feeling the beginnings of a killer headache. "It's really messed up."

Tyson squeezes my shoulder. "Maybe it was an accident?"

My mouth twists. "I don't know. Maybe."

Except I do know. It wasn't an accident. And while having

Hamilton and Tyson at the ready to inflict physical violence on my behalf is nice, one thing is clear.

I need to watch my own back.

～

HOURS LATER, it's determined that the fire started in the Home Economics lab. It totally *did* involve the stoners, only instead of smoking in the bathroom, they were baking weed brownies. Apparently, the brownies sat forgotten in the oven for so long that it halfway burned down the kitchen.

The next day, I open my locker and a piece of paper, folded into a star, falls out. Discreetly, I pick it up and unfold it.

I resisted the other day because I was serious. I want to be with you again.

Come up with a place or I will, not sure if I can hold out much longer.

Heat rushes up my neck and I glance around to see if anyone noticed, which is ridiculous, because I'm still a ghost to most of the school. Even sporting a horrifically bruised nose that's covered poorly with concealer, eyes still pass over me. A few kids on the swim team have relaxed around me, and obviously there's Tyson. But as I glance around, I do meet one pair of eyes.

They're steel gray, dark, and filled with intent.

I head to class, feeling the weight of the note in my pocket like a heady thing. Is this really what we're doing? No longer falling prey to spontaneous lust, but planning it? Admittedly, the fact that Hamilton wants me so badly is thrilling in the most disturbing of ways. He makes me feel good—he makes me *feel*—which is something I've been afraid to do lately.

I think long and hard about answering, my teacher droning at the front of the class, while my heart beats erratically. Just before the bell, I pull out a piece of paper and scribble my reply. I walk down the hallway, jammed between the influx of students, and try to stay focused on my destination. I can't help the anxiety building in my chest at the full hallway, memories of what happened the previous day knocking around in my head.

I duck behind a tall freshman, using him as a shield to get close to my target. When I'm finally in the right position, staring at a perfectly pressed pair of pants, and a perfectly sculpted swimmer's ass, I tuck the note in his back pocket and skitter off, blood pounding in my ears, refusing to look back.

Maybe he'll find it. Maybe he won't.

I'll find out tonight.

THE WAY I SEE IT, there's risk for both of us.

For me, there's the humiliation of realizing this is nothing but a well-orchestrated prank. For him, well...

He has to come to Hayden after curfew and find me. He wanted privacy and a bed. I didn't want him in my room.

Room 216 seemed like a good option.

At least, it did, until now.

I pace the dark room as sweat beads up on my lower back. A sick feeling builds in my stomach and I wring my hands worriedly. *What am I doing? Why am I doing this?*

The door opens and shuts, the hallway light casting a glow on Hamilton's handsome profile.

Right. That's why.

I circle behind his tall frame and lock the door. Turning, I ask, "Did anyone—"

"No," he breathes, pulling me to him. Our bodies meet before our mouths do, his tongue sliding over my lower lip, prodding me to open my mouth. He tastes of mint, and he doesn't waste a moment before walking me backwards, across the room, until we're in front of the bed.

I make a pained sound when our noses push together and he jerks back, hands coming up to cup my face.

"Fuck," he breathes, licking his lips. "Forgot about this shit. Let me see. You okay?"

"It's nothing," I insist, but allow him to look his fill. The bruise is a deep mottled blue that extends under my eyes. "It looks worse than it is, really." The fact that we can't risk turning on the overhead light in this room had been a not-insignificant factor in me choosing it. I figure that seeing it in full light isn't conducive to our goal tonight.

His thumbs raise to gently graze my cheekbones, jaw hardening. "You find out who did this, you tell me."

"I don't know who—"

"But *if* you find out," he presses, holding my gaze. "I mean it. Someone's got a kick to the fucking face coming to them."

I roll my eyes. "You don't have to do anything."

"Don't I?" he mutters, thumbs brushing below my eyes. "I knew this would happen. This is exactly why I told everyone to pretend you didn't exist. Some of the people here are fucking animals."

I shrug, at a loss. Is it better to be kicked in the face than to be ignored for months on end? It's a question that I honestly can't answer. "If I find out who it is," I promise, hands coming up to his wrists, "I'll tell you."

Hamilton nods, finally freeing me from the pin of his fierce stare to look at the bed. "It's a double." He then takes a broader look at the room. "Where are we?"

"Guest room. For visitors or prospective students. It's hardly ever used, but it's private, and yeah." I gesture to the bed. "It has a double, so I figured..."

A wicked grin tugs at his lips. "Smart. Two floors away from your own room."

We stand there for a moment, looking at each other, and it doesn't take long for the air between us to start crackling again. Hamilton's tongue peeks out to wet his lips and I unconsciously mimic him, hands landing on his broad chest.

"So." I breathe, bunching the fabric of his shirt and pulling him to me.

"Yeah, just..." He pushes a slow, wet kiss to my mouth, whispering, "Tell me if it hurts."

I nod, deepening the kiss when his deft fingers pluck at the buttons on my shirt, but it doesn't hurt. It keeps not-hurting when he gets my shirt open, fingers grazing over the lace of my bra. I push at his shirt, eager to feel his skin against me. He yanks it off quickly, rewarding me with a shadowy view of his upper body. I reach out and touch the hard, muscular flesh, dragging my fingers down until I tangle them in the soft hair on his lower belly. Hamilton hisses, his belly caving. I can see his cock already pressing at the fabric of his pants. We move to the bed in unison, my shirt falling from my shoulders. He grabs at the flesh of my hip as he presses between my legs, rocking into me with another deep kiss.

There's no pretense as he reaches back, pulling the condom out of his pocket and clutching it in his hand. He rears back to unbutton his pants, his heavy-lidded eyes dragging down my body as he shoves them down his thighs, kicking them away. I climb over his hips and straddle him, bending to kiss him on my terms, deep and consuming. When I pull back, the spark in his eyes tells me that he's surprised but likes it. My control is fleeting, as he pushes his tongue in my mouth, dominating the kiss and leaving me panting. I grind against him, causing us both to exhale in frustrated bliss.

His hands slide up my legs, up to my hips, where he holds me in place. I feel him grow beneath me, nothing but the thin cotton of our underwear as a barrier, my own growing increasingly damp by the second. He struggles for a moment with my bra, this one clasping different.

His mouth stills against mine as he focuses on the task, huffing out a, "Fucking thing," as he tugs.

I can't help but laugh at his frustration. Hamilton Bates, stumped by a bra. He's diligent though, finally conquering it and tossing it on the floor. I can't even stand the way he looks at my breasts. It's the same as last time—hungry, dark-eyed *want*—and the sound he makes when he slides his hands up to cup them in his warm palms is low and vaguely agonized.

He dips his head to clamp his mouth around my breast, tongue lathing over the peaked nipple. I tilt my head back and he toys with my other breast, making lazy circles. The feel of it is indescribable, something bone-deep and vulnerable in the very best way igniting across my skin, in the pit of my core. I can't restrain my responding moan.

The next thing I know, I'm under him, and he's impatiently tugging off my panties, his own shorts following suit.

His body is a wide expanse of pale, lean perfection, and I can see his abs quaking with his need, the staccato of his breaths shaky and shallow as he rubs two rough hands up my flesh. Gone is the gentleness that took my virginity, replaced by this feral, commanding mess of desire. I pant into his mouth, feeling the same as I had that first night—slightly unhinged and strangely powerful.

"Fuck, I've been thinking about this for days, Adams," he grinds out, breath hot against my ear. "I need to be inside you."

"Yeah. *Yes.*" I buck my hips against his, encouraging, impatient, wanting his body to completely cover mine, wanting to feel his weight, his strength.

He kisses me while he rolls on the condom, his two hands crammed into the space between our bodies, breaths loud in the silence of the room.

When he's ready, my fingers thread in the hair on the back of his neck, tugging him forward. It feels like I can't let him get too far away, like even the thought of him stopping makes something sharp and alarmed go off in my head.

His gray eyes hold mine as I wrap my legs around his waist, inviting him closer, urging him on. He takes himself in hand, pressing his cock into my wet folds as he watches me, and if he's waiting for something, then I'm at a loss for what.

"Come on," I pant, fingers scrabbling at his shoulders, body arching. "*Fuck me.*"

He enters me swiftly, filling me with one solid thrust.

I gasp, mouth agape, time standing still as he stretches me from the inside. Our eyes hold, something that feels far more intimate than his body invading my own. I slide my hand to touch his cheek, his lips, and I rock my hips. His eyes snap shut on a groan and he starts moving inside of me, our hips meeting in teasing, assessing thrusts, looking for our shared rhythm.

"Jesus, Adams." He pulls back only to crash back into me, our hips meeting with a soft clap that has me digging crescents into the skin of his back. "Fuck, you feel so good. I shouldn't have—" he bites down on his bottom lip, a wet, rough sound growling in the back of his throat, "—*we* shouldn't have waited."

I pull his face to mine and lean to the side, breathing hot, and biting down on his ear. "Is this all you've got?"

He shudders with delight, breathing a laugh into my neck, and his next thrust—full of his body's skill and power—nearly pushes me up the bed.

"Ah, God," I gasp, scrabbling at his back. "Like that."

"Yeah?" he asks, adjusting his hands on the bed before driving into me hard. His eyes are wild and heavy, and it's not like the last time. I have to hold on, now, tightening my legs around his hips as the force of his plunges pushes me into the bed. I keep alternating between the need to screw my eyes shut and chase that phantom peak of pleasure, and the desire to keep them open, watching him undo me.

The bed creaks, the old springs crying out with their movements. It's loud, too loud, but I don't care. My orgasm is fast approaching, toes curling with every crash of our hips, and he's obviously too enthralled to stop. I don't *want* him to stop. Now, or maybe ever.

Is this what it's like with everyone? I wonder, but the wave that crashes over me answers that. It's powerful enough to rob me of my breath, chest seizing on a gasp as I tighten around him, head digging back into the pillow. Hamilton makes a low, rough sound and doesn't stop, his eyes drinking in every moment—every shudder and gasp— of my orgasm.

When the overwhelming tide of pleasure ebbs, I wrap my tired arms around him, panting as I watch him.

His face scrunches in something akin to pain—maybe even agony—before he buries it into my neck, his hips pounding away like he's chasing first place. I have no idea how long he'll go, how long he'll last, and I don't care. It could be all night. I could do this *all night*.

When his body tenses, and he shudders deep inside of me, the sound he pushes into my sweaty neck is so raw, so achingly *real*, that I'm already desperate to hear it again.

Hamilton collapses on top of me, weight heavy, our heartbeats racing. I run my hand through his damp hair, then use it to tug his head back. Familiar insecurities creep over me.

"Is that what you wanted?" I ask, wetting my dry lips. "Like, better than before?"

"Jesus, Adams," he mumbles breathlessly against my chest. "Yes, that was better. That was..." He rolls his face against my chest, pushing a kiss into the swell of my breast. "That was the best, actually."

Best.

The compliment makes me smile, even though that's ridiculous. He could be lying. Maybe he says that to every girl he sleeps with. But it still makes my heart kick into rapid gear. It makes me want to fuck him all over again. But I don't. I just lie back on the pillow with the weight of him on top of me, his arms wrapped around my body.

After many long moments spent breathing, my fingers playing through his hair, Hamilton sighs. "I'm definitely going to feel that tomorrow." He shifts his shoulder.

I pause before dropping my hand. The skin of his shoulder is warm, soft, and he makes a low groan when I dig my fingers into it. "Is it joint, muscle, or tendon?"

His breath washes warmly over the center of my chest. "Tendon, they think."

I keep massaging. "Does Janet know it's this bad?"

Silence.

I frown. "You should tell her. You could get a cortisone shot, you know. Remember Bradbury, sophomore year? His was bad, but that helped."

"You know what I remember about Bradbury?" Hamilton lifts himself and rolls to my side, my hand slipping from his shoulder. He looks up at the ceiling, expression slack and relaxed. "I remember coach sitting him out for half the season and he didn't make his qualifiers. Barely any of the recruiters saw him swim and his chances at State were shit."

"Well," I roll to my side, watching him. "Bradbury was different. He couldn't even bend his arm for most of that. You can still swim."

"It's a risk, though." He rolls his head to the side, meeting my gaze. "Once I get a few meets under my belt this year, lure in enough recruiters, it'll get better." He says this like something well-practiced. Like a prayer.

I push a laugh into the pillow, chuckling harder at his questioning gaze. "Look at us. Your shoulder, my nose. We're kind of a mess."

His mouth pulls up into a grin. "It was worth it, though."

"It was," I agree, feeling more at ease than I have in a very long time.

"WHOA," Micha says, once he gets out of the car. He's staring right at my nose. "It looks even worse today. Are you using the concealer with the yellow undertones? Because it'll neutralize those reds and blues under your eyes."

"Hey," I say, shooting him a glare. "Don't forget who taught you about concealer in the first place, pal. The student has not surpassed the master."

"Ignore him," my sister says, linking her fingers with mine. "He's an idiot. You look fine."

My sister is sweet, but my brother is a truth-teller. I do look like crap, and it's not even entirely because of my bruised nose. I woke up with a pounding headache, feeling like I'd been run over by a truck. Admittedly, I *had* been run over by a Hamilton Bates-sized truck, but it was more than that.

"Actually, I think I may be getting a cold or something."

Michaela instantly, heartlessly, drops my hand. "You should go to the nurse."

"It's fine," I assure her and refocus on my brother. "How's show prep going?"

"It's okay. We should be ready." The performance takes place the Saturday after Thanksgiving. "It's a lot of work, though."

"You're going to kill it." I give him a fist-bump. "I know you will."

The bell tower chimes, and we split up. Michaela is right, I probably should go to the nurse, but today is not the day to hide out. After last night with Hamilton, I don't want anything to seem out of place.

We'd met up intentionally. We'd had sex without it being sparked by an argument or fight, and that made it different. I didn't want to behave differently—or to give him a reason to think I was behaving differently.

I sigh as I walk to class. *Why is this so complicated?*

Because you're screwing your enemy, Gwen, that's why, and you really, really like it.

I make my way down the hall, stopping as usual at my locker. There's a white paper cup staring at me, waiting on top of my books. I look behind me to see anyone is watching. It's a force of habit and paranoia, but no one is watching as I reach for the cup and feel the warm liquid through the side. I take a sip—it's a mocha—and the drink warms me from the inside out. Well, I think it's the drink. It may be from the realization that Hamilton Bates did something indisputably nice for me.

Laughter bounces off the crowded hall and I glance back in time to see him and his friends heading toward class. Reagan is glued to his side, and Heston's still nursing his bruised jaw. Hamilton's profile shifts slightly, angling toward me, and he winks—a blip—before following his friends into the classroom.

The two of us hate-screwing is one thing.

Hamilton being nice to me? Well, that's something I'm not sure I can handle.

20

LEANING BACK, I position myself in Dr. Ross' class so that I have a direct view of Gwendolyn. We'd parted quietly the night before, both of us sneaking back to our rooms. If I'd had it my way, I would have stayed all night and taken my time to explore her body, to feel myself inside of her once more. I was already halfway hard again by the time I left. After a bit of consideration, the main one being the nightmare that would happen if we were caught, I managed to get my brain to function better than my cock and forced myself to leave. Back in my own room, I had easily the best night's sleep I'd had in a long time. I woke up early, refreshed for once, and called the coffee shop for a delivery, adding a drink for her. Before the rest of the school was moving, I slipped the mocha into her locker. A little post-booty call thank you.

See? I can be a goddamn gentleman, too.

Suck on that, Tyson.

She looked like hell when I saw her in the hall, eyes tired and nose probably a whole bevy of colors beneath whatever she'd caked over it to hide the bruise. But it worries me, because if any of her look is about what happened, that's no fucking good. Not at all. Gwendolyn is scratching an itch I didn't know I had, filling an ever-growing hole. If she has regrets? Second-thoughts? I don't know what the hell I'll do.

That concern is why I watch her now. Regret leads to guilt. Guilt to confession. A confession that will blow up my world. She seems oblivious to my presence, though, ignoring me so thoroughly that it was almost like last night never happened. Is that good? I don't know. Her hand shakes a little when she takes a sip of her coffee and she rubs her eyes, despite the caffeine.

I remain focused as Dr. Ross hands out packets, one landing on my desk.

"Want to partner up?" Reagan asks, interrupting my thoughts. "Dr. Ross said we could."

"What?" I snap, looking at the girl next to me. She's leaning over the aisle, and I must have something bad for Gwen, because there was a time when Reagan's flash of ample cleavage could draw my eyes like a magnet. Now, I barely glance.

She gives me a long, wary glare. "Never mind." She turns to Rachel Eurbick and starts to work. I look around nervously. Did Reagan just turn her back on me? Holy shit, I need to get it together.

I force myself to focus on my work for the remainder of the period, only periodically checking on Gwendolyn. She works alone —no surprise—and just before the class is over, she gets up, turns in her paper to Dr. Ross, and quietly leaves the room.

Shit, shit, shit. I didn't realize we could *do* that.

I quickly fill out the rest of my sheet, not giving a rat's ass about accuracy, and stand to turn it in. If she can leave, so can I, but just as I grab my backpack, the bell rings. The class jolts up, blocking my access to the door. By the time I turn in my work and get into the hallway, she's long gone, and I'm convinced more than ever that I'm screwed.

～

I don't even make it to my table at lunch. As soon as I see Tyson sitting alone, I know something's up.

"Hey," I say, grabbing him by the sleeve after he dumps his tray in the trashcan. "Where's Adams?"

"I don't know." He's still chewing, shoulder lifting in a shrug. "She never showed for lunch."

"Did you text her?"

"Did you?" he snaps back, eyes narrowed. "Why are you looking for her, anyway?"

Okay.

Getting real tired of this guy.

"Because," I say, struggling to keep my cool. "I need to talk to her before practice."

He exhales. "I did text her. No reply. Don't you have some classes with her?"

"First period." I run my hand through my hair and avoid Reagan looking at me from across the crowded room. "She looked... I don't know. Weird. Tired, sort of."

"Look, Bates, I don't know what's going on with you two—"

"Nothing is going on," I reply too quickly.

Tyson rolls his eyes. "Just don't fuck with her, okay? She's a nice girl and you're..." Tyson makes a sweeping gesture.

I pull myself up. "And I'm what?"

He shrugs. "*You*. A Devil. She's tough, but she's not like you. She's not the manipulative type."

"You've known her for like three weeks," I give him a long, sweeping glance. "What makes you the expert on Gwendolyn Adams."

"I'm not saying I'm an expert on girls like Gwen, but guys like you?" He grimaces. "I know plenty of guys like you, and she doesn't need whatever bullshit you're slinging."

Anger licks at the back of my spine and I react spontaneously, grabbing Tyson by the arm and dragging him into the hall. Once we're away from the crowd, he pushes me off with two hands. "What the hell, Bates?"

"I'm not messing with Gwendolyn," I say in a low voice. Little does he know how much that girl messes with me, intentional or not. "It's not like that. I just need to talk to her—that's all. If you see her, let me know, okay? You should have my number from the team list."

He nods and I storm off, still not finished searching for her. This would be a whole lot easier if everyone would stop jumping to conclusions about my intentions. I check the library and the computer lab. The bell rings and everyone files into their classes. I look in the Chem room—her class after lunch. She's not there, either. I skip my own class, exiting the main doors and walking across the campus. It's not like her to disappear like this, and it wouldn't be such a big deal—not normally—but after what happened to her in the hall the other day, I feel more on edge about it than I should. I'm already in the crazy habit of looking at people's shoes, eyes peeled for any flash of orange.

I'm halfway across the quad, headed toward the fine arts building when I see Gwendolyn's little sister.

"Hey," I say, trotting over. "I'm looking for your sister. Any idea where she may be?"

"Hopefully in the infirmary," she says nonchalantly, eyes fixed to her phone. "She looked like crap this morning."

I blink in surprise. "She's sick?"

"Looked like it. She played it off though, you know she loves to be the mar—"

"Martyr," I echo. We both laugh. "Yeah, she does like that." I scratch my neck, looking around. "Okay, well, thanks. I'll see if she made it there."

"Tell her not to come home and give whatever she's got to the rest of us. I don't want to spend my whole Thanksgiving break sick with whatever plague she's carrying."

This little girl is a piece of work.

"I'll pass that along."

She continues toward the fine arts building and I turn and head the other way. I duck in the nurse's office and ask, "Have you seen Gwendolyn Adams?"

"Not today," Mrs. Tolbert replies. "Should she be here?"

I rap a quick rhythm on the desk. "Not sure."

I walk back out before she asks any more questions. There's only one other place to check—her dorm room—which definitely puts me in the position of obsessing over this. If Gwendolyn is in her room, then she's not regret-confessing what we did last night, and she also isn't being maimed by some wayward Devil. But that doesn't stop me. Something else propels me across the campus toward her dormitory, where I punch in the code and enter the empty building. Since everyone's at class, there's no one around to stop or question me as I climb the stairs to the fourth floor. At her room, I tap on the door.

There's no answer.

I try the knob and it twists, door opening easily.

My eyes sweep around the dark room, and at first glance, it appears empty. Then I distinguish the crumpled mass on the far side of the room, beside the bed, like a mountain of blankets on the floor. My heart thuds when I see feet sticking out, still in shoes. I walk over and drop to my knees, bending next to her. It's Gwendolyn, still in her school uniform, including her shoes, flat on her stomach, fast asleep.

God, please let her just be asleep.

I press my fingers against her forehead. She's burning up.

"Hey," I say quietly, trying to rouse her. "Hey, Adams."

She doesn't budge. My heartrate kicks up and I nudge her again, this time touching her warm cheeks. "Gwendolyn, hey, wake up." She exhales and I do, too. "Listen, wake up, you hear me? Gwen..."

She sighs and shifts, eyes barely opening. "Bates?" she mumbles, voice a harsh rasp. "What are you..."

"I think you're sick," I tell her as she pulls her knees up to her chest. "Can you sit up?"

"No. My head is killing me." She keeps her eyes closed. "Just leave me alone, I'll be better in a while."

I shake my head and lean forward, scooping her up into my arms. I carry her to the bed, laying her in the middle. Her legs flail about, seeking the covers, but her shoes keep getting hung up on the blanket.

"Hey," I sit next to her and pull her foot in my lap, unlacing her shoe. "I'm going to call the nurse. Did you take any medicine or anything?"

"No." She cracks an eye for only a split second, immediately cringing down into the bed.

I take off one shoe, then the other. She pushes at her knee socks and I roll them down. "Do you need anything else?" I try to think of what my mother—or let's face it, my nanny—would do in a situation like this. "Ice? A drink?"

There's a long pause where I'm almost sure she's fallen back to sleep. Then she tilts her head. "Can you get my pajamas? This skirt is so itchy."

"Sure," I say, ruffling the back of my hair. "Where are they?"

She points across the room to the dresser. I take a guess, open the top drawer, and am greeted by lacy bras and panties, one a soft shade of blue. My mind wanders, thinking about what she'd look like wearing them, until she coughs, and I snap back to the present.

"No, on the top of the dresser. The shorts and shirt?"

I shut the drawer, grab the clothes, and bring them back over. It looks like a massive struggle when she gets her hand underneath her body and heaves herself somewhat upright. Her hair is a mess, a total nest, and her cheeks are deeply flushed. She looks gorgeous in the oddest way—vulnerable, her tough exterior completely stripped by the illness and exhaustion.

"Here you go," I say, handing her the clothes. "I'll go call the nurse while you change."

She nods and fumbles with the buttons on her shirt, but quickly gives up, falling back on the pillow. "Fuck my entire life."

I raise an eyebrow. "You okay?"

"Every time I move, I feel like there's a woodpecker stabbing at the back of my eye, trying to drill a hole into my head." She holds the shirt straight up in the air. "A little help?"

I shift my feet, stuffing my hands into my pockets. "You... uh, want me to help you dress?"

"It's not like you haven't seen it already."

Well, she's got a point there. I step closer to the bed, and sit on the edge, taking the clothing back. Gwendolyn lifts herself up again, her uniform shirt wrinkled and twisted at the waist. I reach over and unbutton the top button and make my way down, revealing an ivory bra that closely matches the tone of her skin. Her eyes are closed, as though just opening them is painful. I quickly remove the shirt and direct, "Lift your arms up." She does and I slowly lower the T-shirt over her head, tugging it over the swell of her tits, down her torso. "Okay," I breathe. *Okay.* I can totally do this. I can be the kind of guy who cares for a sick girl. Sure. "Lie back," I instruct. She does as I say, and I proceed to take her skirt off, tugging at the zipper on the side and shimmying it over her hips. It takes a minute, but I get her shorts on, and get her under the covers.

"Now, I'm going to call the nurse."

One of her hands shoots out, nudging blindly at my thigh. "Thank you."

I bite my lip, looking around. "Do you need anything else?"

She opens her eyes. "Thank you for checking on me."

I crouch down, fingers reaching out to graze her warm cheek. I almost tell her that pure paranoia drove me to it, but I don't. It's not true, anyway. Seeing her in here all alone, passed out on the bed, I'm glad I pushed through. "You're welcome."

I stand and pull out my phone, calling the main office to get linked through to the infirmary. When I look back, she's already asleep, covers pulled close under her chin. I wait by the door, not leaving until the nurse arrives, then slip down the back staircase. In that moment, I don't care who finds me here, but I know that she would, so I leave quickly, making sure that no one knows I was ever there.

21

G WEN

"Two days, Mom," I say over the phone. "I'm sure I'll be all better by then. I'll be home with plenty of time to help get ready for Thanksgiving."

My mom's sigh is full of static and worry. "I just hate you being there all alone like this."

"I shouldn't be around anyone right now, anyway." I straighten the quilt over my legs, fighting a shiver at my chill. "The nurse says it's just a nasty, and *very contagious*, virus. It's been going around for a few weeks. I really don't want to get the twins sick, especially with Micha's show coming up. I can order food, have it delivered here, and just rest up."

I hate being sick, but it doesn't happen to me often. The respite is almost a welcomed gift. With the help of my teachers and dorm advisor I've managed to keep up with my schoolwork, so I don't even have to spend the downtime feeling guilty and anxious. I've made myself a comfortable nest of blankets on my bed, laptop open beside me, and spend most of my time sleeping.

My mom says, "I know you like to be independent. It's one of the things I admire most about you. But I want you to know, it's okay to let someone take care of you."

"I will," I promise, hunkering back down into my blanket nest. "In two days. You know Micha would kill me if he got sick before his performance."

She laughs. "No, you're right about that. He's been absolutely off the rails this past week, as it is. But if you need anything—"

I reassure her over and over again, growing tired but more and more determined. Especially after the incident in the hallway during the fire, my mom has been particularly attentive. She'd had a long talk with the dean right after it happened, but I wasn't privy to more than his strained, pale face when they left his office. I still remember the complicated look my mom had given me, something both concerned and scarily protective, and I knew instinctively that she'd threatened to sue the school into the ground if anything like this happened again.

Preston Prep is definitely on her shit list.

It takes a few more minutes until she relents. "You order whatever you need, you hear? Soup, more blankets, junk food, anything. Charge it to the credit card, go nuts."

"I promise to be financially reckless," I oblige, finally hanging up.

It's Saturday morning, and by the time late afternoon rolls around, most of the campus will be gone for the break. A few students always hang around, so the dormitories are still technically open. Faculty will still be here. It's not a big deal for me to rest and recover in the safety and comfort of my room.

I've been in bed since Friday morning. Sometime after second period, I started to feel worse—lightheaded, and feverishly hot. I remember trudging up the stairs to my dorm to change, and not much else. Not until I awoke to Hamilton's worried voice.

I wish I didn't remember what happened next; Hamilton bent over me, picking me up off the floor, and putting me to bed. I cringe at the hazy memory of me pitifully asking him to help me with my pajamas. Almost begging, really. I blame the fever, one hundred percent.

He vanished after calling the nurse and I haven't seen him since. I have no clue what he was doing up here. If he was looking for sex, then he was SOL, although I remember the way he undressed me. It was perfectly clinical, no sense of that crackling tension present when he pulled down my socks or shucked off my shirt— only the gentle, sure touch of efficiency.

Maybe he has matured a little.

After the call with my mom, I take some fever-reducer and pass out again, falling into a deep, dreamless sleep. I've been inwardly referring to it as time-traveling, because it's like I close my eyes, and instantly open them again to find that hours have passed. This time when I wake up, I feel better than I have in days. The light coming through the room tells me it's already early afternoon. I shift on the bed, turning my face into a long beam of sun, basking comfortably.

Saturday afternoon.

I jerk up in the bed.

Shit. Shit. Shit!

I missed detention.

I fumble for my phone. There are no messages from the Dean, and nothing whatsoever from Hamilton. I scroll through my contacts, since I have his number from the swim sheet, and send him off a frantic text.

G: I'm so sorry about detention! I slept right through it. How mad is Dewey? How mad are you?

I stare at the phone, panic building in my chest. I know Dewey would excuse me if I'd brought him a note, but I didn't. I completely forgot about it! I groan miserably into my hands at the thought of him adding more days to my detention. We were so close to being done.

My phone pings and I scramble for it.

H: No worries. I took care of it. How are you feeling?

He took care of it? What does that mean?

G: Better. Alive. Thank you for... you know, yesterday.

H: Picking you up off the floor? You're not the first girl I've had do that for.

I pause, stomach sinking. Of course. He only came in that day because he wanted something. He was probably hoping for a different kind of sweaty moaning than the one he found. I take a controlled breath and pick up my phone, determined to be civil despite the fact he's not being very nice.

G: Well thanks anyway. I hope you have a good Thanksgiving. I'm sticking around here for a few days in quarantine to keep my family from getting sick.

I wait for a reply, phone held limply in my hand, but nothing comes. I curse myself for getting too familiar, too invested. Hamilton's obviously not one for small talk or friendly banter. And even if he were, it's not like we're friends. We're something way less easily defined than that. Enemies who occasionally hook up? Sex enemies? Sexemies?

I toss the phone aside and close my eyes, hoping another nap can provide a distraction from that humiliation. I'm giving him too much, showing him parts of myself that can be used to hurt me, intentionally or not.

Sleep comes easily. I'm not even sure how long I've dozed off when I'm awoken by a quick rap at my door. I squint down at my phone and blearily determine that it's only been fifteen minutes. I also can't help but notice the screaming lack of any reply from Hamilton.

The knock comes again, so I begrudgingly heave myself out of bed. Either the resident has more schoolwork for me, or Mom took it upon herself to order me some food, assuming I wouldn't do it on my own. She knows me almost too well.

I'm still clumsily smoothing down my hair when I swing the door open, my eyes falling on a nonchalant and achingly good-looking Hamilton. He has a paper bag in his hand and a backpack slung over his shoulder.

I almost stumble back a step at the sight of him. "What are you doing here?"

From his tight jaw, he looks as though he doesn't know how to answer that question. His mouth works around an aborted reply before he just thrusts the bag in my direction. "The delivery guy said this was for you. I told him I'd bring it up."

This doesn't actually tell me anything about what he's doing at my dorm in the first place, but I reluctantly take the bag and don't protest when he follows me in the room. I dump the bag on my desk, peeking inside briefly enough to confirm that it's from the pho restaurant in town. Just a whiff of it makes my stomach clench in hunger.

When I face Hamilton, his eyes sweep over me, and I can't even imagine how I look. There he is with his perfect hair and nice clothes, and I'm standing here looking like a zombie in a low-budget horror flick. I'm too worn out to work up the appropriate amount of embarrassment at this.

In fact, I'm too worn out to even stand here locked in some weird power struggle with him at all, so I cross the room and fall back into bed.

"So, really, what are you doing here?" I ask, tugging my blanket back over my legs.

He leans against my dresser, all long and assured. He lowers the backpack to the floor. "You kind of freaked me out the other day, Adams." He says this without any outward sign of self-consciousness, his gaze sweeping over my plague nest. "Guess I wanted to see with my own two eyes that you haven't perished like a wilting Victorian heroine or whatever."

My first instinct is to send him a weak glare. I'll fucking show him a wilting Victorian heroine. Asshole. But then I realize that Hamilton Bates basically just admitted to being worried about me.

I chew on my lip for a moment, watching him. "You ready to tell me why you were looking for me in the first place?"

He shrugs, fidgeting with some of the papers on my desk, glancing over them. "You looked off in first period. At first, I thought it was because of the night before, like maybe you were..." His eyes flick to mine. "You know, having regrets. Then you didn't show for lunch and Tyson didn't know where you were either. Your sister told me you were sick, so I came up here and found you on the floor."

"You talked to Michaela?" I ask in surprise, hugging the blankets around me. That makes twice now.

"She was on the quad. I didn't seek her out or anything." His gaze slides over to the pho, something tight and restless in the shift of his feet. "You want some of that? I can, like... get it for you?" He says this like he's rolling around in his head, testing it, like a question he's asking *himself*.

I open my mouth on an instinctual refusal, but instantly close it. The weirdness of his awkward attempt at, like... *tending* to me, is tempered by the deep pang of hunger clutching my stomach. I ultimately exhale, shoulders drooping. "That would be awesome, actually. Thanks."

He shuffles over to the desk and approaches the bag like it might bite him, fingers reluctantly pulling it open. He pulls out a plastic container of soup, movements growing more sure. I watch as he removes the lid, then takes out a spoon, chopsticks, and napkins. He carries it over and hands it to me. "It's really hot."

"I like it hot," I reply, smiling awkwardly. "Thank you."

He shoves his hands in his pockets and stands over me, watching. I can't quite place the look in his eyes—it's not something I've ever seen directed at me—but if I had to guess, it nearly seems as if he's seeking some sort of approval.

It's more than a little unnerving.

"If you're going to stay, you should sit." I point to the desk chair. After a suspended moment of hesitation, he reaches for it, pulling it out. I twirl the chopsticks around the noodles, blow on it, and take a bite. I moan gratefully. "Oh god, this is so good. I haven't eaten anything in two days." I eye him, lacking the energy to feel embarrassed about the pornographic eating sounds. "So, what did you mean before? About 'taking care' of detention?"

"I told Dewey you were sick," he explains, leaning back more casually in the chair, "then I just did the work myself."

My chopsticks freeze halfway to my mouth, broth dripping from the noodles. "You mean you did the basecoat alone?"

"Yes." His mouth curves into a grin that's more boastful than it has any right to be.

While eating another mouthful of noodles, I glance at his soft, elegant hands. "And you managed to do it without any major injuries?"

"I'm injury-free. Except..."

"What?"

He looks toward the window, scowling. "I was moving the ladder and the paint tray fell off the top. *Luckily,* it landed on the drop cloth. But it was a huge fucking mess. It took me forever to clean up."

"I can only imagine the temper tantrum that followed that." Doing so makes me grin. "How many home improvement supplies were harmed in the making of this detention?"

He narrows his eyes at me, but I can tell it's more playful than anything. "Ha-ha. You like to see me suffer, don't you?"

"I'm sure the masking tape had it coming." I chew on a mouthful of noodles before saying, "But seriously, thank you. That was an impressive amount of work to get done by yourself. I'm proud of you." After a beat of stabbing my soup with the chopsticks, I look up at him cautiously. "Yikes, that sounded super patronizing, didn't it?"

His expression is completely flat, save for the curve of an eyebrow. "Only a lot."

I cover my mouth when I laugh. "Oh God, I'm sorry. I just meant—"

"I know what you meant." He rolls his eyes, but doesn't seem particularly offended about it, so I let it go. "So listen, if you want some company, I can stick around." He clears his throat, shifting. "I brought my laptop, so we can watch a movie or something."

I watch him warily, feeling this odd discomfort in the pit of my stomach. Not that I'm opposed to hanging around Hamilton, because sitting here all day alone, sick, is boring me to tears.

It's the 'or something' I'm worried about.

"Don't you need to get home?"

He exhales loudly, hand raking roughly through his hair. "Honestly, anything to put that off a bit longer is fine by me."

"Okay, but," I hedge, "you're not worried about getting sick?"

He looks at me like I'm dumb. "You were already contagious the other night, when we were together. If I'm going to get it, that ship has sailed. It's halfway to fucking Spain. It sunk in the Atlantic. There's already a tragic mariner's song about it and everything."

I place my bowl on the bedside table. "Look, Bates, I'm feeling better today. But I'm not feeling good enough for—I mean, if you're looking to hook-up, then—"

"I'm not looking for a hook-up." His jaw tightens and a flicker of something new—different—crosses his eyes. A vulnerability, or a weak spot. Something small and stung. "I'm serious about not being ready to go home, and... well, believe it or not, you're not the worst company."

I roll my eyes at the backhanded compliment. "Geez thanks, that's reassuring."

He smirks and reaches for his backpack, unzipping it and pulling out a top-of-the-line laptop. After a few moments spent retrieving the charger and booting it up, he pauses, eyes roaming the room. "Where should I put it?"

"Uh..." I look around, biting my lip. "I guess on the bed?"

I straighten out my blanket nest to give him a flat surface, and he places it at the foot of the bed, streaming service queued up. He drags the chair closer to see, and a battle wars inside of me; one that involves my heart, my body, and my mind. I can invite him to sit with me on the bed, but would that be some kind of signal? Would it be suggesting something I'm not prepared to follow through on? Is what's going on between us primarily a sex thing, or can it also be a friendly thing? I'm not sure where we stand on either. As he fusses with positioning the screen so we can both see it, I decide, "Hey, come on. Just sit with me on the bed."

His eyebrow arcs. "You sure?"

"If you're not afraid of getting sick, then it's fine by me."

I shift over and he kicks off his shoes, lowering himself to the edge of my narrow bed. There's no way for us not to be close, because the bed is too small for all that. But I get the impression he tries his best, even if our hips end up touching. Hamilton pulls the computer to his lap and says, "What do you want to watch?"

I chew on my lip, thinking. "I've been holding out on Stranger Things. Have you seen it yet?"

"You haven't?" His eyebrows climb his forehead in disbelief. "Have you been living under a rock?"

"I don't know. The twins totally got into it. I think I was just..."

Wallowing. Too worried about Sky and my immediate reality at the time to really focus on anything fictional. "I guess you wouldn't want to watch it all over again, would you?"

"Sure I would," he says, queuing it up and pressing play. He shifts the computer so we can both see it, and now his knee is touching mine. I pull the covers up, as much of a shield as anything else.

I'm not a big fan of scary stuff, but this seems to fall somewhere in the middle. It's suspenseful, but funny, campy, and cheesy. We burn through multiple episodes of the first season mindlessly, heedless of the clock, just going from episode to episode. The lingering tension between the two of us slips away so gradually that it doesn't even feel strange or surreal when our arms begin bumping, pressing together. We make conversation, here and there. Hamilton likes Jonathan the most, but Nancy is my favorite.

He scoffs. "You would. You're so Nancy."

"I take that as a compliment." I sniff indignantly. "And you're totally Steve. That guy is such a douchebag."

His laugh is a quiet, bouncing thing. "You're going to be eating your words when season two starts and you find out he's the good guy."

"Dude!" I turn to fake-push him off the bed, heedless of his laughter. "Spoilers!"

As the afternoon light fades into an evening glow outside my window, my eyelids begin growing heavy. I'm so stupidly deep into the story, and so oddly comfortable with Hamilton's company, that I don't even want to go to sleep. But no matter how much I blink, I can't keep my eyes open.

I wake with a start, my neck bearing a sharp ache at even the smallest movement. It's hot under the covers and something heavy is pinning me down. My room is bathed in the darkness of late night, but the lights from the quad cast enough of a glow that I can see Hamilton is still here, his arm flung carelessly across my middle as he sleeps.

The laptop sits abandoned at the foot of the bed, closed now.

I take a moment to absorb the half of his face that isn't buried into my pillow. All the meanness, tension, and caustic cruelty is absent from his expression. All that's left is his beauty, his long eyelashes, sharp cheekbones, stubble-covered jaw. His soft pink lips are parted as he breathes softly, and the urge to lift my hand and touch them is almost too intense to ignore. Though his face is slack, the weight of his arm feels possessive and clutching, like a man holding on to a life preserver.

After all this time, I still don't know who Hamilton Bates really is. Is he the kind, careless boy from the picture in my closet? Is he the golden boy who will stop at nothing to get what he wants? Is he the cruel, ruthless leader of the Devils? Or is he the awkwardly compassionate guy who sometimes saves and protects me?

It probably can't be that easy. Most likely, he's a little bit of all those things, all mashed up into this beautiful, twisted mess of a man. I can't begin to understand how they all reconcile, but I do know that, during moments like this, it's hard to remember why I hate him at all. Or *hated* him. I'm not even sure which tense to use anymore.

I don't dare wake him, instead burrowing back down under the covers, allowing the soft rhythm of his breaths, the weight of his arm around me, to lull me back into slumber. I can't help but think that it's nice not to be alone, even if I am sharing a bed with my biggest enemy.

"So, I'm curious," I say, pausing to take a bite of gooey pizza. "What's the deal with your parents?"

It's late—way past midnight—and we're both wired from sleeping all evening. I'd awoken first, slipping carefully from the bed to take a shower, desperate to wash off the sticky residue of sickness. I returned to find him on the phone with the 24-hour pizza place. He waited outside for the delivery as I stood in front of my mirror, detangling my hair.

When he came back up, I spread a blanket over the floor, and he placed the pizza in the middle of it. Now, we're sitting across from one another; me leaning against the bed, Hamilton stretched out on his side.

"Jesus." He makes a vaguely sour face at my question. "You don't want to listen to all that. It'll take all fucking night."

"Sure I do," I insist. "I asked, didn't I? Plus, it's like two in the morning. 'All night' isn't a huge commitment."

He chews on his feta and artichoke pizza, something I discovered we both like. And clearly, something he *really likes,* because he's on his fourth slice. He sighs, beginning, "Well, this may come as a surprise to you, so don't get the vapors or anything. But my parents— and particularly my father—are pretentious assholes."

"Wow," I fake a gasp. "That *is* a shocker." I dip my crust in the ridiculously delicious butter sauce. "Mostly that you have the self-awareness to acknowledge that."

He takes another bite of pizza, his free hand extending a long, elegant middle finger at me. "For a long time," he continues, swallow-ing, "I thought my dad was a god because he was so smart, successful, and powerful. And in some ways, I still do..."

"But..." I prod.

He takes a breath, wiping his greasy fingers on a napkin. "But some shit went down a few years ago with my sister, and the older I get, the more I think about it. At the time I thought he handled it the right way—the only way—but now... I guess I'm not so sure."

I pull the feta off another piece of pizza and pop it in my mouth. "What happened?"

He sucks his teeth, leaning back on his hands. "Well, my sister, Hollis—I don't think you ever met her—she was always really inde-pendent. And, I mean, my dad loved that about her, practically molded her to be that way. He had really high hopes for her to become some brilliant CEO or lawyer or whatever. But that's the thing about shaping your kid to be independent, right? They rebel against your expectations."

He continues, "When she was sixteen, we were at our place at the beach. I was only twelve at the time. We spent most of the summer there with my mom or our housekeeper. My dad would come down on the weekends. It was kind of boring for two kids, honestly."

I think of the childhood vacations I've had with my own family, having plenty of siblings near enough to my own age to play or hang out with. I nod. "I can see that."

He pushes himself upright, propping his elbows on his knees, and something about the way he curls his shoulders inward seems protective, tempered. "So, Hollis started dating someone who worked at the marina. Just a townie, you know? She kept it secret for a while, until my dad came down one weekend and saw them together on one of the boats. It was bad enough that it was a local, because, well..." He gives me a quick, cautious look.

"Because he didn't have 'pedigree'," I roll my eyes, nostrils flaring hotly. "Because he was a piece of blue-collar, working-class trash?"

"Right," he says slowly. "More or less, I guess. The fact it wasn't a 'he' definitely escalated things."

My head jerks up in surprise. "A girl? Your sister is a lesbian?"

"Yep." He bobs his head. "From there, shit just hit the fan. Like... I know it's a cliché. Rich girl falls in love with a local kid. Father has a meltdown." He looks up at me from under those thick, dark eyelashes. "He gave her a choice, the girl or his legacy—his money, his influence, his support." He shrugs in a way that looks aloof, but I know isn't. "Hollis chose the girl."

"And he followed through on his threats," I guess.

"Big time." He picks at a fray on his jeans, eyes fixed to the thread. "I've only seen her twice since then. She got her GED, and I think she's taking some college classes. Community college, not Duke or Wake Forest like she wanted."

I watch him, frowning. "Is she still with the girl?"

"No, I don't think so." He wraps the thread around a long finger and pulls, fingertip going white. "She's too stubborn to come back, and for a long time, I blamed her. I mean, why would she give up everything for some stupid summer fling? But I was twelve. I'm eighteen now, and I get it."

"Because it wasn't about the girl," I guess, stretching out my legs.

He hums, head shaking. "It was about our father being a controlling asshole. He's a dictator. There's only one way to do things: his way. And Hollis..." He reaches up to scratch at the raspy stubble covering his chin, eyes pensive. "She didn't walk because my dad wouldn't let her date the townie. I don't think it was even because he wouldn't let her date girls. She left because she knew my dad wanted to control every single factor in her life. The girl was just her line in the sand. If she couldn't be who she was—be with who she wanted to be with—then in a sense, nothing could ever really be hers. And what good is any of it—the money, the success, the legacy—if it never really belongs to you?"

I watch him for a long moment, the shadow of something thoughtful and acrid darkening his features. "That really sucks, Bates. I'm sorry."

His gaze jumps to mine, shuttering. "Yeah, I guess that's my real legacy, right? Falling in line. Living like a remote-controlled robot. Doing everything he says."

I shake my head and push my toes against his knee. "Yeah, I don't see that happening."

"No?" He doesn't seem so sure. "Why's that?"

"Because you're the most determined, self-focused, competitive person I've ever met. You don't need your dad to ride your ass about stuff. Like, I'm sure he was pissed about us being co-captains, but you made it work. In the right way. Coach wanted you to do it and so did the headmaster."

He scoffs. "Yeah, well, to my father that makes me... what was it he said?" He uses finger quotes. "An insolent, inadequate screw-up."

I pull a face, because even though I've always known on some level that Mr. Bates was an asshole, that's over-the-top harsh. "Gee, I can't imagine why you didn't want to go home yesterday."

Hamilton nods in agreement. "Exactly. When I do what he says, I'm being a good son. But when I do what the coach and headmaster want, I'm weak."

"But he's wrong." I explain, "Sometimes the best way to get ahead is to play along, and you know that. That's not weak. Your dad just thinks he knows best because he probably tells himself he has your best interests at heart. Even though they're really *his* best interests."

Hamilton gives me a tired smile. "Since when did you get so smart about family dynamics?"

I blink at him. "You're kidding, right?"

"Do I look like I'm kidding?"

He looks like a sex god lounging on my floor, that's what he looks like.

"I live with two flakey parents who, thankfully, found a super nanny to keep us alive, four adopted siblings that each came into the family with their own trauma, and—" I stop short, realizing what I've done. I don't talk about my family at Preston. And I definitely don't talk about them to a Devil.

His forehead creases. "What?"

I shake my head, looking away. "Forget about it."

A slow awareness crosses his face and he sits up, pushing the pizza aside. He shifts until he's in front of me, the knees of our crossed legs touching, and then gently plucks my hands from the floor, lacing our fingers together in the space between us. I let him do this, my eyes warily tracking his controlled movements.

He looks at me with an intent expression, lip caught between his teeth. "Alright, let's make a deal. Whatever we talk about in here, stays in here. No judgements, okay?"

My biggest concern this whole time has been about betraying my family to this boy—this Devil. But over the last few days, I can't deny a shift has taken place. He's been kind. Sweet, even. He's looked out for me and even defended me to the point of making his friends suspicious. If he can do all that, can't I trust him?

Well, he did tell me about his sister.

"Okay," I say, taking a deep breath. "So, my mom is obsessed with us all maintaining relationships with our birth parents. The other kids are open to it, with frankly mixed results. But I've resisted."

"Why?"

"Why do you think?" I say defensively. "Who wants to foster a relationship with someone who sees them as easily disposable garbage? With someone who's been nothing but a source of toxicity and hurt?" Hamilton seems to grow paler, going rigidly still, but I barely register it. "Someone who can't tell their child who their father is, or wouldn't even try to get off drugs, or do any of the things a real parent needs to do in order to raise a child." Hot tears prickle behind my eyelids, vision going blurry. "Why should I? I like the mom I have, because... yeah, she's not perfect, but even her worst traits are just a product of her love for us. My real mother is the person who raised me—not the one who birthed me. I don't want to meet that person and I sure as hell don't want a relationship with her. I don't know why my mom can't understand that."

We're both quiet for a moment, my outburst settling into a heavy silence between us. I've never spoken so freely to him about anything, let alone my very personal baggage, and I instantly regret doing it now—more than any of the other things I've done with him, by far. I try to unlace our fingers, to move away, but he doesn't let me.

"Hey, no," he says coaxingly, gently pulling my hands back. "I get it. That's some really heavy shit, and yours is the only opinion that matters. I'm no expert or anything, but I don't think there's a wrong answer there."

I shrug, trying to sniffle covertly. "It's a whole complicated thing."

His steel gray eyes bore into mine. "Look at that, we do have things in common other than sex."

I let out a surprised laugh. "What? Parents we can't please?"

"That," he lists, fingers playing between mine, "our love of swim, and our unrelenting desire to win." His lips tug in a tentative smile. "Oh, and we both like artichokes and feta, the weirdest combination." He picks up the last piece and pushes it toward my mouth, like he wants me to take a bite.

It's goofy and strange, but so is everything about this moment, so I lean forward. But before I can get to the pizza, he pitches toward me, eyes locked on my mouth. He blindly throws the pizza back to the box, hand coming up to cup my neck. I can't help the staggered, shuddery breath I release as my eyes drop to his lips in anticipation.

He whispers, "Okay?"

I press a palm to his chest to hold him at bay. "We shouldn't," I say.

He licks his lips. "Because you're sick? We already went over that."

"No, because..." I meet his gaze, heart hammering. "Because it's getting really confusing."

His gaze darts between my eyes and my mouth, and I swear I can feel his heart beat faster beneath my hand when he replies, "I'm not confused, Gwendolyn. I know exactly what I want."

I look at him, *really look at him*, and he's a different Hamilton Bates entirely. And maybe some part of me, buried deep inside, still has doubts about this, but in this moment, my heart is running the show. I drop my hand and he ducks his head, finally brushing my lips with a soft, lingering kiss. He pulls back far enough to meet my gaze, assessing my reaction, and I feel the ghost of his kiss like a blaze of heat.

I press forward, returning the kiss, and then climb into his lap. His hands grab my hips and pull me against him, tongue licking into my mouth. I settle in the curve of his hips, and it's nothing like it was. Something's changed. I know, because I can still feel the bright spark of want for him in my belly, but I feel something else, too: The bloom of a breathless swoop in my chest. I knit my fingers into his hair and deepen the kiss, as if I could push the wild swooping feeling into him, share it with him, even though a dark, frightened part of me wants to keep it safe and hidden.

22

Surreal.

That's how I would describe the next 24 hours.

Who knew that eating, sleeping, and binging Netflix while cuddled up next to Gwendolyn Adams would be the best day of my life?

Gwen frowns at the closed laptop. "I can't believe Hopper's dead."

"You did see the extended scene, didn't you?" I reach out to push a strand of hair behind her ear. I've been touching her constantly; I just can't help it. "Because I'm pretty sure you were sitting right next to me when I watched it."

Ever since that kiss on her floor, feeling the weight of her in my lap, I've been perpetually hard. We spent a few long minutes doing that—just trading kisses—but we didn't go any further. And the weird thing is, I don't even mind. I've been enjoying the low-key closeness all the same.

She turns to me and her eyes are so wide and guileless that it's all I can do not to smile. "I did, but what if it's a trick! What if Hopper really is dead? What if Will and his family are moving away, and

Johnathan and Nancy are going long distance and Elle... oh my god, poor Elle."

Truthfully, it had completely escaped my mind that watching that plot point would likely be upsetting to someone who's both adopted and currently entangled in a bunch of emotional stuff surrounding it all. I watch shows like that for the monsters and cool fight scenes, what can I say? It just didn't occur to me. She tried to hide her tears when Elle read the letter from her 'adopted' dad, but I could tell. It didn't feel good. I had no idea what to do.

When she'd revealed her feelings about her birth mother to me, I felt it like a punch in the gut.

Who wants to foster a relationship with someone who sees them as easily disposable garbage? With someone who's been nothing but a source of toxicity and hurt?

The parallels were nauseatingly impossible to miss. How many times have I called her trash? A reject? Tainted blood? How many times have I sneered at her, laughed at her, been a toxic asshole to her? I couldn't count them if I tried, and I sure as hell can't make up for any of it. Which is a hell of a thing to realize just as I began feeling like...

Like maybe we could *be* something?

Only now, I'm not so sure. It's not like I could blame her. Aside from the parentage stuff, I basically fit the same bill as her mom. I'd thrown her away, discarded her, and then rubbed it in for... *Jesus*.

For *years*.

It's only just now that I'm realizing these are probably some serious sticking points, and how completely fucked up is that? It's just that Gwendolyn Adams has always been the picture of self-confidence, strong and assertive, so loyal to her family, and always seeming unconcerned about their different lifestyle. It never occurred to me that there might be pain, trauma even, lurking under the surface. That my actions had bigger, lasting consequences.

Of course, I'd dumped a shitload of unresolved Bates family drama on her as well, so maybe... *maybe* she'll see. Maybe she'll understand that being a Bates has always been about the name, never about the people who bear it. The Adams are a family. The Bates are a *brand*. That's all I've ever known family to be.

I turn to her, deciding to save that introspective nightmare for another time—preferably when I'm not comfortable and enjoying myself. I clear my throat. "It's a TV show, Adams, and a kid's TV show, at that. They're not going to kill the dad." My brow puckers in confusion at her gaping stare. "What?"

"It's like you've never seen The Lion King."

It's the look on her face that makes me drag her in my lap and wrap my arms around her. "When the next season comes out, we'll watch it together, and you'll see that everything will be fine."

The look she gives me is wide-eyed, surprised. I realize a beat too late that I'd accidentally made a declaration about the future. But in the moment, I meant it. Now that I have Gwendolyn Adams in my life, I don't plan on letting her go. Not if I can help it. And I always get what I want. There are a million reasons this wouldn't work, a hundred obstacles, but in this room, just the two of us? Fuck it, why not?

She touches my cheek and lifts up to kiss me, her lips warm and sweet from the candy she'd been eating. She kisses me again, deeper, full of an unmistakable intent. These are not the small, restrained touches we'd shared since that kiss. Her hands rub down my chest, sneaking beneath the hem, her fingers hooking into my waistband. Her teeth tug at my bottom lip, begging for entrance. Happily, I let her in, and when her tongue sweeps against mine, I groan in relief.

Days of pent-up desire well up inside of me, but I shake the lust fog from my head, frame her face with my hands, and ask, "Are you sure? You feel okay?"

"Yep. I had a really good nurse." She straddles my hips, and then pulls her shirt over her head, exposing her perfect tits. Just like that. No frills, no bra, no fanfare. Just instant tits in my face. It's like she knows exactly how to drive me crazy.

I think I know exactly how to make her feel the same.

I roll her over, making sure neither of us fall off the bed, and quickly remove my own shirt. Her eyes rake over me hungrily, lip trapped between her teeth, and I can't help but take my time getting back to her, letting her drink her fill. She likes my body. I see it written all over her face on the regular. It's not much—it's not a long history of me being a good guy who does good deeds—but it's what I've got, something I'm proud of. I put a lot of time into training, staying fit, sculpting my body into an exacting tool. Her eyes gloss over as her gaze sweeps down my chest, fingertips following the reverent path. I wonder if this is how she feels when I look at her— wanted, powerful, triumphant.

I'm only mildly surprised to find that I hope she does.

I start my journey with a kiss, from her mouth to her hips, taking my time, tasting her skin, teasing her flesh. She writhes under me, hips pushing impatiently upward. When I get to her belly, I kiss from one hip bone to the other, smiling when she squirms from the sensitivity. I'm too long, too tall for this little bed, so I hook my hands beneath her knees and pull her toward the foot of it with a single, powerful tug.

She inhales in surprise at the motion, but I don't miss the way her eyes track my shifting muscles. It distracts her long enough for me to shuck her shorts and panties, sliding them down her creamy thighs in one smooth yank.

"Bates," she says, realizing with a start exactly what I plan to do. She pushes up on her elbows and looks at me in alarm. "I don't—"

"Yeah," I say, kissing the insides of her thigh, "I think you do. Come on, let me do this for you, okay?"

I know this is different from that day in the chem lab—that this isn't the dark, shadowy, hasty under-skirt deal we were working with before. This is her spread out before me, as bare as she can be, in the stark light of day. I'm asking her to really trust me, to expose herself in an intimate way—a way I've never even wanted from another girl before. I've eaten out exactly two girls, and each were for nothing more than the novelty of it. The first, for the novelty of just having the experience under my belt, and the second, with Gwen herself, for the novelty of having—taking, *owning*—as much of her as I could get.

Now, I just want to taste her, bring her a pleasure so intense and all-consuming that she calls me by name. My *first* name.

I nudge her legs apart, my palms sweeping up her thighs, never breaking her gaze. This is a question, a request. If she doesn't want it, I'll back off, and I'll never look. I'll let her keep this. I won't take it.

She watches me, and after a long, breathless moment, exhales shakily. "Okay."

I press my thumbs into the juncture where her legs meet her hips, finally allowing my gaze to drop to her center. I wet my lips at the sight of it, shouldering in between her legs, and hold her wide gaze as I press an open-mouthed kiss to her core. She tenses in surprise, mouth parting, but her eyelids grow heavier as my tongue peeks out, prodding into her deep folds. She shivers, fingers twisting hard in the blankets, and releases a soft cry when I flick my tongue against her clit.

She moans, "Jesus, Bates."

Well.

That won't do.

I take my time, and why shouldn't I? It took us weeks—no, *years* —to get here. I set to the task more diligently than I would anything else, learning what makes her tremble, what makes her back arch, what elicits small, agonized sounds from the back of her throat, what makes her buck up against me. Her hands thrust into my hair and her legs gradually relax, falling open around me, completely without shame. Eventually, I learn just the right way to kiss and tease her, and from the way her legs shake and her stomach tenses, I'm certain she's almost to the edge, very nearly ready to topple over.

Until she starts squirming away, whining, "No, no, I want to come with you inside me. *Please.*"

She doesn't have to ask me twice.

I stand and shuck my pants, flinging my shorts off my feet with a clumsy kick. I bend over her, sliding a hand under her back and inching her up the mattress. Her hands grab my ass, pulling me close, her legs spread, hips pushing upward.

I sweep the hair from her sweaty forehead, soothing her. "Wait, *fuck*, I have to—" I fumble to open her bedside drawer and something clatters to the floor in my haste to clutch for the box of condoms, but I eventually find it, quickly rolling one over my aching dick.

Her legs lock around my hips, the heels of her feet pushing me forward, eyes heavy yet demanding. I enter her swiftly, thrusting in deep, and I can tell that she's so close already, hissing at the quiver of her around me, tightening against my cock. I fight every instinct to drive hard and fast into her, instead clenching my teeth with the effort of keeping my movements slow, measured, purposeful. I want to savor her and the way she looks right now, her raptured gaze staring up at me, mouth agape with her panting breaths. I want to have this, and I want to *keep* this, and I want her to—

"Say my name." I press my forehead to hers, hips twisting forward. She gives me a glazed, questioning look. I can't help the way my voice sounds, low and ragged and pulled thin, when I ask, "Call me by my name."

Understanding flickers in her eyes and she opens her mouth, but no words come out. I continue moving, slowly, almost pained with the restraint I need to stop my hips from just slamming mindlessly forward. She cries out and once more I plead, "I want to hear my name, Gwendolyn." *I want to make this real.*

She shudders beneath me, nails puncturing my back. I buck against her, trying desperately to control myself, but every second pushes me closer to the precipice. She groans and presses her mouth to mine, the word "Hamilton," a hot, keening whisper between our lips.

"Oh my fucking—" I shake, eyes screwing closed in pleasure, shocked at the effect it has on me, how much just hearing my name on her lips feels like a physical *wrench*. I bury my face into her neck as my orgasm draws helplessly near, hand cupped possessively around the long column of her throat.

Her breaths are thin and shallow in my ear, and she whispers, "Hamilton," once more before trapping my earlobe between her teeth and tugging, just the way I like it. The combination sets off a wave of feral need that devours all sense. I grab her knee and press it to her chest, spreading her, opening her thighs to me, and giving in to the impulse to thrust wildly into her.

There's something all at once surprised and awestruck in her eyes when they hold mine, and the feeling of her clenching around me, orgasm rippling through her in a full-body convulsion, makes me grunt a low, "Fuck."

I follow her over the edge, coming in a trembling final thrust.

Pleasure turns to ecstasy, and then flows into warm, consuming contentment. I look down at the girl below me, who is gazing at me with dreamy eyes. This isn't someone staring up at me with reluctance and anger. The way her fingers card through my hair isn't the behavior of someone refusing to forgive.

Even if I'm lying to myself, I have to believe that. Because the emotion that shoots through me is unexpected, entirely unfamiliar, but absolute and true.

I'm in love with Gwendolyn Adams.

LEAVING Preston the next day is harder than I thought it would be. Sure, a huge part of it is going home to a dysfunctional family celebrating another empty, joyless holiday, but even I can't deny the biggest factor is Gwendolyn. I really don't want to leave her, but most of all, I can't help the grip of fear that, the second we leave this room, the spell will be broken. That we'll go back to being Adams and Bates, enemies. That we'll return to ignoring each other, at best, and at worst...

I rub a hand down my face.

"Got everything?" she asks, glancing around her room. Her bag is packed on the bed. I'd watched her carefully pick out different shirts and jeans, skipping over the lacy underwear for the more practical—yet still sexy—white. At least that means she's probably not planning on impressing anyone while she's home. That thought made me both anxious and relieved.

"I think so." I look around once more. I'd had to go back to my room once for a change of clothes, but everything fit easily in my backpack. There's not much I need to take home with me, anyway. I have a full closet of clothes there. I look at her and something comes to me. "Oh, wait. Here."

I take my hoodie—black and emblazoned with the crimson

Preston Prep Swim logo—and pull it over her head. She quirks an eyebrow at me, but ultimately pushes her arms through, allowing me to tug it down straight.

"It's cold," I feebly explain. "It'd suck a bag of dicks to get sick again." It's ridiculously oversized on her small frame, and I feel a hot spike of possessiveness at the sight of her swimming in it. It doesn't have my name on it, but anyone with two brain cells to rub together would see that it's a guy's hoodie. Despite that, she still has the element of validity on her side, were anyone to ask. She is on the swim team, after all.

If she realizes any of this, she doesn't say so. She just nods, burying her hands into the hoodie's front pouch. "I'm ready if you are."

It's a loaded statement. It's obvious that neither of us want to go home, to part from one another. I slip an arm around her waist, sweeping her hair back from her neck to press a kiss into the sensitive skin below her ear. "Sure we can't just stay here?"

She laughs, squirming away from me. "You need to shave, and yes. I'm pretty sure if we don't go home, they'll come looking for us at some point."

I cling to her in a last-ditch effort to hold on to what we've got. Once that door opens, either everything changes or it goes back to normal. I want what we have here—now—even if it is impossible.

"Hey." She cups her hand at the back of my neck and nudges my face downward. "It's going to be okay."

She doesn't clarify what 'it' is. She doesn't need to.

I search her eyes. "Are you sure?"

"We're the two smartest kids in the class," she says, smiling, "and you're easily the most nefarious. We've gone this far with no one finding out, and at the very least, we can buy some time to come up with a plan for how we want to handle... you know. Going forward."

I return her smile, some thread of tension deep in my chest suddenly unwinding.

There is a forward, and we're going to it.

I kiss her once more before giving in, slinging my backpack over my shoulder and grabbing her bag off the bed. What she says makes perfect sense. We're smart, and I'm the lead Devil. They'll fall in line, or there will be consequences.

But figuring out what the consequences would be, and for whom, is what makes me so nervous.

~

H: How's it going?

G: Brayden ate the last piece of pie, Micha forced us to watch three musicals, and Michaela has already typed up her Christmas list. #sendhelp

My lips twitch in a smile, more than a little jealous of the silly chaos in her home, but it almost feels strange to do that here—smile. I've been trapped in this oppressively quiet house all day with nothing but my parents, a great aunt and uncle, and some distant cousin who I'm pretty sure is old enough to have lived through Prohibition.

I can probably count on one hand the amount of words I've said after walking through the door. Dinner is over now. The house is tastefully decorated to reflect the season, warm-colored flowers placed in the foyer, a centerpiece on the table so enormous that it was almost impossible to see who sat opposite me, even if there were conversation. It all feels empty and pointlessly festive. The house is too big for the three of us and we seem to just roll around like rubber balls, every now and then bouncing off one another before rolling in different directions.

H: I wish I could. Two more days, right?

G: GTG. We're leaving in a minute to go to the shelter downtown.

H: Of course you are.

G: Hey! I'm not being a goody-two shoes. It's a family tradition.

H: I know you're not. You're just being you, and I like you.

More than like, my mind supplies.

G: Later?

H: Later.

I slide my phone into my pocket and glance down the hall. My father's probably locked up in his office by now. My mom is likely carefully planning all the ways she's going to micromanage the staff into the ground for the post-Thanksgiving, crack-of-dawn Christmas decoration prep tomorrow. My aunt and uncle already took the ancient cousin away, so it's just me now, enveloped in the empty silence of my bedroom.

I'm struck by the lack of close family—of Hollis, of laughter and questions and *life*.

An idea pops into my head. I head into the kitchen where Renata and another woman are cleaning up from dinner. I feel awkward as I enter, like an intruder, suddenly struck with the strange instinct to knock, or apologize, or start washing pans.

A wide assortment of uneaten desserts sit on the counter, and I clear my throat, asking, "Can I have this?"

Renata turns to me with an easy smile. "Whatever you want, sweetie."

I duck my head, feeling like I'm eight years old, all over again. "Thanks, Nata." I pick a pie up to carry it out, but she stops me, hand on my arm.

"Hold your horses, now." She takes it from me and covers it tightly in foil, handing me a small container of whipped cream to take with it. "There you are."

"Thank you," I say again. There have been a lot of times I've dismissed Renata as just the help—simply someone paid to do things for me and my family—and though she's the only source of warmth here, I've often discounted it as likely artificial. But that's unfair. She's also always going the extra mile to do nice things for me. I take it for granted. "I hope you have a happy Thanksgiving."

She gives me a strange look, and then smiles, straightening my collar. "You be good," she says, going back to her cleaning. "And don't you go eating that all by yourself. You'll make yourself sick, you hear?"

I smile. "I won't, promise."

No one notices when I slip out of the house, and once the pie is secure, I head out. The drive isn't long—I'd even venture to call it nice, considering the lack of traffic. I fleetingly wish that Gwendolyn could be with me right now. She'd probably know what to say or how to handle what I'm about to walk into. Her first reaction is to be positive. Mine is to be combative. Although she definitely knows how to fight, she also knows how to defuse, disarm.

I get off the highway and make my way to an apartment complex in an industrial area that's turned mixed-use residential. Five years ago, this area was a certifiable shit-hole. High crime, graffiti-covered facades, burned-out buildings. Back in the day, Ansel used to drive down here to buy weed and other goodies. All of that has changed, now. There are coffee shops and restaurants dotting the old buildings, along with renovated houses here and there, new construction.

I double check the address. I'd gotten it years ago, procured on a whim from an old family friend who had apparently kept sparingly in touch with her. I have no way to be sure if it's still her place, but I park the car in front of the old bungalow and grab the pie. The walk down the long driveway is a little confusing. Her place isn't the bungalow, but instead the carriage house in the back.

I climb up the stairs and hear music coming from inside. Shit. If it is her place, then she has company. A part of me is a little hurt at the idea of Hollis celebrating Thanksgiving on her own. Like it's just proof that she's built this whole different life outside of us—outside of me—and is enjoying it, is all the better for it.

But I know it makes sense. She should have that. I shouldn't expect her to stand still like the rest of the Bates clan.

I take a steeling breath and knock.

I consider making a break for it while I wait, but the door opens and Hollis stands before me, her wide gray eyes matching my own. Her hair is twisted in a complicated knot, and even though she's not a Bates anymore—not in spirit—the threads of our genetics have held strong. She's still got that same elegant and effortless beauty. She's wearing some kind of hippie floral dress that our mother would absolutely loathe.

She looks amazing.

"Hamilton?" she says, totally shocked.

"Hey, sis," I say, dumbly. I remember the pie and hold it up, a weak offering. "Thought I'd drop by and bring you some dessert."

She eyes the pie and her lips curve upward. "Did Renata make that pie?"

I scratch the back of my neck. "Yep."

She grabs the dish in one hand and pulls me into a tight embrace with the other. I'm instantly assaulted with the spicy scents of cinnamon and sage. She leans back and looks into the apartment. "Hey, everyone!" she shouts. The living room is filled with a small collection of colorful people, all vaguely around Hollis' age. "This is my baby brother, Hamilton. He brought pie!"

I'm greeted with a wave of welcoming, celebratory cheers, and for the first time in a long while, I feel like I'm home.

As it turns out, my sister has made her own family. They're an eclectic mix of students, professionals, and hourly workers. One girl, who raved over Renata's pumpkin pie, works at the bakery down the street. Another guy, covered in a wide expanse of colorful ink, is an artist at a tattoo shop. There's a lawyer, a girl getting her MBA, and someone whose pronouns I'm not quite sure of turns out to be the owner of the bungalow out front. No one is like anyone else. That the idea of this confuses me really nails home the fact that I live in a tightly protected bubble, surrounded by nothing but clones of myself.

Except for *her*, of course.

I feel smaller here. Unimportant. Everyone is older than me, more experienced, smarter. It's not exactly a bad feeling. It's hours before everyone leaves, but I hang around until the place clears out and her roommate disappears into her bedroom.

Hollis slides a beer across the kitchen counter to me and says, "Not that I'm complaining, but to what do I owe the pleasure of you showing up on my doorstep?"

"Other than the promise of a long night spent alone in my room, so as to not disrupt Mother's Christmas decoration planning?" Hollis laughs, knowing exactly what I'm talking about. "So, I've been talking to this girl—"

"Ahhh right, it's always a girl, isn't it?" Her eyes are full of bright humor. "No hate. I know the feeling."

"Well, this girl is different," I start, fidgeting with my beer cap. "But like, she has this big family."

"A Preston girl?"

"Yes, but." I take a breath, unsure of how to get across the essence of Gwen. "Not like the other Preston girls."

"Is that even possible?"

I smirk. "I wouldn't think so, but this one is. And not... not just because she's hot." I give Hollis a look. "I mean, she is hot. But the thing is, there's five kids in her family. They're all adopted, like... in this big, open, hippie kind of life. They're all about helping others and community service. Two of the kids are bi-racial, one is flirting with transgender stuff. The oldest brother works for a mechanic and the other sister..." I chew on my lip for a moment, at a loss for how to describe Skylar. "Well, she's been through a lot."

"Okay, you're right." Hollis takes a sip of beer. "That is different from the normal Preston fare."

"Exactly." I nod. "Anyway, I was texting with her, and just hearing about the chaos made me crave some. And we've been at a deficit for that since you left home."

"You're saying I remind you of chaos." Her lips twitch in amusement.

"In the Bates house?" I scoff, tipping the bottle to my lips. "You're a fucking hurricane."

"Speaking of unstoppable natural disasters, how are mommy and daddy dearest?" It's the first time she's brought them up so far. I'm surprised it took this long.

I swallow a gulp of beer, shrugging. "They're the same. Elitist. Controlling. You know, same old, same old."

"Yeah, I do know." She leans over the counter, hair hanging around her face. "I also know that, the last time I checked, you were all-in on their bullshit narrative."

I meet her searching gaze. "People can change."

"Sure." She eyes me warily. "But it's because of the girl."

I stiffen, but don't respond.

"The girl with the family and the alternative lifestyle, she's shown you there's more out there than Ivy League, secret societies, fraternity keggers, and the perfect internship." She grins. "Oh, I bet Daddy just hates her guts."

I pull at the corner of the beer label. "Yeah, he doesn't know." I reconsider. "About us, I mean. But yeah, he does know who she is, and he definitely doesn't approve of anything about her or her family. Truthfully, no one knows about me and Gwendolyn. Except you, now."

Her eyebrow arches. "Gwendolyn, that's a fantastic name."

"Shut up," I mutter.

"I'm serious! So wait, back up. Are you saying you haven't told your Devils?" The Devils have always been a thing. Hollis may have even dated a few herself, back in the day.

"Nope." I tear off half the label.

"Huh." That seems to have surprised her. "So, like, how do you plan on making this relationship work?"

I exhale loudly, admitting, "I don't know. But I really want to." I look up at her with a cautious, beseeching grin. "Any advice?"

She sighs and reaches across the counter to take my hand. "I'm not going to lie, Hamilton. Going against the status quo as it directly relates to our family and community comes at a cost." She looks around the small garage apartment. "Daddy doesn't play games, so if you're going to take a stand, make sure you're ready to go through with it. *All the way*. I'm talking building a new savings account," she lists, "building your own connections, looking at schools, finding out who your real friends are and whether or not they'll support you. Imagine the worst-case scenario, and plan for that."

"Do you regret your decision?" I ask, mind whirling with all the outcomes. "I mean, you're not even seeing that girl anymore."

"It wasn't really about the girl," she replies, basically confirming what I've known all along. "It was about standing up for myself and getting out from under his thumb. I realized that if I caved about some girl, I would cave over and over again about everything else. School, my major, who I married. It wasn't worth it."

I nod. "But what about the guys? The Devils, I mean. It's such a fucked situation, Hollis, you have no idea. She's had run-ins with them before. We're talking one-hundred-percent organic, pasture-raised beef."

"She's a feisty one, huh?" I nod again and she laughs. "I like her already. The Devils are idiots—look, no offense—they're like every other group of bullies. It's all about power and posturing with them. You have to decide if this is really what you want to do, Hamilton. Because if you aren't sure, then you're going to put Gwendolyn in a dangerous position at school. I know what Devils are like."

Hollis is right, exposing the truth about this relationship will be dangerous for Gwendolyn. Heston is looking for an opportunity to challenge me, especially after that day I punched him. I rub my chin.

"I don't want to give her up," I confess.

"Then you two need to come up with a plan. Don't make any rash decisions, but remember, sneaking around won't work forever. Take it from an old pro. I learned that one the hard way."

"Thank you." I exhale, feeling both relieved and more stressed than ever. "I really needed to talk to someone who would get it, you know?"

She walks around the counter and pulls me into a hug. "No problem, baby brother. And you don't have to be a stranger. You've turned out to be a way cooler person than I expected."

I laugh. "Ouch, harsh backhanded compliment."

"Well, I did grow up with Mother. She's an expert at those."

"Right?"

I hug her again and head out, feeling lighter than I have in a while. It's not that anything's resolved, but I do have options. And she's right. Gwendolyn and I, if we're *really* doing this, we need to come up with a plan together. Between the two of us, we should be able to figure something out that won't ostracize both of us from our friends and family.

When I get to the car, I receive a text. It's Reagan.

You coming to Campbell's party tomorrow night? Pick me up?

I stare at the screen, and then type out a quick reply. One decision I can make is to cut things off with Reagan for good, and tomorrow seems like the perfect time to do it.

23

Gwen

Just when I think I've survived Thanksgiving, my mother drops a bomb.

"I have a surprise for everyone," she says, which makes Brayden and I share an uneasy glance. The twins are still young enough to like surprises, but we both know better. "I've invited some special people over for dinner tonight." Dread pools in my stomach and I know what's happening before she even finishes speaking. Her eyes flit nervously toward me before she says, "All of your 'moms' are getting together to celebrate a second Thanksgiving."

"You," my voice is perfectly flat, "have got to be kidding."

The twins glance at one another, their expressions unreadable to anyone but themselves.

"I know this is a lot, but I just posted something on our family group on Facebook and everyone saw it. The next thing I knew, it had spiraled." She looks at me, eyes pleading. "Don't be mad, sweetie. This is a season for thanks, and this is how I want to show my gratitude to them, for bringing you all in my life." She announces, "We're going to meet at the barbeque place in an hour."

I hug my middle, fists clenching. "So they're all coming."

"Yes," my dad says, standing up for my mom. "Bridget, Amanda, Michelle, and Kayla."

My heart bangs hard against my chest, and suddenly, it's hard to breathe. Kayla is my mother. I haven't seen her since I was five years old, when I told my mother that I wouldn't do it again. The magnitude of this betrayal is so extreme that it barely even seems real.

I shake my head, jaw clenching. "You guys can do what you want, but I'm not being a part of this."

"Gwen," Brayden says, reaching for me.

I twist away. "I know you and Michelle get along, Brayden. And that's great." I look at the twins, adding, "If you want to see Bridget that's great, too. But I won't do it. Not today. Not ever."

"Honey—"

"I've made my feelings on this perfectly clear." I look her dead in the eye, doing my best to adopt a facade of calm, because I want her to see that this isn't a tantrum. "You don't respect my feelings, and you don't respect me."

Her face falls. "Of course, I do. It's just that—"

I stop her. "I don't want to hear your mental gymnastics at rationalizing this. You didn't do this for me, you did it for yourself. I'm sorry to be one less kid you can throw in front of their own emotional freight trains for the sake of looking virtuous." I storm out of the room, climbing the stairs. I'll hide out in my room if I have to. Or Michaela's room. Whatever.

I don't expect them to follow me, and they don't. If Debbie had been here, she would have stepped in and supported me. Unfortunately, she's at home with her own family, and that simple fact makes me feel more alone than anything else. The sick, hollow feeling deepens when I hear the front door slam, car eventually revving up outside.

A few moments later, I'm truly alone.

I curl up in my chair and pull out my phone, holding my thumb over my contacts. I want to call Hamilton. I won't deny it. But we just spoke yesterday, and some niggling sense at the back of my mind is afraid of seeming—and being—clingy. Nevertheless, he's been on my mind since I got home, a constant loop of the time we spent holed up in my room. I keep remembering him on my bed, the way it felt to rest my cheek on his shoulder, how sometimes his hand would come up and sweep my hair back as he looked down at me, smiling about something we were looking at on the laptop. I remember the way he kept covertly trying to take my temperature and thinking that he was better at taking care of people than either of us gave him credit for. I remember the way he felt sleeping beside me, curled protectively around me. It was only for two nights, but I somehow find myself missing it, all the same.

And I definitely keep replaying us having sex. It was a new, almost scary level of intensity. Gentle. Overwhelming. When he gazed down at me with those heavy gray eyes, I got that crazy swooping feeling in my chest again, like the second after the drop of a rollercoaster.

He was like a completely different person while we were in my room. Or, maybe not different, just *more*. Better. I want more than anything to believe he'll be the same person outside of it—that *I'll* be the same person, too—but I'm not convinced. There's just so much baggage between us. So much anger and hate, history and bitterness. How can that all just disappear? How can it do anything but keep creeping back like a sickness?

I'm startled by the shrill ring of the phone, jolting in my seat. I look at the screen, thinking that I've somehow summoned him with nothing more than the power of my thoughts. But it's not. It's not even my phone. It's the antiquated landline my parents will probably never get rid of.

I reach over and pick it up. "Um, Adams' residence?"

There's a moment of silence before a voice answers. "Wait, Gwen?"

"Sky?" I straighten in my chair, tucking my hair behind my ear. "Hey! Hi!" I'm a little caught off guard. Usually these calls are planned well ahead of time and Mom is all over them. "Oh my god, How are you?"

"Good," she answers, and her voice is bright, excited. "Mom called earlier, so I was just calling her back."

"Oh, she's..." I bite my lip, looking around the empty room, and decide she's probably better off not knowing where they've went, or what they're doing. "Well, they're all out right now. How was your Thanksgiving?"

"It was really great," she says, bubbling with enthusiasm. "We had a big potluck with the residents and staff, then we got to go on a horseback ride. It's really nice out here."

I smile at the warm happiness in her voice. "I'm really glad to hear that."

"Sooo," she begins, voice growing even more excited. "Since Mom isn't around for once, I'm dying to hear all the dirt from school. Tell me everything!"

Everything?

Ever since she left, Skylar has been on a need-to-know basis concerning the goings-on at Preston Prep, but I understand her curiosity. She's blissfully unaware of my ostracism, and I intend to keep it that way. "Nothing much has changed. It's swim season, so I'm spending a lot of time there."

"Did you make captain?"

I hesitate. "Yeah. Co-captain, actually."

She barks a loud, "Ha! Who's the poor soul that has to work with you?"

"Hey! I'm a pleasure to work with!" Skylar was never a fan of my competitive streak or penchant to overachieve. Many of her afternoons during our childhoods were spent trying to convince me to put down a book and come do something 'fun'. I take a steeling breath, deciding I can at least be honest about this. "You're not going to believe it, but my co-captain is Hamilton."

I brace myself for a reaction. Any reaction. With Skylar, you never know. Even so, I'm a little surprised when she just lets out a thoughtful, "Huh." And then, "Yeah, that makes sense. It was always going to be one of you, right?"

"Yeah." I wrap my arms around my knees. "We've also been stuck in Saturday detention together for the last month."

"Detention? You? What did you do?"

"Well, it's not as rebellious as it sounds. Dr. Ross gave both of us detention for being, like, ten seconds late."

Skylar groans. "Oh, god, Dr. Ross! She's such a total hardass. I'll never forget freshman year, when she put down that line of masking tape, you remember? Anyone who didn't have all appendages on the other side of it, down to the second, instant detention." There's a wistful tone in her voice.

I can't help but wonder, "Do you miss it?"

"Preston?" She sighs but doesn't wait for me to respond. "Sometimes. I like the program out here, though. I think it's helped a lot, and I really love the horses and the farm. There's no judgement from the animals, you know? I realize now that things weren't right. That *I* wasn't right. But out here, I've learned how to put myself first and not worry so much about pleasing others. You know that's always been hard for me."

I nod, frowning. "I know it has."

A long stretch of quiet follows and I panic, captured by the strange worry that we might not have anything else to talk about.

And then Sky lets out a small, tentative, "Gwen?"

"Yeah?"

"How's Xavier?"

"Oh." I lean forward, thinking. "He's doing okay. He actually asked me about you the other day."

"He did?" I'm not sure how I feel about the hope in her voice.

"Yeah, he..." I pause but decide to give her this. "He wanted me to tell you that he's sorry about everything that happened. And that he's sorry he never got to tell you that."

"Oh." I hear the exhale on the other side of the phone. "I really liked him."

"For what it's worth, I think he liked you, too." Again, there's a long beat of silence, so much going unsaid about that night, about how everything imploded. This time, I'm the one to break it. "Sky, I'm really sorry about that night. I should have been there. I should have gone with you, or told you not to go, or—"

"Gwen, I hate to break it to you, but what happened that night had nothing to do with you. I was upset and insecure and drunk, and I let it all drive me to.... do *that*. Xavier and I had that stupid fight, and I think... well, I think maybe I understand now that he was upset and insecure, too. The both of us, feeling the way we did? It was a mess, right from the start." Her sigh is a small, sad thing. "I just liked him so much, all I wanted was for him to like me back. And the thing is, he did. He really liked me. But the other Devils didn't, and they weren't nice like Xavier, but they were his friends, and I thought... if anyone knows him, it'd be one of them." She pauses for a moment but seems to recover. "It just got to my head, Gwen. That's all."

My voice is quiet and careful when I ask, "Was it really your idea to—" but I can't say it. *To give a dozen or more guys a blow job?*

"It isn't important," she insists. "If there's anything I've learned in all these months of therapy, it's that the only thing I have control over is myself. Blame won't fix what happened. I'm stronger now. More self-aware. That need I have to please everyone—I'm working on that. I'm not perfect, and I'm sure I'll do stupid stuff again, but nothing like that. I promise."

Tears prick at my eyes and I'm overcome by a burst of pride in my sister, for facing her demons, for putting in the work. But at the same time, it's all tinged in sorrow that she's had to deal with so much. "You're pretty amazing, you know that?"

She chuckles, sniffing as well. "I had an awesome big sister who was always there for me. That helps."

We talk for a while longer and I feel better about Skylar than I have in a long time—if ever. I do tell her a bit more about school, including meeting Tyson, and I even vaguely mention Hamilton.

"So he covered for you in detention while you were sick?" Her tone is incredulous. "Wow. That's..."

"Surprising?"

"More than surprising. Shocking? Impossible?" She laughs. "Hamilton Bates doesn't do anything nice for anyone."

Warmth floods my chest at her statement, a spoken confirmation of what I've experienced. What Hamilton and I have is different. *He's* different.

I hang up a little while later, and spend even longer in my chair, lost in thought. When I pick up my phone again, I see that there's a text from Tyson, asking if I want to hang out with him and Presley.

I reply quickly and definitively.

Yes.

～

"WAIT, wait! I don't know if I can do this." We've just gotten out of Tyson's truck, but I'm assaulted by a stomach full of nerves. "You really want to go to a Preston Prep party? At Campbell's house?"

Tyson glances at Presley. "Babe, give me and Gwen a second?"

"Sure." She kisses him on the cheek and climbs back into the truck. He and I stand on the sidewalk outside the massive house overlooking the lake.

"I know this isn't what you normally do, but Presley really wanted to come. You know she's into all my school stuff. She just wants to be involved."

I wrinkle my nose. "But Campbell Clarke? You don't know these people, Tyson. They're *the worst*. And beyond that, they really don't like me. And beyond *that*, I'm definitely not invited."

"Well, I *am* invited—by one of the guys on the diving team—and if I want you and Presley to come with me, then there shouldn't be any problem." He cuts his eyes at me. "And, from the way Hamilton's been looking at you lately, I'm not sure I'm buying that they *all* hate you."

My cheeks heat at Hamilton's name, and I'm suddenly very glad it's dark outside. I know Tyson has noticed something going on with us, but I'm no more ready to tell him than anyone else. However, after talking to Skylar and listening to the way she talks about her life, the growing understanding she's gaining about her own issues, I can't help but wonder if maybe I need to accept that I have more control over my place at Preston than anyone else. Including the Devils.

The only thing I have control over is myself.

And then there's Hamilton. I'm not ready any more than he is to go public, but sharing a social space? If we can't manage it at a simple house party, then there's no way we can make this work.

"Okay," I say, exhaling slowly, "but if things go sideways, or if anyone is a mega asshole, I'm leaving."

He smiles and gives me a hug. "You've got it."

I dither for a moment, trying to decide if I should take off Hamilton's hoodie before going in. I'd put it on earlier, partly because I knew it'd be cold outside, wherever we went, and partly because of something far more complicated and difficult to put into words.

It still smells like him.

That harder-to-define part of myself is what eventually decides to leave it on.

Five minutes later, we've made it past the foyer. The pulse of my heart beating in my ears is louder than the bass of the music coming from the speakers wired throughout the house. Campbell's home is massive. Really. Just a true monument to the arrogance of man. Seeing this many people recklessly moving about makes me over-warm, anxious, and uncomfortable.

"Whoa, look at this place," Presley says, verbalizing, sort of, what we're all thinking. She looks at me with wide eyes. "Is your house like this, too?"

"No." I snort, scuffing the toe of my sneaker against the shiny floors. "I mean, we have a nice house, but my parents aren't really into materialism. They'd rather go save a rainforest or build a school or something." She raises her eyebrows, and I concede, "Yeah, those are totally pretentious in their own special way. But it's just different."

"I need a drink," Tyson declares, bringing his hands together in an excited clap. "Anyone else?"

I shake my head, because there is no way I'm drinking around these people. He heads toward the back porch and as I follow, I pretend like I don't notice the stares. The whisper. The elbow-jabs between friends. I also pretend like I'm not searching the room for a particular, tall, broad-shouldered, ridiculously handsome Devil.

I don't see him, but I do see the others. Emory is leaning against the fireplace, arm around Campbell's shoulder. Over by the kitchen, Ansel is chatting up two girls, happily replenishing their cups. Xavier is in the dining room playing beer pong on a massive glass tabletop. We make eye contact, and he seems as surprised as anyone else, but he actually waves.

"See? Not everyone is unhappy to see you," Tyson declares, catching the exchange. We walk onto the back porch, which is a multi-tiered structure that overlooks the glassy lake below. He grabs two cups and fills them with beer, handing one to Presley. A few guys from the diving team bound over to give Tyson bro-handshakes, leaving me and Presley alone. I'm trying to think of a conversation starter when her eyes widen and she asks, "Isn't that Hamilton?"

My body reacts before my mind does, stomach lurching anxiously, but I look across the patio to see Hamilton deep in a conversation with Reagan. His shoulders are tense, jaw tight, and from the way his hair is sticking up, it's obvious he's been running his hand through it. Reagan's arms are crossed over her stomach, her face pale. I'm not sure what's happening, but I don't think it's good.

"If I had to guess," Presley says, reading my mind. "That girl is getting dumped."

Again, my stomach twists. "You really think so?"

"Oh yeah, and she did not see it coming." She takes a sip of beer and watches with fascination.

I start to turn, feeling guilty and intrusive, but not fast enough. Hamilton's eyes flick my way, and he reacts with the slightest twitch of the jaw. Otherwise, he's stone-faced as he focuses back on Reagan. He says something else, something visibly final, and she storms off, swiping a hand over her cheek. This time I *do* turn away before she can see me, not that she'd connect the dots in any way. That's just my own guilt speaking.

"Wow." Presley's eyes keep watching him over my shoulder. My skin itches with its awareness of him.

"Um, what is he doing?"

"Well, he stared at the ground for a second, and then glanced over here. Now he's walking down the steps."

I bite my lip. "Is he gone?"

"Yes."

I look back, needing to know for my own sanity that he's not just lurking in the corner or something. If something did go down with him and Reagan, I'm not sure I want to deal with the possibility of him lashing out. His tantrums are a thing of absolute legend, and I know that from first-hand experience. Despite that, I can't fight the impulse, the niggling need, to make sure he's okay. I don't do anything, not until Tyson comes back over and plants a sloppy kiss on Presley, effectively distracting her. I cross the porch toward the railing and tuck my hand in my back pocket, pulling out my phone.

G: You okay?

I wait, thinking he may ignore me. Who knows where he went, or who he's with. My phone quickly buzzes with his response, however.

H: Yeah, although I'm surprised to see you here.

G: Tyson talked me into it.

There's another long moment that's filled with my racing heart and surreptitious, paranoid glances around the porch, as if someone might be able to determine who I'm texting with. Truthfully, no one is paying me much attention. I suppose, like Skylar said on the phone, not everything is about me.

H: Can you get away?

I peek over to where Tyson and Presley have joined in a game of cards around the fire pit. I can see Reagan inside talking to Campbell, and Emory's expression is irritated. Because he's mad at Hamilton? Or because he's annoyed the party is disrupted by Reagan's upset?

G: Yeah.

H: Come find me. There's a door off the downstairs porch.

My stomach flip-flops, and never before in my life have I been so happy to be invisible. I slowly make my way over to the staircase and follow it down. Fairy lights brighten the way, and when I get down to the landing to another small porch, I search and find the only door. I turn the knob and walk inside.

Hamilton's leaning on the back of a couch that sits just a few feet away. The room is on the dark side, illuminated only by a single lamp. He's holding a plastic cup to his chest, watching me enter the room with shadowed, hooded eyes. Every inch of my body sears with heat, but I'm not sure what I'm supposed to do, or what he asked me down here for.

"So," I say, taking a step into the room, "Reagan? She looked pretty upset."

"I broke it off with her." He sets the cup aside, eyes scanning my body, perhaps noticing his hoodie. "I couldn't put it off any longer. It was time."

There's nothing in there to indicate what made this 'the time'—the thing he has going on with me, or just because he wanted to anyway. I find myself desperately wanting to know the answer, but unsure how to ask.

I hedge, "I'm sorry?"

He breathes a low laugh, lips curving into a smile. "I'd like to think you aren't *that* sorry." He gestures for me to come closer and I do, heart hammering in my chest as his hands hook into the pouch of the hoodie, pulling me into the space between his legs. His heavy-lidded gaze flicks from my mouth to my eyes. "Just to be clear, I never fucked Reagan."

I blink at him, caught off guard. "Seriously?"

He nods. "We never got anywhere near that far. No chemistry."

I'm not sure believing him is the wisest thing I've done—he could totally be lying—but there's no reason for him to bother. He's already gotten into my pants. "Well, I know she liked you."

His pulls a face. "I'm not really sure she did. I think she liked the idea of me, but she's obviously still been playing the field."

My eyebrows hike up in surprise. "How can you be sure?"

"Because," he explains, reaching out to push my hair off my neck, his gray gaze locked to the skin there, "someone keeps giving her a Devil's mark and it sure as hell isn't me."

I swallow loudly when his fingers press to my neck. "She's been cheating on you?"

"Ironic, huh?" He finally ducks his head, planting a soft, teasing kiss under my ear. "Guess that makes me a free man."

A shiver runs down my spine, spreading goosebumps over my skin. I run my hands down his chest, feeling the firm muscles beneath his shirt. Whatever tension he'd had upstairs seems to be gone now, replaced by the languorous line of his body as he mouths lazily at my neck. This isn't the Hamilton Bates from upstairs, at all. This is the boy who spent days taking care of me in my dorm room, and god, I've missed him.

He pushes, walking me backward, hands guiding my hips as he leads me around to the front of the couch. He doesn't even need to pull me down with him. The second he folds himself down into the sofa, I straddle his waist, capturing his mouth in a slow kiss. He's already hard and eager beneath me, and something inside me swells with pride that I'm able to arouse him so easily. His fingers thread in my hair, tugging me close to deepen the kiss. I think maybe he missed me, too.

He tucks his hand beneath the hoodie, fingertips cold on my belly and making me squirm, grinding down on his erection. He groans into my mouth, hips pushing up into me. His lips roam, sucking, licking. The flicker of an idea, of a *want*, tickles at my brain. I act before I talk myself out of it and ease off his lap.

"Where are you going?" He pouts.

I push at his chest. "Stay still."

He does, watching me carefully as I drop to my knees and bend forward. I reach for his waistband. His eyebrow rises, accentuating the angle of his face sharp in the shadowy room. His hand stills mine. "Gwendolyn."

I look into his eyes. "Yes?"

His eyes tighten, searching mine. "You don't have to do this."

"I want to." I wriggle my hand out of his grip. His abs tense when I dig my thumb beneath the waistband of his jeans, popping the button and lowering his zipper. "Don't worry, this isn't about your bullshit test. I'm not auditioning to be your girlfriend." I reach into his pants and feel him, his cock warm and hard. I pull it free and look. It looks bigger from here, almost intimidating. I tentatively stroke down the surprisingly soft, taut skin. I look back at him again and he's got his head pressed back into the couch, dark eyes watching me, mouth parted. His eyes seem conflicted, like he's caught in some battle between his mind and his hormones.

He runs his fingers along my cheek, thumb pulling at my bottom lip. His cock pulses in my hand. "You get that there isn't a test, right? It *is* bullshit. Campbell made it up, it's not..." He wets his lips, squirming. "I don't actually do that."

I'm not sure why he tells me this. To get it off his chest? To make himself look better? It doesn't change anything for me.

"Let me do this," I say quietly, running my hand down his shaft. "You did it for me."

His jaw tightens, but he drops his hand, eyes heavy and watchful. I stroke him a few more times, getting used to the weight of him in my hand, adjusting to the sound of his breathing, and the way he slowly relaxes.

"Is this okay?" I ask, shifting.

"Fuck yes," he mumbles. "Harder is okay, too. It won't break, Gwendolyn."

Although he'd been the one begging for me to say his name, I'm surprised to discover how much I love hearing mine come from his lips. I tighten my grip and run my thumb over the tip. His fingers curl into fists against the couch and I repeat the motion, feeling a bit more confident.

"Take off your top?" he asks, chest moving with slow, shallow breaths. "I want to see your tits."

His mouth his filthy, and he's bossy as hell, but I don't really mind. I do as he asks, pulling the hoodie shirt over my head in one go. His eyes grow heavier as he takes me in, reaching out and running a finger over the lacy strap of my bra. "Blue. Thought you left this one at school."

"Are you checking my underwear drawer?" I laugh, and he smiles in reply, cock bobbing between us. "I had another at home."

I reach for him again, but this time I work up the courage to lean over his lap and take a careful lick at the tip.

He shudders beneath me, hissing out a low, strained, "Fuck, *shit*."

I can't help my smile, because there's nothing I like better than getting a rise out of him, and apparently that extends to far more than just fighting. Bolstered by this, I don't hesitate to put my mouth all the way over him, slowly taking him in my mouth.

I can hear his head falling back, his breaths growing more strained as his hand shoots out to clutch my shoulder. I experiment a little, sucking with my lips, licking with my tongue, careful to keep my teeth out of the equation. I can't tell what he likes better—the slow, tongue-laving strokes, or the quick, hard-sucking bobs. I get the feeling if I asked him, the answer might just be 'yes'.

It's not long before I feel the tremble in his thighs. His hips keep making these small, aborted jerks, as if he wants to thrust into my mouth but is holding back, restraining himself. I don't protest when his hand winds into my hair, cupped against my skull, not guiding, but just resting there, thumb rubbing against my temple.

Eventually, his breath catches, and he starts going rigid. "Fuck, Gwen, I'm going to come. If you don't want..."

I should release him, but our eyes connect, and the strangest wave of intimacy washes over me. *I do want*, I think, sucking a little harder, feeling him losing control. He groans loudly and holds my gaze as he comes into my mouth, eyes little more than two lazy slits as he watches himself pulse, salty and warm, between my lips. For a second, I think I can't do it, I can't take it, but I do, swallowing quickly, thoroughly.

He watches the whole thing and my face heats, feeling exposed and weirdly shy for someone who just sucked a dick. But he tucks himself back into his pants and pulls me off the floor, guiding me back into his lap.

"Jesus, Adams," he breathes, pressing a hot, open-mouthed kiss to my lips, my neck, between my breasts. His mouth twists into a grin against my collarbone. "That was unexpected."

"We're back to last names?" I ask, tugging at the hair at the back of his neck.

"Absolutely not." He kisses my sore, swollen lips again and laughs. "And for the record, I was serious about there not being a test, but if there was one? You not only passed it, you fucking aced it."

I have no idea why that makes me happy, why any of this makes me happy, including Hamilton himself, but it does. *He* does.

Can it last?

We're about to find out.

24

"MICHA, YOU HAVE TO EAT!" My mom looks down at Micha pleadingly, but the day of any show with him is always a chaotic mess.

He flaps a frantic, dismissive hand at her. "You know I don't eat the morning of a show!" He and Michaela are sitting at the counter, a whole variety of makeup and supplies spread out before them. He says matter-of-factly, "Two hours before curtain call, I'll eat—"

We all chime in a tired unison, "Seven crackers, six slices of Swiss cheese, five slices of pepperoni, four grapes, three peanuts, two M&Ms, and a Capri Sun." We all pause, and then add, "Strawberry-Kiwi flavor."

Micha's pre-show superstitions are a thing of legend.

He straightens his back primly. "It's all my stomach can handle."

None of us were able to sleep in today, as it's all hands on deck, despite him being packed and ready to go the night before.

"I've got this." Brayden, awake much too early to witness both the standoff itself and anything greasy going to waste, picks up Micha's plate and dumps it onto his own. "Problem solved."

Michaela's plate is already empty, and at the moment, pushed aside in favor of an eyeshadow palette. "I think green and purple."

Micha scoffs. "No way. Purple and turquoise, silver highlights, glitter in the corners."

Michaela tilts her head, eyebrows pulled together in deep thought. She ultimately nods. "Yeah, that could work."

Micha had probably had his look chosen and perfected weeks ago, but nobody says so.

An hour later, after we've all had the appropriate amount of caffeine, Micha's face is in fine form. I know that he'll just end up re-doing it all prior to the show, but no pre-show look can be tolerated if it hasn't withstood his afternoon test.

Micha studies his face in a hand mirror, tilting his head from side to side. "What do you think, Gwen?"

This is a trick question. I know for certain there is never too much for Micha. If I tell him it's too much, he'll apply more. If I tell him it's too little, he'll apply more. If I refuse to answer, he'll apply more. I venture, "I think you look fantastic."

He narrows his eyes at the mirror and purses his lips. He declares. "More gloss, I think."

I roll my eyes and add all the necessary pre-show snacks to his bag. Ten minutes later, my mom and dad are shuffling the twins out the door.

"We'll meet you there," I call, waving as they pull out of the drive-way. I walk back into the house and collapse heavily onto the couch next to Brayden. "Wow. Is it just me or does that get crazier every time? I need a nap."

Brayden holds an orange in one hand and flips through the TV channels with the remote in the other, stopping on some kind of sports ball. "It could be the fact you got home so late last night."

I glance over at my brother and despite willing otherwise, heat creeps up my cheeks. "It wasn't that late."

"For anyone else? No." He lifts an eyebrow. "For you? Definitely late."

I'd gotten home after midnight and the house was quiet. We don't have curfews. Mom and Dad feel like we should be responsible for our own time. In general, it's not a big deal. But like Brayden said, staying out late isn't something I do.

I shrug as casually as I can. "I went out with a friend from the swim team."

Brayden leans over to put the remote on the coffee table. "A guy?"

"Yes," I say slowly, eyes narrowing. "But his girlfriend was with us."

"Hmm." He starts to peel the orange, eyes trained on the task. "Michaela says some guy has been asking about you at school."

I shake my head. "Michaela is a gossip."

"We're just worried about you." He tosses me a glance, eyes tight. "Everyone knows things have been tough the last few months. Especially after what happened that day, with you getting kicked, it seems like it's getting worse. Even the twins have noticed things are bad."

I inwardly wince. Sharing a campus with the twins makes it really difficult to hide the fact that I'm a social leper. "Well, things are fine. Swim, classes, all that stuff. It's fine."

"So, no one is messing with you?" Out of all my siblings, he knows the most about my ostracization. He knows exactly how the Devils work.

"No more than usual."

He gives me a dark look. "And no one is hurting you?"

"What happened that day in the hall was a one-off. Nothing like that's happened since." I huff in frustration, because it'd just figure when things started looking up, everyone would look at me like a silly victim. "Honestly, things have actually been a little better. Hamilton —" I snap my mouth closed around his name, afraid I've said too much.

He glances over, eyes narrowed. "Hamilton *what*?"

I exhale, explaining, "Look, we're co-captains now, and I have to give him credit. He's really stepped up. He's just..." I pause, unable to really explain the change in him without admitting things I have to keep hidden.

Brayden gives me a complicated look—something full of dread and anger. "Please tell me you're not involved with Hamilton Bates, Gwen."

"What? Why would you say that?" But my ears are flaming, and I may be sweating through my shirt. "We're co-captains. The school made it very clear they wanted us to cooperate." I reluctantly try testing the waters with, "But if you want to know the truth, we are friendlier now. Actually, I think calling us friends wouldn't even be wildly inaccurate."

"I saw the car that dropped you off last night," he says, and my breath gets trapped in my chest, like a frightened bird. He looks like he's giving me the chance to fess up before he finally says, "It looked a lot like Hamilton's BMW."

I work my mouth around a reply but find that I can't.

He places the orange on the coffee table and wipes his fingers on his jeans. "And don't think I can't see that mark on your neck."

My hand shoots up to cover it, eyes averted.

He sighs. "Do you know why I quit the football team?"

I think back, and come up blank, shaking my head. "No, not really."

"It was fine until my senior year. The guys and I had grown up together. They knew me—trusted me. Sure, I may have been a little different, an *Adams*, but most of them were willing to overlook that since I was a steady, reliable player, and plus, I'd been their friend for so long already. They were weird about it, but they still liked me." He shifts, kicking his feet up onto the coffee table. His voice is quiet and bitter. "And then Hamilton stepped in. Even though he doesn't play football, the other Devils do, and you know how it goes. You know how they're all his little puppets. He made a lot of comments about the team's standards, and how I was only good because my father probably came from the projects or something. He twisted everything and turned the younger players against me. They complained so much, the older guys told me I was too much of a distraction to have on the team. They wanted unity. I was an outsider. It was best for the team if I quit."

My stomach twists uncomfortably. There's no reason to doubt what he's saying. It sounds exactly like Hamilton.

At least, the *old* Hamilton.

My brother continues. "Hamilton is a player, Gwen. He knows

how to get what he wants, from who he wants, all the time. I know you think he's just an asshole, but it's more than that. He's really *skilled* at being an asshole. Manipulating people is his superpower. He comes by it honestly, from a long line of snobby-assed rich dudes who get off on the oppression of others. And no matter what he says, he will never see you, or any of us, as anything other than freaks."

I chew on my lip as I sit there with a heavy, sinking feeling in the pit of my stomach. "Don't you think it's possible for people to change? To grow and become better people?"

His eyes are filled with disbelief, and I know that he sees right through me. "Do *I* think that?! What I think doesn't matter! You're the one who refused to come to dinner last night with our moms. You're the one who's made it very clear that you *don't* think people are capable of change. You're the one who says they don't deserve second chances. If you can't give your mother that benefit, does someone like Hamilton fucking Bates deserve it?"

I stand up and walk away, the truth of his words stinging more than they should. Comparing Hamilton to my mother isn't fair. Yes, Hamilton has been awful to me—to my family—for years. But what is Hamilton to me? He's no one. He didn't bring me into this world. He didn't choose to abandon an inherent responsibility to me.

He stepped up, revealed himself, and he even showed some self-awareness. He grew. He changed. He *defended* me. My mother never did any of those things.

And that's the difference.

Micha, on stage, is a *force*.

The dance performance is a modern version of *The Nutcracker*. Part ballet, part hip-hop, and a heavy dose of artistic license. It's clever and filled with bright, vivid colors. Roles are gender-bent, and Micha has the lead as Clara. Or rather, in this version, Clarence.

His costume is elegantly androgynous. He was right—he *did* need more gloss. It perfectly matches the glitter on his tutu. The fight with Brayden fades away as I sink into the performance. Seeing Micha do something he loves—*truly loves*—is magnificent. And the thing is, he's so utterly good at it. He moves like something fluid and wind-driven, yet also so amazingly strong and solid. He is a true performer, and I can tell from being part of the audience that he has them all in the palm of his hands. It's not just because he's adorable and charismatic, either. He's incredibly skilled, technically-speaking, and it's obvious by the way he moves that he's put in the work training, that this is so much more than some childhood whim of his. It's something he was born to do.

"Want a drink or some candy?" I ask Michaela during intermission. From the way she's looking at her phone, texting with Micha, it's clear that she's planning on sneaking backstage. Sometimes I wonder if any of the others worry about her, like I do. I imagine it'd be easy to find yourself constantly feeling drowned out, having a twin brother with such a big personality.

But if that's the case, she never shows it—is never anything but his biggest cheerleader. She looks at me, nodding. "Water and some Skittles?"

"You got it."

Dad passes me some money and I head to the lobby, stretching my legs gratefully. As I head up the aisle, I pass a few people I recognize. Emory's family is here, including his sister Vandy. Two years younger, she gives me a small, friendly-ish smile. As the other systematically isolated student at Preston, we've had an unspoken bond. Hers is out of protection, her brother making it clear no one is to mess with her. Me? I'd never think protection was part of the way people treat me at school, but Hamilton did say that was part of it, didn't he? To make things easier on me than worse?

The concessions are a fundraiser for the dance program, so it's packed. I wait in line for a long while, scrolling down my phone and ignoring the circus going on around me. That is, until I hear shrill laughter from across the room. I know that voice.

"Oh my god, right?" she cackles. "He doesn't even pretend he's not a fucking misfit. No wonder he had to have the lead. He just wanted an excuse to wear a skirt."

Casually, I turn, tilting my head in the direction of Campbell's obnoxious laughter. She's standing next to one of the large promotional posters that have Micha front and center. It's not surprising that she's not alone. Emory is with her, as well as Heston, Reagan, and Ansel. I scan the area for Hamilton, but I don't see him.

"I'm sure at their house this is the norm." Heston says, flicking poster-Micha in the face. "It's like all of them go out of their way to be massive freaks. Can you imagine living in that human reject pile, with the slutty blowjob freak and Morticia the robot freak?"

Campbell laughs. "It's no wonder the other kids' freaks are emerging."

Heston looks at the poster and then frames it with his fingers, as if setting up a camera shot. "Queen of the freaks."

Ansel cries, "Hear ye, hear ye!" and they all say, "All hail the queen!"

It's my turn at the counter. My hands shake when I grab two waters out of the cooler, giving the student behind the table a limp smile as I request a pack of Skittles. I hand over the money and try to figure out how to get away without them seeing me. I know I shouldn't hide, but honestly, it would take almost nothing right now for me to walk up and start throwing punches, and I don't need the trouble that such an escalation would bring.

I cut through the crowd, paying more attention to the jerks behind me than where I'm going, and end up slamming right into someone.

"Sorry—" Strong hands steady my arms. I look up and grimace.

Hamilton stares back at me. "Watch where you're going, Adams."

Adams. I blink at him and see the aloof distance in his eyes. They dart to the side and that's when I notice Xavier. He gives me a small smile and I twist out of Hamilton's grip.

"Dude, your brother is awesome," Xavier says. "I'm not a big fan of dance or anything, but he's killing it."

I try to smile back at him, but my face isn't working. "Thank you, Xavier."

A beat of awkwardness ebbs between the three of us.

He nods and looks between us. "I'll, uh, meet you in few minutes." He slaps Hamilton on the shoulder and strolls off. Before I can take another breath, I'm dragged into a small storage closet off the lobby.

"What's wrong?" he asks, eyes searching my face.

My laugh is a tight, acerbic thing. God, so many things are wrong. Too many to go into here. "Nothing."

He rolls his beautiful gray eyes. "Gwendolyn."

I look away. "Oh, so now I'm Gwendolyn."

He sighs, face pinching sourly. "That's what you're mad about? Xavier was right there. I panicked."

I cross my arms over my chest. "Your friends are jerks."

"This, and other news at ten." He sighs and rakes his long fingers through his hair. "Seriously? We know they're jerks. What did they do this time?"

I purse my lips, wondering if it would even do any good to explain. I eventually say, "They were out there in the lobby, mocking Micha. Loudly. I don't think I need to tell you why they were making fun of him."

He holds my eye. "Campbell is just bitchy because her sister wanted the part. You know the Clarkes can't handle being told no. So yeah, she's going to take it out on whoever she can—in this case, a kid."

I shake my head, feeling my nostrils flare in frustration. "I don't like it. This wasn't your garden-variety childish, playful bullshit. They're really, aggressively mean about it, and it makes me worried for him. Micha's not like other kids—"

He snorts. "No, he's not."

I blink at him, mouth parting in shock, before turning on my heel.

He reaches for my waist, turning me back to him. "No, I didn't mean it like—I didn't mean it like anything. Micha *is* different. You just said so." The next thing I know he's got his arms around me, pulling me against his chest. "They're assholes, Gwendolyn. Micha's a fucking rock star, okay? He's authentic and completely true to himself. That drives them crazy, because it's something they can never have."

My arms are between us, acting as a barrier, and I can feel his heartbeat notching up before he even begins bending to kiss me.

I turn my face away before he can, his lips crashing clumsily into my jaw.

There's a beat of silence before he asks, "What, are you mad at me?"

"No." I sigh, eyes fixed to the collar of his shirt. "I just… I need to get back to my seat. They'll be looking for me."

He inhales deeply but doesn't let go. "Please don't be mad about all this. That's exactly what they want."

"I'm getting really tired of you telling me not to get upset about upsetting things." The frustration returns, my jaw tightening. "It's easy for you to say that. You don't have any vulnerabilities. You're Teflon. If someone calls you a slur, you have the privilege of not actually being that slur. Stop telling me this shit isn't a big deal. It's not a big deal *to you*. Let it be a big deal to me, because my little brother isn't fucking Teflon, Hamilton."

When I shoulder out of his embrace, his arms land heavily against his thighs, mouth flattening into a grim line. "I didn't mean it like that. I just meant, having been there…" He sighs, shoving his hands into his pockets. "Well, never mind what I meant. I'm not saying it excuses it."

"It's just that this is going to be really hard, you know?" I say, gesturing between us. "With the Devils, and school, and our families… it's going to be hard enough without you dismissing their antics all the time."

He nods in understanding. "I'm sorry, okay? I promise, we'll figure it out." And then he stresses, "*I'll* figure it out. Baby steps, right?" Since when does Hamilton Bates have patience? He'll tire of this situation and me long before anything gets resolved. "Just work with me, here," he pleads.

I sigh, finally meeting his gaze. The line of his shoulders is curved dejectedly, jaw tight, as if he's waiting for the worst. I ultimately give in, threading my arms around his waist, and fall into his embrace when he pulls me closer.

His exhale into my hair sounds more relieved than anything. "Will you meet me tomorrow? Early, before everyone gets back at school? We can hang out a little."

A smile tugs at my lips. "My room?"

"Yep."

When he bends to kiss me, I let him, wanting to feel his lips on mine for one tiny moment of bliss, wanting to let them wash away the bitterness I feel. His kiss could tell the whole story of the last few minutes. Soft at first, gentle and tentative; an apology. Harder then, head tilted as he deepens the kiss. And finally, a handful of aborted pull-aways, his mouth dipping back in after every hesitant pause.

I pull away sooner than I'd like, slipping back into the lobby. The Devils are gone now, the sparse lobby signaling the end of intermission. At my seat, I reach into my pockets and pull out Michaela's water and candy, passing it over.

"Why are your lips so red?" Michaela asks, tearing at the package.

The lights go low just then, granting me a reprieve, but not before I glance down the row at Brayden, who'd heard our sister. Guilt flickers heavily in my belly.

I touch my lips as the music starts to play. That kiss was a confirmation—one that we're both willing to make this work.

25

HAMILTON

"WHAT ARE YOU DOING UP HERE?" I ask as I duck under the center beam of the Devil's tower.

It's early, eight a.m. I left before either of my parents were up, figuring I'd get here way before the rest of the students will arrive. No one willingly wants to come back to Preston after a long break, especially with exams on the horizon. It feels longer than a week since I left Preston Prep for the break. Those days in Gwendolyn's bed feel like a foggy memory, but if she manages to get back to campus early, hopefully we can have a little more time together before we fall back into our routine. I'd come up here hoping to sneak a covert peek of her dorm building.

Xavier's perched on one of the open arched windows, looking down at his phone. "Parents sent me off early. Just enjoying some peace and quiet before I have to go back to the dorm."

I pause. "Want me to fuck off?"

But he just says, "Nah, you're cool," finally putting away his phone. "Is it just me, or does it get harder and harder every time we have to come back? Let me tell you how much I'm not looking forward to being subjected to Ansel's weird music genre flavor of the week."

I grimace. "God, remember his dumb 'core' phase?"

"Mathcore. What the hell even is that?" Xavier snorts. "Still better than the ragtime jug band phase, though."

I look around the space—it's gotten sort of excessively gross over the past couple years—and kick an empty beer can into the corner. "It does, though." At his inquisitive glance, I elaborate, "Get harder, coming back."

"Well, it's probably different for you, you don't even like it at home," Xavier says, kicking back against the side of the window. "Did you know I have two dogs?"

I raise an eyebrow. "No."

"Piper and Melon," he says, turning his gaze to the empty court-yard below. "Black labs. I barely get to see them anymore."

I roll my eyes. "If this is supposed to be a guilt trip, then I'm disappointed. You can do better than missing your dogs. Aren't you leaving behind three hot tubs and a yacht?"

Xavier catches my smile and laughs. "No, not a guilt trip. Let's face it, my parents would have found a reason to ship me off eventually, with or without your dad sending you here."

I'm momentarily caught off guard. "Yeah, but you've been pinning that shit on me for months."

"Well, I was pissed at you because of all that stuff with Skylar." He shrugs nonchalantly. "But I'm a Devil. I'm not allowed to be mad at you for that. So, I just found something I could be mad about."

"Wait." I blink at him, stunned. "Really?"

He nods. "Yeah, I'm not going to pretend I'm a pillar of maturity or anything. It's weird, isn't it? All the dumb shit we hide to save face with all these jackasses." He looks me dead in the eye. "Kind of like how you've been fucking Gwen."

I go utterly still, an aborted exhale dropping like a brick in my chest. He's looking at me like he's daring me to lie, and I probably should. I should at least *try*. But a bigger part of me wants to say 'fuck it', and just go to one of those windows and tell the whole goddamned campus that, yes, she's *mine*.

I want to tell them that it's not just about the sex. What I feel for her goes way beyond that, now. This girl... she's in my head all the time. When was the last time I had to tell myself that things would get better? That I'd just need to make it to the next achievement, the next grade, the next label, and then it would get better?

It already is better.

Being with her—being challenged by her, seen by her, liked by her—makes it better. It makes *me* better.

Last night, at the play, she'd looked so hurt, and the last thing I want is to hurt her more. That's what fuels the instinct of shutting down when we're around others. It's a shield of protection. For her. For me. For us.

But I know one thing for certain; I never want this to stop.

It's a big move for me, but after talking to Hollis, I'm ready to take it. I'm going to have to let the Devils know, but I have to go about it carefully. Strategically. Once they find out, so will my father, and from there my life shifts dramatically. For both me and Gwendolyn. I need more time to get it right, to lay out a plan.

So, I can't tell the Devils.

But maybe I can tell a friend.

"You're wrong," I tell Xavier, something unwinding in my chest. "It's more than fucking."

Xavier watches me for a long moment, hands flexing around his phone. "Don't fucking do this, Hamilton." He drops from the window's ledge, stone-faced as he turns to me. "We've put those people through enough of our bullshit. And more than a little of that was at *your command*. Now, what? What happens after the shine wears off of this exciting conquest of yours, huh? What are you going to do to her then? How ugly is it going to be?"

"She isn't a conquest," I insist.

"Bullshit, dude. I know you." He gives me a long look, an edge of disgust curling against his mouth. "She was the one girl at this school you couldn't have. It's so typical of you, I don't know how we all didn't see it coming a mile away."

"You're wrong," I say, shrugging, and I'm not even mad, because

Xavier has my number. That's exactly how all this shit started. But it's sure as hell not how it's going to end.

He looks at me in disbelief. "How am I wrong?"

"If people found out we were together," I explain, "do you know what I risk? My family, probably. My dad would shit a brick. I wouldn't be the leader of the Devils anymore, that's for damn sure. My trust fund, my eligibility for college, all of it."

Xavier rolls his eyes. "Is this where you tell me that you're still doing it, even though you could lose everything? Because dude, I know you. The bigger the risk, the more you enjoy it."

"No, I was going to say," I narrow my eyes. "That despite all that, the thing that scares me the most about this getting out is what it'd do to her. Losing all that shit would suck, my entire life would be turned upside down. But I could take it." I look out the arched window, toward her dorm, just in time to catch her figure disappearing through the door of the building. "But I couldn't take it if something happened to her—especially because of me."

Xavier is silent, watching me closely.

"Which is why I need to know..." I look at him carefully. "Are you really my friend?" Before he can answer, I clarify, "I mean, *really* my friend, not just someone who falls in line because they know I can make life harder for them if they don't."

"Well." His eyebrows pull together in thought. "Yeah, I guess. If you're really not screwing with Gwen, that is. Because I don't want to be friends with the kind of person who'd do that. Not anymore. I'm fucking over it, Hamilton, I mean it."

I nod in understanding. "Then you can't tell anyone. I'm serious, not even Pippin and Melanie."

His head tilts in confusion. "Who the fuck are Pippin and Melanie?"

I give him a long-suffering look. "Your dogs."

"My dogs are Piper and Melon, you fuckwit." He laughs and I can't help the way my mouth curves into a grin.

I remember Hollis' advice.

'Find out who your real friends are and whether or not they'll support you.'

This at least puts me on the path.

~

THE BEST WAY TO get to Hayden from the Devil's tower is to cut through the entrance to the athletic fields. I start down the path that curves around the side of the stadium, thrumming with the anticipation of getting to Gwendolyn's dorm room. Just as I pass the gate, I hear the sounds of clatter and clinking, smell the harsh scent of chemicals in the air. The unmistakable smell of spray paint. The thing that really draws my attention, however, is the sound of muffled laughter.

I go through the gate and am greeted by the sight of Heston, holding a can of spray paint, and standing right in front of the massive wall that Gwendolyn and I have spent weeks prepping and painting. He's got this dumb, shit-eating grin on his face, which never bodes well. My stomach drops when I see Ansel up on a ladder, a paint brush in his hand. Emory stands underneath him, a cigarette in one hand and a stack of papers in the other.

None of them see me as I walk toward them, which is probably good because there's no fucking way I can hide the shock and building rage on my face. Are they seriously screwing up all of our hard work?

"What *the fuck* are you doing?" It comes out in a low growl.

"Dude," Heston turns to me and laughs, oblivious to my anger. "You're early. We were going to present it as a surprise, but you've got to see this. It's completely epic."

I finally get a good view of the wall and I just stand there, staring at it in disbelief, because it can't be real.

Plastered there is a massive poster from yesterday's performance. It features Gwendolyn's little brother dressed in his flamboyant costume. Dozens of smaller photos surround him—programs from the show. There's a tag overhead in hot pink paint. "*Queen of the Freaks!*"

I lunge at Heston and grab the spray paint, then shout to the guys, "Get the fuck down, *now!*"

Ansel looks at me like I've lost my mind, but Emory just stands there with a dumbass look on his face.

"Dude, what's your fucking deal?" Heston says, looking like he wants to take me. I can see him measuring me up, wondering if he'd come out on top. We both know he won't.

"What's my deal? Are you fucking kidding me?" I take a gulping breath. "For one, I spent four Saturdays getting this wall prepped and ready. Four. Goddamned. Saturdays. And you come in here and fuck it up?" I slam my hand into Heston's shoulder, sending him stumbling back. "For two, this is a *twelve-year-old*. A twelve-year-old who has fuck-all to do with you!"

Ansel, seeming entirely unconcerned, says, "But look at it? It's absolutely hilarious. That picture of the kid? How could we not?"

Even the old Hamilton would have found this stupid. Picking on a twelve-year-old? Where is the fucking victory in that? Where is the challenge in punching down like this? What's the fucking point? Bashing someone because they're gay—because they're different—that's never been my thing.

Heston comes charging back to me, fists clenched. "We just know you had to spend *all that time* with Adams, and we figured this would make it worth it. Don't you think?" His smile is cutting. "Unless, you know, you actually like hanging out with her." His blue eyes hold mine. "Do you?"

I step up to him, nostrils flared as I challenge, "Why? You looking to steal another girl from me?"

He huffs a laugh. "What are you talking about?"

"Don't think I don't know about Reagan. You've been marking her up for weeks now."

"You were stringing her along," he spits. "Either that or using her for a cover. Maybe you learned something from your sister—like how to stay on the downlow when you're fucking the town trash."

Heston's eyes dart above my shoulder and widen before I can even get my fist in the air, which seems strange enough to stop me.

I hear Ansel mutter a sharp, "Fuck."

I close my eyes, inhaling deep and measured. "Dewey's behind me, isn't he?" And that's it. I'm even more screwed. I grimace and turn around, mind racing to come up with an excuse, but it doesn't matter.

It's *not* Dewey.

Gwendolyn stands five feet away, staring up at the poster with a pale, horrified expression, blue eyes swimming with something devastated and stunned.

I hear the guys scrambling behind me, the ladder creaking. In that moment, I'm aware of two things. One, that they're about to run and leave me holding the paint can. And two, that Gwendolyn has this all wrong.

"Do you think this is funny?" Her gaze drops to me, and her voice. *Fuck*, her voice. It's rough with unshed tears and so much hurt that it's like a physical blow. The intensity is a punch in the gut.

"Please, just wait!" I hold up a palm, beseeching. "This isn't what it seems."

It looks like it's an actual effort for her to lift her arm, to extend a finger toward the wall. "There's not a poster making fun of my brother on the wall?" Her eyes flick to the can in my hand. "And you're not holding that paint can?"

I dart my gaze down to the can and chuck it toward the ladder. I hold up both my hands. "I just got here and saw them doing this. I swear. I'm as pissed as you are. They completely wrecked all the work we did."

"Shut up." Her words are a harsh whisper. "Shut the fuck up, Bates. Don't you dare blame this on someone else. *Oh, my god.*" She presses her fists into her stomach like she's staving off a sob, eyes shining with unshed tears. "This is about Friday night, isn't it? You finally got me to take your disgusting 'test', and that's all this was about, wasn't it? This whole time. Tricking Gwendolyn 'The Freak' Adams into getting on her knees and debasing herself for you."

"Holy shit," Heston says from beside me, voice cracking. "She gave you a blow job? Oh, shit, this just keeps getting better." He laughs, leaning forward to peer at her. "And is that a mark on her neck? Jesus, this is *gold.*"

I turn around, shoulders heaving, and feel my face crumple into something murderous. Heston looks over at the others, and then back at me, a bitter smirk plastered on his face as he backs away. A second later they're all gone, bolting across campus.

When I face Gwendolyn again, it's the most painful thing I've ever seen. Her expression is pure devastation, tears now tracking down her cheeks. She looks broken.

My heart clenches painfully, because I wasn't lying to Xavier before. Seeing her hurt? It's agony to me. But another part of me is incredulous and pissed off.

I scream, "I didn't trick you!" and wave my arm around erratically. "This wasn't me. I would never do that to you, and I'd never fucking do that to Micha. If you'd just calm down and listen to me, you'd—" Nothing I'm saying is working, I can tell from the anguish in her eyes, and that's the scary thing. I'm used to her being mad at me, hating me, fighting me, tooth and nail and piss and vinegar. But the heartbroken defeat in her eyes? Desperation runs through me. I swallow thickly. "Gwendolyn, I lov—"

"No!" She sobs, stepping back. "Shut up! You do *not* get to say that to me. What is wrong with you?"

I step toward her. "But—"

"Did you know it was him, all along?" She keeps backing away, no matter how many steps I take toward her.

I stop, face falling as I watch the tears stream down her cheeks. "What are you talking about?"

"Heston's shoes!" she cries. "You can't tell me you didn't know! He's your friend, you live with him. How many people have orange shoes?"

It suddenly dawns on me. "Wait, Heston's the one who kicked you?" I can't even fathom the disbelief in my voice. It makes perfect sense. Nevertheless, it's still a lot to wrap my head around. This is a guy I've spent serious amounts of time with. If he were capable of something fucked up, shouldn't I know?

I'm still processing this when Gwen shakes her head, backing away once again.

"Fuck you, Bates." She swipes the tears from her cheeks, and draws her spine up straight, looking me in the eye. "Never speak to me, or anyone in my family again."

In a blink, her shield is clicked firmly back in place, effectively shutting me out. I don't try to stop her when she walks away. Why bother? Everything is stacked against me.

I should have known.

It was all too easy, the way we could just fall into each other like that. Too easy to think she could love me back. Too easy to think that she could trust me. If it hadn't been this, it would have been something else, and I don't deserve any less. Hadn't I already decided that?

The rage I felt toward Heston is dwarfed by the jagged, sharp things rattling around in my empty chest, a multitude of *'could have been'*s and *'shouldn't have'*s.

But I should have seen them coming. Gwendolyn Adams hit me like a hurricane and now that she's gone, there's nothing but pain and destruction in her wake.

I have no fucking idea how to clean up this mess.

THEY'RE ALL in the suite when I arrive. Emory and Ansel are on the couch, Xavier is in the kitchenette, and Heston is just walking out of his room.

Gwen was right.

His shoes have a wide, orange stripe around the soles.

"So you beat up on girls now," I say, letting my rage simmer just under the surface. Everyone stops to look at me, but Heston doesn't even have the sense to look worried. "Between that and picking on twelve-year-olds, it's almost like you're a complete chicken-shit."

Xavier's eyes ping between us. "Did I miss something?"

Emory pipes in, "You're blowing the poster thing out of proportion. It's just a joke."

"What if it'd been Vandy up there?" I turn to him, blood boiling. "You think she's safe just because you're a Devil? You think these guys aren't whispering behind your back all the time about how she's pathetic and crippled, but—and I'm quoting Ansel verbatim here—perfectly bangable?"

Emory looks at Ansel, jaw clenching. "Is that a fact?"

Ansel gapes at me like a fish. "Bro, what the fuck?"

"Time out!" Xavier makes a 'T' with his arms. "What poster? What girl? What the hell is going on?"

Heston steps in. "Our boy here got him some rotten-ass pussy, and now he thinks he's better than us."

My lip curls. "I've always been better than you, Heston. Gwen had nothing to do with it." I shrug out of my jacket and turn to the others, ordering, "Here's what you're going to do. The two of you are going to go down to the field and take that fucking poster down before people start seeing it. The poster, the programs, all of it."

Emory rolls his eyes, still eyeing Ansel with an edge of hostility. "Why the fuck do we have to do it?"

Ansel agrees, "It was Heston's idea."

"Because," I explain, rolling up my sleeves, "in about three minutes, Heston's not going to be moving very much."

I don't miss the gleam of anticipation in their eyes, and I'm not even surprised. Animals. They're all fucking whacked-out, high on the whiff of their own testosterone, and will turn on one another at the drop of a hat. For all the talk of the Devils being about integrity to our families' legacies, there's no actual loyalty here.

"Jesus, another fight?" Xavier huffs. "Is violence really necessary here?"

Without breaking my gaze from Heston's, I say, "He kicked Gwen in the face, and then vandalized the school by committing a hate crime against her little brother."

There's a moment of stillness, silence.

Xavier exhales. "Yeah. So that's all systems go on the violence thing, I guess. Come on, guys, help me move this."

Xavier, Ansel, and Emory start moving the couch, butting it against the wall. They move the coffee table next, clearing the middle of the floor.

Heston scoffs at me. "I'm not fighting you."

"Oh, I know." I bend down to tighten my shoelaces, just in case. "I'm neither a girl nor a twelve-year-old. You're too much of a pussy to take someone your own size." I straighten, shrugging. "Doesn't exactly put a damper on my plans."

His face is stony and blank, but I can see in his eyes that he's starting to get nervous. "Lay a finger on me, and I'm not going to bother with the dean. I'll just call the cops."

"Seems smart, given the mountain of charges *you'd* be facing." I glance at the others. "I mean, we have witnesses and a mountain of evidence. You've got jack shit."

Emory narrows his eyes at Heston. "Are you really that much of a little bitch?"

Heston's jaw clenches as he looks between us all, realizing that the only way to even remotely save face here is to take it like a man. "You're pathetic," he says to me, walking to the middle of the room. "You think beating my ass is going to prove anything? At the end of the day, you're still the piece of shit who turned his back on his own fucking people. You don't deserve to be leader of the Devils."

"There are no Devils anymore." I step up to him, letting the searing anger boil under my skin, imagining what his face is going to look like after all this is over, and how satisfying that'll be.

Once I do that, it'll be better.

It has to get better.

When my fist crashes against the hard edge of his jaw, I don't feel a thing.

26

I BARELY REMEMBER GETTING to my room. My bag's still sitting on my bed, unpacked, from when I'd arrived back at Preston. For no real reason, I suddenly remember my first night in here, feeling as though it wouldn't be so bad. It was a nice room. Private. It had everything I needed, allowed me to live minimalistically, without the threat of other people clawing their way in. I look around the space and something about it feels terminally small now, as if the walls could close in and crush me if I stood here long enough.

I feel the sour taste of bile rising in my throat long before my stomach even finishes churning. I bolt for the door, darting down the hall to the communal bathroom, and crash into the nearest stall. My knees crack against the floor as I fall, emptying my breakfast into the toilet bowl. It feels like my insides are being pulled out, and I wouldn't even really mind it if they were. There's something black and sickening in there, roiling around, and I want nothing more than to purge it.

Because these are the noxious remnants of what I felt for Hamilton Bates.

The toilet gurgles loudly when I flush, and I sit there on the floor, gazing listlessly at the graffiti littering the stall.

Priscilla Yates farts in her sleep.

These boys ain't shit

TJ + MB 4eva

Raise your hand if you've ever felt personally victimized by Dr. Ross

Gwendolyn Adams is in room 418. Stay frosty!

I blink at the jagged scrawl. Much like TJ and MB, it'd been scratched into the metal instead of just scribbled with a marker. It's not something that can be painted over or erased. It'll always be there.

Always.

Just then, I hear someone enter the bathroom, door closing heavily behind them. I hear footsteps—the delicate 'clack' of heels—and the sounds of shifting fabric. I close my eyes and wait for them to enter a stall so I can sneak out unseen. But whoever it is, they must be at the mirrors instead. With a steeling breath, I stand, brush off my pants, and push the stall door open.

Reagan's gaze jumps to mine in the reflection of the mirror. It only lasts a split second before her eyes return to her face, carefully applying a coat of lipstick. She doesn't live here like I do, but I know she has friends in the dorm. It's not my first time seeing her here.

It's the first time she ever says anything to me, though.

"Well, that didn't last long."

I blink at her, feeling a distant sense of confusion. "Excuse me?"

She puts her lipstick away, her eyes jumping to mine again. "You and Hamilton." She leans back and fluffs her curls, arranging them carefully over her shoulder. "Not that I'm surprised. It's just that when a guy dumps you for another girl, you generally hope they have a longer shelf-life than a gallon of milk." She looks at me, those ruby red lips pressing together. "But I know that look, so let me be the first to welcome you to the Hamilton Bates cast-off club. It's a lot less exclusive than it used to be," she mutters.

I hug my arms around my middle. "How did you—"

"You can't really think I'm that stupid," she says, eyes narrowing. "The two of you were about as subtle as a sledgehammer."

I shift my gaze to the floor, swallowing against the sour taste in my mouth. "I'm sorry."

She snorts a laugh. "No, you're not. And if you're going to go around poaching from other girls, at least have the decency to own it."

"It wasn't—" My throat seizes around the sad, messed up truth of it all. That it wasn't what she thinks. That it wasn't real.

She doesn't seem to care, anyway. She picks up her bag and finally turns to me, looking me in the eye. "You want to know what the most screwed up thing was? When I realized that his obsession with you was no longer just about his long-standing hatred of freaks, I actually asked myself 'what does she have that I don't'. And there for a moment, I thought that was the way. To piss him off, like you did. One second of him glaring a hole into your head was more emotion than he ever showed toward me. But no." She smiles snidely. "Not even parading around with someone else's Devil's mark could get a rise out of him. And do you want to know why?" She pushes off the counter, sauntering forward until she's close enough that I can count her perfectly curled eyelashes. "Because Hamilton Bates is a black hole of nothing. You scratch the surface, you just find more surface. The problem wasn't that you had something I didn't." Her grin is a dark, twisted thing. "It was that you didn't have anything at all. So, if he chewed you up and spat you out, then I'm curious. What exactly does that make you now?"

I stand there for a long time after she leaves, watching my own tear-stained face in the mirror, and I don't make a sound.

No one would hear it, anyway.

I SPEND the next hour locked inside my room. I can't go to classes. Just the thought of it is enough to make my stomach heave again. The only reason I end up leaving at all is for Micha—because I know that poster is still up, and I don't want others to see. When I know I can go out without a total breakdown, I drag myself out to the athletic field right after first period has begun but find that someone's already cleared it. There's nothing left but a few torn corners of yellow program paper.

My relief is two-fold; that hardly anyone would have seen it, and that I won't have to report it, as clearly the administration already knows.

For this, at least, I won't be the snitch who ruined everything.

I go back to my room and collapse onto my bed. I tell myself that this will be the last of the tears, that I can just get it out now, it's only right, and aren't I owed this? Aren't I allowed to be human, just for one day? To hurt and feel and be *something*.

My mind keeps running back to that moment in front of the wall, the moment he was caught. He'd started to say *"I lov—"*

The lengths, the sheer cruel lengths, Hamilton Bates will go to ruin a person is a level of commitment impossible for me to comprehend.

When did he decide to do it? The day after the locker room? When coach told us about the co-captainship? Or was it earlier? After the party with Sky?

I cry myself to sleep, paranoia swirling in my brain.

I have no idea how much time passes. For a long time, my dreams waver between utter monotony and horrific nightmares, but neither is powerful enough to jolt me awake. Eventually, my sleep grows dreamless, an eerie feeling of vacancy permeating my mind. I float there for a long while, long enough that I awaken thirsty, with a pit of hunger nagging my hindbrain. I fall back into sleep, instead. There's nothing here for me. No one to protect and nothing to look forward to, just the endless expanse of ugliness and shame.

The knock comes so late that it's already dark outside my window. My bladder and I aren't on the best of terms, and my joints feel creaky and disused when I finally climb out of the bed and cross the room.

I'm not sure who I'm expecting to find on the other side of the door. Reagan, maybe, coming to push some more salt in the wound. Maybe she's found more creative ways of telling me I'm nothing. All the same, it could be Hamilton, or any one of his Devils, coming to gloat. It could be my dorm resident coming to ask why I missed

classes today. It could be Dewey coming to tell me that I have a thou-
sand years of detention for skipping classes.

The reality is all at once far less dramatic and way more
surprising.

My mom gives me a small, sad smile, holding up a bag. "I brought
pho."

~

My mom and I eat on the floor. I think how similar this is to the time I
spent in here with Hamilton, and then I can't help jerking violently
away from the memory. At first, my mom doesn't talk at all, just
busies herself with unpacking the food and drinks. Nevertheless, I
can see the question in her eyes, the intensity of her concern. She
doesn't verbalize it, though. She gives me a pair of chopsticks and lets
me distract myself with the business of eating.

I eat mechanically. The soup seems tasteless. The motions of
chewing feel foreign and strange, all of a sudden. My stomach accepts
the offering, anyway. I can see her in my periphery, eyes searching,
waiting, but I don't have anything left. I feel numb now, like something came when I was sleeping and hollowed out my insides, and
now I'm just a brittle shell made of dead nerves and unfamiliar skin.

My mom sighs. "Got a call today."

I push a chopstick-full of noodles into my mouth.

There's a beat of silence before she continues, "I take it you
saw it?"

I stab my chopsticks into my soup, offering only a single,
heavy nod.

"Oh, Gwen." She sighs again, pushing her cup of soup away.
"Sometimes I really hate my commitment to letting all of you make
your own choices. If it were up to me, I'd pull the three of you out of
this place so fast."

Despite the broth and the iced tea I'm drinking, my throat still
feels dry when I swallow. "Does Micha know?"

Her face falls. "There were pictures. Online."

I nod. "Is he okay?"

She reaches out to sweep my hair away from my face, arranging it behind one of my slumped shoulders. "We spent the day with him and Michaela. Had a nice, long talk with them. He seems to be taking it as well as can be expected. I think Michaela took it harder than him, truth be told. It seems like maybe you did, too." Her smile is rueful. "I suspect I've raised some really amazing girls."

I push my own food away. "I don't think I can handle any more."

She doesn't ask which I mean—the soup or the antics. Instead, she asks, "Do you know why I asked the moms for Thanksgiving dinner?"

I give her a look that I'm pretty sure says it all for me.

"I know you think my insistence is selfish." She scoots until she's beside me, our backs against my bed. "And I suppose you aren't wrong. It is selfish, in many ways. I know what you all go through here. I also know that you are all the stubbornest, most resilient kids I've ever met. But I feel so helpless." She takes my hand in hers. "I can't make things better for you here—I can't give you my blood— and I worry that, at some point, you'll all start internalizing this nonsense. That maybe you'll start feeling like something really is missing. Sharing you with your biological mothers is the only power I have over this." She ducks her head until our gazes meet, eyes shining. "Gwen, I never wanted to make you feel like I don't respect you. I can't promise that I'll always be perfect, but I can promise this: I will never again put you in a position where you feel forced to face her." Her hand comes up, thumb swiping at my cheek, and I become aware of the wetness there in a detached, surreal sort of way.

I hadn't thought I had any tears left.

"Mom?"

She tucks my hair behind my ear. "Yes?"

I shift my gaze to darkness beyond the window. I know that this school is a machine, that it has moving pieces that never cease, and I know that I'm tired—so very tired—of being crushed between the rusty cogs.

I look at her and say, "I don't want to be here anymore," and then break into a wet, broken sob.

She instantly pulls me into her arms, cupping a warm palm over my head, as if shielding me from it all. I want to tell her that it's not what she thinks, and how guilty it makes me feel. That what happened to Micha and Skylar was awful, but that this gaping void in my chest is the result of me stupidly giving my heart to a guy who could never want it. I want to tell her that it *hurts*, and that it doesn't seem like it'll ever end. Instead, I bury my sobs into her shoulder, hands fisted into her cardigan as if I could force it into her through osmosis, this ghoulish truth that I brought it upon myself.

Her fingers card through my hair as she soothes me through it, and the only thing that calms me are her soft, whispered words.

"Pack a bag."

27

IT DOESN'T TAKE LONG to burn, at all.

The metal barrel flashes sharply when I throw the match into it, and then a few moments of leaping flame. It calms into an almost serene glow, the paper of the poster and programs curling into dark smolders. I watch, transfixed as the halo of fire gets consumed by the ashes, until the barrel finally goes dark again.

The whole thing is disappointing.

It should have been bigger, brighter, something worthy of the catastrophe it caused. Instead, I'm bathed in darkness once again, with nothing but the sounds of tree limbs rattling in the chilled breeze. I should have brought more shit to burn. It's late enough that the whole campus is dead. Even Buster, the floppy old security guard, is probably taking a nap somewhere. It seemed like a good time to come down and destroy the evidence.

Well, that and I got sick of the pervasive and weirdly angry silence in the suite since I'd beaten the shit out of Heston and declared the Devils dissolved.

Ansel and Emory aren't talking to me. Heston spent four hours in

305

the infirmary, and then got sent home, even though nothing was broken, and it wasn't all that bad. I probably hurt myself more than anything, my shoulder throbbing wildly with even the slightest movement. I rotate it now, just to feel the pull and ache, letting the pain anchor me.

For a long time, I wonder where I went wrong.

"What are you doing out here?"

I flinch in surprise, whirling around. I'd been so lost in thought, staring into the black pit of the barrel, that I didn't even hear anyone approaching. I squint against the brightness of the flashlight, holding up my hand to block it.

"Buster?"

So much for his nap.

He lowers the beam enough that I can actually see his face. "You're breaking curfew, young man." He points the flashlight into the barrel, face stern. "And I saw that fire."

I explain, "I was just getting rid of something. It wasn't..." I push my hands into my pockets, frowning. "It wasn't a big fire."

"Nevertheless," he says, "I think you and yours have left your mark on school property enough for one day. Don't you?"

I stare blankly at his sharp, disapproving frown, and it's probably a good thing that the Devils are done, because in a single day, we've lost every bit of favor. Even after getting Ansel and Emory immediately down there to clean it up, and even with Xavier standing guard to divert any attention, it didn't matter. Since we live in a society where everyone has to document everything—even stupid illegal, expellable things—*someone* took pictures, and *someone* shared them on social media.

"Yeah, I guess we have."

"Back to bed, Mr. Bates." He grabs my arm and starts marching me back toward Cresswell. "Word has it you've got a big day tomorrow." And while I wouldn't describe the fissure of buoyancy in his voice as *delight*, it isn't far off.

I never really gave much thought to it before—how much of a burden the Devils have been on the staff here. There are pranks, of course. There's the initiations. There's the sneaking out, and the booze, and the girls, and the vandalism. Pissing off the staff has never been anything more than a childish game, as far as the Devils are concerned.

When we reach the dorm, I turn to him. "I'm really sorry if we caused you trouble, Mr.—er, Buster."

He peers at me through his thick glasses, mustache twitching. "No use sucking up to me, son. Administration doesn't give a hoot how I feel. If they did, all of you would have been expelled years ago."

"No, I'm not—" But the rest of it gets blown away on a tired exhale. "Never mind. Good night."

I'm halfway up the steps when he says, "A bit of wisdom, Mr. Bates?" and I turn back, lifting an eyebrow. "If you think nothing you do matters, one day you're going to wake up and find out that what you've done is *all* that matters." He turns, waddling away. "Make it out count, kid."

AT EIGHT A.M. THE following day, I'm sitting in Headmaster Collins' office with my father.

Even he can't fix this.

I stare at my hands as the Headmaster lists the charges accumulated in the last twenty-four hours. It's quite the laundry list. Setting aside the context and severity of the crime, the old me would have probably been a touch proud. But all leniency for the Devils is gone. The acts of vandalism, bullying, and general violations of the school's code of conduct are in direct defiance of the deal we made last year. Targeting Micha Adams was more than just abhorrent. It goes beyond even the cowardice of the thing. It was just plain fucking *stupid*.

Off limits. That was the rule about the Adams family. And we all broke it.

By all accounts, I'm the worst offender.

I wait patiently for him to bring up my treatment of Gwendolyn, an accusation of sexual misconduct looming stark on the horizon. That'll really be the cherry on this shit pie. I spent all night thinking of what I'd say. The way I see it, I have two choices. I can either insist that there's been a huge misunderstanding and drag her in here to give her full account, or I can just... sit back and take it.

I decided long ago to simply roll with the punch.

I'm mentally preparing to prostrate myself in the face of it all—obviously, some of Gwendolyn's martyr complex must have rubbed off on me—but it's all for nothing.

It never comes up.

"It's my understanding, Hamilton," the Headmaster says, "that you spearheaded the clean-up of the wall."

Well, at least the guys told him that. "Yes, sir."

"Can you explain why you'd vandalize something only to immediately clean it off?"

I'd shrug if my shoulder didn't hurt so much. "No."

"No?" My father shifts in his seat, turning his irate gaze on me. "You can't explain your own senseless actions?"

I flick my eyes toward him, wishing I could muster even a fraction of the fury I see in his eyes, because seriously, join the club. Despite having been boiling with rage about this for twenty-four hours, it's buried so deep beneath my apathy that all I can manage is a nod.

"Look, just give me my punishment. I can accept the consequences." I glance at the Headmaster, asking plainly, "Are you kicking me out?"

He sighs, folding his hands on the desk. "Can you give me a terribly compelling reason why I shouldn't?"

Again, I say, "No."

"Hamilton!" My dad fumes at me for a few solid seconds before turning to the Headmaster. "He's the top of his class, Victor. You know his record."

"You're right," he says, raising an eyebrow. "I do."

"A few disciplinary problems don't cancel out years of academic, athletic, and creative excellence. Hamilton is a pillar of this institution. A legacy. I defy you to look me in the eye and say that Preston Prep won't be losing more than it gains by being rid of him."

The Headmaster's gaze turns to me. "Academics, athletics, and creativity are an important part of this institution. But you cleaned up the vandalism and there's no evidence that you participated in the social media bullying campaign. Those are the only reasons I'm giving your continued enrollment here any thought. Do you understand?"

I nod. "Yes, sir."

He sighs, watching me closely. "I'm willing to let you remain on campus, but there will be conditions. For one," I don't miss his weary glance at my father, "you'll have to resign your position as co-captain of the swim team, and this will go on your permanent record, which means you'll have to reveal this as a disciplinary action on your college applications."

"Now, you wait—" my father begins, but the Headmaster cuts him off.

"This isn't going away, Martin. I've done it once. I can't do it again."

"It's fine," I say, no longer caring about swim or college or anything else. Why should I? I found something more important to me than any of that, and before I ever truly made her mine, I lost her. I deserve this and so much more. "Whatever you think. I accept it."

"There is one more thing," he adds.

"Yes, sir?"

"The Devils are to be disbanded and—"

"Already done," I reply.

My father's gaze whips to mine, wide and shocked, and if I thought he'd understand, maybe I would explain. I'd tell him how serious their actions were, how even Xavier got caught up in this, despite having nothing to do with it, and how completely fucked that is. I'd tell him that I'm over it, and that the Devils harm more than they help. What's that line? With friends like these, who needs enemies?

That's how I feel about the Devils right now.

But he wouldn't understand—wouldn't even bother trying to. This diminishes me. This makes me weak. This makes me powerless and yadda yadda, blah blah.

Moments later, I'm excused. I walk out of the office, passing Emory on the way out. He's a junior and losing the Devils is going to hurt—he undoubtedly would have been coronated their next leader. He looks at me hopefully, but I clench my jaw and walk on. My father catches up to me outside the front door.

"Stop and turn around," he demands when he sees that I have no interest in listening.

I slowly turn on my heel, levelling him with a bored look. "I have a lot of shit to do today, so if this is going to be your regular oral history on the magnitude of my fuck-ups, can you just skip to the part where you get in your car and speed off?"

"I don't know what's going on with you, Hamilton," he strides forward, eyebrows pulled low in anger, "but this streak of defiance has been going on for months, and I won't tolerate it anymore. I told you weeks ago to stay away from that girl—that just being near her would cause you trouble."

"Sure, it was her," I look away, eyes scanning the hall to make sure we're alone. "It wasn't the Devils. They never cause problems. We're a fucking bastion of best behavior." I say, laughing humorlessly. "When are you going to open your damn eyes?"

"Oh, my eyes are open." He steps closer. "I know you went to see your sister at Thanksgiving. I can only imagine what kind of garbage she's filling your head with. Is that what made you think you could throw it all away? I've half a mind to pull you out of this school and send you to Sparrowood Academy for the rest of the goddamned year."

"Do whatever you want, Dad. I don't give a shit anymore." Even though it hurts, I shrug. "I'm done with the Devils, I'm done trying to be a leader, and most of all, I'm done trying to satisfy you. I could drop out, for all I care."

His jaw drops and his eyes widen, and I think for a minute he may lash out. But he seems to recover, simply shaking his head. "I don't know what's come over you, son. But whatever it is, you'd better work it out before you ruin everything."

I gape at him, flinging my arms out wide, gesturing broadly. "Everything is already ruined."

He argues, "Nothing has happened here today that can't be fixed."

The worst thing is that, as it relates directly to his goals, he's completely right. None of this will make a mark on him, and if he has it his way, none of this will leave a mark on me. Oh, it'll have to be creative, for sure. Maybe this time he could donate a new gym, a new library, a new science wing, tennis courts, lacrosse field. It doesn't matter. He'll throw money at it until everything is perfectly smooth.

The thought of it makes me want to scream. It makes me want to go get that metal barrel, throw my entire life into it, and just burn it the fuck down.

"I think—" I pause, wondering if I really want to do this. But honestly, what the hell do I have to lose? "I think I'm learning that there's more to this world than your legacy and this..." I struggle, thinking, "...this constant clawing rat race for prestige. Blood doesn't make you a family, Dad. If it did, you never would have cut Hollis out."

His nostrils flare as he surges forward. "Family is about loyalty!"

But I stop him. "Yeah, and I'm learning that loyalty is about more than just what someone can do for you. I know you might not want to hear it, but I don't want to be loyal to you. Not the way you want me to be, at least."

His eyes bore into mine. "I've never done anything but guide you on the path to success. I don't care whether or not you *want* to be loyal. You will be."

"No, I won't." I shrug again, stepping back. "I know you think you're just helping me—maybe you've really convinced yourself of that. But we don't share the same beliefs, Dad. Right now, I don't deserve to lead the Devils or the swim team. I accept that, even if you don't."

"Deserve?" He scoffs, giving me a snide look. "This isn't something you deserve, it's something you're entitled to."

It's then that I realize I won't get through to him. I can see it on his face. He still thinks he has me, that he can still control and reason with me on the merit of our last name. He hasn't heard a single word I've said.

"Father." I put my hand on his shoulder and look him in the eye. "I love you, but right now, I don't respect you. Maybe that bothers you, maybe it doesn't. Either way, I don't want to be you. I want to be someone who can look at himself in the mirror every day, and that's not a path you're equipped to guide me to."

With that, I turn and walk away, because it really doesn't matter what he thinks. It only matters what one person thinks, and she already hates me. The only way forward is to come to terms with that, even if I'm not sure I can.

28

Gwen

"Are you sure this is what you want to do?"

"Yes, sir." I stand before Coach, my stomach a twist of anxiety. This isn't about what I want to do. Nothing could ever be so easy as that. This is what I *have* to do. I can't stay at Preston Prep another second. Every moment I remain on this campus, it takes another little part of me, chipping away, bit by bit. Maybe there isn't much of me left, but whatever is there? I'm taking it away from this place.

"You're aware that Hamilton has been removed from his position as captain by the administration, right?" He frowns at me, eyes searching. "This leaves me with no leadership on the team."

I think I do a pretty good job of hiding my shock at this news. I hadn't known. Aside from the talk with my mom, no one's really mentioned the fallout to me. The sense of justice I feel is only bittersweet. It probably won't make much of a difference in the long run, and anyway, it doesn't change anything for me.

"I'm sorry for letting you down, but let's face it. The effectiveness of my leadership here has always been questionable. As much as I hate to admit it, without Bates next to me, no one will respect me. On top of that, now they'd just blame me for him getting removed." I twist my hands behind my back, eyes dropping. "Thank you for giving me a chance, but I feel like it's a no-win situation for any of us."

He sighs, face falling. "You're a good kid, Gwendolyn. You'll leave this place and go on to better things and never look back. I have no doubt you'll be amazing at whatever you do."

Tears prick at my eyes, but I blink them back. I'm tired of crying. I spent all of yesterday, and then all of last night, curled up on my bed at home, a complete blubbering mess. I'm done wasting my tears on these people. "Thank you. I hope you guys have a great season."

I cross the pool deck, thankful that it's empty, and enter the office to collect my things. Although some part of me feels like this is a failure—like I'm giving in—a bigger part of me knows this is best. I pushed through this with Skylar, but I can't do it again. Sitting in class with Hamilton, knowing what he did to me—to Micha—would be horrible. I can just see it in my mind now, the long stretch of days to graduation, the creeping, black sickness of anxiety, the constant dread. That isn't healthy.

Worse still is the way everyone seems almost grateful for it. My mom and dad are obviously relieved, and the Headmaster offered me the option of finishing the school year online. It was almost as if he'd been prepared. It didn't matter to me, though. I gladly took him up on it.

I search the desk first, scooping up my pens and notebooks. Then, the locker, where my bathing suit, goggles, and towel are hanging from hooks. After that, the bathroom, for the special chlorine removal shampoo I'd left in the shower. I'm pulling the strings on my bag, cinching it tight, when I walk out, oblivious to the fact I'm not alone.

Hamilton stands in the doorway.

I freeze when I see his form, wide shoulders filling the gap of the entrance. He's got this strange, dull look in his eyes as he watches me, and it's not the first time I've found him imposing, intimidating. But now, it's different. How odd to remember a time where I was afraid of his size and physicality—as if that could be his most effective way of harming me. Standing here now, just facing him, is like having a knife shoved through my heart.

"Don't worry," I say, hoping that my words drip with sarcasm rather than hurt. "I'll be out of your way in a second."

His eyes dart between my empty locker and the bag in my hands, brows knitting together in confusion. "What are you doing?"

"Packing up." I spot my swim cap on the shelf near him.

His gaze follows mine and he picks it up, holds it in the palm of his hand, as if he's testing the weight of it. "Why are you packing? I'm the one who's no longer a captain."

I'm flooded with so many emotions at once, that it's nearly a struggle to breathe. The humiliation and anger, the betrayal, the ache —the chest-hollowing, all-consuming *grief*—all come to the surface. My voice sounds as staggered and ragged as I feel. "You're going to make me say it, aren't you?"

He stares at me blankly.

"You beat me." I toss my hands up, letting them fall limply against my thighs. "Isn't that what you wanted? To make me think it was all okay, that you actually cared for me? To make me think that maybe you'd changed?" I look up at the ceiling, blinking to hold in tears, and chuckle thickly. "Well, congratulations, you won. You proved I'm just like every other girl at this school. Willing to debase herself for a chance to be with the Devil himself."

He watches me, gaze swimming with emotions that I refuse to read. "Gwen—"

"Don't," I hiss, fists clenching, and something flickers through his eyes. I'd be foolish to think it was shame. "Do not say my name. *Ever again*. Isn't this enough?" I'm resentful of the way my voice cracks, but can't help the thread of a plea that emerges. "Isn't breaking my spirit —breaking *my heart*—enough for you? Or are you just not going to stop until there's nothing left?"

"If you'd just stop for a minute and listen—" His eyes shutter then, and if I watch carefully enough, I swear I can see him packing away every emotion, nice and tidy, until they become that dull gray once again. He speaks, empty gaze holding mine, as if coming to a realization. "You were never going to forgive me, were you? You were never going to trust me."

"Forgiveness?" I spit. "*Trust*?" My face twists in disgust, knuckles white where I'm clutching my bag. "I guess we found one way that I'm not like every other girl at this school. Because I'm done with you, Bates. Never speak to me, or anyone in my family, ever again."

I wait for a retort—for whatever mean, twisted response he has prepared—but he just watches me, face still full of that carefully arranged blankness. I wait, and wait, but nothing greets me except the still silence of the room. I've never known him to let anyone get the last word, but he watches me, and doesn't speak.

This must be what Hamilton Bates is like when he realizes that he's finally gone too far.

I sling my bag over my shoulder and meet his gaze, teeth gnashing as I wait for him to move. He's effectively cornered me, but I'm not afraid. That's the thing about becoming this vacant, empty shell. There's nothing left to hurt.

He looks away then, jaw clenching as he steps to the side, allowing me space to pass. My body trembles as I catch his clean, soapy scent, and I know that I was wrong. The mere scent of him fills me with a hurt so acute that it shocks me. Heart thundering painfully inside my chest, I feel like an open, walking wound when I stride away. Away from everything I struggled so hard to gain. Away from this toxic place and all its creeping ugliness and pervasive dread. Away from Hamilton Bates, for good.

I don't look back.

MOVING home isn't without bumps.

Michaela tells me she's fine about moving back to her old room, and then spends the next four hours slamming drawers and angrily snatching her things up to carry next door. I try apologizing, but she just gives me a strained look and says, "It's okay."

It's clearly not.

But at least she tries to lie.

Mom turns into a handwringing, eye-wrinkled mess every time I walk into the room. It's clear that she wants to talk to me, obvious that she understands now that there's something more happening here than I'm saying. She at least does me the favor of not trying to coax it from me. Perhaps we both sense how futile that would be. I'm not ready to admit what happened between Hamilton and me, and I'm not sure if I ever will be. I just want to box it up, shove it into a dark closet somewhere, and never see it again.

Dad's constantly uncomfortable around me, often approaching me like I'm a ticking time bomb who must be treated with delicate care. He takes to offering me snacks, to letting me run errands, to giving me the remote control. Sometimes when he looks at me, I can see a thread of fear in his eyes. He already had one daughter fall apart. I don't think he can handle a second.

Debbie, as usual, is a godsend. She does none of these things. She gives me time, space, and chocolate, and doesn't seem as if she's asking a question every time our gazes meet.

Brayden gives me a wide berth at first, until late one night, he finds me sitting alone on the back porch. I fully expect his well-earned '*I told you so*', but it never comes. He sits down beside me, silent, and the weight of his palm, warm against my back, means he probably feels the hitch in my breath when I struggle to choke down my tears. We sit out there for over an hour, just staring into the darkness of the backyard, and it's nothing, really. No words are spoken. Nothing gets resolved. But it's the first night I fall asleep without shedding a single tear.

Then there's Micha.

Micha is, by all accounts, perfectly fine. He's still riding a high from the show, and if he's upset with me or anyone else, then he isn't showing it. I watch him for days, waiting to see a sign of resentment or detachment, but they're never there. Nevertheless, I stew in the need to comfort him while I wait, carefully composing my apology in my head.

Eventually, I take the plunge.

"Hey," I say, walking into his room. Michaela's stuff is back on her side, but you'd never know it was a boy and a girl who shared the space. There's pink and glitter everywhere. He's watching something on his laptop and barely flicks his eyes in my direction. "Can we talk?"

He sighs, flicking me a long-suffering gaze as he presses pause. "Sure."

I walk in the room and sit gingerly on the edge of his bed. I lean to take a peek at what he's watching on YouTube, and see the still frame of a dancer leaping across a dark stage.

I look away, lacing my fingers into my lap. "About what happened at school—"

"What about it?" His eyes are shrewd, completely unguarded.

He's not going to make this easy.

With a composing breath, I confess, "I think the Devils targeted you because of me. And if that's the case, then I'm really sorry. I know that seeing the pictures of you floating around like that has to hurt, and nothing would hurt me more than seeing you feel self-conscious or—"

"Gwen, stop."

"What?" I look at him, sighing. "I'm just trying to clear this up because I feel really shitty—"

"Well, this isn't actually about you." He closes the laptop, pushing it aside to level me with a frank gaze. "I don't care about that graffiti, okay? Honestly it was pretty cool."

I blink at him for a moment before openly gaping. "Excuse me. What?"

He shrugs. "I looked amazing in that costume. I did amazing in the show. I don't have anything to be ashamed of here. I crushed it."

"I know, but—"

"There's no 'but'." He rolls his eyes. "Are those guys assholes? Yes. They're also jealous haters who can't stand the fact that us middle school kids don't care about all their Devil bullshit. I have friends, Gwen. Real friends, who love me for who I am." He pulls out his phone and opens the ChattySnap app. He goes to a hashtag—*#queenofthefreaks*—and I see hundreds, if not *thousands*, of posts. Each and every one is something positive; demands for more pictures, celebratory gifs, kids showcasing their own uniqueness. I look at it in awe, realizing that he's already got support—a tribe of his own. He explains, "It went *viral*. The freaks shall inherit the Earth, sis, and I'm proud to be one."

I stare at the photos and feel my cheeks heat. Leave it to Micha to see this as good publicity. "I'm proud of you too, Micha, so much. I just didn't want you to get hurt like—"

"Like Skylar got hurt at that party?" My gaze jerks to his, widening in surprise. The twins aren't supposed to know anything about Skylar and that party. "Please," he scoffs, watching me. "With as much of a snoop as Michaela is? Did you really think we were just sitting around, not even trying to find out what happened to our own sister? We might be younger than you, but we're not dumb, and we don't love Sky any less."

"I know that." I frown at him. "I wasn't meaning—"

But Micha just continues, "What happened to Sky was bad, and I hate that she had to go through it. But that's not who I am."

"You're strong," I agree. *Way stronger than I am.* "But people like the Devils? They see that strength and they want to break it."

He rolls his eyes, seeming entirely unconcerned. "I'm not scared of the Devils—or whatever is left of them, anyway. Every day, I walk out the door and make the choice to defy assholes like that." He turns to me, eyebrow raising. "Like, come on, Gwen. Do you have any idea how much bad bitch energy it takes to pull off some of the outfits I wear?"

I can't help but laugh, feeling something in my chest slowly loosen at the sight of his twinkling eyes. "You really are the baddest bitch I know."

"And don't you forget it." He smiles back and it warms my heart. "Now, can I tell *you* something? From one bad bitch to another."

I nod. "Of course."

"You worry too much about what other people think," he kicks back on his bed, scrolling through his phone again. "You think those people target you because you're strong, but you're wrong." He says this matter-of-factly, nodding his head. "It's because they know you care. It makes it easy for them."

I give him a weary look. "Are you saying I should just stop caring when the people I love get hurt?"

He shakes his head. "No, I'm saying that it's not your baggage. You don't have to burn and salt the earth for us. You hold grudges like it's your job."

"So, what?" I scoff. "I should just go and be friends with the people who bully you?"

He gives me a look like he knows exactly how stupid I'm being. "I might be twelve—almost thirteen, thank you very much—but even I know there's a difference between being friends with assholes and not being friends with anyone, *ever*."

"I do have a—" I start, but stop when he gives me a glare. I exhale. "When I drop my guard, people get hurt." *I get hurt.*

"When you drop your guard, you let people see the real you, and I think that scares you—just like it scares you to see the real them." He sighs, those big eyes boring into mine. "People are flawed, Gwen. Sometimes they need to be forgiven for the stupid stuff they've done. But the way you hold grudges... you never want to listen to the apology. It just makes it hard, you know?"

I stare at my twelve-year-old brother and wonder how he got to be the mature one. He's right, I don't want to listen to apologies. They've always sounded like excuses to me. I don't think people deserve a second chance. Should a mother get a second opportunity to hurt a child? Should a boy get another shot at breaking a girl's heart? Do they even want to?

I give Micha a tight smile. "I'm really glad you're doing okay." I pull him into a hug, smiling when he tolerates it with a roll of his eyes. "I'm so proud that you're my brother."

"I know," he says, giving me a grin. "That's one of the reasons I'm able to be this strong. You're a badass, Gwen, but you can still be a badass and live your life. Don't let it isolate you."

"I won't," I tell him, but I don't add that I'm pretty sure it's probably too late.

∼

TYSON WHINES PATHETICALLY, "Gwen, I need your help."

I purse my lips, looking at him skeptically. "I'm really not sure I'm the one you should ask."

"You're a girl." He gestures to me, expression befuddled. "Presley is a girl. You have the golden ticket. You have the inside scoop."

I flip through the hangers, looking for the right size. Tyson and I are at the mall. I'm here to get an Atlanta United soccer jersey as Brayden's Christmas gift. Tyson apparently has no idea what to get Presley, and assumes that simply having a vagina somehow makes me an expert on her tastes.

"I barely know Presley. How in the world would I know what she wants?"

He groans. "But you must have the general gist! Come on, you know how it is. Jewelry seems like it's too much for where we are, status-wise. Clothing is tricky. Trinkets seem lame."

"Well, what does she like?" I find the right size and pull it free from the rack. "Food? Experiences? Sentimentality? Something practical?"

He rubs his chin, expression thoughtful. He's let his beard grow out since school began winter break a week ago. It's depressingly thin. "She likes stuffed animals."

I raise a dubious eyebrow. "Seriously?"

"Yeah. Those really soft ones. She has, like, this whole collection." He frowns. "There's a pretty alarming amount of penguins."

"Well, there you go." I carry the shirt over to the checkout counter. "There's a shop downstairs the twins used to love. I bet they'll have something she'd like."

We get in the long line and I idly check my phone, curious if I have any messages. Skylar's coming home today for the first time since she left for the program. It's just a visit, but it's a big step. It's also the first thing I've felt excited about in a long time.

"Hey, guys."

I turn and see Xavier is standing behind us, a bundle of sweat-shirts in his arms.

Tyson grins and they bump fists, which, in my opinion, seems a little friendly for their relationship. "Hey man, what's up?"

"Christmas shopping."

"Same," Tyson says miserably.

Xavier's gaze flits to me. "Hey, Gwen. How are you doing?"

"Fine." It's my understanding that Xavier had nothing to do with the vandalism at school, and unlike the other guys, he didn't even get punished. Regardless, I can't help that my hackles rise in his presence. But in the spirit of trying to be a more forgiving person, like Micha suggested, I'm willing to give Xavier a pass. "You?"

"Okay, I guess. Things have been a little weird the last few weeks." He scratches the back of his neck. "You know, since shit hit the fan."

A look passes between the two of them. A long, *meaningful* look.

I raise an eyebrow at this. "Am I missing something?"

Tyson wrinkles his nose. "I just didn't really think you wanted to know what was going on at Preston, and you know, particularly with certain people."

"And you'd be right," I say, turning back around. I chew on my lip for a moment before whirling back around. "Okay, nevermind. Spill."

"Well," Xavier hesitantly begins, "it's just that it's about Hamilton."

"What did he do now?" I grunt in distaste, firmly ignoring the way my heart squeezes painfully at just the mention of him. "Did he, like... record me when I wasn't looking? Is there a sex tape out there or something?" Oh, god. *Is there a sex tape?* I wouldn't even know. I shut off all my social media.

"There's not a sex tape," Xavier assures me. "It's just... well, I guess it all started that day. Before we cleaned up the wall, you know? He was spoiling for a fight with Heston, and—" he gives Tyson and I a significant look, "—I use the word 'fight' very loosely here. Heston didn't even want to, but he couldn't back down. Long story short, Hamilton absolutely pummeled him. It took three of us just to pull him off. It was really ugly."

I grimace, guessing, "Because Heston found out about us."

He shakes his head. "No. It wasn't like that. For Heston, it probably wasn't even about you. He just wanted to challenge Hamilton's place. But for Hamilton? It was mostly about what Heston did to you."

My stomach flip flops traitorously. "I doubt that."

"No, I'm serious," he says, eyes wide and earnest. "After taking out his rage on Heston, he kind of just...well, Hamilton's just lost now. Barely recognizable." I must look skeptical because he adds, "Well, for one, he quit the swim team."

I'm not sure I do a good job of hiding my shock. I look at Tyson and he nods in confirmation.

"And," Xavier continues, "he's completely cut off his parents. Not to mention, he skipped the deadline for turning in his applications for Duke and Wake Forest."

My heart thuds. "*What*? But those are his dream schools."

"Hamilton made it pretty clear that those are his *father's* dream schools. Honestly, I don't even know if he's going to college at all anymore. I don't know what he's doing." A line creases his forehead. "He's living with his sister over the break. It wouldn't surprise me if he didn't even come back to Preston in January."

"Is this true?" I ask Tyson. It's not that I don't believe Xavier... I just can't comprehend a universe in which Hamilton quits swim, doesn't care about college, and could drop out. "But what about valedictorian? I practically handed it to him."

Xavier shrugs. "Yeah, well, turns out that when you left, so did his motivation." He holds my eye. "You're the only person who ever really challenged him, Gwen. The Devils just did what he wanted. You know he had the faculty there in the palm of his hand. And girls?" He snorts. "They gave him whatever he wanted. Academics came easy to him. His father didn't challenge him so much as make demands. But you? You pushed him. You made him hold a line." He laughs. "And I suspect you were the first girl to ever make him work for it."

My cheeks heat. The "it" is implied. And he's right. I did.

"Next."

I glance over at the cashier and realize it's my turn to check out. The exchange goes quickly, and Xavier also pays at the register next to mine. We all leave the store at the same time.

"Have a good holiday," Xavier says, offering me a grin. "And please tell Skylar I said hello?"

"I will." I give him a tight smile. My head is reeling from everything he just revealed, but something else pops in my mind. "I told her what you said before—your apology and everything."

"Yeah?" His eyebrows shoot up his forehead, something nervous and hopeful illuminating his expression when he asks, "And?"

"I think..." I shift my gaze to my shoes, swallowing thickly. "I think that Skylar is better than I am at forgiveness."

He exhales loudly, seeming relieved. "That's good to hear. Do you think it'd be out of line for me to call her some time?"

"I think she'd probably appreciate that." His face lights up. "Merry Christmas, Xavier."

He's smiling as he walks off, and I possibly have a better understanding of what Micha was trying to tell me. Forgiveness doesn't have to be a show of weakness, or an invitation for more hurt. It can also bring people together, help them heal those gaping, invisible wounds that fester into something deeper and lasting.

Maybe it's time for me to offer a little of my own.

29

HAMILTON

"ARE YOU SERIOUSLY WATCHING THAT AGAIN?" Hollis mutters, walking across the room. She stops to pick up a pair of shoes—my shoes—and dumps them on top of my suitcase. "Isn't that like, the third time?"

"Only the second," I say, but she has a point. It's not like I didn't just binge watch Stranger Things three weeks ago. There are a few reasons I keep going back to the show. It's easy, first of all. I don't have to pay attention. But it's also a nice distraction. I need something to keep me from remembering the look on Gwendolyn's face the last time I saw her. I thought I knew what hatred looked like, and especially from her, but that had been so much worse. It had been betrayal, and emptiness, and pain. Even if I hadn't meant to, I'd hurt her, and she'd made it clear that there was no going back.

My sister stops in front of the TV. Babysitter Steve is in a battle with a Demogorgon and I don't need to look too deeply into why the *'douchey boyfriend turns into the unexpected hero'* trope is so appealing to me right now.

Hollis says, "Hamilton."

I tilt to the side to peer around her. Steve is kicking some serious ass here. "Hmm?"

"We need to talk."

I nod distractedly. "Sure."

She shifts into my line of vision. She's got her hands on her hips, and her jaw is stubbornly set.

Oh.

I grimace and turn off the TV. "Sorry."

She circles the coffee table and sits on the couch next to me. "Look, you know I don't mind you being here. In fact, I love that you've come to me. I will always be here for you, even when you don't tell me what's going on."

I give her a dubious look. "But..."

"But I would be able to help you better if I knew what was going on."

"It's nothing." I shrug, shifting my gaze to the dark TV. "Just school bullshit. You know how it is."

She nods. "I do. Or, well, *did*. But this is obviously a whole new caliber of 'school bullshit'. I can tell, because..." She trails off, eyes sliding reluctantly to me.

"Because what?"

"Because, dude, you are *rank*. You need a shower." She looks me up and down, grimacing. "And to change your clothes, and to get off the couch and do something—*anything*. And if you wanted to start by cleaning up the mess you made in the kitchen, then I'm just saying, I wouldn't have any immediate objections."

My late-night attempt at cooking hadn't turned out particularly well.

I rub my chin—there's at least a week's growth there—and sniff my shirt. When was the last time I took a shower? Honestly, I can't remember. I guess I am a little gross.

"It's winter break." She says, shaking my shoulder. "Go do something fun with your friends. Call the girl you told me about."

I suck on my teeth and reach for the remote. "Not possible."

She grabs the controller from me. "Why?"

"Because I fucked it up, that's why."

"It can't be that bad," she says, and I snort, shaking my head. "Have you talked to her?"

I run my hand through my greasy hair. "Hol, she doesn't want to talk to me. I screwed up. Big time."

My sister isn't an imposing person. She inherited my mother's grace and beauty, but her face shifts, eyes flashing in something sharp and vaguely terrifying. "If you did something to hurt that girl, you need to apologize. Right now."

"Yeah, that's the thing." My laugh is entirely without humor. "I didn't actually do anything. She *thinks* I did it. The school thinks I did it. Dad thinks I did it. But I didn't. Figures, right? All the shit I've gotten away with over the years, and I end up going down for something I didn't even do." I give her a bitter grin. "Guess that's like karma or something, right?" My smile falls. "But how do you apologize for something you didn't do?"

She blinks at me. "I'm going to need more information. And possibly wine." She stands up and heads to the kitchen, deciding, "A lot of wine."

So, I tell her. I dump it all on the table. The last month—hell, the last *year*. I tell her about the party and Skylar. I tell her about canceling Gwendolyn. I even tell her about the sex—how at first it was rough and maybe questionably consensual. How she got under my skin, and how I think I got under hers. How slowly, we became more than enemies, more than competitors. How we became partners, and then possibly even friends. At some point, lovers. And then, with my head in my hands, I tell her how it all imploded.

It feels like something gnarled and parasitic is being pulled out of me with every breath I take to get the words out. I wonder if maybe this isn't the best thing I can do; just exorcise it from myself, lay it bare, let someone else do the judging for once.

When I finish, Hollis has a sad, pitying gleam in her eyes.

"So, I should apologize, right? But where do I even start? Do I apologize for a month ago? Six months? Five years? Do I take the blame for what Heston and the guys did at school? For the fact she thinks I used her?"

Hollis has waited patiently for me to stop. Her wine glass is empty. "If I'm reading this right—which... god knows, I may not be—I think that it's less about apologizing and more about proving to her that you really do care for her. That you *see* her. And that you're not ashamed to be with her."

"I'm not," I insist, feeling the first spark of defiance in a long time. "I only wanted to protect her."

"You can't protect someone by keeping them a secret. Own your feelings, Hamilton. Actions speak louder than words, you know this."

I think miserably back to Buster's words that night. *'What you've done is all that matters.'*

My phone buzzes and Xavier's name flashes on the screen. Hollis retrieves it from the table and purposefully hands it to me. "Talk to your friend, Hamilton. This wallowing thing you're doing? I get it. But the sooner it ends, the better you'll feel. Clean up and get some fresh air."

I frown at the phone. "And then what?"

"If you want her, figure out how to get her, bro." She gives my shoulder one last pat. "It's the only way."

So, going to Gwendolyn's house was a mistake.

This is made clear to me when her brother, Brayden, intercepts me before I can even step a foot off the driveway.

"Nope," he says, thrusting a finger at my car. "You're going to want to get back in there and drive away." When I just stand there, staring blankly at him, he adds, "Or you can stay here and get your ass kicked. Up to you."

I could take Brayden.

Like.

Possibly.

"I'm here for Gwen," I explain, squinting against the late evening sun. "I just wanted to talk to her, try to clear up some—"

Brayden looks at me like I'm an idiot. "Are you deaf?"

I sigh, face falling. "Come on, man. I'm not here to start anything, I'm just—"

"Wasting your time." Brayden steps closer. His hand slams into my shoulder, making me stagger back two steps. I can't help the yelp I make, nor the way my hand comes up to protectively cradle it. The pain is sharp enough that my eyes prickle, teeth clenched against the stabbing tide of it. He scoffs. "Seriously? This is the great Hamilton Bates? Can't even handle a push to the shoulder? Pathetic."

I gnash my teeth as I straighten, swallowing against the nausea building in my gut. "Brayden, just—"

"She doesn't want to talk to you. *None of us* want to talk to you." He looks me up and down, mouth curled in disgust. "You know what the messed-up thing is? I'm not even sure what to beat your ass for. For Skylar, for Micha, for Gwen? Maybe just for having the nerve to show up here."

"I'm not trying to—"

"I don't care."

"Would you shut up!" I explode, heedless of the surge of red rage on his face. "Jesus Christ, none of you will let me finish a fucking sentence."

"Because we don't want to hear—"

Now, I get to interrupt. "I didn't do it!" I pitch forward, feeling another one of those little surges of defiance. I clutch it like a lifeline. "I had nothing to do with what happened to Micha! Trust me, I was just as pissed as you were when I found out. Would you just—" I press my fingers to my temples, battling the impulse to tear out my own hair. "Just please, listen to me?"

"I don't want to hear your excuses, Bates." Brayden crosses his arms, a challenging look in his eyes. He shrugs aggressively. "I don't care. You're a shit person with shit friends and a shit personality. That's all I need to know."

I look at him, suddenly feeling the urge to laugh. "Are you *sure* you and Gwen aren't genetically related?" His eyes flash again, but before he can get started, I hold up a hand. "I'm sorry, okay? I'm sorry for what happened to Skylar, and I'm sorry for what happened to Micha. Even though I didn't have anything to do with either of those, it doesn't make me any less sorry about it." I take a deep breath, relieved just to see he's letting me talk. "I know you don't think I'm a good person, and that's... that's fine. That's fair. But I swear to you, Brayden, I didn't have anything to do with it."

I'm not sure. Maybe he can see the plea in my eyes. Maybe he can hear the tremor of remorse in my voice. Maybe he can feel that I'm being sincere. Either way, he finally drops his gaze, jaw going tight. "Even if what you're saying is true, it doesn't matter. I know you, Bates, and I know the Devils. You might not have put the poster of Micha up, or put Skylar into that room," He looks at me, eyes blazing, "but you created the environments, the situations. So how exactly does that make you blameless?"

"It doesn't." I shake my head, conceding, "I'm accountable for that, and I *am* trying. I'm trying to make it better." Brayden raises a skeptical eyebrow and I remember my sister's advice. Actions, not words. I add, "I got that wall cleaned up as soon as possible. I mean... after beating the shit out of Heston, but that's—" Probably best to skirt around the bloody violence. "And I dissolved the Devils. And I already apologized to Micha."

Brayden looks taken aback by this, arms dropping. "What? When?"

"About a week after it happened." I shrug, remembering how awkward the moment had been. I'd cornered him after his nanny had driven away, and Michaela looked about three seconds away from kicking me in the nuts and yelling some scary Stranger Danger shit. But Micha had been surprisingly forgiving for a kid living in the Adams house. He looked me right in the eye and said, "Just keep me out of your dumb straight white boy drama from now on," and then walked off.

"He never said anything to us about that," Brayden argues.

I nod. "We pretty much agreed it'd be best if he didn't. Considering, you know."

"And Gwen?" Brayden asks, face stony. "Do you really think an apology is going to make things better for her? Do you realize you're the first guy she was ever with? And the messed-up thing is that I told her—I *told her* you were playing her—and she actually defended you." He shakes his head, cold gaze boring into mine. "She really thought you'd changed, you know."

"But I did!" I insist, willing him with my eyes to listen. "She thinks it was a trick, but it wasn't."

He laughs. "Sure, you were hooking up with my sister for weeks because you *liked her*." He watches me for a long moment before his expressions falls, transforming into something flat and blank. "You've got to be fucking kidding me."

"Yeah." I give him a sad, defeated smile. "I'm sort of stupidly in love with her, actually."

I don't react soon enough to protect my shoulder when Brayden pitches forward, shoving it again, growling, "You're such an *idiot*."

This time, I don't even try to hide my cry. The pain is swift and intense enough that it bends me back and makes me stumble to my knees. "Son of a bitch!"

Brayden gapes down at me in disbelief. "Have you been watching too much soccer or something? It was just a shove, give me a break!"

"It was already injured." I pant through clenched teeth as I climb to my feet. "Fucked it up swimming and just made it worse when I—" Right, skirting around the violence. "*Jesus*."

Brayden watches me nurse my shoulder with a series of very complicated winces, before huffing. "I can't believe I'm about to do this, but get in the damn car."

LITTLE KIDS RUN PAST ME, shrieking and squealing. The room looks like North Pole vomited all over it. Twinkling lights, crafts and glitter, elves, music, and of course... Santa.

"Why are we here again?" I ask, flinching when another little kid runs by.

"It's called *volunteering*," Xavier says obnoxiously. "Nice people do it because they like helping others. People like you and me do it in an attempt to clean up our karma." He shoves his hands in his jacket, rolling his eyes. "Look, my grandma comes to this community center. She signed me up. And then I signed you up."

I nod, swiping a cookie from the cotton-snow-covered snack table. I grumble, "I guess I could use a little karma repairing."

Xavier snorts and leads us over to a table manned by a woman in a festive red smock. He gives her our names, and her beady eyes closely assess us.

"You two look like strong, strapping fellows. How about helping with the tree lot out back? They'll need assistance getting trees tied onto the top of cars."

"Great," Xavier says, handing me a name tag.

"You seriously want me to spend the afternoon throwing trees on the top of cars?" I aggressively slap the sticker on my chest, flat across the PP on my letter jacket.

Xavier elbows me. "I want you to chill out, relax, and just focus on something other than your personal drama for once." His eyes dart around the room before leading me out the back door.

I guess it could be worse. We could have to wear one of those elf costumes. And ever since that day I tried going to the Adams house, my shoulder is feeling a lot better. Apparently, Brayden still has a lot of contacts from his varsity football days. He took me straight to an office that specializes in sports injuries. After a fucking painful massage, and an assessment where they determined at least half my problem was from holding in too much stress, he took me back to Hollis' with sheets of instructions. It's not one-hundred-percent—I suspect this is going to be one of those things I'll need to patient about—but the freedom I feel just being able to lift something like a Christmas tree is a potent thing.

An hour later, I have to admit that Xavier and Hollis are right. I needed to take a shower and get out of the house. Strapping down trees all day turns out to be a stupidly satisfying experience. It feels good to work again, to feel the pull and burn of my muscles, to do something solid and tangible with my body again. And watching those little kids' eyes light up when they see their tree tied to the top of the car is surprisingly cool, too.

"Guys," the coordinator of the tree lot says, "there's a couple of girls two rows over who need help."

"I've got it," Xavier says, patting the hood of the car we're just finishing with.

I've tied down two trees before I realize he still hasn't come back. I wander down the rows and hear his voice, alongside a girl's, one over. I should've known. This fucker bailed on his own karmic project to flirt, leaving me to do all the work. I start around the corner when someone grabs me by the arm, pulling me back.

"Watch it—" I say, but swallow the rest as my eyes fall on the face of the person tightly gripping my arm. It's the face that's haunted my dreams for the last few weeks. "Oh. Hey."

She looks amazing. She's wearing a bright red hat pulled low over her ears, despite it not being cold enough here to merit one, as if it was done for the mere novelty of it. Her cheeks are pink, and her lips have a bit of a shine, like she's wearing Chapstick. She looks better than the last time I saw her, lacking the dark circles beneath her eyes and the stark deadness within them.

She gazes up at me, those long eyelashes of hers blinking. She blurts, "You have a beard."

I slowly raise my hand to my chin, stroking it idly. "Yeah, uh... I just—"

Her gaze jumps to the side, her hand squeezing my forearm. "Shhh! Don't interrupt them."

I glance around the corner to catch sight of Xavier and the girl he's talking to. She's cute, with long blonde hair and bright green eyes. She tilts her face toward Xavier's and grins. His own face lights up with a bright smile in response.

"Who—" I start but stop myself. It hits me like a ton of bricks. I look down at Gwendolyn. "Is that Skylar?"

"Yes." She takes another quick fire glance at them before using her grip on my arm to drag me a row over. Finally, she releases me, explaining, "Just give them a minute to talk?"

I stare at her. "You're okay with them talking?"

Her smile is small and rueful. "They need some time to work things out. It's not really my business." Her gaze flicks down to my name tag, and then the work gloves. "You're working here?"

"*Volunteering*," I correct her, eyes rolling. "Or, more accurately, it's really volun-*tolding*. I got tricked." I rock back on my heels, pretending with all my might that I'm not sweating under my jacket. "It's not so bad."

"Huh." She tugs at her winter hat. "I would've thought community service. You know, for kicking Heston's ass." One of her perfect eyebrows vanishes under the edge of the hat. "I guess I owe you a thanks for that."

"You don't owe me anything," I say, but then decide to take a chance. "I've been wanting to talk to you, actually. Do you think—"

"Not now," she says quietly as Xavier walks around the corner, lugging a tree on his back. "Hey!" she says to him, a touch too brightly. Her eyes dart between her sister and Xavier. "Look who I ran into. It's like a class reunion."

"Oh! Hi, Hamilton." Skylar gives me a reluctant grin—although it's nowhere near as bright as the one she gives Xavier.

I manage a weak wave. "Hi."

Xavier senses the tension and claps his hands together, turning toward the check out. "Come on, I'll get this tied down for you."

"Great," Skylar says and they both walk off.

I look back at Gwendolyn, but she speaks before I get a chance. "I hear you're staying with your sister."

I huff out a feeble laugh. "Xavier is such a gossip."

"He really is." Her expression turns concerned. "And you quit swim? And you didn't turn in your college applications?"

I shrug, looking away. "That's more or less accurate."

She punches me in the arm. "Ow! What the hell, Adams!" Despite the fact that she didn't even hit the arm with the bad shoulder, I growl, "You and Brayden seriously need to get DNA tested."

She ignores this, eyes flashing as she throws her hands up. "Why did you give all of it up? I handed it to you, dumbass. All you had to do was coast."

I rub my arm dramatically. It doesn't really hurt, or if it does, I can't tell over the feeling of my heart banging a wild percussion in my chest. I confess, "I guess after you left, I realized it's not as fun with no one there to compete with. What's the point if I'm not kicking your metaphorical ass?"

I see a spark in her eye—that competitive spirit that's always drawn me in. Something passes between us, and it's familiar, heated, and just as strong as it ever was.

"Gwen? You ready?" Skylar calls.

"Yeah, I'm ready," she calls back. She starts off but I grab her arm, tugging her back. She blinks at me. "What?"

"I really do want to talk," I say, begging her with my eyes.

"Well," she says, holding my gaze, "if that's something you really want, then you'll have to figure out how to make it happen."

Her response surprises me, *jolts* me, and I drop her arm.

She walks toward the car, hopping in the driver's seat. Skylar gets in next to her, the tree tied securely on top. Xavier walks back to my side, waving as their doors close.

"What did she say?" he asks out of the corner of his mouth.

"I think she just issued me a challenge."

"Oh yeah?" His gaze flits briefly to me. "You going to take it?"

I nod, watching the car pull out of the parking lot. "Since when have I said no to a challenge?"

30

THE DAYS before Christmas pass quickly, filled with shopping, baking, and all of our family traditions. They're also filled with something unexpected. Little gifts begin showing up for me on the front step. They're wrapped shoddily—too much tape, jaggedly cut paper—like it was either done by a child or someone who has never wrapped a gift in their entire life.

Someone with delicate hands.

The first day is a T-shirt, personalized to '*Monkey Bar President*', and it's randomly cryptic enough that it takes me a few solid hours to work up a good suspicion regarding who it's from, and what it's a reference to.

The second day is a box of Eggos, which erased all my doubt as to who was sending them.

The third day, a pizza arrives, and it's feta and artichoke, prompting a lot of questions from my family.

"Care to share who this secret admirer is?" Mom asks as I take a bite, making it impossible to reply.

"Is it Tyson?" Michaela wonders, propping her chin on her fists. "I like him."

"I like him, too. I also like his *girlfriend*," I reply, not wanting my sister to run with a new rumor.

"Well, who else could it be?" she asks, picking off a piece of feta. "You don't know anyone else."

Micha stays conspicuously silent about it all, while Brayden just sends me significant looks. They both must know. I'm pretty sure I know how Micha feels about it, given his whole forgiveness lecture, but Brayden's a bit of a mystery. Granted, that alone is saying a lot. A few days prior, he'd gone with me to the store to find a joint gift for Dad, and had brought Hamilton up. It was jarring, to say the least, especially when he turned to me and said, "I don't know if he's a good person, and you definitely deserve better. But that guy is a complete fucking mess over you, Gwen. You need to hear him out. Woman up and let him tell his side. You both need it."

When he told me about Hamilton coming over to see me, I was stunned speechless. When he told me that Hamilton had nothing to do with what happened to Micha, I realized that he didn't even need to. Deep down, I suppose I already suspected—already knew that Hamilton was better than that, even at his worst. Then Brayden confessed that he'd taken Hamilton to have that damn shoulder finally looked at. What is going on here?

It's not a blessing, but it isn't *not* a blessing, either. I get the feeling Brayden has absolved Hamilton for the crimes he had no part in, and feels the rest could be forgiven, for someone who really wanted it, really *earned* it.

Other than the gifts, I haven't heard a word from Hamilton. That's not unusual, but these new tactics definitely are. Before, when he wanted something, he either took it or hounded me into giving it to him. This is something way different. This is a marathon, not a sprint, and Hamilton Bates has always been a sprinter.

Something has changed.

On Christmas Eve, I make increasingly pathetic excuses to go outside and check the porch. I pretend I'm looking for a UPS package. I need to get something out of the car. I need to put a card in the mailbox, despite knowing the mail won't even run tomorrow. But each time I go out there, the front step is annoyingly void of any gifts, and I begin to worry that the game is over.

This upsets me more than I'd like.

Maybe those three things are all he knows about me? Maybe that's all there is. Maybe our relationship is hollow and predicated on nothing more than years of competitive angst toward each other. All the same, maybe he's just been waiting for me to respond in some way? How would I go about doing that? Where would I leave the presents? I don't even know where his sister lives.

There are no rules here. Hamilton and I are in the wilderness.

I try not to let it get me down, instead determined to focus on my family for the remainder of the day. Every Christmas Eve since the dawn of mankind, my mom has made a big pot of her incredible potato soup, and for the last couple years, Skylar and Michaela have made fresh bread to go with it. Brayden and my dad spend each year making bets on the football game, and Micha adds another move to the rather ambitious Christmas dance routine he's been building on since he was six. We already have way too many desserts, and we gather around to watch classic Christmas movies in our matching pajamas, which is another Adams tradition. It started as a way to get the twins to settle down and go to bed, but now that everyone is older, it's just something we have to do every year.

We're in the middle of *A Year Without Santa Claus* when there's a knock on the front door. Dad's in the kitchen getting *more* cookies, and a few minutes later he calls, "Gwen, can you come in here?"

"Sure," I reply, gathering my dishes. I walk into the room, but stop abruptly, nearly dropping the china to the floor.

Hamilton Bates is in my kitchen.

"I'll take those," Dad says, gently removing the dishes from my hands. "And give you two some privacy."

"Thank you, sir," Hamilton says. My first thought is to mentally acknowledge that he still hasn't shaved that beard. My second thought is '*good*'. It makes him alarmingly attractive. Which is not to say that he wasn't already alarmingly attractive, but this makes him look more rugged, less pretty.

His eyes sweep over my red pajamas.

"Um," I look around, face heating, "let's go in the living room."

The living room is a formal space off the front of the house. It's currently housing the tree we got from the lot, which has been horrendously draped in so much tinsel and glitter that even Micha had said, "This may be a bit much." There's a low fire going in the fireplace, more for the festive ambiance than anything else. This is the only time of the year it ever sees any use. This, plus the lights on the tree, cast the room in a warm, twinkling glow. The stockings hanging from the mantle, and most of the tree's ornaments are handmade. This is something that I probably would have been embarrassed for Hamilton to see in the past, but I'm not anymore. He can see the real me—my real family. Glittery ornaments, badly sewn stockings, and all.

"I like your pajamas," he says, lips lifting in a smile.

"Mom has this thing about matching PJs." I tug at the hem of my shirt and try not to cringe. There's a dancing reindeer on the front. It's not exactly my first choice of things I want Hamilton to see me in at this moment.

The warmth of the lights reflects in his eyes as he watches me. "They're cute."

My stomach flip-flops and I lace my fingers together, pressing my fists into my belly like a stern warning. *Behave.* "I like your beard."

His hand comes up to rub his chin, and it's quiet enough that I can hear the soft rasp of it against his fingertips. "Yeah?"

"It's sexy." The compliment slips out before I can stop myself. I close my eyes in mortification, but Hamilton just grins.

He gestures at me. "To be fair, I wanted to say your pajamas looked sexy, too, but I was restraining myself."

I snort a laugh. "Yeah, I'm sure the prancing reindeer are really doing it for you."

"It's not the reindeer that make it sexy," he says, his dark gaze holding mine.

That flicker of heat that always ebbs between us sparks to life. I stutter out, "Thank you for the gifts. I probably should have texted you or—"

"No." He shakes his head. "You told me to figure out what I want, and first and foremost, I want to apologize for everything. All the bad shit. I had this... this thought, right? That it was too many things to list." His mouth curves into a wry smirk. "But then that just made it seem like a challenge." He reaches into his pocket and pulls out a thick square of paper. As he's unfolding the pages, he says, "Now, my memory is aces, but I'll confess to bribing Emory with tickets to my dad's box seats for the Falcons if he helped me remember some of the older stuff. You know how he is."

He clears his throat, eyes jumping to mine as he reads, "When we had that district-wide 'talented and gifted' luncheon in fourth grade, I ate the entire apple pie from the dessert cart, and then I told everyone that you did it." He pauses, adding, "I feel like I already paid my karmic debt with that one, because I was sick the whole night, but —" He takes a pen from his pocket, crossing it out.

"Number two," he continues. "That same week, at recess, I more or less organized a very strong opposition to your position at the monkey bars. If you'll recall, it got excessively heated."

I've had my hand over my mouth, fighting a smile, but at this, I pipe in, "It's true. Fourth graders take monkey bars politics very seriously."

He nods in agreement, crossing it out. "Number three. Two weeks later—or it could have been after spring break, I'm not sure—that time I stepped on your doll's hair so you couldn't pick it up. You were—"

"Hamilton." I reach out, gingerly taking the papers between two fingers and sliding them out of his hand. "This isn't necessary."

He frowns as he watches me take the papers away, reluctantly tucking the pen back into his pocket. He nods. "You can read it later, I guess."

"I don't need to read it," I insist, folding the pages back into their thick square. "I forgive you."

His frown deepens and he looks away. "It can't be that simple, Gwen."

"Sure it can," I argue, shrugging. I hold up the square of paper, waiting for him to meet my gaze, and then I chuck it into the fire. "See?"

His eyes follow it, face gone slack as we both watch the pages burn. "I—" His mouth works around something silent and complicated enough that his eyes go wide. "I didn't even get to the real shit yet."

"This *is* the real shit." When he meets my gaze, I let out a gusty sigh. "I'm done living in the past, Hamilton. It's exhausting."

He's silent for a few long moments, just staring back at me, and I can't tell what's going through his head, but those eyes—the ones that are always schooled into cool distance—brim with life.

"I—" he starts, but stops, running his hand through his hair before reaching into his pocket. He pulls out a small package wrapped in red and green paper and hands it over. "Here."

I take the gift. It's heavy and wrapped just as haphazardly as the others, and he gestures with a nod for me to open it. My heart hammers as I slide a finger under the tape and pull away the paper. From the back, I see that it's a silver frame. I turn it over and my chest constricts.

"Where did you get this?" I ask, wide eyes drinking in the picture.

He shrugs, burying his hands into his pockets. "I've always had it."

It's a photo similar to the one I have upstairs—a snapshot in time of the two of us. We're wearing matching team suits. His hair is wet, plastered over his forehead. Mine's in narrow, dripping pigtails. Neither of us are looking at the camera, but instead smiling at one another. We're both displaying the champion medals that hang heavily around our necks.

"I want—" He exhales and shuffles closer, voice dropping as his gray eyes lock with mine. "I want you in my life, Gwendolyn. If all I can ever be to you is a friend, then I'll take that. It's selfish of me, but you hold me accountable. You challenge me. You make me better. You make *everything better*."

His words rock me, leaving me trembling and breathless. These are the words of the man who cared for me when I was sick, who stood by me with the swim team, who defended me to Heston, over and over again. I don't wonder anymore which version of Hamilton is the real one, because the way he's looking at me right now—hopeful and impatient and terrified—could never be anything less than real.

I flex my fingers around the frame, inspecting the photo. These two kids were fearless and ready to tackle anything that life had to throw at them. I'm not sure where they lost their way.

But I think I may know how they find their way back.

"You're not the only one figuring out what you need," I confess, meeting his gaze. "I don't need Preston Prep, or the swim team, or to be valedictorian. But I know the kind of person you can be, and that guy? I don't want to lose him." I give him a watery smile. "Because he's funny and clever, and he made me feel special and cared for. And maybe also because he needs a little tending to himself, and I like that he can do that—listen and question and grow. People take for granted how hard that is to do. But not me." I glance down at the photo, then back at his face. "Not anymore. So now it's my turn to apologize. I jumped to conclusions and made assumptions that day at school. I knew being with you was going to be hard and I bailed without giving you a chance to explain."

He shakes his head. "Don't, okay? It's alright."

I nod, pressing the frame to my stomach, feeling the knot in my chest unwind.

He wets his lips, shuffling forward once more. "Now that we've agreed we're all sorry and forgiven and everything, where do we go from here?"

I want to kiss him—so bad. I threw those papers into the fire so we could start fresh, and it's almost embarrassing how much I want everything we missed. I want the dates and the fumbling, and a new first kiss—one that isn't the product of anger and resentment and doesn't end in shame. I want it all.

I walk to the mantle, move a paper mâché snowman a few inches to the left, and place the frame there. "Want to come hang out?" I ask, turning to him with a cautious smile. "We're watching cheesy movies and there's, like," I roll my eyes, "a gazillion cookies."

His gaze skitters to the entry, expression heavy with anxiety. "With your family?"

I nod. "We're kind of a package deal."

It's a stretch for Hamilton to not only accept me, but the rest of the Adams family, too. I think of all the hateful, cruel things he's said in the past. If he really wants this, wants me, this is his moment to prove it.

He exhales shakily, but moves forward, slipping his warm hand into mine. "I think I'd like that." His gaze cuts uncertainly to me. "If you think I'd even be welcome, that is."

I laugh, squeezing his hand. "We're talking about my family, Bates. We love nothing more than a good stray."

He smiles and it lights up his face. I start toward the den, but he yanks me back, crashing me into his chest. His eyes are warm but intense, darting between my eyes and my mouth. I know that look. God, I've missed it. He takes my face in his hands and spends a torturously long moment gazing into my eyes, thumbs brushing my cheeks. We meet in the middle, lips brushing against one another, and it's everything I want from a new first kiss—sweet and gentle and warm and Hamilton.

THIRTY MINUTES.

That's the length of time Hamilton, my family, and I sit in a tense, awkward silence. Mom and Dad are on the couch, while Hamilton and I share a loveseat. Brayden is slouched in the armchair, and Micha is on the floor, painting Michaela's nails over the coffee table. Skylar is sprawled out in front of the TV, cramming popcorn into her mouth.

Hamilton feels so tense beside me that I grab his hand and squeeze in what I hope is a reassuring manner. If anything, it seems to make it worse, his gaze darting nervously to my mom and dad, to Brayden. When his jump to mine, the question in them screamingly obvious, I just smile, lifting a shoulder in a shrug.

Naturally, it's Micha who breaks the ice.

"Can I paint your nails?" he asks, staring at Hamilton with an expectant look.

Hamilton looks around, eventually realizing that Micha is talking to him. "Me?"

Micha nods.

"Well, that depends," he says, eyebrows knitting together. "Do I get to choose the color?"

Micha shrugs. "Yeah, 'course."

Hamilton spends the next ten minutes going through Micha and Michaela's ridiculously extensive palette of polish. Everyone else in the room spends the same ten minutes watching him closely.

"What about a green?" he says, considering. "Like a dark green, not a neon green. Like this one—" He plucks a bottle from the menagerie.

Micha pushes his mouth to the side in thought. "I like that one. It'll go good with a glitter coat."

Hamilton's eyes narrow. "No glitter."

I can practically feel everyone holding their breath.

Micha asks, "Why not?!"

"Because it gets everywhere," Hamilton explains, "and you spend the next week spreading it like the glitter-flu."

Micha snorts a laugh. "It's nail polish, not craft glitter." He lifts his chin, sounding obnoxiously formal when he promises, "I personally guarantee this glitter isn't going anywhere but your nails."

Hamilton looks skeptical, but ultimately agrees, "Fine, but it has to be this," and plucks out a purple glitter coat that, in my opinion, is chosen a touch too quickly and decisively for someone who claims to hate glitter.

After that, things relax immensely. We all finish the movie as Micha carefully paints Hamilton's nails, only commenting once that he's got really nice cuticles for a jock. Later, when the polish is finished drying and Micha and Michaela have both begged off to bed, Brayden and Skylar follow, and my dad's not very far behind them.

Before my mom clears out, she gives me a look that's meant to be meaningful but goes completely ignored. "Good night, you two. Hamilton, please send your family our Christmas wishes."

Hamilton shoots to his feet and for a split second, looks utterly ridiculous, like he's about to shake her hand or possibly bow. "Thanks for letting me stay, Mrs. Adams. I'm sorry if I imposed."

She watches him, something in her face softening and—*ah ha!*

There it is. Mom is realizing that he's a stray. "Do you have some-where to go tonight?"

Hamilton looks briefly confused by this question. "I, ah—I've been staying with my sister."

My mom smiles and nods like she expected as much. "Well, if you get tired and don't mind Michaela waking everyone up at precisely sunrise to open her gifts, then you're more than welcome to our sofa."

Hamilton's still got a stunned look on his face when she leaves the room. "Did your mom just offer to let me stay the night?"

I stand up, stretching lazily. "Yep."

"But she knows that I'm—"

"Yes."

He gestures between us. "And she knows that *we*—"

I nod, taking his hand. "Most definitely."

"Don't take this the wrong way," he says, watching my face even as I lead him to the stairs. "Because they seem really nice. But your parents are kind of..."

"Crazy?" I ask, smiling as I lead him up the stairs. "Recklessly lenient? Overly trusting?"

Hamilton doesn't understand where I'm taking him until we arrive in my bedroom. When he does, he freezes, two steps inside the room, watching me close and lock the door. "Whoa, wait."

I look at him, lifting an eyebrow. "What's the problem."

He looks shiftily around, like he's casing the place. "Is this a good idea? What if they find out I'm in here?"

I shrug. "Trust me, it's fine." At his worried expression, I sigh, explaining, "Their room is on the bottom floor, all the way on the other side of the house. They never get up during the night, espe-cially the night before Christmas. You can go back down before Michaela wakes everyone up. But even if they did catch me, like... these are my parents." I roll me eyes. "I'm sure there will be some very psychology-approved talks about contraception and responsibility and how to handle one's emotions in a healthy way. But that'll be it."

He gnaws on his lip for a long moment, eventually meeting my gaze. "You're sure?"

"Yes."

His shoulders slowly lose all of that back-rigid tension as he approaches me, hands landing loosely on my hips. "We don't have to do anything, it's not—"

I cut him off with a kiss, sighing when his hand comes up to gently cup my jaw. This kiss is careful, testing, as if we're asking a question, wondering how well we still know this. But it comes to us as easy as breathing, him deepening the kiss, me tugging him back toward the bed.

It's a little reckless of me, having him here, pulling him down onto the bed with me, and guiding his hips until they're between my legs, his body surging into me. All I can think is '*Yes. This*'. God, I've missed this. I've missed the way he pushes open-mouthed kisses to my neck, and I've missed the solid length of him, hard and insistent, pressing into my center. I've missed the white-hot zing of burning lust I feel when he does. I've missed the way his hand snakes up my shirt and grabs a handful of my breast, and I've definitely missed the rough groan he muffles into my kiss at the feel of it.

He pulls back when I grab at his shirt, letting me shuck it over his head. His chest is heaving with his every breath, much like mine, and the look on his face when I pull off my own shirt is full of something unguarded and *wanting*.

He touches me like someone who's afraid it might be snatched away. Slow and careful, trembling.

I run the tips of my fingers down the hard planes of his chest, over the ripple of his abs, and then hook them into his waistband. "Do you have a condom?"

He stares down at me with hooded eyes, lips wet and red. "Uh." It seems to take him a moment to shake the fog, eyebrows wrinkling together. "I don't know." Before I can question that, he reaches back, sliding his wallet from his pocket. I know the answer just from the relief in his eyes when he peers into one of the folds, but he pulls it out with a victorious smirk.

We finish undressing one another slowly, and I'm not sure if it's because we want to take our time, or because we're both weirdly nervous. Either way, it seems like it takes hours before his fingers finally make their way up my bare thighs, hooking into the elastic of my panties. He holds my gaze as he slides them off and keeps pinning me there as his fingers find my bare center, fingers sliding into my wet folds.

I spread my legs and bite my lip, letting my eyes close at the feel of him. His mouth drops to my neck, breath washing warm across my skin as he kisses the skin below my ear. Suddenly, the world seems very small, reduced down to all the places we're separated; narrowed in on the way he feels, hard and eager against my thigh; shrunken down to the curl of his shoulder as his arm works between us, fingers sending me to the edge and back again.

I have to nudge him impatiently before he finally opens the condom and rolls it carefully over the hard length of himself. He holds my gaze as he pushes inside, and I can tell by the strained, desperate look on his face that this isn't going to last long.

He can probably tell by the look on mine that it really, *really* won't need to.

He makes a ragged sound when he's fully seated, elbows digging caverns into the bed as they bracket my head, and I feel like all the air has been sucked right out of my chest. He moves in these short, grinding thrusts that make me dig my fingers into his back, biting hard on my lip to keep myself quiet. He watches me with those heavy gray eyes, and we haven't lost this—the crackling intensity that's all at once thrilling and terrifying—only now, it's a different kind of fear.

It's not long before I feel my toes curling with the mounting pleasure blooming in the pit of my core. I know he feels it, too, by the way he rocks into me, punctuating every thrust of his hips with a lingering push against me, the friction bringing me right to the precipice.

My orgasm hits me with a sharp gasp into his mouth, eyes slamming closed with the overwhelming tide of it. I feel him following me, hips crashing mindlessly into mine as I swallow his rough groan.

Later, we catch our breath while curled into one another, having tucked myself beneath his arm, head resting on his shoulder. We stay on top of the blankets, leaving it all bare. He curls his fingers and brushes his knuckles over the side of my breast, eyes heavy, as if lost deep in thought.

"Hey," I whisper, reaching up to run my fingertips over his new beard. "What are you thinking about?"

Instantly, and without any shame, he answers, "Your tits." He looks up when I laugh, mouth curving into a smile. "Well, you asked." After a beat, he adds, "I'm also thinking about how you burned my list. You have no idea how long that took me."

I shrug. "I'm not sorry."

"Now there's a list I can give you, right off the top of my head," he says, fingers carding through my hair. "Things I'm not sorry for."

I peer up at him, exhausted and yet somehow too excited to fully fall into sleep. "Is this going to be more stuff about fourth grade?"

His chest bounces with a soft laugh. "Nah, it's only got one thing." He pushes a kiss into my hair and lingers there, inhaling. "I'm not sorry for falling in love with you."

My breath stutters and stalls, and then escapes me in a hard *whoosh*. If I could find a way to put it into words, I'd explain that breathless swooping-chest feeling to him, that I know what it is, and what it means, and how much I want to keep it safe. Because when you're running with a Devil, you might get tattered and torn and broken and bruised.

"Neither am I."

Alternatively, the Devil may care.

EPILOGUE

I've heard the word so many times, it's starting to do that thing where it stops sounding like an actual word in your head. Nevertheless, every time I hear it, I feel pride swell in my chest. Earning Valedictorian wasn't easy—not when you've got Hamilton Bates chasing your tail the whole time.

Literally and figuratively.

"One tenth of a point," he reminds me constantly. Ironically, the class that pushed me over the edge was Dr. Ross'. He thinks I had the upper hand because I sit in the front of the class, "wearing those little goddamned skirts every day. It's a fucking miracle I came in second place."

"That's when I knew," Hollis says to me over the crystal punch bowl. We're on the expansive back patio of the Bates house, overlooking the lake on a warm evening. His parents wanted to throw him a graduation party and had been hounding him about it for weeks. Hamilton ultimately agreed, but only on the condition that it be for the two of us, together. "Anyone who can beat my brother and earn his respect at the same time? You're perfect for him."

I flush, trying and failing to hide my pleased smile.

Hearing her say it means a lot. And having his parents accept our relationship means even more. Not that it was easy, but they've had a big turn-around in the past few months. They could shift the blame when one kid walked away from the family, but two? It was time for a little introspection.

Across the room, my parents are talking to his. This isn't a huge deal. We've all coexisted in the same community for ages. Our dads are both Preston Prep alumni. The difference now, is that they're talking because their kids are dating. We're public now and have been since we both agreed to go back to school in January.

No more secrets.

No more hiding.

I won't pretend it didn't cause a ripple in the social structure at school. That first day back, Hamilton waited for me in the quad as I parted from the twins. I was nervous—terrified, actually—of going from the girl everyone ignored to the girl walking hand in hand with Hamilton Bates, my sworn enemy, down the hall.

Not only did he hold my hand, but he backed me up against my locker and kissed me long and hard. Long and hard enough that Dean Dewey threatened another month of detention if we didn't keep the PDA to a respectable minimum. I didn't even care. It was worth it to see Reagan and Campbell's shocked expressions. It was perfection watching Heston's jaw drop in disbelief. But we didn't do it alone. Tyson was great. Xavier was awesome. And everyone else?

They fell in line.

Because the Devils may have disbanded, but that didn't take away from the power structure at the school. Hamilton Bates will always be at the top. He can't help it. It's in his genes.

The only thing that's changed is that, from now on, I'll be by his side.

~

"WHEN IS YOUR FLIGHT?" Presley asks, popping a chocolate-covered strawberry in her mouth.

I hum. "Tomorrow night."

"I can't believe you're spending six weeks in Puerto Rico." Tyson wrinkles his nose. "I've got a full summer of training ahead of me."

"It was a compromise," Hamilton says, hand slipping around my back. "I wanted to go to Hawaii. She talked me into some half-vacation, half-work situation, where apparently we'll be digging wells or something."

I roll my eyes, looking at him long-sufferingly. "It's not 'work'. We're going to volunteer at a program my mother has contacts with while we're there, and no one said you had to dig a well."

"Unpaid work." He makes a series of overdramatic, fake gagging sounds. "Like a fucking socialist. Even better."

We talk with our friends, and I realize that I'll miss them. But I'm also really excited about going on this adventure with Hamilton. It'll be a good test for the fall.

We both committed to Vanderbilt and secured spots on the swim team.

We'll be around one another *a lot*.

"We're going to go," Tyson says, shrugging into his dress blazer, "but we'll see you tonight at the end-of-year bonfire, right?"

I nod. "Yep."

Presley gives me a hug, and over her shoulder, I see Hamilton across the room talking to an older couple I don't know. I take the break to head to the restroom off the kitchen. I'm only just returning to the party when a hallway door opens, and I'm pulled inside.

I'm engulfed in the spicy warmth of Hamilton's scent before the door even clicks shut.

"What are you—"

There's no need to finish my question. His wolfish grin tells me everything I need to know.

"I just needed a minute alone with you. You know I hate crowds." His nose nuzzles in the crook of my neck. "All the small talk and chit-chat. Really, you're the only one here I like. I don't need a big fuck-you party to have that."

It's true. For the last six months, we've spent most of our time together. In all the years I'd seen Hamilton dating different girls, the

Devils or sports or whatever he was interested in, those things always came first.

He's done a thorough job of making it very clear that I'm his main priority.

Although, the fantastic sex is probably a contributing factor. That's one thing that hasn't changed. He's insatiable, still as wicked as they come. He pushes at the hem of my sundress, fingertips dragging a blazing trail up my thigh.

"Please?" he says, planting a slow, teasing kiss to my lips. "It's been, like... *days*."

I laugh but can't help but push into his hands. "It's been *two* days."

"Jesus, that's like a lifetime." His insistent fingers dip under the lace of my panties, searching.

"What if Renata or someone comes in here?" I say, knees weak from the feel of his lips on my neck. "Or *god*, your mom?"

He breathlessly explains, "I locked the door."

There was really no talking him out of this—not that I ever planned on trying very hard. It's just so much fun—so satisfying and empowering—to see him beg like this, eyes strained and pleading, hands so gentle yet demanding.

He grabs my waist and picks me up, sliding me onto the counter. It takes me a moment to understand that we're in the laundry room. It's absolutely absurd. It's probably bigger than most peoples' living rooms.

I kiss him, suppressing a frown at the feel of his smooth chin against mine. He's shaved his beard, and although he promises to grow it back out in Puerto Rico, I still miss it. I thread my fingers into the hair on the back of his neck and moan when he deepens the kiss, his hips pushing persistently between my thighs. I run my hands over his chest—his button-down is the color of his eyes—and feel a small object in his breast pocket.

I pull back with a breathless sound, asking, "What's that?"

He licks my lips and then his own, giving my thighs one last squeeze before reaching into his pocket. It's a small box. "It's a gift. For you."

My stomach flips in excitement and awe. Hamilton gives the best gifts, and even though it's a semi-regular occurrence to get one, I still get a fissure of pleased surprise every time.

I slide off the gold string and open the lid.

Inside, there's a silver ring. It's shiny and polished, and the design is familiar—a pitchfork wrapped in a circle.

I raise an eyebrow, and he lifts his chin.

"Before we head off, I wanted to mark you properly. Stake my claim, Devil style. Will you wear it?"

"Yes." I grin so wide it almost hurts.

He smiles in return and slides it onto my finger. After, he presses a lingering kiss to it. "It's a promise," he explains. "One day I'm going to give you the real thing. Conflict-free diamonds, of course." He wraps his arms around me and pulls me flush against his body. My legs wrap instinctively around his waist and he speaks into my hair, voice rough with emotion. "You're my everything, Gwendolyn. My best friend. My future. My compass." He tucks my hair behind my ear. "I love you."

It's not the first time he's said it, but my heart still swoops excitedly the same way, each and every time.

"I love you, too."

AFTERWORD

Thank you for reading Devil May Care, the first standalone novel in the Boys of Preston Prep series.

Keep an eye out for book 2 of the *Boys of Preston Prep: A Deal With The Devil*, available on Amazon for pre-order and sale in August 2020.

If you liked Devil May Care, you may also like Angel's reverse harem series, Sparrowood Academy or Thistle Cove, both contemporary, dark, bully romance. Check out chapter one below!

A Deal With The Devil

Prologue

The night it all changes begins like a fairytale.

It's warm for late spring, even for the south, and it's the first time I've seen fireflies this year. They twinkle across the rolling green of the golf course, like tiny fairy lights beckoning me into the dark. I watch them for a long moment, transfixed, feeling the bloom of awareness that always arrives with the changing of the season, as if suddenly realizing the world has taken a gulp of time. Without thinking, I wander away from the patio, the dessert buffet, and my parents, to follow the blinking bugs in an attempt to catch one.

Even at thirteen, I'm still the kind of kid who's more interested in chasing fireflies than talking about gossip, looks, and boys. I'm just not into hanging out with the other tweens at The Club, which is not to imply that my parents would let me anyway. In a world of excess and privilege, I've been blessed with two obnoxiously overbearing parents who expect—no, demand—good, *appropriate* behavior. Especially for a girl. If others think I'm bland and boring, then it just means my parents are succeeding.

It doesn't really matter to me. I'm more comfortable on my own, anyway. I can't compete with the other girls my age, with their push-up bras from Victoria's Secret, or their high-heeled wedges that make them three inches taller. My best friend, Sydney, is all in the thick of it, a cornerstone of their whispered bathroom conversations about sneaking alcohol and giving guys blow jobs. Along with all the stuffed bras, I suspect they're making it up—well, I *know* Sydney is—but regardless, there has to be a certain level of confidence to even pretend to live that life. It's something I definitely lack.

The firefly slips through the cracks in the wrought iron gate leading out to the parking lot. I push through unthinkingly, continuing to follow it, but jolt to a stop when I hear a voice.

"I bet you can't do it," I hear a boy whisper.

No, not just a boy. My brother, Emory.

Someone else scoffs. "Sure, I can."

I freeze at the sound of *this* voice, my heartbeat stuttering at the low cadence. Reynolds McAllister is many things. He's our next-door neighbor. He's my brother's best friend. He's our neighborhood's biggest troublemaker. He is, I suspect, the focus of many of those whispered bathroom discussions among the girls. But most of all, Reynolds McAllister is this:

My soul mate.

Reynolds whispers, "I just need a distraction."

I shift a little so I can get a better view. It's already dark out—hence the fireflies—but the moon is bright and full enough that I can see both of their profiles in a thicket of sculpted bushes. They're crouched low, peering out at the parking lot, and I can just barely make out the confident, loose smile curving Reynold's lips.

"Are you down, or what?" he challenges.

I watch as Emory gnaws at a thumbnail, silent for a moment, before agreeing, "I'll distract the attendant and you'll snag the keys."

Reynolds turns to him to say, "Remember what I taught you. Nothing too big. Don't draw outside attention."

"Yeah, yeah." My brother flaps a dismissive hand, adding, "And you can't just grab any key. It has to be something really nice, like a Porsche or Tesla."

"Hey, hold the fuck up. Now there's criteria?" Reynolds' voice is already deep for a fourteen-year-old. He makes my brother sound like he's still in middle school, with me—not a freshman at Preston Prep. His deep voice and penchant for curse words always makes Reynolds sound confident and a little commanding, like he's the one in charge, older somehow. It also frequently makes my cheeks heat, but that started long before he hit puberty.

Since as far back as I can remember, I've always had a crush on Reynolds McAllister. It isn't just his easy smile, nor is it the deep-set dimples on his cheeks, both of which are likely a useful distraction, as once he sets them loose, you're rendered temporarily unable to wonder what he's up to—though the answer is usually 'stealing something'. It's not his messy hair, or that he's got the dreamiest green eyes, or the way he always slouches when he sits, with his legs spread wide, like he's just too cool to care about anything. It's not even that he somehow knows a lot about things that fourteen-year-olds shouldn't.

It's about the way he looks at me sometimes, assured and trusting, like I'm not a child—like I'm more than the neighbor's bratty kid sister. Emory and the rest of his friends have no tolerance for me. I can't even count the amount of times Emory has wanted to do something and our parents have asked him to take me along. I can't ignore the way my brother and his friends react with deep groans and barely-veiled glowers.

But not *him*.

Reynolds will just give me one of those easy smiles, gesture with a nod at the door, and wait for me to follow.

"Bro, look," Emory explains, "If we're going to jack one of these cars, it may as well be worth it. We're both already on strike two."

I gape at their shadowy forms, knowing that one of the biggest reasons my parents are so overprotective is that my idiot brother can't seem to stay out of trouble. It's like a moth to a flame. Which is why, despite the fact I'm not the least bit surprised the guys are talking about stealing a car, I *am* surprised they're stupid enough to actually do it.

Again.

This has been going on for a year now already, and they're both close to getting into real trouble—the *serious* kind of trouble that can't just be wiped away with a phone call from our dad and a donation to whatever institution has fallen victim to their next antic. It comes at no surprise that Reynolds is orchestrating it, though. There are a finite amount of certainties in life; the grass is green, the sky is blue, and Reynolds McAllister will steal anything that isn't bolted down.

Not that bolts would stop him from trying.

It'd started as a running joke in the community—little Sticky Fingers McAllister—but Reynolds isn't little anymore, and no one is laughing now. It's grown obvious that this is more than good natured pranks, more than material desire. Reynolds just keeps taking things, no matter the punishment. Whether it's for the fun of it, the challenge of it, or some weird compulsion, this is what it's escalated to, and he's dragging my brother along.

But Emory isn't stupid, and unlike many of our other friends' parents, ours would follow through on a serious punishment if he got busted one more time.

But I don't need to wonder why they're taking the risk. They've both been vying for a chance to be part of the exclusive group of Devils at the high school. The Devils are a bunch of popular jocks, which is something Emory and Reynolds already are, so it doesn't even make sense to me. They've already made the football team. They've dated the prettiest girls, have worn the matching letterman jackets, and have driven the expensive cars. They're already legendary, even by middle school standards. But, from what I understand, trivial schoolyard shenanigans are far below the cruel caliber of the Devils' usual fare.

A prank like this would look great on their resume.

The second I decide to step in and do something, my heart starts pounding, palms growing sweaty, but I have to stop them before this goes too far. I don't want either of them to get a third strike—whatever that means, it doesn't sound good.

I take a deep breath and march down the sidewalk, having to cut around the shrubbery to meet them. But when I reach the bush, the only person I see is Reynolds, peering over at the valet attendant's stand.

"Where's Emory?" I whisper.

Reynolds jerks in surprise, whipping around to meet my gaze. When he does, he releases a slow exhale, shoulders slumping in relief. His green eyes sweep over me, then dart back to the attendant's stand where my brother has suddenly appeared. "Get out of here, Baby V."

Ugh, I hate when he calls me that. "I know what you're doing," I say, crossing my arms defiantly, "and you two need to stop."

"If you know what we're doing," he says, sparing me a rapid glance, "then you need to get the hell out of here."

From the attendant's stand, my brother suddenly shouts, "God Dammit, Bryan!" sounding much older than fourteen. "There's a scratch on my father's BMW! Do you want to explain how that got there?"

We come to this country club often enough to know that Bryan is new. "A scratch? Where?" Bryan narrows his eyes suspiciously at my brother, but it's clear from the way they dart around that he's worried.

Emory gestures wildly. "Down the whole side panel!"

My teeth grind in frustration at having been blown off by Reynolds, so I give up and just march toward the valet stand instead. If I can't stop Reynolds, maybe I can talk some sense into my idiot brother.

"Why were you at the car, anyway?" the guy checked his clipboard. "I still have the keys here."

Emory's gaze jumps to mine as I approach, never flinching. "I was getting a sweater out of the car for my sister, and that's when I saw it. If you don't believe me, come see it for yourself."

Bryan argues, "I can't leave the stand and Jeremy is on a break."

Emory rolls his eyes, and I wonder if maybe he hasn't been spending a bit too much time around Reynolds. He's putting on a really convincing act. "My sister will wait here and just tell everyone you'll be right back. Trust me, that's a better option than my dad being the one to see that scratch first."

I freeze.

Did he just drag me into this?

Bryan assesses me for a long moment, fingers carding through the papers on the clipboard, and must decide that I look trustworthy. Which, of course, I am. I'm just innocent little Baby V. Nothing to see here but an awkward thirteen-year-old giving her brother the stink-eye. Bryan mutters a curse under his breath but concedes to my worryingly persuasive brother. I'm left standing by the curb, arms crossed, as my brother walks toward the parking lot. He turns back to wink at me.

Before I can react, Reynolds darts out of the bushes, his dress shirt wrinkled and his Club mandated tie askew. He brushes past me without any acknowledgment, ducking behind the valet stand to run his finger down the clipboard. I watch uselessly a slow, wicked smile appears on his face. A heartbeat later, he's snatched a set of keys bearing a Tesla logo from the board at his back.

"This is a bad idea," I say, wringing my hands to stop them from shaking. "I don't want you guys to get in trouble."

Every time Emory does something, my parents clamp down even more, and I'm usually the one who gets the brunt of their frustrations. It's not fair. It's not right. But that's the way it's always been.

Reynolds pauses just then, staring pensively at the keys in his hand, and for a moment I think maybe—just maybe—he'll actually listen to me. Instead, he turns his mischievous smile, dimples and all, right on me. "You should come with me."

I blink at him, gulping. "What?"

"Come on, Baby V." He reaches out, grazing the soft knuckle of a curled forefinger beneath my chin. I'm momentarily struck speechless. Breathless. Senseless. He cocks his head, watching me. "Aren't you tired of being the good girl who watches us have all the fun? Come with me, you'll have a blast." He holds out his hand, gesturing with a nod toward the parking lot. "It's just one joyride, it'll be fine."

Through the thick fog of my screeching internal '*oh my god, he touched me*', I'm only distantly aware of what he's doing. Reynolds wants me, at the very least, out of the way. And at the very most... *complicit*. Reynolds may be a thief and a troublemaker, but he isn't dumb. I'm a witness now, a liability. What better way to shut me up than to make me an accomplice?

Even more distant is the awareness that Reynolds *must* know how hard it is for me to say no to him. It always has been, and it certainly isn't the first time he's leveled me with one of those dimpled grins and found a convenient blind eye to his and my brother's antics.

It is, however, the first time he's asked me to go along for the ride.

I look at his outstretched hand, at long fingers that have picked pockets and locks and pretty high school girls, and I know it's not real, but this is Reynolds.

This is Reynolds picking *me*.

My heart bangs wildly as I slip my hand into his, finally meeting his gaze, and I wonder if I look as panicked and unhinged as I feel. "Okay."

"Sweet." He grasps my hand and turns, leading me away, and I follow without question.

Because the thing about Reynolds McAllister is that even when he's doing bad things—even if being nice to me is merely a means to an end—he still has a way of making me feel like I'm special.

Later—after the sirens and the pain and the tears—I'll look back on this moment and remember how it all began. I'll remember the way his smile makes me go all soft inside, and I'll remember the way he laughs—low and breathless—when I stumble over a dip in the asphalt. I'll remember the way my heart feels like a hummingbird when he squeezes my hand, and feeling scared and thrilled and like

I'm finally a part of something. I'll remember all of it, and I'll wonder how I ever thought the beginning of my own personal nightmare had ever felt like a fairytale.

In my periphery, I see a firefly hovering just within reach.

I walk faster.

Chapter 1

Vandy

You'd never know from looking at me that I'm broken.

In fact, on the surface, I'm probably quite enviable. I've got long, blonde hair that isn't too straight, nor too curly. My teeth are perfect, the result of extensive adolescent orthodontia. My nose is thin and aligned. More than once my eyes have been described as 'strikingly blue', and spoken with tones of wonderment. I have a nice body. I know I look good in a one-piece bathing suit, when my scars are hidden. Once, over the summer, I caught the lifeguard checking me out by the pool. Even the basic school uniform is flattering on my figure. So yeah, on the outside—at least the visible parts—Vandy Hall is the kind of seventeen-year-old most girls want to be.

At least, I am until I walk.

There was a time during Freshman and Sophomore years that I used a cane, but I've gotten well enough to not need it. Even so, my limp is severe enough to draw stares. And if people could see past my normal exterior, and even further, past the stilted way I walk, all the way deep into the heart of me? It's ugliness, all the way down.

People somehow see it, regardless. I inspect my face in the mirror and try to find out how, but I don't really need to wonder. I'm not just the girl who survived the accident. I'm the girl with the scars. The girl with a secret. The quiet girl with the dead eyes who has to be treated ever-so-carefully.

"Vandy!" my brother shouts down the hall. "I'm leaving in five minutes! AIS or I'm leaving."

I roll my eyes at my own reflection.

AIS: *Ass In Seat.*

He'll do it, too. God forbid Emory miss the five minutes before the bell rings to ogle and flirt with girls on the quad before class starts. It's always been bad, but now that he's a senior, he's completely unbearable.

"I'm coming!" I yell, running my fingers through my hair one last time. Yes. Shiny hair, spotless face, and crisp uniform. Everything seemingly in order, I reach for the little pouch hidden in my jewelry box, pulling it open. I don't need to count, but I do anyway, like some kind of compulsion. Fourteen pills for fourteen days. Two per day. One in the morning, one at night. No more. No less.

Or at least, that's what I promise myself.

I'd spent all summer weaning myself to an acceptable amount of Oxycontin. Two pills isn't a problem—not when you've been through what I've been through. I swallow the small circular pill dry, then tuck the pouch back in the box, snapping the lid shut. I walk across the room, one leg refusing to function the same as the other, and grab my backpack, heavy with first day essentials.

My mother waits in the kitchen, already dressed in her bright, camera-ready outfit. I know she has a big interview today—something to do with a collapsed multi-million dollar utility project that has possibly been the front for some shady dealings. The thing about our mom being a big time news reporter is that she's brushed fame a few too many times, but has never been able to really hold on to it. Instead, she has to constantly search for the next big scoop, hoping something juicy and significant will fall into her lap.

In many ways, I really respect that about her. My mom is the hardest-working parent I know who's also still involved in, like, *parenting.*

"I made your lunch!" She says as she closes the fridge. The stainless steel door is covered in an enormous, post-it riddled, color-coded calendar. Every single activity has been micromanaged down to the minute, up to and including 'pick up lunch for the kids'. My mom cuts her eyes to the bag on the island. "Well, I *packed* your lunch. Spicy tuna roll, a little bit of rice, and that yogurt with the honey that you like."

"Thanks, mom," I say, kissing her on the cheek. I take the bag and tuck it in my backpack. She leans over to help and I jerk around in a twist to prevent it. The horn blares from the garage, eliciting my groan.

"Your brother is anxious," she says, rolling her eyes, as well. "You know how he gets."

"Oh, I know." I dig a fist into the small of my beck, trying to reacquaint my spine with the weight of a backpack. "Now that Campbell's in college and they are 'keeping their options open'," I use finger quotes here, "he's on the prowl."

Mom's nose wrinkles. "Honey, don't talk about your brother like that. And Campbell is a sweet girl." She frowns as she says this, as if she could will it to be true.

"Uh huh."

Sometimes it's easier for my mom to live in a delusion than face reality, especially when it comes to my brother. Campbell Clarke is a bitch, through and through. She has my brother completely wrapped around her well-manicured finger. But if Mom looked beneath the surface of that choice, she'd have to acknowledge a lot of the other crap my brother does, and that would take the attention off me for a second. *God forbid.*

Preston Prep is everything to Emory. He'd been instantly accepted when he arrived as a freshman, his social status secured by his position on the football team and admittance into the quasi-legit fraternity, The Devils. He lived and breathed Preston Prep, the letterman jacket, and the older, more experienced girlfriend. He fully embraced the entitled, privileged attitude of the majority of our classmates.

He'd live in the dorms if he could—if he were allowed to. But there was no way my parents would allow *me* to live on campus, which meant there was no way he could live there either. Even for my parents, some tit-for-tats are just inevitable. Ultimately, that was probably a good decision. Last year, during Emory's junior and my sophomore year, the Devils outdid themselves, ultimately getting disbanded. The administration finally stepped in after a series of events that not only violated school policy, but brushed with illegal. To be honest, I wasn't paying much attention at the time. I spent my days trying to catch up on the schoolwork I fell behind on as a freshman, and my afternoons in physical therapy. I also spent the majority of time blissed out on painkillers, to the point that most of my classmates thought I was an idiot.

Or, so I learned over summer break. I'd been in the country club locker room when I overheard Amanda Brown ask Sydney if the accident had caused a brain injury. Apparently, she didn't remember me being *so slow*.

Ouch.

It was only through hushed talks between my parents and gossip at the swimming pool this summer that I learned what the Devils, including my brother, had really been up to for the last couple of years. None of it was necessarily good.

"I can't wait to hear about your first day tonight at dinner." Mom runs a hand through her hair, something she does when she's a little nervous. It's hard, sometimes, feeling all this bitterness toward her when she cares so much. She adds, "I'm making your favorite. Shrimp and grits."

I force a smile. "That sounds good." It seems a little much for the first day of junior year, but I've learned by now that if my mom wants to spoil me, the path of least resistance is to just let her.

The horn blasts again in the garage, and I roll my eyes, heading through the door.

"Finally," Emory says, as I climb into his truck. It's a beast. My parents only relented to getting it for him if he agreed to the lower running board so that I could step up to get into the cab. "I mean, what do you even do up there? It's not like you spend a bunch of time doing yourself up like the other girls."

Double ouch.

I scowl out the window. "You know mom doesn't let me wear a lot of makeup." She also doesn't let me wear anything revealing, or go out with boys, or stay out past nine.

"Exactly," he replies, backing out of the garage and swinging the car around, "it shouldn't take you so long."

"My leg hurt this morning," I mutter, looking away. "I had to do some stretches."

"Oh." I notice how his fingers grip the steering wheel, his knuckles turning white. "Right, yeah." The 'sorry' is implied.

It's not totally a lie. My leg didn't hurt, but I did have to do stretches. I know from experience just how difficult it is going from a summer free of academics to suddenly having to haul books around on my back all day. The administration gives me plenty of time allowances to travel to and from my locker, but if I accepted all of them, I'd miss half of every class. Being stuck with back pain, a limp, and disfiguring scars the rest of my life was bad enough without throwing 'never graduated high school' into the mix.

Aside from that, I'd also been working on my newspaper proposal. Every year, Mr. Lee, the Chronicle sponsor, chose a student to do a deep dive for an investigative topic. This topic had to cover something current and gritty, something worthy of six months of focus, and something that was of interest to the Preston Prep community without actually offending anyone or making the school look bad.

I know people will assume I want to follow in my mother's footsteps, and why wouldn't they? She's a moderately popular investigative journalist who's made quite a name for herself. But the reality is, I've seen what my mother does, and while she works hard and rails about things like justice and truth, her work is just a numbers game. The number of people who care, the number of viewers it can get, the number of ads they can run during the program, the number of dollars they can earn.

I don't want to follow in her footsteps.

I want to recreate them. The right way.

I'd been considering ideas all summer long and had finally settled on what I believe to be an amazing topic; the systematic classism and bigotry that has permeated a school like Preston Prep through the generations. I want to explore how that type of environment is a hotbed for racist and classist behavior—specifically the incidents leading to the Devils being disbanded. It's a tough topic, but one I think Mr. Lee, and the school at large, may finally be willing to address.

I keep my topic and the idea of proposing it to myself. This would be the kind of thing my family would cling to if I told them, feeding into their desperate hope that I'm doing more than just surviving. I don't want that kind of pressure.

I glance out the window as Emory drives past the McAllister house, next door. There's a black jeep in the driveway and it gives me a moment of pause. I wonder if Mr. McAllister got a new car. Seems a little juvenile for him, but he's been flirting with a mid-life crisis for years, part of which is likely courtesy of his delinquent son.

I shift uncomfortably, the pain in my back flaring, and divert my eyes. Although I don't like to think about Reyn, he's on my mind constantly. I can never forget that smile on his face as he held out his hand, daring me to go for a joyride with him. The way he confidently sat behind the wheel, peeling out of the parking lot. That moment, right before the world spun, with his wide eyes and locked jaw as he slammed on the brakes.

And, of course, I can never forget the last time I saw him—fighting through a wall of nurses, doctors, and emergency room security—pale-faced, covered in blood, eyes wild like a man possessed as he struggled to get to me. I still hear his screams in my nightmares, sometimes. *"What are you doing to her? Tell me what's fucking happening! Is she okay?"*

Emory cranks up the music as he drives the ten miles to school, and I let it drown out my thoughts. My brother and I don't talk much anymore. I don't blame him. The oxy made it easy for me to check out, and he's been focused on actually having a social life, unlike me. I know things kind of derailed for him when the Devils were disbanded. With most of the other guys—particularly Hamilton Bates—graduating last year, Emory had been in the position to take over the group. Even I had been stunned when Hamilton fell in love with his arch-nemesis, Gwendolyn Adams. The entire social eco-system had been shattered. Emory no longer had a girlfriend, nor his group. He was understandably a little adrift.

Welcome to my world.

He turns into the Preston Prep parking lot, securing a spot in the senior section.

"Don't forget," he says, unbuckling his seat belt, "I have football practice."

I nod, gathering my bag. "I'm going to a meeting for the Chronicle, so I'll probably get out around the same time."

His nose wrinkles. I know he hates that I'm involved with "nerdy" stuff, but good grief, what does he expect me to do? It's not exactly like I can be an athlete or try out for the cheer squad with Syd.

"Okay." He commands, "Meet me out here when you're done."

Sydney's for me waiting at the edge of the parking lot. Her eyes are glued to her phone until she sees us walking over.

Well, until she sees *my brother*, which will always catch her attention.

"Heya, Em," she says, beaming at him. He gives her a quick nod and strides across the quad, unmoved by her batting eyelashes. Sydney turns to me, fanning herself with her phone. "If it's possible, I think your brother actually got cuter over the summer."

I grimace. "Hmm..."

Syd has had a crush on Emory since before we even got to Preston Prep. There's really no nice way to tell her that he's not interested, and frankly, he doesn't even like us being friends. But unlike him, I don't have a million people lining up to become my buddies, and sure, Sydney has issues, but she's also stuck by my side during everything. Even if it means I have to put up with a lot of her self-inflicted drama.

Speaking of, Syd's phone buzzes and she glances down. "Oh my god."

"What?" I ask, taking an awkward step over the curb.

"Fucking Caleb. He just texted me to say that *everyone* is talking about me."

"What now?" People 'talking' about Sydney is a common occurrence.

"Some insane rumor that I fucked two guys from North Ridge, *at the same time*, last weekend. As if." She laughs and shakes her head. "God, when are people going to stop being so interested in my sex life?"

I grip the straps on my backpack and don't reply to what is obviously a rhetorical question. Sydney's social life—her *sex* life—has been a constant source of gossip and fascination for years. She's either a slut, or a tease, or a sex goddess, or a virgin, at any given moment. I stopped keeping up years ago, and after the blow up with Skylar Adams a couple years back, it seemed like maybe it would slow down, but nope. According to Syd, the rumors keep flying.

"Whatever," she mumbles, pushing her phone in her backpack. She turns to face me, her eyes searching my face. "How are you? You ready for this?"

Sydney is the one person who knows how much I've struggled the past few years. There's part of me that knows her interest in me is probably driven by a desire to be tragedy adjacent. But there's another part that's grateful to just have someone around. I haven't told her the truth about the painkillers—not exactly—but I have told her that I do have plans to get more involved this year. It all starts with the Chronicle.

I take a steeling breath, nodding. "I have my proposal ready."

"Awesome, I think you're going to kill it, and then next year you'll get to be editor-in-chief." I reluctantly accept her high-five.

We walk through the clusters of students and my eyes track them all. I see Emory and his jock friends, all in their letter jackets despite it still being hot outside. A few kids say hello before side-stepping to give me space. As we head down the sidewalk, I can't help but notice everyone taking great care to give me a wide berth. Their smiles are friendly, if distant. There's a twinge of pity on every face, and some people won't even meet my eyes.

I grab Sydney's arm to get her attention. "What's that all about?"

"What's *what* all about?" She's got her eye on Tyson Riggins, who is leaning against the brick wall by the main building. He's adorable, and if social media is accurate, very much already taken by a girl at another school.

"Everyone is looking at me," I explain, eyes warily taking in the students around me. "And they're all giving me room. I know I have the gimpy leg and all, but it's not like that's new."

"Uh," Syd says, looking around, "This is pretty much how people have always treated you. You were probably just too stoned to realize it."

I turn to her, mouth parted in surprise. "Seriously?"

Wow.

I'd known I was out of it. Almost all of my high school experience up to now can be described as just that—*high*. Months and months of sitting in the classroom, walking the halls, lost in a delicious fog of sweet nothingness, and this is probably only scratching the surface of things I've missed.

It's so much worse than I thought.

Before I can process this information any further, the bell in the tower tolls, signaling that we have five minutes to get to class. Syd gives me an apologetic smile and peels away, heading toward her homeroom. I do the same, taking the path toward the same homeroom I've had for three years now, but everything is different this year. My mind is clearer, like I can see things in a way I haven't in a long time. I run two rough palms over my cheeks, wanting more than anything to go back to my safe place, back to when I didn't realize how people looked at me. And the thing is, I could do it. I have enough meds stashed away in various hiding places in my room that I could probably medicate a small village. It would be so easy.

No.

The dead, nothing-eyed quiet girl isn't who I want to be anymore. I'd made a commitment to see this year through, clear-headed and decidedly *present*. For one reason or another, my life was spared that night.

It's time for me to start living it again.

ACKNOWLEDGMENTS

Readers,

It took me eleven years to talk Sam into co-authoring a novel with me. We'd dabbled here and there but when Hamilton Bates, Gwen Adams and Skylar took over my brain I lured her in good. The truth is that I knew I couldn't do this story justice without her help. Sam is the queen of angst and I knew she could turn my idea of the worst guy ever (Hamilton) into reality.

Many years ago, I used to wait for Sam to update chapters. Writing this book was like that all over again. I couldn't wait to see what she did to my words. I can't wait to do it again!

Quick thank you to Lisa and Jennifer for beta reading, VCEdits and the members of Angel's Antics for keeping me inspired.

Angel

&

Readers,

It took me eleven years to talk Angel into talking me into co-authoring a novel with her. Our previous forays into writing assholes are a thing of legend to my cruel withered soul. Angel is the goddess of plotting, structure, pacing, and—I cannot stress this enough—actually making me get shit done. She has always been my #1 creative cheerleader and I hope I did her ideas justice. I look very much forward to torturing future fictional douchebags, as is clearly our shared destiny!

My thanks go out to Angel, my Discord memers, all the cover clients who cheer for me, and my husband for being a super bro on Team Crush It.

Sam

* To follow me or Sam on facebook go to Angel Lawson Author or Samantha Rue

www.ingramcontent.com/pod-product-compliance
Lightning Source LLC
Chambersburg PA
CBHW031844310726
48972CB00005B/1400